LOVE
it's messy

JEANNINE COLETTE

For Jill Meister and Nanci Weaver

one

ALL I WANTED WAS a Coke.

"Miss, you need to step aside now! This is an active scene, and you're going to get hurt."

I scrunch my nose at the fire captain who's attempting to usher me away from the hotel where I'm staying … well, was staying until it was lit ablaze by a raging inferno.

My slippered feet try not to trip on the thick hose snaking from a hydrant as I follow the fire captain. Sirens blare from an ambulance rounding the corner. The deep, grumbling honk of a fire truck echoes from where a convoy of engines has descended. It's a madhouse of a scene, and while everyone is running away from the blazing hellfire, I want to go into it.

I tap on the fire captain's shoulder and smile as he turns around with an exasperated expression, which I ignore.

"Excuse me, sir, but if I could just get inside for one moment and grab something—"

"Are you serious?"

"Deadly," I state with a point of my finger up toward my hotel room window, which is just below where a fireman is standing on a ladder. "My phone, computer, wallet, car keys … my clothes are all up in that room."

"Are you a guest at the hotel?"

I look down at my attire—a plush white robe, matching slippers, and the metallic-gold ice bucket I'm holding like a teddy bear. His eyes do a double take, clearly answering his own question. My free hand clasps around the folds of my robe that are threatening to open from a gust of wind barreling down the small-town avenue. The fact that I'm not wearing underwear is plaguing me big time, yet I'm trying not to harp on that detail.

"Please," I beg with the kindest, most pleading voice. After all, my mother always says you get more with sugar than vinegar. "Just two minutes inside. I can pop right in, grab my phone, which I'm certain is on the nightstand, and my purse, which is definitely on the desk. Oh, there's also the box of monogrammed favors for a brunch. I need to get those too."

Seriously, at this rate, I don't even care about my clothes. My phone, car keys—so that I can hightail it out of here—and the favors my business partner, Melissa, made for our clients are all I need. A bra and a pair of underwear wouldn't hurt, but in the grand scheme of things, I can forgo modesty for necessity.

"The building has been evacuated," he yells as two firemen run toward the building, forcing me and the captain to step back. He gives me a stern warning. "Get out of here before you get yourself injured."

His name is called, so he turns around to answer someone's question.

Despite the breeze in the air, the heat radiating from the building is toasting my skin and doing nothing to calm the urgency inside me. I clear my throat and keep the plastered, closed-mouth smile on my face, and tap on his shoulder.

He turns around, looking quite displeased. "You're still here?"

"Perhaps I'm not explaining myself correctly. I'm a wedding planner with an event in the morning, and all of my contacts are on my phone. You're not looking at a woman who wants to log on to social media. This is business, and it's imperative I get into my room, which isn't even on fire. I'm looking at it now. It's below the smoke and barely touched by flames. I just need to slip in and get my car keys at the very least."

No sooner are my words spoken than a loud popping sound rings out as the fireman on the ladder uses an axe to break the window to none other than my hotel room.

I let out a whimper.

"The elevators are down. The building is closed to everyone, except the Walden Fire Department."

My desperation rises to the surface. "Maybe you can walkie one of your men and have them zip into room 519 for me. Like that man right there on the ladder—"

"Are you out of your mind?"

"Mildly," I answer, straight-faced, because at this moment, I have no clothes, communication, way home, money, or dignity.

The breeze picks up, and my eyes widen as it threatens to lift the hem of the robe. My free arm makes a desperate attempt to keep my robe from opening around the crotch area. I must look like a deranged woman despite my failing attempt to maintain decorum.

When I checked in to the Walden Hotel, it was to have a decent night's sleep after being on my feet all day. It wasn't to stand outside on the windiest night of the year with nothing but an ice bucket and borrowed cotton as I watch plumes of smoke billow out the room above mine.

"There's a waiting area set up in the restaurant across the street. Stay there. Get yourself something warm to drink."

"Do I look like I have money on me?"

"I'm pretty sure it's free. Call a family member."

I take a deep, cleansing breath and pinch the bridge of my nose. "I don't have my cell phone on me. It's up in my room."

"I'm sure someone will let you use their phone."

"If it were that simple, I would have asked to use yours by now!" Another bout of wind dances in the air, kicking the flaps of my robe apart. I push the ice bucket into his arms and grip my robe with both hands.

He looks down at the bucket like I just handed him a grenade that's about to blow. "Miss, please, you can spectate from across the street."

"I don't want to stand over there."

"We need the area clear."

"And I need to get into my room and get my things."

"I can't let you do that."

"I have to."

"Why?"

"Because I'm not wearing any underwear!" I yell entirely too loud, as I'm pretty sure everyone heard me over the sounds of engines roaring, water gushing, flames blazing, and people scurrying.

How is it that I, Jillian Hathaway—loving mother, fierce wedding planner, friend extraordinaire, and someone who does the right thing, lives a proper life, crosses her *t*'s and dots her *i*'s, and avoids all things troublesome—have found myself in the biggest pickle of a lifetime?

I squeeze my fists and scrunch my face as I beg the universe for a solution to this nightmare of a situation.

"Jillian?"

My heart, which is already thumping a million beats per second, goes into overdrive as my name is said by a man behind me. The voice is deep and gravelly—that low, sexually charged frequency that makes the hair on your arms rise and your chest quicken.

I turn slowly, wondering who could know me in this town three hours away from my home of Greenwood Village and say my name with such potent familiarity.

Then, I see him.

Tall. Broad-shouldered. Dressed in heavy firefighter equipment, sweaty and covered in the faintest amount of soot. Despite the helmet casting a shadow on his face, I can see his eyes clear as day. They're hypnotic, soul-searing eyes. Dark blue with sparkles of gold and tiny crinkles on the sides. They're the kind that ooze charisma as they flirt and sizzle and make you drop your panties … if I were wearing any, that is.

My jaw falls to the pavement, and my stomach plunges as my heart lands right in the pit of my belly.

"Luke," I utter in disbelief.

Three swoonworthy days, one sinful night, and a ghosting that could frighten a vampire. It's been years since I saw this man, and here he is, on the streets of Walden.

"What are you doing here?" He assesses my robe, which I'm still clinging to for dear life.

"Oh. You know, just, um … work." I swallow the lump in my throat.

He appears just as stunned to see me, and I scowl, wondering how on earth out of all the firemen in all the world, the one I met over a three-day wedding and then threw myself into bed with like a whore in church, is standing here. Here. In Walden. In front of the Walden Hotel as I wear nothing but a damn bathrobe with my hooha feeling the midnight breeze.

"How did you know it was me?"

He hesitates before replying, "Your auburn hair. Only woman I know with that shade of red and who pulls it back as tight as you do."

I lift a hand to my head, as if needing to make sure it is indeed pulled back.

"Can you handle this, Incendio?" The fire captain hands Luke the ice bucket. "I need to attend to matters on the ladder. Get your friend here to remove herself before she gets trampled."

Luke nods as his eyes remain on mine.

The captain leaves, and we're still standing here, entirely too close to a burning building.

He's looking at me like I'm a mirage in the desert. Since he blocked me from all forms of communication, I'd have assumed I was the last woman on earth he'd want to run into again.

To make matters worse, while I look like a wild woman, he's all gruff and handsome with his dark, arched brows, high cheekbones, and full mouth that quirks on the side in a permanent smirk, dressed in a fireman's uniform, looking like a wet dream.

"Jillian ..." He pauses, shifting his feet as his lips purse and a deep V forms on his brow. "It's been a long time."

His comment is enough to snap me out of my haze.

I blink rapidly and shake my head. "Nope. We are not doing this. And by this, I mean, reminiscing. You are going to treat me like I'm the stranger you forced me to be, and we'll pretend this meet-cute never happened." I start to walk away and then realize the bastard owes me, so I spin on my heel and march right back and look up into his ridiculously attractive face. "Scratch that. I need you to get me into that building."

"No chance. I won't let you risk your life."

"Then, risk yours."

A small smile lifts on his face and disappears just as fast. "Why don't you tell me what's going on, starting with why you're standing outside in nothing but a robe? Are you even wearing anything under that?"

I let out an unrefined growl. "I was in the lobby when the fire alarm went off."

He lifts a brow and looks down at the ice bucket in his hands. "Naked?"

I grab the bucket from him, albeit forcefully, and clench it tight in my arms. It's my lifeline and the only thing I own in this moment.

"Not that it's any of your business, but I was about to get into the bath when I remembered there was a vending machine down the hall. I really, really wanted a Coke, and wouldn't it be nice with some ice? I thought I deserved that, you know? A nice cup of ice-cold soda while taking a long soak in a bath after working an eleven-hour wedding sounded like heaven. Should have reconsidered leaving the room in just my robe, but getting dressed merely to walk down the hall was a waste of time. I'm seriously regretting my decision."

Why I'm sharing these details with this man is beyond me. I suppose it's easier to talk about soda and ice than tell him I was completely unprepared to see him since he had broken my heart and ruined men for me for the past five years.

"When I stepped into the hallway, the door locked behind me, and I realized I'd forgotten my room key, so I went down to the lobby to get a new one when the fire alarm rang. They wouldn't let me back upstairs, so that's why I'm standing in the middle of the street in nothing but a robe with an ice bucket—and I didn't even get my darn soda!"

I want to slap the amused look off his face. I would, except my hands are busy holding on to the damn bucket and making sure I don't flash all of Walden.

A woman in a red windbreaker walks by with a tower of plastic bags in her arms. Luke stops her and grabs one off the top of the pile. He pries the plastic off and unravels a dark blue wooly blanket, weaving it over my shoulders and wrapping me in it.

"It's too cold for you to be standing out here."

His kind gesture is disarming.

"I wasn't planning on being outside, half-naked."

"Well, there's no way you're getting back inside for at least a couple of hours—possibly ever. What's your plan?"

"You speak as if there's one to be had. I couldn't even call someone if I had the means. I don't have a single number memorized, except for my parents' home phone—and trust me, they're the last people I want to call right now. Besides, it's after midnight, and their ringer is definitely off. My business partner, Melissa, is probably awake, but I'm so used to clicking on a name in my Contacts list that I haven't memorized a number since the year 2004."

He lifts a shoulder in agreement as he places a hand on my back and gently steers me away from the burning building. "Do you have anywhere to go?"

"I have a car, but my keys are upstairs. I can't even check into a hotel if I tried. My credit card, money … everything is in my room. And while my personal needs are pretty dire right now, the absolute worst part is, I have a farewell brunch I'm hosting tomorrow and a couple who is counting on me to close out the best weekend of their lives. Now, I won't be there because I have no clothes, no car, no money, and every contact is currently in a raging inferno."

I would cry. I should cry. I want to cry. But I don't.

I am not a woman who sheds tears easily. In fact, I've only cried three times in the last decade. The birth of my daughter. The death of my grandmother. And when Luke left me, afraid and alone on the worst day of my life.

"Incendio!" someone shouts, and Luke looks over with a nod but gives his attention back to me.

My pulse beats erratically at the concern in his gaze. It stirs something in my belly, and the thought makes me uncomfortable.

"Jillian, you can't be outside like this. Let me take you to—"

I hold a hand up and halt that statement. "You know what? I'm good. There's a restaurant across the street. I'm going to wait there with the other hotel guests until this blows over."

There's a hardness to his stare, and his brow furrows with concern. I think he wants to add more to whatever he was going to say but appears to think better of it.

Part of me would love to see him fall to his knees and grovel for the pain he put me through. Another part wishes he'd just walk away.

I look to the side because I can't stare at him any longer. He takes the cue and fearlessly runs toward the burning building as I stare at the letters on his back and the name that I've thought of more times than I can count.

Turning on my toes, I spin in my wooly blanket cape and take myself and the stupid ice bucket to the restaurant across the street.

By two o'clock in the morning, most of the guests have left the restaurant. There are a few stragglers here with me, presumably displaced travelers with nowhere to go.

Apparently, Walden is so small a town that there are no vacant rooms. I know for certain that the wedding I planned and worked last night had sold out the hotel the reception took place in. The only other hotel is currently under an arson investigation. The closest motels are in neighboring towns about thirty minutes away, and a bus is on the way to bring people there.

I just want to go home.

I managed to borrow someone's cell phone to email Melissa, letting her know what happened and the number to the restaurant. She's clearly sleeping—rightfully so—as she hasn't called to rescue me.

I asked a Walden police officer if I could get a ride back to Greenwood Village. Because the drive would take an officer out of duty for six hours round trip, he didn't have anyone at the moment, but would try to send someone sometime in the morning. Taxis won't drive that far, and I can't even Uber without my phone.

My head is down on the table, and I'm inhaling the linen of the tablecloth, feeling rather desolate and depressed when something cold brushes up against my forearm. Startled, I bolt upright and look curiously at the offending object. I'm bone-tired and slightly delirious, so when I see a red soda can on the table, I question my sanity.

Blinking a few times, I run my hand over my eyes and confirm there's a can of Coca-Cola on the table, then roll my head over to the man standing intimidatingly close to me.

Luke has changed his clothes, no longer in his firefighter ensemble. He's in sweatpants and a T-shirt with his ladder number on it. Skin sooted and hair dirty and mussed up, he still looks far more put together than I feel.

My mouth opens to ask him what the hell he's doing here, but he just stares at me ... strong, commanding, imposing.

My words fail me.

Those dark blue eyes glare down at me, looking sinister and sexy at the same time. His stance is one of a man who spent the evening being heroic in a fire, and his job isn't close to being done.

As his lips part, I swallow, wondering how on earth he could now rescue this redhead in a robe.

"Let's go, Jillian. You're coming with me."

two

WHEN LUKE SAID TO come with him, I assumed it was to drive me back to my home. That was why I shouted my address at him before curling into a ball and falling asleep in the passenger side of his pickup truck.

Under any other circumstances, I'd rather lie on the pavement all night than let this man bring me home, but I was desperate and exhausted.

The time on the dashboard shows I haven't been asleep long. I rub my eyes and look out the window to where we're parked in front of a ranch-style home that is definitely not my condo building. Actually, we're not even in Greenwood Village. If I'm correct, we're still in Walden.

Shaking the grogginess off, I sit up just as Luke rounds the truck. He opens the passenger door and holds out a hand, which I refuse.

"This isn't my house. I live at 733—"

"Cherry Street. Yes, I remember. But it's late, I worked all day and night, and I'm not driving three hours to bring you home."

I look behind him at the house he's gesturing toward and shake my head. "I'm not going home with you."

"You're already home with me. Whether you walk through that door or not, this is my curb and my property. I wasn't going to leave you in that restaurant all night. One, you're a woman, alone. Two, you're practically naked. I know this isn't perfect, but it's all I can offer. If you prefer, you can go inside, and I'll sleep out here in the backseat. Either way, this situation ends with you walking through my front door and going to sleep where I know you're safe."

He tosses me his keys, and I'm impressed I have the wherewithal to catch them.

"There is no way I'm staying with you. I need to go home. I need clothes. I have to go to my office and salvage what I can for this brunch tomorrow … today. Oh God, it's in eight hours."

His brows draw together as he looks down at me. "After everything that happened tonight, you're more worried about the wedding you have to work tomorrow?"

I nod with pleading eyes.

A deep, weighted groan escapes his lips. "I can't do the drive now safely."

My lips pout. I might despise the guy, but I don't want him to crash on the highway due to sleep deprivation.

Luke takes a step forward and leans against the open car door, folds his arms, his forearms flexing pure muscle as he takes a deep breath. "Go inside, get some sleep, shower in the morning. You can't go to this thing smelling like a chimney. I'll see what I can do about clothes for you, and we'll get you to that brunch on time."

"The favors," I mumble.

"Jillian." He lowers his forehead and raises his brows. His tone softens. "I wasn't at the wedding you planned yesterday, but if it's anything like the one I met you at—the wedding that was so over the top and the best three days of my life—then I can guarantee when the couple learns what happened to you tonight, they'll be more than understanding that you don't have parting favors for their guests."

I sigh. If there's one thing about this man, it's that he has a way of swaying your attitude from one of dismay to conquering the impossible. Even when it's the middle of the night and he's tired, dirty, and has a serious case of helmet hair, he has the ability to influence me to do almost anything.

I lift my chin to the sky, and bow my back with closed eyes and whisper, "Fine."

The wooly blue blanket is dragging on the pavers as I walk toward the front door. His house keys jingle in my hand as I put one in the lock, opening the front door. I turn around and notice Luke isn't behind me.

I roll my eyes at the sight of him hopping into the backseat of his truck, puffing up what appears to be a jacket of sorts into a makeshift pillow. He closes the door, and I wait for a moment before realizing he's making good on his offer. Luke is planning to sleep in his truck.

With a drop of my shoulders, I pad back down the pavers to his truck and knock on the back passenger door.

He opens it with his brows peaked with interest, and his hand is up, as if to stop me from making a declaration.

"Jillian, I meant it. You go inside, and I'll sleep out here. I don't want you feeling uncomfortable with me in the house. Yes, we have history, but I'm still a man you barely know, and things didn't end as we'd hoped. I understand if you need your space tonight. Thank you for offering, but I'm good."

I scowl as I take the blanket off my shoulders and hand it to him. "I wasn't offering for you to come inside. Just thought you might be cold."

His lips form an O as he takes the blanket and nods. "Good. Thanks." With a clearing of his throat, he leans forward. "I don't have a spare bed, so you can take mine. Or the couch. Just don't be startled by the cat. His name is Joe. I think he has anthropomorphism. Acts more human than tomcat. He's a good man though. You should be aware that he likes to snuggle. The bedroom is best so you can lock him out."

"Joe, the cat, is anthropomorphic and likes to snuggle. Good to know. Good night, Luke."

I turn around and head back inside, close the front door, and stare at the dead bolt. It's probably wrong to lock a man out of his own home, but he's in his car and comfortable. If he needs to get in, he can knock. Unless I'm dead asleep and he has to get in for an emergency.

As I'm internally deciding the proper etiquette for a situation like this, I'm startled out of my skin as a soft, vibrating object rubs up against my leg. I scream as I thrust myself back so fast that my spine hits the wall, knocking over a picture frame that thumps my head before landing on the floor.

My hands are flush against the wall as I look down stiffly.

I can only assume this is Joe, the cat. He is sauntering around me in his feline glory, going straight for my ankle again and rubbing his orange tabby head up against it.

A loud pounding on the door makes my heart race for the second time in mere moments, and I shout, "Who's there?"

"It's Luke. Who the hell else would it be?"

I unlock the door and open it, clutching my chest as I catch my breath and tame my erratic heartbeat. "What do you want?"

His hand slams against the front door, pushing it open while those hypnotic eyes dart around the foyer. Rough and rugged, he takes on a proactive stance of protection.

"Are you okay? I heard you scream."

"Joe tried to get to second base with my ankle."

His fists unclench as he looks down at Joe with a condescending growl.

My back is pressed against the wall once again as Luke turns his attention from Joe and looks at me intently. His tall, heavy frame walks forward, stopping in front of me. I stare at the numbers on his chest and trace the shield emblem with my eyes. Anything to ignore the unhurried way he drops to the floor, forcing me to inhale sharply as he picks up the picture that had fallen.

His broad chest brushes against mine as he hangs the frame back on the nail just above my head. This close, I can feel the heat pouring from him, the scent of burned embers. This is a man who worked a long, tireless night putting out a fire. It's a heady feeling that has me closing my eyes, for fear if I look up at him, he'll see into my soul.

"Are you sure you're okay?" he asks.

"You walk into a pitch-black house that's not yours and have something warm and hard rub against you."

My comment has him smirking in a devilish way. I place my hands on his chest and push him back out the front door before he can make a joke about warm and hard things.

"Out!"

Luke doesn't argue as he walks backward, a low chuckle humming from his throat. I close the door before he makes it back to the truck.

While I am still quite tired from the long day and night, between the cat scaring me and Luke's pounding, I am now startled awake. Awake enough to begin to process exactly what transpired over the last two and a half hours.

I should be dwelling on my lack of clothes, possessions, and the massive fire that took over the hotel I was staying in.

Yet none of that seems to matter, as my brain is completely obsessed with the fact that I'm standing in Luke Incendio's home.

I grip my robe and bite on my thumbnail as I walk farther into the house. The streetlamps cast a glow through the large picture window in the living room so I can meander around in the twilight.

It's a small single-story home, yet it feels big because there isn't a ton of furniture in here, just a sofa set and a television on a stand. The dining room features a table big enough for four, yet there are only two chairs. His kitchen is neat and tidy.

There isn't an abundance of knickknacks or personal effects, aside from a few picture frames on a credenza between the living and dining rooms. I walk over and look at the photos. A picture of a boy, who I assume is Luke, splashing in a lake with a teenage girl and another girl about his age, has me smiling. It's no surprise he was a cute kid. He stares at the camera and beams a toothless grin, and those almond-shaped eyes of his were as mischievous then as they are now.

Beside that photo is another of Luke and who are most likely his parents and sisters. I lift the picture frame and look at the faces. The couple is definitely his parents because Luke looks just like his mom. Same wavy, dark hair, vibrant eyes, and height. She's a tall woman, taller than his father, and it makes me smile for some reason. There aren't many couples you see where the man is shorter. While Luke looks like his mom, he has his father's grin. It's smooth and wicked and deepens with a Y-shaped dimple in the chin. It reminds me of my daughter, Ainsley's, smile.

Ainsley has a cleft in her chin that she refers to as her chin butt. I hate when she says that. I think a boy at preschool made fun of her, and that's why she's so wary of it. At only four, she's too young to harp on her physical features.

I place the photo down with a sigh and walk around some more.

Joe is back at my feet and purring like an engine. I kneel down and give him a rub on the head, which only serves as foreplay to the heavy petting this little guy seems to want. He rolls onto his back and inches his body closer to my hand, eliciting a belly scratch.

"You are an affectionate little guy, aren't you?"

Joe hops back to his feet and then up onto my knee, placing his head under my chin. I can feel the vibration from deep within his chest as he nuzzles my neck.

"Daddy was right. You do like to snuggle."

My words halt me, and I suddenly have a pang of guilt. I stand, this time with Joe in my arms. There's a crocheted afghan on the top of the love seat. The colors are navy, white, and teal. I run my hand over the wool, and it reminds me of the blanket I gave to Luke, who is sleeping outside in the truck.

Peering out the blinds of the picture window, I look at the truck and can see Luke's shadow moving about and then falling back down. It must be uncomfortable in there. He's not a huge man, but he's brawny. About five-eleven, lean yet muscular. My much smaller frame would hate to sleep in the backseat. I can feel the phantom crick in my back that would come from having to lie in a scrunched position all night.

Joe hops out of my arm and onto the windowsill, meowing out the window. He paws at the glass, as if begging for his owner to come inside.

"You think he should come in, don't you?" I ask Joe, who looks up at me with pleading eyes. "I understand it's his house, but he's practically a stranger to me. It's not proper for a man to be alone with a woman in a home. Especially when they don't know each other well. He could be an axe murderer for all I know. Have you seen the Dahmer movie?"

Joe's eyes slant, and I give him the same expression back.

"Yes, I know it didn't stop me from hopping into bed with him all those years ago, but I was drunk on lust and charisma. He's funny—you know that?" I take a seat on the couch and look out the glass with Joe, the two of us staring at the truck.

"I met your dad in Aruba. At the time, I was working for an event company that had a contract with a hotel chain down there. We got a bonus if we booked a wedding at the venue and got to travel for the event. I'm a wedding planner, so being able to coordinate a destination wedding is a dream. I flew in early to make sure everything was prepped for the rehearsal dinner. I met him at the restaurant where the dinner would take place."

I run my hand down Joe's back and think about that night. I was overwhelmed, to say the least. My first destination wedding, and of course, the hotel overbooked the venue. I was young, feisty, and delirious with party-planning anxiety.

"You look like you could use a drink," a man said as I approached the bar.

"An old-fashioned," I asked the bartender, ignoring the question from the gentleman next to me. I wasn't trying to be rude, but I had a lot on my mind, being the only person from my company at the resort. If things went wrong, the onus was on me.

"Cat got your tongue?"

The stranger leaned into my personal space, and I was hit with the scent of musk that had me looking up into his face. It was a good-looking face. Strong jaw, gleaming eyes, and that damn smile. I thought I'd stared at his teeth for a beat too long because he lowered his gaze to mine, and I was mesmerized by that twinkle.

Yes, Luke twinkles and shines with just a glance.

"Sorry. I'm lost in my head."

"Good news. I happen to be an expert in being a head case." He inched closer, ignoring my standoffish vibes.

In the mirror behind the bar, I watched as his eyes drifted down to the V-neck of my blouse, and I did a double take at him, admonishing him with my eyes.

"You're blatantly staring at my boobs."

"On the contrary. I was looking at your heart."

"You're slick."

The bartender slid my drink on the bar, and the handsome stranger grabbed it, bringing it closer to me.

"I'm Luke."

I took it out of his hand and downed a few sips too many, too soon. Luke had his elbow on the bar as he casually leaned and stared at me. It was a debonaire look. A strapping man with windswept hair and a shirt unbuttoned one too many, his body pressed into a bar like a pose in a catalog.

I looked back at him and tilted my head. "You're staring."

"Sorry." He grinned, seemingly embarrassed. "I think I need a map because I keep getting lost in your eyes."

"The cheese," I said incredulously at his line, fighting the smile that wanted to let loose. "I'm sure the next thing you're gonna tell me is that I'm a perfect ten."

He slid those navy-blues my way and twisted his lips with a shrug. "You are not a ten."

I scrunched my nose at the audacity.

"You're a nine. At best," he stated.

I rolled my eyes, and he laughed with the mouth of the bottle at his lips and then took a drink.

My body tingled. The liquor was clearly going to my head, and I'd only had a sip. "You're one for pickup lines, aren't you? I bet you're quite the player."

"I usually play the field, but I'd hit a grand slam with you."

A laugh bubbled from my belly, and I shook my head, giving in to his charm. "While your corny lines are not something I ever give the time of day for, I admit, it's working. I need a distraction. And, please, before you give some sort of line about the distraction you could provide, I promise you, there is no way in hell I'm going to bed with you."

His hand landed on his chest as he feigned insult. "That's harsh. Not in the least did I ask you to go to bed with me, nor did I even say I was interested. I just said you had nice eyes." He lifted his beer from the bar and halted before taking a sip. "Nice boobs too."

I had to look away, for the way he was making my head spin was new to me. I liked men. Dated regularly. But there was something about Luke. Okay, I could admit, he was easy on the eyes. He had a smile that was practically Colgate and a roguish cleft in his chin. There was even this self-deprecating way he delivered his cheesy pickup lines. It had been seconds, and yet I was completely overwhelmed by this man.

"You're incorrigible."

"I prefer charming."

He took a step away from me, which was a relief. It wasn't that I didn't like how he had been invading my space. I hated it and craved it, all at once.

"All kidding aside, what's a beautiful woman doing, drinking alone, too late at night in a near-empty restaurant at a Caribbean resort?"

"This feels like a future episode of Dateline. The kind where the redhead goes missing and everyone questions the handsome stranger with an alibi."

"So, you think I'm handsome? I can work with this."

I pushed him away playfully.

He called over the waiter, "Garçon!" He used a French accent, which was ridiculous.

"Aruba isn't French."

"I know. It's part of the Netherlands, but I just like the way the word sounds."

The bartender came over.

Luke explained, "I'm gonna need you to take a picture of my license with your phone." When the bartender looked at him quizzically, Luke added, "I'm going to make this woman fall in love with me this weekend, and when she does, I'm gonna need her to know where to find me when it's over."

I'd never danced on a beach before, yet in the next hour, this man had me in his arms, dancing under the moonlight. The sound of crashing waves was our music, and the beating of our hearts was the tempo. Yes, I—a girl who had been raised in the upper crust of Connecticut, who summered in Maine and lived the pristine and poised lifestyle of the Hathaway family—was barefoot in the sand with my arms around a stranger, giggling like a schoolgirl.

There was something about Luke that overwhelmed me.

Surprisingly, I wasn't afraid of the rush.

We didn't kiss that night.

I didn't go back to his hotel room.

I didn't know if anything—other than this awesome guy with wild words and a zest for life, who had shown me a fun hour and a half before returning me to my room—would come of it.

And yet …

"Your daddy swept me off my feet," I sigh to Joe, who gives a nod and a purr, as if he understands.

I drop my head into my hand.

I shouldn't be having this discussion with a cat.

There's a huge part of me that is so angry with Luke for breaking my heart. He doesn't know I fell for him over the next forty-eight hours. He doesn't know I often think of him at midnight—when the moon is high, the house is quiet, and I'm alone with my thoughts.

My thoughts are always of him.

Joe leaps off my lap and jumps onto the coffee table, then to the love seat, and down to the ground like an acrobat. He stops by the half-wall that leads toward the foyer, looks over his shoulder, and lets out a loud mewl in my direction.

Puffing my cheeks with a large exhale, I rise from the couch and follow Joe to the front door.

"I know; I know."

I tighten the belt on my robe, push my shoulders back, and march outside and up to the back passenger door of the truck.

My knock is forceful and loud enough that I hear a rustling inside and then a loud thump that sounds like it came from the roof.

Luke opens the door, and I step back. He's rubbing the top of his mop of hair and squinting his groggy eyes at me.

"You should come inside," I suggest.

"Why the change of heart?"

"For the record, I never asked you to sleep here. You offered and made the first move. I merely gave you a blanket." I shift on my heels and cross my arms over my chest. "A grown man shouldn't sleep in the back of a truck. You need a couch and to sleep in your own home."

"All right. You don't have to beg," he jokes, and I squint my eyes at him. "You know I was fine out here, but if you're so desperate for me to come inside, who am I to go against the wishes of a beautiful woman?"

"For the record, these aren't my wishes. They're Joe's."

"The cat told you to let me inside?"

"Yes." I smash my lips together and then head inside the house.

In the living room, I stand and watch as Luke walks in and kicks off his shoes. He looks exhausted as he lifts his arms up in a yawn, exposing a sliver of taut skin and the faint lines of his lower abdomen.

His eyes are glazed over as he looks back at me. "Do you want me to take the couch, or does Joe think I should sleep in the bedroom with you?"

Ignoring him, I walk my fine robed ass straight into the master bedroom and close the door. There's a soft padding at the base of the door, followed by a meow.

Luke's voice echoes from the other side of the house. "Joe, you rascal, leave her alone. Come snuggle with me on the couch."

The padding continues, so I open the door and see Joe is in the hallway, staring up at me with pleading eyes and a swishing tail, waiting for an invitation. I appreciate he's such a gentleman and not assuming he's allowed in here just because he's cute.

Down the hall, I see Luke standing at the end. He looks sleepy and rumpled. Kind of like how he looks after making love in a canopy bed with the ocean breeze blowing through the windows. His eyes are hooded, and I swear I see a semblance of a lusty haze. I adored that haze once.

I bend down and scoop the tomcat off the ground. "Joe's sleeping with me tonight."

I close the door and then snuggle with the only man in the house worthy of my affection. The worst part is, this is the first man I've shared a bed with in five years.

three

"MORNING, BUDDY," LUKE CROONS in a soft whisper. "I see you gave me up for the first pretty girl to enter the bedroom. So much for do-or-die brothers, huh?"

I wake to the sound of Luke's voice as he talks to the kitty on the dresser. His back is to me as he rummages through a drawer in nothing but a towel. His broad back is on display, and every muscle ripples as he flexes and moves.

I need to know the time, yet I don't want to move. If I do, he'll realize I'm awake. I'm not a voyeur. It's just that this situation would be awkward, to say the least, should he turn round and see I'm staring at his half-naked frame.

My jaw hits the duvet as his towel falls to the floor, and I'm now staring at Luke's well-defined and very muscular behind. He has two divots on the sides of his rear. Plump, round. Perfect. It's not appropriate for me to be gawking the way I am, so as he grabs a pair of black boxer briefs from his dresser, I close my eyes and pretend to be sleeping so as not to cause any unwanted attention toward the bed.

I'm saving us both the embarrassment, you see.

Joe lets out a loud mew, as if shouting at his owner that there's a peeping Tom nearby. Another drawer closes, and I hear a slight moving about when the door to his bedroom closes.

I roll over, and Joe is now on my chest, meowing in my face, as if to ask, *Did you like the show?*

The clock on the bedside table dictates I don't have a lot of time until I have to be at the brunch, and I desperately need to get to a store to find something to wear.

The stench of smoke from last night is pouring off me, so I get up and use Luke's bathroom. The mirror is still foggy from his shower. With my index finger, I make a smiley face in the mirror. It's a habit of mine from when I was little and something Ainsley and I do often. Lately, we've taken to playing tic-tac-toe and hope there's a winner before the steam fades.

I turn on the faucet and walk into the shower and wash away the horror of last night. Luke doesn't have feminine-smelling shampoo or soap. He doesn't even have conditioner. I do my best with Old Spice and Irish Spring.

Turning the water off, I realize there isn't a towel on the bar. I move the curtain to look around the bathroom, but don't see one in sight. My hair drips down my back as I step onto the mat and look briskly around the room, but to no avail. There might be something in Luke's room, so I open the bathroom door, only to scream at the top of my lungs at the sight of a man standing in the doorway.

My hands make quick work to cover my sexy bits as I hunch over to hide my body from the prying yet seemingly amused eyes of Luke Incendio.

His palm flies to cover his face. "I heard the water and figured you needed these." He holds out a towel and a clean robe while his hand does nothing to cover the smile on his face.

I rip them from his grasp and cover my body. My own eyes squint at him in accusation. "Your eyes had better be clenched tightly."

"A gentleman would never."

"A gentleman you are not."

"I'm not the one who was pretending to be asleep ten minutes ago," he states with an amused tone.

I close the door in his face and catch my breath from the flourish of nerves and embarrassment I feel. Joe is now standing on the hamper. I turn around and slide Luke's robe on.

"Well, Joe, hopefully, that's it for the morning theatrics. It's only eight, and I'm already over the day."

There's a hair dryer under the sink beside a small, unmarked bottle. I lift the bottle of what looks like sand and inspect it. It could be from anywhere, yet there's something about the color and the fine texture of each grain that reminds me of the Caribbean. I shake off the idea that it has anything to do with the white sands of Aruba and a wistful night on the beach. Thoughts like that can get a girl in trouble.

I blow out my long red hair and think of Ainsley and how I should be calling her now and singing our good-morning song. It's a melody I came up with when she was a baby, and it's now something she looks forward to. Who am I kidding? The day she's too big for a sunshine song from her mama will be the saddest day for me.

Joe jumps on the counter and tilts his head, as if asking for my thoughts. I pet his head.

"I miss my little girl. She's a lot like you. Demanding, opinionated, and the sweetest snuggler ever. Too bad you'll never meet."

I can't go to the store in a robe, so I fluff my hair and walk into the living room to ask Luke if I can borrow clothes.

Imagine my surprise to see we have company.

"There she is," Luke announces as I walk down the short hallway to where he's standing in his living room, holding a coffee mug, like he didn't just see me in my birthday suit.

Next to Luke is a woman, about our age, with a large tote bag in her hand. She smiles at the sight of me, and I do a double take. I wasn't expecting a visitor.

"Morning." I give a kind smile to the woman and spin toward Luke. "Can you give me a ride to town? I have to pick up some clothes and be at the restaurant by nine. I don't know what's open at this hour on a Sunday, so we should leave soon and drive around a bit."

He's leaning against the back of the couch, ankles crossed, with no sense of urgency about him as he nods toward the woman. "Jillian, this is Stella, my neighbor."

"Hi, Stella. It's nice to meet you. So, Luke, I need to get out of here. I can borrow your car and drop it off at noon."

He quirks a brow. "Will you be going commando to Target?"

I glance down at the navy waffle knit covering. "Of course not. I'm not picky though. I'll wear anything you can loan me. A pair of jogging pants and a sweatshirt will do."

"I promised you last night that I'd take care of getting you clothes. Stella brought over a few things."

I frown at his response and then turn to the woman. "I can't take your clothes."

The cherub-faced woman smiles, taking a step forward. "It's no problem. Luke texted last night about what happened. As soon as I woke up and saw the message, I put this bag together. You can return them anytime. Heck, you can keep it all. You've been through a hell of an ordeal. The fire and being stranded naked on the street until sweet Luke came to your rescue. You must have been petrified."

I give a sideways look to Luke and the depiction of what transpired last night and then turn back to Stella. "I couldn't impose—"

"I happen to be one of those girls who goes up and down in weight. My closet is literally filled with everything from a six to a twelve. I brought an option in every size. Luke said you're classy, so I picked out all dresses. I also ran to the drugstore this morning and got you all the unmentionables. Luke said to get a bunch of stuff and he'd return the rest."

Her selflessness pours out of her heart through her bright eyes and outstretched arm. I take the proffered bag from her and grin in disbelief.

"Stella, you're … a gem. I'm not one to take handouts. Actually, I'm usually the one handing out, but I am in quite the rush. You're very kind to help."

"What am I, chopped liver?" Luke asks with his arms stretched out in question, which I ignore, and Stella laughs.

"Why don't you try them on first and see what works?" she says. "You're also welcome to come to my house and pick something else out. Oh! There's a pair of black heels in the bag. I'm a size nine in shoes, so I don't have any other options."

"Luck would have it, I'm an eight, so nine is fine."

I excuse myself and head to Luke's bedroom and take out the contents of the bag. The size-eight dress is a long-sleeved brown jersey dress with a V-neckline and a hem that falls just above the knee. Everything fits rather well, even the sports bra, which I'm sure is the only thing she could find at this hour. She even bought me mascara, lip gloss, eye shadow, bronzer, and concealer. I don't know who this Stella woman is, but she's already my new favorite person.

When I exit the bedroom again, Luke is sitting alone at the kitchen table. Stella can be seen out the picture window, crossing the street back to her home with a swish to her hips and a sway of her long blonde hair.

Luke rises when he sees me. The color of his eyes does nothing to give away the enlarging of his pupils as they appraise the neckline.

"Wow. You ..." He pauses as he slides his hands into his pockets and takes on an air of nonchalance. "You clean up well."

"The bar was set rather low."

"You looked pretty good in my robe."

"I look good in everything, Luke."

He clears his throat and gestures to the devices he has set on his living room table and starts pacing toward the kitchen. "I set up my laptop and cell phone so you can make whatever calls you need. I'll get you a coffee. I asked Stella to grab you French vanilla creamer. She didn't get the sugar-free."

My head shoots over to where he's now standing in the kitchen by the open refrigerator door. I'm amazed he knows how I take my coffee.

He halts. "Did I say something wrong?"

"No," I mutter. "The regular is fine."

I shake off the familiar feeling simmering in my chest and take a seat by his laptop.

I open a browser and log in to my email account and see Melissa replied, assuring me she contacted all the vendors and urging me to call her immediately now that she's awake. Since Luke said I could use his phone, I take his cell and dial her number.

"This is a new version of *Naked and Afraid!*" Melissa gasps on the other end of the phone after she picks up. "That is some pickle you got yourself into, my friend. More like something I'd do. Were you high on rosé? I've made some questionable decisions while on the vino."

"Absolutely not," I admonish and then sigh. "I just wanted to use the vending machine."

Melissa's laugh echoes through the phone. "That's karma coming for you because you won't let Ainsley drink any. Someday, she's gonna find out you're a closet soda head."

"Am not."

"I saw you down that Big Gulp when we were driving back from Pennsylvania for the Bristol wedding last month."

"That was a five-hour drive. I needed the caffeine."

"Just as believable as the news that you stayed with a friend last night. What friends do you have in Walden?"

I lower my head and move my hair in front of my face, like a veil, so as to cover my voice from traveling to the kitchen. "A firefighter I met a long time ago."

"Oh my God!" Her shriek has me holding the phone away from my ear before placing it back. "You went home with a man last night."

I glance at Luke again. As my eyes rise, his lock with mine, and he lifts his brows. I give a small smile, then get up and scurry down the hall and into the bedroom for some privacy.

"Get your head out of the gutter." I close the door and lean against it.

"Can't. It's already so far down that I'm in sewage. I have to call Tara."

"Please don't. She has Ainsley with her, and I don't need her harping all morning about this with little four-year-old ears hearing it all."

"You're right. Ainsley is young, but she's four going on forty. You really need to get that kid evaluated as a child prodigy."

"Just let her be a normal kid in a normal town."

Melissa laughs, and I can picture her walking around her kitchen as she talks. Unless she's working, the woman doesn't know how to sit still. "Should I have Tara call this number? Ainsley will be surprised you haven't called."

"No," I say rather quickly. "Let her know I'll be home in … shoot. I don't know how I'm getting home."

"I'll bring you your spare keys. Where are they?"

Placing a hand on my forehead, I shake my head and reply, "I don't know where the key fob is. Maybe the kitchen drawer. Never mind. Forget about me. You have your daughter's art show. That's important and why we decided I was staying the night and you were going back. Be with your family. I'll figure out something. Maybe there's a dealership in the area, and I can have a key made. Just check in with Tara and make sure she's okay to keep Ainsley for another few hours should it come to it."

"I'll touch base with Tara, and between the two of us, Ainsley will be taken care of, and one of us will come and get you," she assures. "We are the two best girlfriends a woman could have. And we're definitely going to want to hear all about this guy. Oh, why doesn't he drive you back?"

"Absolutely not. For a hot second last night, I wanted him to drive me home, but I was delirious. Trust me when I say, I don't want Luke anywhere near Greenwood Village. The faster I get out of Walden, the better."

"Luke?" She says his name with a hum. "I vaguely remember you talking about Luke one night over too much bourbon." She pauses, and I can feel the revelation coming from the intake of air she takes. "Oh. Shit. He's the one, isn't he?"

I bang my head against the door and close my eyes. "He's the one all right. The one I never thought I'd see again. The one who destroyed me."

"How are you handling this? I would have burned all his underwear by now."

"I'm fine. He means nothing to me, so I feel nothing."

"Damn, woman. You are a pillar of strength. I swear, nothing gets you unraveled. Well, except your mom, but we all know she's a bitch. Otherwise, you're so stoic, which I'm calling out as major bullshit. Okay, this is more a Saturday night convo over lots of drinks than a Sunday powwow. You do what you need to do today, and we'll unload all of the things—emotionally, that is—at a later date."

We hang up, and I take a moment to compose myself. Waning over exes while on the phone with your best friend can certainly affect your complexion, and no one wants a sallow complexion when trying to appear put together, headstrong, and fabulous in front of your ex ... if I can even call him that. Ex-fling perhaps.

With my shoulders back and chin held high, I exit the room and walk back to the kitchen, where Luke is taking a pan out of the oven.

He doesn't look at me as I enter.

"Smells good," I offer as I place the phone on the counter.

"I hope you like it. I slaved all morning."

"You did?" I ask.

"No. It's a quiche, the kind you buy premade at the store. Fooled you though."

I look over at the dining table. It's set for two with plates, napkins, and silverware. It's sweet. Like a mini date in the morning. I twist my fingers around each other at the thought.

He clears his throat and runs his hand in circles over his chest. "Yeah. I thought we'd have time to sit and talk for a while, but you have to get to that thing. It could take a while to get there with traffic, so we should leave now."

Placing a piece of quiche in a napkin, he walks around the kitchen half-wall, hands it to me, and grabs his keys. A mug, freshly filled with coffee, is on the counter. The French vanilla creamer beside it. It's left forgotten as I follow Luke outside to his car.

Someone really wants me out of his house and fast.

Luke slides into the driver's side, and we head to the hotel in silence. It's an odd kind of silence. A forced staleness in the air that I should be happy about, yet it has my mind confused as to where the shift in energy came from. His hands are both on the wheel, and his gaze is fixed forward, jaw stiff and those cheekbones perturbing. He looks mad and yet … kind of sad at the same time.

The quiche is hot in my hands and looks perfectly golden. I fiddle with the crust and roll the dough, crumbling it between my fingers until it's almost nonexistent. Like the piece of quiche never was.

To my surprise, we're at the hotel in moments. At the house, he made it seem like we'd be in the car for twenty minutes, not two. I suppose he just wanted me out of his house and out of his life.

I remember that feeling.

I open the door and lay a foot on the pavement, about to hoist myself out when he calls me back.

"Wait."

My heart pauses in my throat as I settle back in the seat. Turning, I am caught in the intense stare of a man who wooed me with cheesy pickup lines and a screw-top bottle of wine.

After a short silence, he asks, his voice low and gruff, "How are you?"

"I'm fine. Yesterday was a lot but—"

"I'm not talking about yesterday. I mean … with what happened … between us."

Of all the impromptu times to be reminiscing about the past, now—when I'm about to go into a hotel to work while wearing another woman's dress and drugstore panties, holding a crumbling quiche in my hands—is not the moment.

Still, there is never—and will never be—a good time for us to talk.

For me to talk.

Some would say I owe the explanation in this situation. While I have many things I want to tell him, I'm not sure it would do any good. In fact, a whole lot of awful could come from me confessing my feelings to him.

Instead of answering his question, I ask him my own. "Do you regret anything that transpired between us?" I watch as his eyes dart downward.

He swallows hard, his Adam's apple bobbing as the lines on his forehead form into deep, pensive canyons.

I keep my attention on him and ask it in another way. "Is there any morsel of doubt—a single, tiniest bit of regret—you have about the choices we made?"

My question simmers with him for a moment longer than I expected. When he looks up at me, it's with eyes bearing so much conviction that I know he's about to tell me the absolute truth.

"No."

A slow, quivering breath escapes my throat, and I blink away, trying to get my bearings. His answer is a devastating knife to my chest, and yet it's confirmation that I made the right decision all those years ago.

"Same," I lie. "Thank you for helping last night."

I get out of the car and head into the hotel. When I turn around, Luke's car is gone just as fast as he left the last time I saw him.

four

"EXCUSE ME, MS. HATHAWAY, there is a package for you, waiting in the lobby." The hotel manager comes up to me at the end of the brunch event.

It's amazing; it all went off without a hitch. Just as Luke predicated, the bride and groom were understanding that the favors weren't here, as everyone had heard about the hotel fire. It still bothers me though. If there is one thing I pride myself on, it's being punctual, professional, and always coming through when needed.

To say I would have walked into a burning building to make my clients happy is an understatement.

I follow the hotel manager to the reception desk, where she lifts an envelope off the counter. Inside are my car keys. I know the fob is mine because of the diamond encrusted butterfly key chain attached.

"Who delivered this?"

"A man. Tall. Brown hair, blue eyes. I don't know if that helps. He asked we not alert you of his arrival. Your car is in the main lot, aisle two. He said the fob won't work due to water damage, but you can take out the valet key to enter your car and the magnet in the fob will start it."

I look back in the envelope and see my credit cards and license are inside.

"Thank you," I say, bewildered that Luke went to the hotel for my keys. I'm assuming the rest was destroyed. I'm grateful to at least have a way home.

I find my car where she said it would be. Inside, I sigh in relief at no longer feeling stranded in a faraway town.

In the console is a can of Coke. It's warm. The one he brought me last night and I never drank. My shoulders fall at the nice things Luke has done in the past twelve hours despite words he can't take back. I open the can and take a long gulp.

Melissa's right. I'm a closeted soda fiend.

I'm also a recovering Luke addict.

I need to kick the cravings for good.

"Mommy!" Ainsley comes barreling down the hall with her arms outstretched and long brown hair flowing around her shoulders. "I missed you. I waited for you to call and sing to me."

I lift my girl up and give her the hug of a lifetime. "My phone was lost last night. There was a fire at the hotel I was staying at."

"A fire!" She pushes against my shoulders to look at me with wide eyes. "Were you rescued by a fireman?"

"Kind of. What does Mommy always say about emergencies?"

"Look for a police officer, firefighter, doctor, or teacher. They're there to help."

"That's right. Hey, guess what," I say to her, and she grins, knowing what I'm about to say.

"I love you!" she answers for me with a laugh, and I tickle her in reward. "You say that every time."

"It's because I mean it." I give her about ten kisses on her cheeks and neck, which makes her giggle even more, and then put her down on the floor.

Being a wedding planner as a single mom has had its advantages. Ainsley and I are close because I've had her by my side since the moment she was born.

When Ainsley was a baby, I was home with her during the day and even brought her to appointments. Turns out, brides love a cooing, swaddled newborn. Grooms, not as much.

As she entered the toddler years, babysitters would watch her while I worked a weekend wedding. It's only recently that I started working out-of-town weddings.

Occasionally, my parents will take her, stating she's "self-managed," which I always read as, *Ainsley doesn't need someone to hand-feed or change her anymore, so we can now tolerate having our granddaughter in the house without your supervision.* I'm also well aware my mother enjoys the alone time with Ainsley because she feels she messed up certain "family values" with me and wants to make sure their sole grandchild sees what a "proper home" is.

This is why when Tara offered to stay with Ainsley overnight, stating it keeps her tied down from making bad decisions—which she does often—I accepted the offer right away. Sure, Tara is loud, a bit wild, says inappropriate things, and has a knack for getting others in trouble, but she's a confident, independent woman, and that's who I want my daughter to be around.

Ainsley scurries toward her room as I walk to the kitchen, where Tara is standing with a glass of wine in her hand, her hair up in a messy bun with long black tendrils falling around her face.

"I love your kid, but not gonna lie. Thirty-six hours together is a lot."

I nod toward the glass. "Drinking on the job?"

"I waited until I heard the garage door open. This bad boy has been chilling since eight o'clock this morning."

"A little dramatic, don't you think?"

"Who would I be without my dramatics?" She taps her chin, as if pondering the question, then replies with a grin, "Oh. You." She holds up the bottle of wine and asks if I want some.

"You say that like it's a bad thing," I say with a nod, sliding off the shoes that are too big for me. "Thanks again for watching Ainsley overnight. You need to let me know if it's too much."

She pours a glass and hands it to me.

"After my past few fiasco-filled weekends, I need to be tied down. Last month, I met a man who asked if I liked chain mail. I thought he was talking about pen-pal shit, so I was like, 'Yeah of course.' He mentioned he dressed up, and I'm wondering if he meant, you know, in bed. Next thing I know, I accidentally have this guy thinking I'm a huge fan of the Renaissance, and I spent the next two days in a corset, making bracelets and chest protectors in a role-playing Renaissance festival upstate. I was surrounded by people saying, 'Good morrow,' and, 'Prithee attend me,' while trying to get me to play bar wench and join some orgy in the backwoods. Trust me, I needed a girls' weekend with my favorite four-year-old."

"You never cease to amaze me."

"Maybe I should write a book. I'd call it *The Misadventures of Tara Parsons*. One woman's quest to meet a tall, gorgeous, and very funny man who will travel the world with her." She takes a sip and lets out a sigh. "If only such man existed."

I lean against the counter. "Still no luck on the dating apps?"

"I had a few pings last night. They probably just wanted a one-night stand, but I'm over that."

"What about that guy you dated last year?"

"Kent?" She takes another long swig. "Mr. Celibate? No, thank you. I might not want a one-night stand, but there has to be a happy medium. Men don't understand that sex and intimacy are two different things. Some want only sex without the intimacy while others, like Kent, think kissing and cuddling are enough. It's a disaster out there, Jillian."

"That's why I don't date."

"Okay, I said it was a disaster. Not avoidable. Seriously, woman, it must take some resilience to abstain from love as long as you have."

"That's because love is stupid."

"It is. But not everyone has the balls like you to go to a sperm bank to be a single mom before the age of thirty just to avoid the dating scene altogether."

"Some people have priorities. Being a mom was mine."

Ainsley's footsteps patter down the hall, but she doesn't appear. "Mommy! Cover your eyes."

Tara's face lights up. "I forgot to tell you. We went out for a little dinner and shopping spree last night. I couldn't help myself."

I close my eyes and smile, wondering what Tara could have bought my little girl that's such a showstopper.

After a beat, Ainsley's tiny voice shouts, "Open!"

When I do, I see my sweet, brown-haired cutie grinning up at me in a mermaid costume, equipped with a feather boa that looks like algae.

"You bought her an Ariel costume?" I ask through my tight smile.

"Doesn't she look beautiful?"

I beam as Ainsley does a twirl. "You are the most gorgeous sea princess I've ever seen! What made you want this costume?"

"I saw *The Little Mermaid* yesterday. It was raining, so Tara and I watched it, and I loved it! Then, we went out for egg rolls, and she bought me this!" Ainsley does another spin and nearly falls over with how her feet are virtually bound together in the costume.

Tara leans forward. "I couldn't believe she'd never seen *The Little Mermaid* before."

"That's because we don't watch movies with misogynistic views of women," I explain.

"What are you talking about? She had a *Moana*-themed birthday party last month."

Ainsley lifts her arm, and I twirl her again as I explain, "Moana's different. She left her family to bring life back to the island of Tafiti. Ariel left for some hot guy."

Tara looks up at the ceiling, pressing the wineglass to her chin as she muses, "You're right. Moana left to save her island. Ariel left for dick."

"What's dick?" Ainsley asks, and my eyes practically bulge out of my head.

"Dick's!" I grip her shoulders and move her out of the kitchen. "She said Dick's, as in the sporting goods store."

Ainsley looks over her shoulder and squints her eyes at me. "Ariel left for soccer cleats?"

"Yep. Why don't you go change into your Elsa costume? I love how beautiful you look, like the Snow Queen."

Ainsley shifts carefully down the hall, and Tara groans.

"Sure. Let her dress as the one who isolates herself in an ice castle, not to be loved by anyone."

"Better than the sister who marries the first man she meets."

"At least she takes chances." Tara smiles and bats her eyelashes.

"You're a bad influence." I accusingly point at her while grinning.

"Hey, everyone needs a fun Aunt Tara." She places her now-empty glass on the counter and then lifts her purse off the stool. "Okay, I'm off the clock and ready to let loose. It's ladies' night at Lone Tavern. Gonna go see if I can find me a cowboy."

I walk Tara to the door and convince her to keep the jeans and tank she has on and not switch to the minidress and boots that was her sexy cowgirl costume from last Halloween. I want her to meet a nice man, not get groped in a stall by the bad-boy sheriff.

With her gone, I head back into my kitchen and clean up. Tara is an awesome friend and babysitter, but she certainly makes a mess wherever she goes. Remnants of the brownies she baked are still on the counter and sink.

I'm finished cleaning when Ainsley comes back into the living area. I do a double take at her next costume of choice.

"I'm a firewoman!" she declares as she runs around the couch, making siren sounds, and then stops at my feet. "When I grow up, I want to be a firefighter, like the one who saved you last night. Was it a lady firefighter? Do I look like her?"

With her little grin, chin cleft, and precocious sense of humor, my little girl does indeed resemble the fireman who rescued me last night.

I take a seat on the couch and pull my daughter onto my lap. "Him. It was a him."

"Was he handsome?"

"Does that matter?"

"Answer the question, Mom."

"Yes, baby. He was very handsome," I say with a smile and brush her hair behind her ear. That information seems to appease her. "Any more questions?"

"No. I'm good. I love you." She taps my nose and then runs off into her room with a hand on her firefighter's helmet so it doesn't slip off her head.

Raising an independent woman is going to be the death of me. Especially one who reminds me a little too much of the man who she is dressing up as.

To my surprise, I liked the mermaid costume better.

five

"REALLY, JILLIAN, YOU COULD pretend to be coy. Jonathan is a catch and someone you should be eager to have a drink with."

I sigh into the phone as my hands sink deep into a dirty pot in my kitchen sink. It's been three days since I lost my phone in the fire, and I finally have a new cell phone.

"Absolutely not, Mother. I have no desire to go out with Jonathan Longbottom. The man has a thing for young twenty-somethings who think Smirnoff Ice is a luxury cocktail."

"You were a young twenty-something once. Wouldn't have hurt for you to flirt a little when you were a desirable young woman and could meet a suitable man."

"I'm still quite desirable now." I scrub tomato sauce off the sides of the pot. I brush a little too rough, and my fist punches the water, sending dirty suds into my face. I gag a little.

"You're my gorgeous, amazing daughter who is a trailblazer. That said, you can't deny it's a hard sell when you're a thirty-two-year-old single mother. Not to mention one who conceived in the most unnatural of ways." She says the final statement as if she were sucking on a sour candy.

"Tell me how you really feel."

"It makes you appear cold and dreary. If you were a lesbian, people would understand. Married yet infertile, you're a medical marvel. Otherwise, you just seem like a man-hater."

"Women who conceive or raise children on their own are badasses and should be applauded. Revered. Put on a pedestal."

"A twenty-six-year-old who goes to a sperm bank is diabolical. Your lifestyle is unconventional at best. I try to spin it."

"I'm not a headline, Mother."

"You should be. You're a showstopper of a woman. A Hathaway and the mother of my beautiful grandchild. I just wish you'd stop being so close-minded and let me set you up with one of these handsome gentlemen. It's not proper for a woman to do everything on her own. Ainsley deserves a nuclear family. She needs a male role model to show her how a woman should be provided for."

I remain quiet as I continue to scrub the pot, pausing from my weekly conversation, where my mother calls with another stab at my lifestyle.

"Jillian? Hello? Did I lose you? I think the line went dead. Are you there?"

"I'm here. I was looking up the date. I wanted to confirm it's no longer 1945."

"Clever," she muses with a disappointed harrumph. "What about companionship? I don't want to see you die alone." Her tone takes on a whisper-like volume. "I mean, seriously, who tends to your needs, dear?"

"Battery-operated toys."

"A lady shouldn't be so crass. Ainsley needs a father."

"She has a mother."

"Please, Jillian, you act like you have it all figured out. You wouldn't have been able to provide her with your cozy lifestyle if your grandmother hadn't given you a handout. What wedding planner can afford to live in Greenwood Village?"

"A successful one."

I scrub harder at the pot, scouring it until it looks brand-new. It's easier to take my frustrations out on a dirty piece of cookware than tell my mother to go to hell. In fact, I did that once, and she told me not to scowl because it was giving me wrinkles. Then, she proceeded to write down the business information for her plastic surgeon.

My mother, Kathleen Hathaway, is uptight and overbearing with an unrealistic, outdated vision of what a woman's lifestyle should be. She's also fiercely protective with a strong moral compass. She's the only mom I have, so I put up with her comments because, despite her callous attitude, I love her.

She huffs. "If you can't stand Jonathan, then consider Eric Hollenford. He's a geneticist, following in his father's footsteps, and recently divorced. Handsome as can be, and if you don't snag this one, I promise you, he will be taken off the market quickly."

I sigh as I remove the pot and dry it with a hand towel, balancing my phone between my shoulder and ear. "What will it take for you to stop your incessant desire to play matchmaker?"

"If you stopped fighting me on this, I'd consider the reality that there is no man good enough for you."

For the last four years, my mother has been on a mission: find Jillian a successful husband. I do not want a husband, nor do I care if he has money. I can take care of myself.

Doesn't mean I didn't once dream of having someone by my side.

My mother's words are cruel in their delivery, but they are sometimes true. I can provide a beautiful life for my little girl because of my grandmother's financial support when I found out I was pregnant with Ainsley. It was our little secret until my grandmother passed away last year. Perhaps my grandmother's support has given me too much power to feel independent, yet I have worked incredibly hard at creating the life I have. I own my own home, my business is thriving, and my daughter is living a life comparable to the one my parents provided me.

I wanted to fall in love. Then, I had Ainsley and was given all the love I could ever need. I've been on a few dates, but my time is very limited, and so is my patience. I have yet to find a man who has piqued my interest in any way.

My mother believes my lack of a husband is because my pickings are limited due to my "situation."

It'll be years before she stops pestering me, so perhaps if I stop fighting her, she'll realize I'm not interested in any of the men she parades in front of me every chance she gets.

"Fine," I say in defeat.

"Before I get my hopes up, I'd like to know what you are fine-ing?"

"A date with someone of your choosing. It cannot be Jonathan Longbottom. Really, Mother, it's insulting that you think he'd be a good match for me. And if it's the divorced one, I need to know why he's divorced, as I won't tolerate infidelity. Nor can I spend a moment with someone who doesn't like children."

"Fair and fair. Anything else?"

I bite down on my lip. "No one too charming. I need a realist."

"I have no idea what that means, but I'll do my best."

As I hang up with my mother, I finish tidying up my kitchen from the dinner I made for me and Ainsley. I'm not a good cook, but there are a few things I've mastered through the years. Two nights a week, Ainsley and I go out to dinner, somewhere refined, where she can learn how to sit like a lady and have manners, as any Hathaway should. Other nights, I have her in the kitchen, cooking with me, because, while I might be raising her with etiquette and against the social norms, I don't want her to be reliant on a live-in maid to cook her meals, like my mother.

I walk around the living room and pick up the toys Ainsley has left around. Our townhome is quite lovely. A three-bedroom brick home with dark hardwood floors and white cabinetry. I keep it tidy with the help of the extra bedroom being a playroom for Ainsley. I look down the first-floor hall to the room Ainsley uses for her toys and playthings. It's a sweet room. Pink walls with faux picket fencing and a mural of a fairy garden. It's similar to her bedroom upstairs, except that one is a deep purple with hand-painted hot-air balloons over a magical land below.

While Ainsley plays with her stuffed animals, set up for a tea party, I put the laundry away. I'm in Ainsley's room when the doorbell rings, and I look at the time, wondering who could be at my door this late on a Wednesday night. I look at the doorbell app on my phone to see who the visitor is, but it's not working—hasn't been for the past week.

"I'll get it!" Ainsley's voice squeaks from the floor below.

I call down to my daughter, "Wait. I'm not expecting company. That could be a package I have to sign for."

As I'm jogging down the stairs, I hear her talking.

"Who are you?" Ainsley asks, which clearly means she opened the front door after I told her not to.

"I think I have the wrong address," a man drawls.

I know that baritone voice—deep and gravelly, calm and smooth.

The hair on my arms rises, and my chest quickens.

I hadn't heard it in five years, and then recently, the owner of said voice quasi-rescued me from being stranded at a restaurant in a non-panty-wearing night of abandonment.

"If you want 733 Cherry Street, this is it," Ainsley states, having recently learned our address during a lesson on the importance of the post office in school.

I should be walking over there, but I'm currently frozen, stunned. Maybe Luke will get confused and walk away. I shouted my address at him the other night in his truck. Perhaps he'll think he wrote it down wrong.

"I'm looking for Jillian Hathaway. Does she live here?"

Please say no. I send telepathic signals to Ainsley and hope some mother-daughter connection will help her hear me. *Ainsley, remember what Mommy said about talking to strangers. Close the door and walk away.*

"Yep! That's my mom. Stay. I'll get her. Mommy! There's a man at the door for you!"

I slam my hand on my forehead and make a mental note to go over the importance of not talking to random men who show up at our front door. Stranger Danger 101 was clearly a failed lecture in the Hathaway household.

I pinch the bridge of my nose.

Luke is here.

Why is Luke here?

He shouldn't be here.

But he is.

six

GET IT TOGETHER, JILLIAN.

I look in the mirror and take note of my beige jogging suit and topknot bun. I need to change. This makes the second occurrence in recent memory where this man is catching me looking less than my most fabulous self. I don't want to impress him per se. It's just when one sees the man who deserted her years ago, she usually prefers a *don't you wish you could have me back* look over *yeah, sometimes, I wear this to bed and lounge in it all day because I'm too lazy* ensemble.

I take a deep, cleansing breath, dragging it down to my ribs in order to calm myself, then walk down the hall.

Ainsley is standing at the doorway. Her squished eyebrows match that of the man she's staring up at.

"Hi," I say, stepping in front of Ainsley and swooping her behind me. "Why are you here?"

Luke blinks back at me and shifts from one foot to the other. His arched brows are furrowed, and his full lips are pursed, as if he, too, doesn't know why he's here. In his hands is the gold ice bucket. I haven't seen it since he walked me out of the restaurant and tossed it into the backseat of his truck.

"You have a daughter?"

"Yes." My answer is quick. "What do you want?"

"I brought you this." He holds up the ice bucket.

"That belongs to the Walden Hotel."

"They won't be needing it for a long time. I, uh …" He hands the bucket to me, and I take it in bewilderment. "I thought you might want it."

I quirk a brow. "You drove three hours to bring me an ice bucket that's not mine?"

He stands there, leaning back on his heels and seriously glaring back at me. "Yes."

I look down at the bucket. Its exterior is pristine with a shiny gold mirror-like covering that reflects everything around it while the white interior is scratched and stained from years of wear by guests, only to be left behind in a hotel room. I can oddly relate to this piece of tin and plastic.

"Thanks."

I go to close the door, but he takes a step forward, halting me.

"Can we talk?" he asks.

I grip the bucket close to me and shake my head. "I don't think that's a good idea. I'm on my way out."

"Dressed like that?"

My jaw drops at the audacity of him making such a rude comment. It's something I'd expect from my mother, not Luke Incendio.

He must notice my objection because he quickly adds, "What I mean is, from what I remember … you don't like to leave the house unless you're dressed for the occasion. Skirts and blouses and all that. Classic. But I'm not here to talk about your attire. Truth is, I haven't been able to stop thinking about something you said. I just wanted to … fuck."

"Bad word!" Ainsley shouts with a giggle.

"Crap. Shoot. Sorry." Luke shakes his head and tries again. "I used to have all the lines, and words came easily, yet now, standing here, I …"

"Don't know what to say?"

"I don't know where to start."

His honesty catches me off guard. My inhale is thick, and I hold the air in my chest. Turns out, Luke and I have something in common.

"Are you going to invite me in?" he asks.

"No."

"Why not?" Ainsley chimes in from behind me. "We never have friends here. Well ... Melissa and Hunter and Izzy. Oh, and Tara. She's Mommy's friend and sometimes she babysits. She needs a boyfriend. Do you need a girlfriend?"

"No," he answers as Ainsley pulls him over the threshold rather forcefully.

"We always go to everyone else's house, which is fun, but I don't get to show anyone my house. I hope you like costumes because I have the best. Wanna see my new tea set?"

"Luke doesn't want to play tea," I interject.

"Says who?" He looks at me like I'm insane and then down at Ainsley. "I'm Luke. What's your name?"

"Ainsley Lisette Hathaway. Pleasure to meet you. That's what my grandmother says I have to say when I meet adults. If you see her, tell her I did a good job."

"I will." His amused grin is so different from the nervous energy he was exuding from the doorway.

"It's a school night. Ainsley needs to get in bed," I state.

"No. Not true," she argues. "The sky isn't fully dark yet. Luke wants to play tea party."

"He was just being nice. Grown men don't play tea."

"Not true." He leans down toward Ainsley with his hands on his knees and meets her eyes. "When I was little, my big sister made me play with her every day. I didn't get to play with dinosaurs and monster trucks, like most boys. I was usually playing house."

She giggles. "Were you the daddy?"

"I was the baby. Every time. My sister pretended to change my diaper and feed me bottles until I was at least four years old. Then, we graduated to supermarket and diner. I made an excellent cook."

She claps her hands together and widens her eyes. "You're going to love my playroom!"

With her small hand in his large one, Ainsley drags Luke into the house, and I suddenly have an empty feeling in the pit of my stomach.

I wipe my sweaty hands on my pants, then carry the ice bucket into the kitchen and place it on the counter before moving quickly down the hall to the playroom.

They've each taken a seat at the play table. On Luke's lap is the elephant that usually occupies the seat. There are only two chairs, so I settle on my knees, which keeps them from bouncing.

Ainsley pours the tea.

Luke eyes her with interest. "How old are you, Ainsley?"

"Four. How old are you?"

"Would you believe me if I said I was twenty?"

"No. You're old, like my mom. I'd say forty. If you want to date Tara, you need to muster-eyes. She likes pretty boys."

"Moisturize," I interpret for Luke.

His hands clench an invisible dagger in his chest, and he makes a show of pulling it out of his heart. "Damn, I'm gonna have to up my game. Here I thought, I was doing pretty well for thirty-two."

"You're too young to be talking to Tara about pretty boys." I blanch at her.

Ainsley pauses mid–tea pour to give me the stare-down. "Mom, I am a lady. Me and Tara … we have A and B conversations. You can C your way out of it."

"That's not kind. A real lady doesn't talk to her mother like that," I scold.

"Sorry, Mommy." Her bottom lip puffs out as she looks down with her shoulders sinking.

Sensing the energy in the room has shifted, Luke holds his cup up and takes a pretend sip. "This is delicious. And it's such a cool color."

Ainsley perks up. "It's blue. I used magical blueberries when I made it," she replies matter-of-factly regarding the invisible tea.

He takes another sip and offers some to the elephant. "Looks like my cup is empty. Can I have more?"

"Why, yes, sir. Please hold." Ainsley scurries to her play kitchen and pretends to boil another cup of tea.

As we wait, Luke looks around the playroom. His long legs are bent with his knees practically at his chin while his elbows try to find a comfortable spot on the table.

While those dark, daring eyes flicker around the room, I take the opportunity to appraise him.

He's still so very handsome with his wide-jawline bone structure. Today, he's sporting a very light scruff, making him look manly and rugged. At this small child's table, the bold exterior of the man looks extra absurd yet absolutely adorable.

"Your place is nice," he comments.

"Thank you. Been here a few years. Ainsley and I needed the space."

"Your apartment would never have held all this stuff." He gestures around the playroom, and I flinch.

"You've never been to my apartment."

"Assuming," he says quickly and adds, "it's very feminine. Lots of pink. Is there a man cave around here for your husband?"

"I'm not married."

"Ainsley's dad lives far?"

"She doesn't have one."

Luke looks back at me with a discerning stare, and I shiver. There's a small draft that comes in through the playroom window. I get up and make sure the window is closed tight. I shift the conversation back in his direction.

"Your place was rather devoid of a feminine quality. Surprised Stella didn't add some floral pillows or something."

"Surprised myself."

Ainsley is back with the teapot, along with her milk and sugar play set. "Would you like some sugar?"

Luke accepts but holds his hand up in refusal of the milk. "I don't take milk in my tea. Real or pretend."

"Me neither. Gives me a tummy ache. That's why I only serve almond milk at my tea parties." She lifts her palm up in the air, like the sassy child she is. "It's only my favorite with French vanilla in it."

"Chocolate almond milk is even better."

Ainsley's eyes widen at me. "You never told me there's chocolate almond milk!"

"You have enough treats in your life," I explain.

She leans into Luke and whispers rather loudly, "She won't even let me drink soda."

He lifts a brow and gives me a bemused look. "You don't say."

Ainsley places a hand on her hip. "She hates it and says it rots your teeth. I really want to try the black soda. My friend Hunter said it's so good and his mom lets him drink it at birthday parties."

Luke leans back with his arms crossed. "I bet your mom drinks soda on the sly when no one is looking."

I clear my throat, interrupting their powwow. Luke smiles at me. My stare back is a reprimanding one.

"What?" he asks with a laugh as Ainsley runs back to her play kitchen.

"No one gives away my secret soda obsession." My scolding is in a loud whisper.

"Good to know I have blackmail."

I scrunch my nose at him as she reappears with plates.

While she serves us, something on the other side of the room catches Luke's eye. There's a floating bookshelf on the wall that I've recently rotated out with books appropriate for an emerging reader. The covers of the books face the room, as it's a shallow shelf made for the covers to be displayed that way.

"That's a pretty impressive book list up there. Are those all autobiographies?" he asks.

"Mommy got me a new book on some lady who wears a black cape and looks real mean."

"Ruth Bader Ginsburg is a national treasure," I defend. "I encourage her to read books on real-world icons. Preferably women."

He gives an agreeable nod. "You need a book on Molly Williams. First female firefighter."

Ainsley jumps up with her hands clasped together. "A girl fireman?"

"Molly Williams was a former slave in New York City, who bought her freedom and was braver than most men."

"Mommy was rescued by a fireman. A very handsome one."

Her comment has Luke's head swiveling slowly in my direction with an arched brow and a devilish smirk. "Good to know." He leans forward and asks Ainsley, "I'm a firefighter. Do you think I'm handsome?"

"You're okay, but you have a butt chin, like me."

His eyes narrow. "Look at that. I never heard it called a butt chin before."

"Mikey—he sits in front of me in school—called it that. He's a meanie. I want to sew my chin closed and make it look like a normal chin."

"Absolutely not." He slaps his knee. "Chin clefts are dignified. They command respect."

"It's ugly, and no one else has them. Especially girls."

"They are rare. I got mine from my dad." He runs his hand over the back of his neck and glances at me for a beat and then back to Ainsley.

My heart feels like it's in my throat, and I wipe my hands on my jeans.

"Ainsley, I think you've been chewing Luke's ear off. He just came for a quick visit and has a long drive back home. Besides, you have to get to bed. School tomorrow."

She grumbles as she rises to her feet. My girl might be sassy, but she's a good kid when it comes to doing as she's told. Well, except when it's direct orders to not open the front door.

Luke takes the hint and rises. I'm thankful he moves easily to the front door. Ainsley and I are fast behind him—her wanting to be near our new visitor for as long as possible and me needing him to get him out the door as quickly as possible.

Luke opens the front door but stops, spins around, and takes a knee, making him Ainsley's height. The two stare at each other, eye to eye. His dark blue to her light green.

His hand reaches up and brushes her untamed hair behind her ear as he takes her in with a silent look. I rest a hand on my belly. There's a narrowing of his eyes and a tilt of his chin. He's studying her face, as if trying to commit it to memory.

"Ainsley Lisette Hathaway, I'm glad I got to meet you. I hope we get to see each other again."

She smiles bigly. "Can you bring your fire truck next time?"

"Maybe. I'll see what I can do." Luke winks, and I swear my little girl internally faints with happiness.

He stands erect, taking up the doorway, and I place a hand on the door and start to close it. His feet are steadfast as he pauses a beat longer than is comfortable.

Mouth pursed, eyes slanted, and chin raised.

"Good night, Jillian."

I close the door as fast as I can and usher Ainsley to go upstairs to get ready for bed. While she's upstairs, I'm still standing here in the hallway with my back up against the door, wondering why his good night felt so triggering.

Probably because it wasn't a good-bye.

It's a promise.

When Luke gets something in his head, he won't stop until he sees it through.

"Heard you're off the clock until two." Luke, the handsome stranger in Aruba who had me dancing on the beach the night before, practically jumped out of the bushes along the path I was walking on.

My hand rose to my chest as I closed my eyes and caught my breath.

"You scared the heck out of me," I reprimanded.

With teeth skimming his bottom lip, he leaned down and waited for me to open my eyes. When I did, it was to the sight of his gloriously shirtless and sun-drenched body. Firm pectorals with a chiseled torso and arms that looked like they could carry me for days without him breaking a sweat. I had a faint vision of just where I would like to be carried, then shook the feeling away … fast.

"You're cute as hell. Did you just say heck? Please tell me you curse."

"There are plenty of words in the English language. No need to use profanity."

"Fuck is in the English language."

"I don't think you need to use it for everything."

"That's something someone who's uptight would say."

"I'm not—" I dropped my shoulders and placed a hand on my hip. "You're a child. Fine." I let out a breath before saying, "Fuck."

With a tap on my nose, he grinned. "You're adorable. Now, let's go. We have a boat to catch."

"I'm not getting on a boat. I have work today. There's a ceremony rehearsal, followed by a sunset dinner. I can't get on a boat. Why is there a boat?"

He grabbed my hand and started walking me off the path. "I booked us a catamaran tour of the island. I asked the concierge desk, and they said the rehearsal dinner you're working isn't until five and that you aren't supposed to be on the beach until two. So, I figure that gives us two hours to have some fun."

My feet halted, although my hand was still in his. "Luke, you're sweet, and I had a nice time last night, but I'm here to work a very expensive, very upscale, and very high-profile wedding. I can't disappear on a catamaran for two hours with a guy who's here for a bachelor party."

"Why not?"

"Because I have to work."

His mouth pursed as he nodded in understanding. "You know what we are. Grumpy and sunshine. My twin sister says she likes to read books where the romantic characters are opposites attracted to one another. You're grumpy, and I'm sunshine."

"I'm not grumpy. And I'm not attracted to you." My words were ones he clearly disagreed with as he raised a brow and wore the wickedest grin I'd ever seen in my life.

I leaned back, raised my face to the sky, and groaned in defeat. "Fine. I'll go. For one hour."

"You're gonna love it. And, Jillian, go grab a suit—unless you plan on skinny-dipping."

"I can't get my hair wet."

"What? My girl has to try cliff jumping."

I swallowed with nervous energy. "I don't cliff jump, and I'm not your girl."

"Not yet, you're not."

"Not yet to what?"

"All of the above." He winked and slapped me on the ass. "Countdown starts now."

The next two hours—yes, I gave in and stayed for the duration—were ones I'd never forget. We sunned, splashed, and laughed. He charmed me with his stories of living in Boston, growing up in the rural pastures of New York, his buddies who were always into mischief, and life as a bartender with dreams of someday owning his own restaurant and bar. He sailed that catamaran like a pro and sang into the open ocean. Nay, he crooned. The man sang country music so well I became a fan of the genre I once hated. He was charismatic, charming, and so damn beautiful in the sunshine.

I was putty for Luke after that.

Yes, I'd tried to fight it, but it was only a matter of time until I was completely gone for him.

What transpired soon after was a tragic love story.

My cell phone vibrates in my pocket, pulling me from reminiscing about a lazy afternoon in the Caribbean Sea. The number on the screen is one I don't recognize, but the words in the text message let me know exactly who it is.

Luke.

The reason I know it's him is something that has my legs feeling like jelly and a chill running down my chest.

When were you going to tell me we have a daughter?

seven

"Lavish Events," Melissa answers the phone at our office in downtown Greenwood Village. She gives a little shimmy as she says our company name. It's as if she still can't believe we have our own office for the wedding and design company we started four years ago.

Our new office is three rooms of awesome. We share a desk in our office above a bridal boutique on Main Street, and it's been a godsend for our business. No longer is my garage a place for storage, and meetings at the local coffee shop were getting harder to hold without random patrons eavesdropping on party-planning discussions with clients.

Working with Melissa is the icing on the cake. She's smart, funny, and far more free-spirited than I ever have been. It's fun, living vicariously through her whirlwind of a soap-opera-drama life. Hopefully, she has some good stories for me today because I could use a little distraction. A Mack truck–sized distraction actually, but I'll settle for a Kia.

While she's on the phone, I'm working on my laptop, trying my best to focus on an upcoming wedding but I can't concentrate.

I lift my phone and look for any text messages.

None.

I never responded to Luke last night. I mean, how does one respond to a text like that? It's jarring, to say the least, and yet—

"You okay over there, killer?" Melissa asks as she hangs up the phone.

"Yeah. Fine."

She looks down through the glass-top dining table we use as a joint desk. "Could've fooled me. Your knee has been bouncing like crazy. I fear you'll shatter the glass."

"Just trying to work through logistics. Do you have everything set with the imported woodland tables?"

"I had to practically sell my lastborn on the black market for them, but I got 'em! Seriously, I don't think anyone understands the stress that goes into wedding planning and designing. Bridezillas get a bad rep. Well, some might deserve it. They can be monsters to the family. We, however, are professionals and put in hundreds of hours of work to make the six most magical hours of a couple's life."

I lean across the table and give her a high five.

"Speaking of bridezillas, how is your own wedding design coming along?"

Melissa's engagement ring shines in the sunlight pouring through the window as she groans at the thought of designing her upcoming nuptials. She's so theatrical that it makes me giggle.

"Trying to throw a very small, very laid-back wedding in a barn is actually turning out to be far more intricate than I thought," she explains. "It's my second wedding, so I don't want it to be over the top, yet it's Will's first, so it should be special. His mother seems to think this is the most important wedding of her life and keeps on trying to make it bigger and bigger. I can't believe I let her talk me into having an engagement party."

"Doesn't she have a bunch of kids who are already married?"

"Yes! Will is one of five and has eleven nieces and nephews. That family is in no shortage of parties. Only one of his siblings has never been married. Cade is the consummate bachelor. He's never home long enough to date anyway. Oh! I should hook you two up. I bet you could get him to settle down."

Holding up my palms, I declare, "No, thank you. A bachelor who doesn't have kids is not a good look for me. Besides, I can get my own dates. I have absolutely no desire to be set up with anyone." I go back to typing on my computer and then drop my head in my hand when I remember what I promised my mother last night. "Strike that. I told my mother I'd let her set me up. One time."

"Letting your mother hook you up with someone is a big deal, Jillian. Are you sure about that? It's not gonna stop at one date. She can be a bit—"

"Overbearing," I say before she can use another adjective.

My mother is many things, but I'm trying to stay calm today. Just the thought of why I'm trying to stay Zen, distract myself, and overall forget about my current life drama has me sighing in a cry-like whimper.

Melissa brushes her long blonde hair over her shoulder and opens her laptop. "You know you can always call if the date goes south."

"No need. I know how to walk away from a bad date. No reason to waste his time or mine."

She looks up from her screen and smiles. "I wish I had your disposition. I feel like I was a walking punching bag for years. Just kept rolling over and playing dead so everyone else didn't have to deal with my issues."

"You were trying to make your children's world stress-free."

"True, but I was a total people-pleaser. Took me a while to take my life back."

Melissa Jones is a divorced mom of two who has a jerk of an ex-husband, who she remains close to for the sake of her kids, Isabella and Hunter. A little over a year ago, she was arrested for breaking into her ex-husband's mistress's salon for her hair-color card and met her knight in shining armor. Her fiancé, William Bronson, is the real deal ... if I still believed in that sort of thing.

"Took your life back is right!" I lean back with a smile. "You, my darling friend, are worthy of every bit of happiness this world has to offer."

"That's sweet. Write that down. Izzy's gonna need help writing her maid-of-honor speech. Tara's trying to convince my twelve-year-old to do a hip hop and rap performance."

"Tara has already started writing it for her," I say with a laugh. In fact, I heard some of her ideas, and it's going to be ridiculous, if not kinda cute, if her daughter, Isabella, can pull it off. "What kind of speech did Tara make at your first wedding?"

"A drunken one, where she hit on my dad, told Tyler his balls would be in a vise if he hurt me, and then had a mariachi band come in and play 'Celebration' by Kool & the Gang because she thought it was the happiest song in the world."

I fall to the side in a fit of laughter, feeling lighter than I did a few moments ago. That's what a good friendship will do. Melissa doesn't know the anxiety I have in my life right now, but her mere presence and simple conversation can put me at ease.

If only I felt comfortable enough to confide in her. Sadly, I've never had that comfort with anyone.

The intercom buzzes, so Melissa picks up the phone to see who could be at our front door. "Lavish Events!"

While she shimmies, I rise and walk into the other room that we use as a storage space for the items we like to keep on hand. We also happen to keep a small refrigerator in here, where I'm currently getting a bottle of water. As I take a sip, Melissa appears at the doorway.

"You have a visitor." Her eyes are shining with giddiness. "A tall, strapping fireman is here to see you. I know good-looking men because I happen to be engaged to one, and this guy is salivatingly hot. Beware that, if he's a potential groom, it's best not to make out with him. I learned that lesson the hard way."

I nearly spit out my water. Okay, I actually do, and Melissa has to take a step back to protect herself from the spray.

"Come again?" I ask with a cough.

Her brows narrow as she wipes down her arm and looks slightly amused. "Someone is nervous. I've never seen nervous Jillian. That is more my style."

"How do you know he's a fireman? Is he wearing his uniform? Maybe the building's on fire and we have to evacuate."

"Nope. He's wearing one of those T-shirts with the engine number and logo on it."

"Does the man own any other clothing?" I mutter to myself, which makes Melissa raise a brow.

"You know him and his clothing well then?"

I give her a deadpan expression and then look behind her. I don't see him, so he mustn't see me. "Tell him I'm not here."

"Too late. As my daughter, Izzy, would say, that would be super sus. I hate preteen lingo, but sus for suspicious works."

I play with the collar of my button-down and weigh my options. Behind me is a window I could climb out of. The fire escape seems easy to manage, but my heels would get stuck in the grating. My pencil skirt might make it a tad difficult to climb down the ladder, yet I could make it.

Escaping Luke's presence is tempting, but that would imply I did something wrong when I know, without a doubt, I'm not in the wrong here.

Chest out, chin high, I walk past Melissa and into the main office. It's a beautiful room with a wooden accent wall, pastel colors, and crystal chandeliers. A very feminine space that is currently bearing way too much testosterone as Luke Incendio stands in the middle of it.

His hair is wild today, as are his eyes, dark and daring. He looks even taller today with the way his chest is barreled and shoulders squared. His Wranglers hug his thighs, and his T-shirt accents the ripples in his chest and biceps without it being too tight. It's a silly time to be appreciating his body, but it's easier than looking into those eyes, which are so overwhelming that my heart is working its way into my stomach and is about to explode.

I press down the sides of my pencil skirt and square my own shoulders, matching his stance. Even though his hands are casually in his pockets, his frame is tense.

"Jillian." My name is gruff on his lips.

"Luke," I say back.

Melissa's eyes practically bulge out of her head as she appears, realizing that the Luke, who I apparently rambled on about one night over drinks, is the same Luke I stayed with this past weekend, and he's now in our front office.

While Luke and I do some sort of mental game of chicken, waiting for the other to say something of importance, Melissa fiddles with her ring and starts to pace.

"For the record, I am not good in situations like this unless it has to do with my children. My heart says I should leave you two alone to talk about whatever it is that is brewing in this moment, but my head says not to leave Jillian alone with a strange man who looks like he either wants to kiss her or kill her. Am I reading the room right?"

I shrug my shoulders while Luke's stance relaxes a touch, and he stares at her, wondering if this girl is for real. I give him an assuring nod.

Melissa grabs her purse from the table. "I'm going to walk to Beans and Leaves for a coffee. Luke, pleasure to meet you. In case this goes awry"—she lifts her cell phone and takes a picture of us standing on different sides of the table—"I'm gonna use this as evidence. Also, Luke, please know that while I am not the type to hide a body, we have a friend named Tara who will be here with a .45 and a shovel and has no shame in burying you in Newbury Woods." She takes a quick breath and then smiles brightly. "Okay then. I'll be back in twenty."

Like a bolt of nervous energy, Melissa is gone, and I'm left wondering what kind of loyalty my friend truly has that she's left me with a man she assumes is either going to murder me or maul me with his mouth. If the roles were reversed, I'd have parked myself on a chair and watched the confrontation.

"You didn't answer my text," he says almost immediately upon being alone.

"Wasn't aware you were waiting for a reply."

There's a conference table in the room, creating a barrier between us. He starts to walk around the table in my direction. I move in the opposite direction.

"Your daughter has wild brown hair," he states.

"As does about twenty percent of the world's population."

"She's lactose intolerant."

"Again, not an anomaly."

"There's a prominent cleft in her chin."

"Just like Henry Cavill, Ben Affleck, Matt Damon—"

"Me."

He halts his prowl around the table.

I stop.

"You," I breathe.

His hands grip the top of a chair as he looks down and arches his back. His eyes close with a sharp squint, and I can see his jaw muscles protruding through the sides of his face. As he looks up, that powerful posture is now replaced with the picture of a man defeated yet determined.

"Jillian, please. Be honest with me. Is Ainsley ..." His eyes hold steady while he parts his mouth with an inhale, preparing himself for his world to fall apart or be put together. There's a shaky vulnerability to his staggered words, the weight of them felt with every syllable. "Is Ainsley my daughter?"

There are many reasons why I'm a single mother. Choosing to bring a little girl into the world without a man in my life was not an easy decision. While the reasons are justified, there is nothing in this moment that can keep me from answering his question truthfully.

"Biologically, yes."

My words hit him in the face like a freight train, and I can sense the overwhelming sensation of him being hit by it. He came here with a purpose. He saw the train coming, and yet the impact of the truth is evident.

Luke gasps so hard that his chest rises. He lays a hand over his heart, and the look on his face that was so sharp, so wild, and so annoyed just moments ago has been replaced. With two simple words, Luke's demeanor has gone from hardened to softened, with eyes shiny and a throat that contracts with a hard swallow. His mouth is pursed, and his brows furrow as he looks down and processes the news.

"I have a daughter."

"Your sperm contributed to her creation, yes."

"She looks like my mom. I saw it in her as soon as we met. Same smile too. Everyone always said I favored my mom, but I never really saw it until I met Ainsley."

"Believe me, I know the similarities," I mumble.

"She's so smart."

"Her preschool said she's very advanced for her age. You gave her the looks. I'll take credit for the brains."

"And her eyes. They're so pretty."

I'm taken aback by the proud-papa vibes he's giving off. I nod as I fold my arms across my chest and take a step back.

"Is she ..." he starts, his voice almost pained as his fist rises to his mouth. "I know I met her, but is she ..." He swallows so hard that his Adam's apple looks like it's going to pop out of his neck. "Is she healthy?"

"Yes."

His gaze flicks upward. They're glassy with remorse, affection, and—dare I say—anger. "Why didn't you tell me?"

"You know exactly why."

"Do I?" His jaw juts out, his features like stone as he shoots me a hardened stare. "Pardon me if I can't find a proper reason why a woman wouldn't tell a man she brought his child into the world."

Heat flushes through my body at his accusation. "Because you didn't want her."

"That's not true."

"Do you need a history lesson? Because I'm happy to teach it."

"What you remember and what really happened are two different things."

"Let's start with you leaving me alone in a hotel room with a text for a *great lay* and a *see ya later*."

"That's not what I wrote. It wasn't like that."

I push off the back of one of the chairs. "You're right. It wasn't. It was followed by a sweet voice mail and then the ghosting of a lifetime." I start to move about the conference table, no longer needing the space from him as a surge of pent-up anger rages through me. "I should have known you were too good to be true with your corny lines and charisma, practically stalking me for three days until you got me spread-eagle in the damn canopy bed. I thought you were the real deal, Luke, and then you vanished. I wasn't planning on ever talking to you again, and yet two weeks later, I got the surprise of a lifetime. The first thing I did was call you, but lo and behold, you blocked my number."

His eyes close in response, as if he's mentally scolding himself.

"I was tempted to just leave you in the dust, but I couldn't do that. You had a right to know. You have no idea how impossible it was to hunt you down. Incendio isn't exactly the easiest name to spell. I had to track down some part-time bartender in a foreign country who had taken a picture of your license in order to get it. Of course, there was no number listed for that address in Boston. I should be a detective if this wedding planning life doesn't pan out because I called every Incendio in the book."

"You called my parents' house," he says, his dark brows clenched together.

He clearly remembers me calling years ago and him telling his family to tell me he was unavailable.

"I was pregnant, alone, scared, and you made me go on a wild goose chase for you. I found you. I did the right thing, and I found you."

"I wasn't ignoring you. Jillian. You have no idea what happened back then."

"Neither do you, and it was awful. I had no one. I might have been a grown woman, but I couldn't tell my judgmental parents I had gotten impregnated by some guy I'd met in Aruba who vanished into thin air. Who does that? You, Luke. You cut me off completely."

His hands rise to his head, and he turns away from me, probably because I must look like a wild, raging lunatic of a woman. My finger is in the air in an accusatory pose. My chest heaves, and I feel my cheeks rising to stop my emotions from spilling down my face.

I will not cry for this man. I will not let him know what happened next utterly destroyed me.

"It didn't stop you," he says over his shoulder.

He knows this story well.

He knows just how tragic it became.

After a week of calling his parents' home and being given the cold shoulder, I finally heard his voice when he answered that goddamn phone.

My jaw quivers as I ask, "Do you remember what you said to me? The horrible, awful words you sputtered?"

This beautiful man with his smooth skin, chiseled features, and pouty lips looks heartbroken and shattered as he faces me with a dire expression. Too bad there's no amount of beauty that can hide the ugly we hold inside.

Since he's not going to answer my question, I answer it for him.

"You told me you didn't want our baby. You said to get rid of it."

There's a mist of dread that falls upon his face as he relives the moment that absolutely crushed my soul.

With a step forward, he declares, "I was drunk, Jillian. I didn't mean it. That wasn't me speaking. It was grief. And whiskey."

"It doesn't matter what you were going through or feeling at the moment. All that matters was, you had a choice to make, and you did it with conviction and never turned back."

The clench of his jaw hardens as he shakes his head. His stance widens. The muscles in his arms flex with his sudden change of physical emotion.

"Never turned back?" His voice rises. "That's what you think? You believe that all these years, I had zero regrets about how things ended between us? That I haven't—" The lines in his forehead deepen as he shakes his head and lifts his chin. "No. None of this matters. Those eyes of yours, they fucking struck me dead the first time I saw you in that bar and have always shown exactly what you're thinking. Right now, they're saying all that needs to be said. No matter what comes out of my mouth, you'll never believe me. There is so much more to this story, but right now, all that matters is Ainsley. I'm her father, and I'll be damned if I'm not in her life."

"You can't swoop in and disrupt her world."

"I protect what's mine."

His fist barrels into his chest as his lips curl. He glares down at me like he's not just talking about Ainsley. The hair on my arms rises, and my fingers run over the nape of my neck as my pulse speeds up.

"You didn't protect me. Not when I was scared and alone and had to make the choice of a lifetime. Not when I was emotionally broken in the back room of a family planning clinic. Not when I was bringing an infant home and wondering how I was going to do this by myself. Then again, I wasn't yours, so why protect me?"

"I fucked up."

"You did, and now, you want to be the hero. That's not how it works. You can say all the right things, but your actions are what count. You walked away a long time ago."

He closes the space between us. The heat of his body pours off him, the fire of his conviction coming dangerously close. "I'm here now."

I step back. There's no way this man is going to come crashing into Ainsley's life—my life—five years too late. Anxiety insidiously infiltrates my thoughts.

"How do I know you won't hurt her again?"

"To me, family is everything. If you don't know that, then you never knew a thing about me."

I want to laugh at that comment. "Turns out, I know nothing about you, Luke."

"We have a lifetime to get to know each other. Let me prove my words with my actions. I want to see my daughter."

My hands rise and try to push him back without touching him. "You're going too fast. I need to think this through."

I make my way to the other side of the room, closest to the window overlooking Main Street.

When Luke banished me from his life and threw away his chance to be a father, I came back to this town to be safe. Greenwood Village has always been my home, the place where I planned to raise my daughter and keep her away from the hurt of the outside world.

I never wanted to do it alone. I wanted Luke. An eternity has happened in the time he walked away from me, and yet the years passed by in a flash. He might have given up on me, but I hunted him down because not only did he have a right to know he was going to have a child, but our child also deserved to have a father.

He threw her away before he even knew her.

Why now? Why hasn't he tried finding me before? Perhaps it doesn't matter. This isn't about me. He's here, wanting to know her and not walking away.

I might hate this man, and yet I am so grateful to him. He gave me Ainsley. And no matter how I feel, the fact is, he's standing here with the knowledge that he has a daughter, and he's not running from it.

He's demanding his presence in her life.

There are so many ways this could go wrong. I could stand to lose a lot. I could lose her. I could lose myself. Yet I have to do what's right.

I turn around and face Luke, the gorgeous man who gave my daughter her beauty and—let's face it—her whole personality.

"You're right. I don't know you, and while you might have created her, I can't just have you barging into her life. She's feisty, but she's fragile. She's still a baby in many ways. This could be too much for her."

He swallows and walks toward me. His hands are open. His voice is softer than before. "I'm not looking to brand her like cattle. I just want to spend time with my daughter."

His daughter.

"Okay." My sigh is one of defeat for so many reasons. "The park. We can meet there. I'll look at my and Ainsley's calendar and tell you what works for us."

The corners of his eyes drop, and his lip rises in anticipation.

"Jillian, this is only the beginning."

That's what I'm afraid of.

eight

THE GREENWOOD VILLAGE PARK is vast in space and unlimited in activities. Like a mini Central Park, it boasts a lake, a playground, baseball fields, and even a carousel. Living in a tiny town like this has its advantages, and this beautiful recreational area is one.

I told Ainsley that Luke was meeting us today, so she spent an inordinate amount of time selecting the perfect outfit. When she appeared in a red dress and heels, I ushered her back to her room to change. She looked beautiful, but the attire was in no way appropriate for monkey bars. After some fierce negotiations, we settled on her still wearing the dress but with shorts underneath and her sneakers instead of heels.

As we walk down the knoll hill that leads from our townhouse to the playground section of the park, my heart skips a beat when I see Luke's already here. He's seated on a bench, wearing jeans, a button-down, and leather dress shoes, and his wild mane is brushed back. He even shaved off the stubble.

Looks like Ainsley isn't the only one who was excited about today, although Luke appears to be nervous as hell.

He's looking down and fiddling with his hands. His fingers weave in and out of each other while he mumbles to himself, as if reciting a speech.

Ainsley squeezes my hand and points her outstretched arm. "There's Luke." She waves wildly. "Hey!"

When he hears her, he looks up with a wide smile. He stands up quickly and lifts a small bouquet of flowers that was lying on the bench beside him.

Ainsley runs down the hill, and I try my best to slow her down, worried she'll tumble ass over teakettle. It's no use because she's sprinting toward Luke, and she comes to a halt just a few feet before him.

I jog behind her and am catching my breath as I take in the exchange.

Luke is staring at her like he didn't just meet her a few nights ago. In fact, he's gazing at her like she's a marvel, the likes of which he's never witnessed before.

"Those are pretty flowers!" She points at the loosely clustered, cup-shaped buds.

His navy eyes blink, and then he looks down at the bouquet in his hand. "Yes. Didn't know what you'd like. Or if you had allergies. These are ranunculus. They were my mother's favorite."

"Ran-onnu-loose? That's a silly name."

He laughs and hands them to her. "You're right; it is a silly name, but the flower is beautiful. Like you."

She smiles and gives the bouquet a hug, which has me nervous for the petals. "Wanna play sorbet truck?"

"Sounds fancy," he declares.

"Come." She takes his hand and pulls him with her tiny might over to the smaller of the two playgrounds on-site. The one they're walking to has a window-sized cutout that Ainsley and I pretend is a diner, fast-food place, or even a sorbet truck.

"Mommy, play with us!" she calls out when they get to the window, dropping the bouquet onto the ground.

Luke takes a knee as she runs up the stairs and over a bridge to get to the inside part of the window.

"What can I get you?" she asks him with a smile when she reappears.

Luke leans back, acting in character of someone ordering. "What flavors do you have?"

Her tiny fist rises to her chin as she thinks. "Cherry, lemon, mango, and chocolate."

"Mango, please," I say, noticing the bouquet of flowers down on the ground. I lift them and lean them against the plastic structure.

"Chocolate," Luke orders and then looks to me as Ainsley rushes off somewhere. "I guess this is how the lactose-free kids play these days?"

"She has quite the palate. There's a shop on Main Street that has a whole line of dairy-free ice cream and sorbet. She frequents there." I roll my eyes. "Too much actually. I blame my friends. Melissa and Tara indulge her."

"When I was a kid, there weren't many options. My sisters loved ice cream, and my dad had a huge sweet tooth. I spent years salivating over their desserts."

"Sounds awful."

"Wasn't so bad." He shrugs. "My mom always kept a bag of Oreos in the freezer for me."

"Freezer?" I blanch. "That's ... different. Ainsley's not crazy about Oreos. Neither am I unless they're with milk. They're too dry."

"My girl has to try Oreos in the freezer."

A zing rushes through my chest and settles in my stomach.

"Your orders are ready!" Ainsley appears at the window. Her brown waves are flying out of her barrette as she hands us our make-believe sorbets. "What can I get you for lunch?"

"Lunch after dessert?" he asks.

She oozes sass as she speaks with a swish of her arm and head. "It's a pretend diner."

"Oh. I thought it was a sorbet truck." He nods and looks to me in confusion, but I smile, letting him know to just roll with the role-playing. Preschoolers can be quite the pivot masters of activity. He places his order. "Can I get a hamburger and fries?"

I lean down so she can see my face as I ask, "Chicken Caesar salad."

Luke looks up at me. "It's pretend. Would it kill you to order fast food?"

"Not good for the figure. Real or pretend."

He laughs at my use of the line he said while playing tea party the other night as his eyes roam up and down my body. The slight widening of his pupils and the quirk of his lips show just what he thinks of my figure.

"Eyes up," I admonish. "Besides, there's not much to see."

"Digging for compliments is beneath you. I remember a certain catamaran ride around the island. You wore a one-piece, and I almost lost my cool in the middle of the Caribbean."

"Luke, you had zero chill in Aruba."

"You're right." He smiles. It's bright and luminous, making him look carefree and youthful—very much like the one he wore on that boat while he sang into the wind, shirtless, fearless, golden.

Sure, he's smiled and even laughed lightly a time or two the past few times I've seen him, but this look right here has me inhaling sharply.

"What's the face for?" he asks.

"Your smile," I answer honestly. "You just … it's the first time since reconnecting that you've looked like … well, you."

My words settle on him as Ainsley serves our orders.

"Boring salad for Mom. Burger and Frenchie fries for Luke."

His brows shoot up. Luke's tongue sits behind his front teeth as he tilts his head toward me with narrowed eyes. I plaster on a smile and ask Ainsley for ketchup. She scurries away to her imaginary kitchen.

Luke stands tall, his tall frame imposing as I turn to face him.

I already know what he's going to say.

"You thought I told her. Luke, this needs some easing into."

"It's pretty simple. *Ainsley, Luke is your father.*"

My hands settle on my hips. "This isn't *Maury*. You don't make blanket statements like that to a little kid."

He matches my stance. "It's the truth."

"She could get hurt. I did a lot of research the past few days about this situation."

"What did you Google—*how to introduce a kid to a dad who didn't know she existed?*"

"Kind of. The most important thing is to prepare her by talking about you, which I have been. Not as her dad, but as a man and a friend. We're supposed to avoid a sudden meeting, but you already met her. I want her to get to know you first and then ease her into it."

"I'm her dad, Jillian."

"You don't get to claim the term until you prove to her that you're worthy. You didn't want her once. How do I know you're going to be everything she wishes you to be?"

His mouth is in a flat line as he looks up to the clear sky and lets out an exasperated groan. "I'll just have to prove you wrong."

"There was no ketchup." Ainsley appears back at the window in a huff. Her tiny breaths are fast and harsh.

Luke and I lean down and look into the picture window at the little girl with bright red cheeks and hair that's sticking to the sides of her face.

"What is going in that kitchen of yours? You running a marathon back there?" he asks.

"I was playing a game. Every time I have to go to the kitchen, I run through the entire jungle gym. This little boy asked me to race him. I won."

"That's my girl!" he says loudly, and my eyes widen.

Ainsley doesn't seem to think twice of it.

"Bet I can beat you too." Her challenge is way too confident for her pint-sized frame.

"Luke's a grown man. His size alone inside those tunnels would hold him back," I state.

He throws down his invisible napkin or gauntlet. Honestly, I don't know what kind of gesture it is, but it is one of determination. "Challenge accepted."

Ainsley claps her hands and squeals as Luke struts up the stairs to the side of us, taking all three in one step. He follows the very excited little girl with a matching chin into the confines of the smaller jungle gym. The two start at a red tunnel. Ainsley allows Luke to have a head start since he's, as she says, old and slow. He takes the concession.

"On your mark! Get set. Go!" she bellows, and Luke starts crab-walking through the tunnel.

I stroll around the playground to follow their progress.

Luke emerges on the other side first with Ainsley quickly behind him, barreling past to get to the slide. She's at the bottom quickly with him practically walking down behind her with how much longer he is than the plastic slide, and he chases her around a bend.

Her legs kick up off the ground as she whizzes down the zip line. Luke lifts his feet, but he doesn't move, his body weight holding the mechanism in place at the top of the zip line. He places his feet on the ground, crouches, and walks the ten feet to the end.

I let out a bark-like laugh and lift a hand to hide my smile.

Ainsley leads them up a chain-link ladder to the larger playground with a series of tunnels, drawbridges, and slides. A parade of children is also playing on the structure, so while Ainsley makes her way around, Luke has to do his best not to knock over kids as he tries—quite hard—to win this mini version of *American Ninja Warrior*.

Seeing Ainsley is far in the front, Luke hops over the railing and lands about six feet below, racing alongside the structure to cut Ainsley off at the monkey bars. She blows air out of her nose at his cheating, but doesn't let it deter her.

Luke walks the monkey bars while she uses all her might and muscle to get across behind him. When she does, she races him to the swings, which is their official obstacle-course ending spot. As she flies past him, his feet slow down in his obvious attempt to let her win.

The two are laughing. Luke leans forward with his hands on his knees to catch his breath. Ainsley is doing a dance of victory and kissing her bicep muscles, which are lined up in display.

She flops down on a swing, and Luke takes the spot behind her. He pushes her much higher than I'm used to. I raise an arm to get his attention and give the universal *slow down* sign to say not so high. He rolls his eyes, then decreases the power of his push and sets my daughter at a normal speed.

I have a desire to stand next to them, but my feet don't move. With a deep breath, I take a moment and just let them be.

The flowers Luke brought Ainsley are still in my hand. The pinks and purples are stunning. They don't really have a scent, but their beauty is unparalleled with their lush foliage and fern-like leaves. A charming little flower. Just like the girl they're for and the man who gave them to her.

My teeth graze my lower lip.

I can't believe this is happening.

I take a deep breath, and it's temporarily bottled up in my chest. It's a lighthearted feeling with a fluttering in my belly. I can't let this hopeful sensation settle too long, for the facts of the past are too potent to forget.

"Jillian," he breathed heavily into the phone. "Beautiful Jillian, who I was a fool for. My gorgeous girl with green eyes and the smartest woman I've ever met."

"Are you drunk?"

"Not enough."

It was easy to hear he'd been on a bender. Had it been easier to get him on the phone, I would have said we'd have this conversation another night. After weeks of trying to find him, I wasn't losing my chance now. I had to make a choice soon, and time was of the essence.

"Luke, I wanted to tell you face-to-face, but you've gone out of your way to never see me again so—"

"You think I don't want to see you? Jillian, I ache for you. I'm obsessed with you. I need you."

"Funny way of showing it."

For a second, I almost let my heart believe those words. I had to remind myself of the hunt I'd gone on for him. I hadn't had Facebook or Instagram, but I'd tried to find him there anyway. He'd ignored my messages there too.

"I'm not the man for you," he drawled hopelessly. "You deserve so much more than this. I'm so scared, Jillian. I wish I were strong enough to get through this, but I'm a mess."

"Stop speaking in code. What are you talking about?"

"Good-bye, Jillian."

"I'm pregnant," I spit it out, desperate for him not to hang up the phone. I'd tried too hard to reach him.

Silence fell upon his end of the phone, yet I could hear his heavy breaths. A part of me hoped his actions would turn around, and he'd go back to being the man who had wooed me not too long before.

I was a fool to wish such a thing.

"No." Panic etched his words. "You can't be."

"I can, and I am. I have an appointment tomorrow at a clinic."

"Get rid of it."

His harsh tone was a shot to my chest. I gasped, unable to breathe. It wasn't that I was completely against the idea. I was almost six weeks along. I had options.

Still, his adamant tone was crippling.

"What?"

"Get rid of it. Make it go away. It's tainted. It's bad. You can't have that baby."

"Why?"

"Because it's mine."

I stifled the gasp of a woman who had just been struck in the heart with cruelty. I had to be sure. "You don't want our baby?"

His answer took longer than needed, and when he answered, our fate was sealed.

"No."

Now, he's here, and while the past has been foiled with choices we made, I can only hope the ones we make today are the best for my daughter.

Yes, I still say she's mine because even though Luke is doing and saying all the right things, I can't fight this nagging feeling that something is about to go horribly wrong.

That he'll abandon her.

That he won't want her … again.

Until I can be sure, protecting her heart is the most important thing. The walls around my own were put up with steel cages long ago. I can handle Luke.

Ainsley's going to fall in love.

She'll be shattered.

My cell phone vibrates with a text. I groan when I see my mother's name and click to read the message.

> *You're having dinner with Dr. Eric Hollenford Thursday night at 7 p.m. Meet him at the Wolfson Estate. Don't cancel. Wear something pretty.*

She doesn't even have the courtesy to ask if I'm even available on Thursday. Her order has been given, and I desperately want to reply back that I can't go. But after one look up at Luke with Ainsley at the swings and the way my heart is thumping with enough hope to make my stomach spin, I look down at the phone and send a simple text back.

> *I'll be there.*

nine

WEARING MY BEST COCKTAIL dress and a pair of very high heels, I walk down the cobblestone path to the Wolfson Estate on time for my date with the doctor.

I glide my hands down the navy form fitting dress that compliments my curves. The rest of my wardrobe consists of silk blouses, pencil skirts, and slacks. And it's mostly black. I own so much black clothing; you'd think I went to funerals for a living.

The Wolfson Estate is a familiar venue for me, as I've planned many weddings here. There's a ballroom in the back with a vast domed ceiling. In the front is a restaurant where I've dined with my parents many times. I step down the front entryway to a reception area. The hostess takes me to a table for two in the center of the room. I let out a breath in relief that it's vacant.

I'm only seated for a few minutes when a gentleman walks into the reception area, and from the gesture the hostess makes toward me, I know he is my date.

Dr. Eric Hollenford is thirty-eight, divorced, and a world-renowned geneticist. What my mother alluded to, but failed to properly mention, was how lovely he is to look at. He steps into the dining room, and it's like a music video, where everything around him is in slow motion as he walks with a gentlemanly gait.

Not too short, not too tall, and a lean figure that shows he works out regularly and eats right. His hair is light and cut short. His eyes are dark, and when he approaches the table, he flashes a grin that could awaken a corpse.

I take his offered hand. It's cool yet soft. "Pleasure to meet you."

"Likewise." He holds back his tie as he takes a seat across from me. "Your mother was eager for us to meet. I'm happy I was able to make this happen. I had an appointment that went longer than I'd hoped, and I didn't want to cancel."

"For fear of my mother's incessant calls?" I tease as I place my napkin on my lap.

"Guilty."

"I understand. My mother can be a bit … much."

He has a nice laugh. "True, but she's not the only one. My mother is just as concerned for my well-being. And by well-being, I mean, my lack of a wife and children. My divorce didn't sit well with her. I think she would have handled it better if I'd had a few kids. The woman is desperate for grandchildren … which I probably shouldn't have just said to a woman I'm on a first date with."

I laugh, then smash my lips together in complete understanding. "My single-mom status doesn't sit well with my mother. I know she would have handled it better if there were an ex-husband in the picture. Easier to justify things to the masses."

"It's so old school."

"That's what I say! And my mom's not even that old. She was born in a time when women were conquering the world and burning their bras. Clearly, she missed the women's lib memo."

"Good to know we have at least one thing in common. Overbearing mothers." He lifts his water glass. "Cheers to burning our bras."

I giggle like an idiot and lift my water glass and cheers him as well. As he takes a sip, I see his eyes gazing gingerly my way. With the clearing of my throat, I place my glass back on the table to reset the mood.

"This is the only time I've agreed to a date my mother's offered. She's recently taken to springing men on me at social gatherings. I think she's getting desperate."

"Jillian, you're the third woman mine's set me up with this month. I'm kind of a pro at first dates. The pressure is greater than telling a patient they have a rare and incurable disease."

"How do you handle it?"

"Pot," he deadpans.

"Seriously?" I gasp.

"It has its medical benefits."

"I'm not so brazen as to smoke. Wish I were. Perhaps I could try a gummy or two."

"Do-gooder?" he asks.

"Kind of."

"What do you do to relax?"

"Work. I'm a wedding planner, and it's kind of my Zen. I get lost in the details, and it's good for me. That and kickboxing. My friend Tara is an instructor as a side job, so I try to get to her class twice a week."

"I do jiu jitsu. Maybe I'll spar with you one day."

"I'm far from being able to actually fight someone. I mostly go to zone out."

"I feel the same way when I'm working. I have a playlist I listen to and get lost in the mechanics of the surgery. I'm known as Dr. Rock around the office."

The nickname makes me laugh, and I mentally slap myself for being so giggly. "Do you also have wheelies on your sneakers and zip around the hospital on your heels?"

"Not cool enough for that. Although I do have a tie with pictures of tacos all over it. My nurses got it for me for my birthday as a gag gift, and I wear it now and again to bring some levity to the office."

"That's awesome. I'd love to see that." My eyes widen as I realize how brazen I sound.

Eric seems to appreciate my offer. "I hope, someday, you will."

The waitress appears at our table with menus, interrupting our banter, and the break in momentum gives me a chance to assess the feelings I'm exhibiting right now. Namely the ones caused by the way he's looking at me like there will be a someday.

Eric is nice, successful, handsome ... the kind of man a woman like me should want to date, and yet there's something tugging at my back, pulling me away.

"Can I get you anything from the bar?" the waitress asks.

I open my mouth but fail to speak. My mouth has gone dry, and I'm not quite sure what I want. And I'm not just talking about what to drink.

Eric slightly narrows his gaze at me with a thin smile before asking the waitress for a moment. She smiles and says she'll be back.

My date is looking at me with kind eyes and patience.

"Eric, listen, the thing is, I'm not looking for anything. Not a fling or a proposal. You seem like a great guy. I'm an idiot for saying this, but I just want you to know that before I give you the wrong impression. I'm not interested in a someday."

He settles into this information and leans his hand on the table, strumming it lightly with his fingers. A gentle smile graces his face as he nods.

"Okay. Thank you for your honesty. Now, if I can be open with you as well. Of all the women I've been set up with, you're the easiest to talk to. The prettiest too. I've only been here five minutes, and it's the most enjoyable five minutes I've had in a while. I'm not looking for a fling or to propose to anyone either. I do, however, love the steak au poivre here, and they make a killer espresso martini. I'd really like the chance to sit and talk with you a little while longer. If you can stand that, I'd like to continue this non-date with zero expectations, other than a good evening between new friends."

I let out a long breath I didn't realize I had been holding.

"I like that."

He opens his menu and smiles. "Besides, this could get our mothers to relent a little."

I open my menu as well. "I like the way you think."

"How was your date with the good doctor?" Melissa asks as I walk into her house to pick Ainsley up. "I swear I had my phone on, waiting for you to need a rescue."

Her fiancé, Will, comes walking down the stairs. "She kept checking it. Worked for me because she was too distracted that it cost her the triple points round in *Family Feud*." He gives her a kiss on the cheek and then walks toward the kitchen.

She's quickly at his feet. "*Name something you put on a hamburger* has way too many good answers for soup to be number two."

"You need to think out of the box," he bellows over his shoulder.

Melissa groans. "I don't know why I play it."

"Because you love it."

She pouts, and he gives her a smolder that I know melts her on the spot.

Melissa and Will are a really cute couple. Not perfect, yet they give me a glimmer of hope that not all relationships are doomed. My parents have one of convenience. My father works hard while my mother tends to their social needs. They don't hold hands, kiss, or joke. They are merely Mr. and Mrs. Hathaway. A couple that appears warm on the outside, yet inside their home, they're frigid. Makes me wonder why my mother is obsessed with me meeting a man. It's not like what she has with my father is like what Melissa has with Will. At least when Melissa tells me to give love a chance, I know it's coming from a place of happiness.

Ainsley and Hunter come running into the living room with capes on their backs and swords in their hands. Hunter is two years older than Ainsley, has a heart of gold, and still enjoys pretend play. He's not the kind of kid to walk around the house, bouncing a ball. You're more likely to see him pulling a coin from behind your ear in a well-done magic trick.

It drives his father crazy, which is why we all encourage it.

"Hey there, kiddo!" I grab Ainsley as she runs past me, lift her into a superhero pose and nuzzle her neck.

She giggles as she kicks her legs, desperate to get back to playing with Hunter.

"Guess what?" I say to her.

"I love you!" she yells at the top of her lungs.

I kiss her neck and put her down and let her finish playing before we leave in a few minutes.

Placing my purse on the kitchen island, I take a seat on a stool. "Thanks for watching her tonight."

"It was the first date I've seen you go on since I've known you. I would have kept her for a week if you needed me to." Melissa lets out a whistle as she looks at my attire. "Sexy dress. Was the good doctor worth it?"

"Will you stop calling him that?" I admonish, and then roll my eyes at her playful stare. "For the record, he wasn't horrible. Eric was actually really great."

Her jaw practically hits the granite. "Shut the front door."

"It's not open, Mom!" Hunter calls from his spot by the couch.

She answers him, "It's an expression for something I can't say in the presence of children." With excited eyes, she gives her attention back to me. "Tell me everything."

"Not much to tell. We ate steak, drank martinis, and talked. It was … lovely."

"Lovely." Her brows lift. "You're blushing an awful lot for lovely."

Will calls out from his place by the sink, "You don't blush for lovely. You blush for amazing."

"Incredible," Melissa adds with a pointed finger.

"Hot," he adds.

"Sexy."

"Unbelievable." He builds on to their list of things that should make me blush.

I hush them both, to which Will laughs his deep chuckle.

"If Melissa ever referred to me as lovely, I'd check my man card at the door."

I shoo him away, and Melissa gives him a slap on the butt.

"Girl-talk time. No boys allowed."

"Yes, ma'am." He gives her a kiss on the head and walks into the living room to take a seat on the couch near the kids.

With him out of the way, Melissa leans on the counter, her chest halfway across the stone, to get closer to me as she speaks in a hushed tone. "Hey, I have a question for you, and it's kind of personal."

"Ask me anything."

"So, Will and I are ready to start a family and have pulled the guard from the gate, if you know what I mean."

"Wow. That's awesome. I'm surprised you're willing to do it before the wedding."

"I'm not getting any younger, and he really wants to be a dad."

"I get it," I say, and I do. I was only twenty-seven when I gave birth to Ainsley and wasn't about to let the chance to become a mother pass me by. "What's the question?"

She waves her hands around, figuring out where to start. "When my ex-husband and I tried for Izzy and Hunter, I got pregnant right away. But with Will, we've been trying for a few months, and nothing's happened. I'm wondering if we need an intervention."

"A few months isn't long. Just give it time."

"I will, but I'm thirty-five. I don't think it hurts to get checked out by a specialist. Who did you use to have Ainsley?"

"I went to my OB/GYN. The same one you use."

She lowers her voice even more. "I mean, for the ... *insemination.* Didn't you have to go to a fertility center?"

This is where my life gets murky.

I've never actually told anyone I used medical advancements to have my child. I simply allowed them to believe it. The details of why are convoluted at best, yet it was what needed to be done.

"Melissa, I didn't go to a fertility center to have Ainsley."

Her mouth frowns in confusion. "I thought you had a sperm donor."

"I did. Tara likes to refer to him as Bobo the Sperm Guy. I really hate that term, but she's a force to be reckoned with when you try to reprimand that woman, so I just let her say what she wants."

"If you didn't go to a sperm bank, where did you get the sperm?"

"From a man," I answer slowly. It's not that I'm keeping information from her. I've just gotten so used to not having to explain it to anyone.

"I think I'm following. Do you know who this man is?"

"I do."

"Does he know he has a daughter?"

"He does now."

Her eyes bulge out of her head as she stares at me for a minute and starts to put the pieces together. Melissa is a highly intelligent woman. An emotional wreck at times, but she knows how to read the writing on the wall. This writing seems to be blaring at her in neon lights.

"Holy shit!" she says way too loud, causing Will, Hunter, and Ainsley to stop what they're doing and look our way. "Sorry. Just got a little excited."

Melissa lowers her head back down and talks in her lowest tone again. "Jillian ..." She swallows as she tries to digest the information. "Are you saying that Luke, the guy who came to our office the other day is"—she glances up and looks at the kids now playing and not paying attention—"Bobo the Sperm Guy?"

My palms feel clammy as I run them through my hair and state with an air of nonchalance, "Yes. Luke gave up his chance to be in her life years ago, but appears to now want to be ... in her life."

"Does she know? Have they met?"

"They have met. Twice. But she doesn't know. She just thinks he's a cool firefighter who likes to play games with her."

"A smoking-hot fireman," she says as she rises and places a hand on her hip. "Come on. I can say it. Dark hair and light eyes are my kryptonite. You picked a good one to procreate with."

My hand rises to nudge her because she is entirely too loud for this conversation even though she's speaking just above a whisper.

"Please keep this between us. It's no one's business how my child came to be, and the condescending stares from my parents are bad enough."

Her shoulders drop as she looks at me with a tilted head and sad puppy-dog eyes. There's a nod of complete understanding as she bends down to the counter and grabs my hands.

"I get it. You and I haven't been friends that long, but it's been long enough for me to know that it was easier for you to explain to your judgmental parents that you chose to have a child on your own than to tell them you got pregnant by some guy who walked away."

Her accurate description of my life events is jarring.

"Didn't know you paid such close attention."

"You also value privacy and don't care for town gossip or whispers at parties. Being part of that nonsensical fuss would be painful for you. Jillian, you're one of my best friends. You and Tara are my yin and yang. You and I haven't been friends as long as Tara and I have, but our bond is just as strong. You're an amazing mother and a pillar of strength. It's okay if you want to be vulnerable with me. I'm here for it."

I bite my lip, then let out a shaky breath before pulling my head back up, and I look at her confidently in the eyes.

"I know. And I'm good. I promise. Just keep this between us. I adore Tara, but she's not the best with keeping secrets. Ainsley needs to find out gently."

"Of course." She lets go of my hands and crosses her arms.

"As for your original question, just give it time. Besides, it must be fun trying." I wink at her and watch as she gives a sway to her body.

"Oh, yeah. Making babies with Will is a lot of fun. Raising them … not so much."

We laugh, and I think about that night in a canopy bed.

Yeah, making a baby wasn't so bad.

In fact, it was really, really good.

ten

"GO FISH!" AINSLEY SHOUTS after Luke asks her if she has the seahorse card for the third turn in a row.

With a puffed-out lip, he draws yet another card from the deck, theatrically placing the new card into the growing stack in his hands.

She rises to her knees with eager anticipation and looks at the one card left in her chubby palm. "Do you have a crab?"

Putting on a complete show for Ainsley's benefit, Luke whimpers as he slowly pulls the crab card out of the pile and hesitantly hands it over. She grabs the card lightning quick and holds it in the air along with the matching crab card as she does a victory dance.

"I won! I won!" Her feet kick up. The checkered blanket Luke and I are lying on bunches up. "I won again!"

While she sings, he looks up at her with a beaming smile. His cards are flung onto the blanket, and I take a look at them with a shake of my head. His eyes twinkle as they turn from Ainsley to me. I sit up and tilt my head at him while narrowing my eyes.

Luke's eyes have a mischievous crinkle to them as he sits up as well and opens the cooler. He takes out a chocolate almond milk, opens the top, and hands it to Ainsley.

"That's her second one today," I assess.

"She's fine. The calcium is healthy for her bones."

I scrunch my nose and watch as she gulps down half the bottle, leaving a chocolaty mustache on her face. Luke asks her to come to him, then uses his thumb to wipe the milk residue from her upper lip.

My chest quakes. I grab my cardigan and slide it over my shoulders to fight the cool breeze that's obviously in the air.

"Can I go play on the seesaw?" she asks me.

I look over at the playground and the amount of children playing. There are a few, but not too many. "Yes. Stay close. Remember, if you can't see me, I can't see you."

"I'll come," Luke offers, but she places a hand on her hip and shakes her head.

"You're too big. Last time, I was stuck in the air forever, remember?"

"I figured it out for us, didn't I? Did about a hundred squats, making sure I could manually lift my side up and down for you."

Her hands rest at her sides as she looks down at him. "Then, you made a big deal for the next hour about how much your legs hurt. I'm gonna go play with the kids. Bye!"

Ainsley takes off toward the seesaw and the crowd of young children appropriately sized to share a ride with.

Luke leans back on his arms, his long legs stretched out, and stares at her skipping along the grass. His eyes brim with tenderness when he watches her. I wonder if that magic will ever dissipate from his face. When the burden of being a parent will overpower the wistful way you see your young.

"She's amazing," he croons as his lips part in a dazzling display of straight white teeth.

"You could let her lose a game every once in a while. She's amazing when she's drunk on chocolate milk and winning at Go Fish. Try getting her to sit still when you have to brush the knots out of her hair."

His broad shoulders rise as he looks over at the playground. "We should stand closer to her. I don't like that she's so far away."

"Helicopter parent much?"

"Is that what I am?" His hand lands on his chest, and he rubs it in circles. "I've been a dad for two weeks, and I'm already turning into an overprotective asshole. What will I do when she dates?"

"Way to put the carriage before the horse. Maybe you should just ease into letting her go on a seesaw first. As for dating, I already have a plan for that. She can't date until she's sixteen."

"Thirty," he says at the same time, and I give him an incredulous look.

"Thirty? We were twenty-six when we met, and I know you were with many women before then."

"Exactly." His voice rises at the end, which is jarring for the deep baritone he has.

There's something in his delivery that sounds off.

His eyes narrow as he watches her play. "Is she athletic?"

"I don't know. I haven't put her in sports yet."

"I mean ... does she have good balance and coordination?"

"Yes," I answer slowly. His question is valid, I suppose. "Does she look off to you?"

"No. Just asking." He jerks his leg, and it's writhing as he flexes. Luke's brows are drawn together, and the skin between them is wrinkled. "Let's go for a walk," he declares.

"A minute ago, you needed to be on top of Ainsley, and now, you want to go walking."

"The path makes a circle around the playground. If I can watch from here, I can walk around and keep an eye on her from the path. Besides, my leg is falling asleep." He shakes out his calf and squeezes the thick muscle of his thigh. "Yep, I need to stand."

Luke rises and gives a long stretch. His arms are behind his back as he stretches, causing him to puff out his broad chest. The way he checks on every muscle of his body looks like an athlete about to perform a race. His movements are swift, full of grace and virility.

Staring up at him, I take in his frame with the sun shining from behind, casting him in shadow. There's an ethereal light surrounding him. From this angle, he appears larger than normal, like a Roman god atop a mountain. A handsome face with a passionate beauty.

When he holds out a hand, I stare at it in wonder.

"You coming?" he asks.

His brawny fist is hot and slightly callused at the knuckles.

I use his leverage to rise to my feet and slide my shoes back on. I took them off when we sat down for the lunch Luke had brought for us—three turkey, tomato, and lettuce baguettes, a fruit bowl, and almond milk—packed at his home in Walden and driven here for his day with Ainsley.

We leave our things on the blanket and pad through the grass to the concrete path. People on bikes whiz by us, and other pedestrians keep their varied paces, so we stay to the right and move over when necessary.

A gentle breeze is in the air. Nothing like the night of the fire, yet enough to make your hair dance. Luke's hair flips up a little, making him seem carefree as his watchful eye stays on the playground, where Ainsley is bopping up and down with another kid.

I slide my arms into my cardigan. Luke's hands are in the pockets of his khakis as he strolls beside me. Our sweater-clad shoulders are close as we keep a slow pace in the sunshine.

"How's that leg doing?" I ask for small talk.

"Saved from what could have been an uncomfortable hobble of pins and needles."

"Glad you were saved."

I fold my arms across my chest and breathe in the crisp scent of a fall day.

We walk in a shared quiet around the bend in the path. The trees have recently started to change colors. I stare up at the foliage that lines the path.

"The trees are beautiful this time of year. Makes you dread the winter because the beauty of the trees will fade," I say.

"They change in their own time, at their own pace."

His comment intrigues me, so I look to him for clarification.

He points toward a tree in the wooded section near us. "The maple will let its leaves go in a whoosh. The first decent rainstorm will blow most away in a cyclone of wind. The oak, on the other hand, will cling to its leaves with crunchy brown ones holding on till the very last turn of the season. Then, there's the evergreen with its constant flow of dropping needles and creation of new ones. You don't see the change because it stays an everlasting green."

"You know a lot about trees," I muse. "Horticulture enthusiast?"

"Just a kid who grew up playing in the woods. I like the way they're all the same yet different. My dad says trees are like people. Some give up easily, others try to hold on to things they need to let go of, and then there are those that are constantly reinventing themselves. No matter what, no matter the difficulty, the trials and tribulations … hell, even the best parts of our lives … will fade. We all change and renew if we just give it time."

"That's insightful. Your dad's a wise man."

"He's great. Kept me from falling apart far too many times. In case you were wondering, I'm a maple. My father has been pretty strong in his assessment."

I never thought about comparing myself to a tree, but as Luke talks about his father's analogy, I think of where I fit into the idea. I think I'm an evergreen. Constantly changing and going with the flow, always appearing green on the outside yet making quick changes on the outside.

A golden retriever comes up to Luke, and we stop so he can kneel down and rub the large head of the friendly animal as he makes small talk with its owner. As the retriever and its owner walk away, a park table of elderly women—all curly-haired with canes resting against the table, playing a game and chatting loudly—has us turning our heads.

"I saw that show on Netflix. The one about love and sex. What was it called?" one of the women, who appears to be in her eighties with a large cross around her neck, states rather loudly to someone at her table.

"*Love Sex*," another in a buttoned-up sweater says as she takes a tile from the pile in the center of the table.

Luke and I look at each other quizzically. I try not to laugh, especially when he looks at me with a brow raised very high and his mouth tipped up on one side.

"It was filthy. Naked people and adultery. You see all the naked bits of everyone. When I got to the finale, I nearly fainted," the first lady states, to which another agrees with a disapproving hum.

"Did you see episode seven? I had to rewatch it to see if I saw things correctly!"

Luke and I fight smiles as we continue our stroll. After a few steps, I can't help but let the laugh out.

"Older women talking about raunchy shows on Netflix is not something you hear every day," I say with a smile still on my face. "I like how the one woman pretty much said it was trash yet stated she watched the whole series."

He grins. "Apparently, it was so dirty that she had to rewatch it to see the sex scenes."

I laugh. "I know exactly what scene she's talking about. It was quite taboo, to say the least. Lots of eggplants in that one, if you know what I mean."

Luke leans back and stares at me with incredulity as we stride. "Jillian Hathaway, do you watch porn?"

I scrunch my nose at him. "Don't be shocked that I watch romance. Most women do."

"What's your favorite show?"

"*Bridgerton*. I can rewatch every season."

Tilting his head to one side, he steals a slanted look at me. "You act all buttoned up, but you're really a romantic on the inside."

His words have me nodding and looking at the path in front of me.

"Everyone knows romance is only believable in books and films. Real life doesn't roll the credits."

"Can't say I disagree. Life can be pretty ugly. That's why I'm not the forever kinda guy."

"Yeah, well, that makes you an even hotter commodity. A man who swears off love and maintains his distance is a heartthrob who women swoon over and can't wait to tie down."

He laughs in agreement. "My sister used to read these books where the guys were total assholes, and she was so obsessed that she'd make these fan graphics and everything. She said bad boys were her jam."

"Exactly my point!" I stop walking and turn to him, lifting my hands as I declare, "a woman who doesn't seek relationships and maintains her distance is cold and frigid. A guy like that is a romantic hero."

"I recall things pretty well, and I'd say the workaholic in Aruba who swore off men had a pretty great romance even if it did last only a few nights." He steps closer to me to avoid a child on a tricycle. His hand finds my lower back as he steers me out of the child's path.

That comment has me taking long breaths and settling the excited feeling that was going through my chest from talking so much.

He takes a breath of a step closer, yet it feels like the warmth of his body is seeping through the air and into me, pulling me closer.

I clear my throat and start walking again. Luke follows suit, those long, easy strides at my side.

"So, you don't date at all?"

My dating life isn't his business. While I don't owe him an explanation, I very well can't have him believe I work myself to the bone most weekends in order to avoid the dating scene altogether.

"I've gone on a few dates since Ainsley was a year old. Nothing that made it past dessert. I don't have time to waste on a relationship that might go somewhere. The other night, for example, I went out with a very nice doctor."

He clears his throat. "Will there be a second date?"

"No," I state simply.

Luke acts like he understands why. "Dull date, huh? Bummer."

"The opposite. He was really lovely. Please don't make fun of me. Melissa gave me grief for my adjective of *lovely* when describing my date with Eric. For me, lovely is good."

Luke pauses. I stop as well and look up into his navy eyes, then at his firm features and the confident set of his shoulders.

"Can I ask you a question?" he asks, and I raise my shoulders with a nod. "When I took you out on the beach ..." He broods, and I wonder where this is going. "Would you have considered that night we danced with our toes in the sand and laughed until the tide rolled in lovely?"

I fight the shaky way my breath wants to come out and remain steady. "No."

"Better than lovely?"

"Luke—"

"Just helping you compare it to something. What would you have said it was?"

Different, I want to say. *Sweet. Sexy. Exhilarating. Absolutely perfect.*

"It wasn't a date, but it was fun."

"Fun," he muses. "Okay, I need to know then, if that wasn't a date, what about the afternoon we spent on a catamaran, laughing our asses off in the sun and drinking in the salty air? You were too scared to do it, but you jumped off that cliff. When you hit the water, I was certain you were going to scream at me for pushing you off. I followed and climbed onto the catamaran, ready for a scolding. Instead, you kissed me, and it was the wildest, most passionate kiss in the world. If that wasn't a first date, then I don't know what is."

I want to punch him for bringing up what was single-handedly the best kiss I'd ever had in my life. I also want to kiss him for remembering it all. I was sure he had forgotten the details.

"Exciting," I answer. "Too exciting, if I recall."

The glimmer in his eyes dissipates as he takes in my words.

"Exciting didn't seem to pan out. Maybe lovely is good for you." Luke turns away but waits for me to start walking before following in step. "Do I make you uncomfortable when I bring up the past?"

I look up into his eyes. "Yes, but not in a way that you probably think. I don't need exciting or lovely. I have Ainsley. She's my everything. If I'm going to give her time with me away to a man, I won't settle for less than perfect."

His gaze drops from my eyes to my shoulders and then up to my clavicle.

"So, Mr. Incendio, where has life taken you the past few years?"

He runs his hand over the back of his neck, then slides it back into his pocket. "Same as you, I suppose. I work a lot. Max out my shifts and overtime. I wasn't caring for a child, but my mom was sick for a long time. I spent my free time taking care of her. She passed away last year."

"I'm sorry. You've mentioned her a few times. You really think Ainsley looks like her?"

He sighs. "So much like her. It sounds corny, but when I met her, I felt like my mom came back to me. Like she sent me this gift. Her name was Annie. I kept thinking Ainsley even sounds like Annie. How did you come up with Ainsley's name?"

"I just thought it was beautiful. It means solitary clearing, which isn't profound, yet the name sounded serene and peaceful. A pretty name for a pretty girl. Her middle name, Lisette, is my grandmother's name. Ainsley Lisette Hathaway."

Luke drifts off as he calmly stares at the pavement. I don't know if I said something to offend him.

I look at my feet moving and add, "Knowing your mom was Annie makes the name even more special. You loved her very much."

"Yes. She was my whole world."

"Are you close to your dad?"

"He's my best friend. I wish I lived closer. I moved from Boston to Walden because it's where I was able to find a full-time job as a fireman. Where I grew up in New York state it's volunteer only, unlike the city. In Connecticut, eighty-three percent of our state's firefighters are volunteers, so I couldn't lose the opportunity or the benefits."

"I recall you having a dream of opening a bar and restaurant. What changed your mind?"

"It was a lifestyle choice. Being available for my mother was the main reason. I still go back to my dad's house often. It's just over the New York-Connecticut border. We're kind of all each other has right now."

"Do you think he'll move to Connecticut to be closer to you?"

"Hopefully, he won't have to." He turns his body toward me as we walk. "He's itching to meet Ainsley. When I told him about her, he was in shock and then went out and bought her a softball glove."

My feet halt on the path. "Really? That's all so—"

"I know you're worried about all of this impacting Ainsley. My dad knows he has to wait to meet her until you're ready. It's just that he never thought he'd ever be a grandfather. The man has had a lot of pain in his life, yet he's the most optimistic guy you'll ever meet. He's a good man, I swear. He's just really excited, and he hasn't had a lot to be excited about in the last few years."

I place a hand on his arm. His chest puffs in reaction, and his bicep flexes.

"I was going to say, it's sweet," I say. His shoulders relax, and the trepidation in his eyes disappears. "My parents have never bought anything like that for Ainsley. They've never played a game with her or taken to her interests. We go to dinner with them a lot, and they've watched her overnight, but that's the extent of it. She says they usually watch documentaries or have her play alone in her room when she's there. My parents aren't very kid-friendly. They're *children should be seen, not heard* kind of people."

"Be warned. Mitch Incendio is ready for a game of catch with his granddaughter. I told him she likes to play dress-up, so he got her a Rockford Peaches costume from *A League of Their Own*."

I squeeze his arm as I smile. "She's gonna love it."

"I hope so."

His eyes twinkle. I get lost in that twinkle for a beat too long. His features turn smooth as his lips part. My hand is still clinging to his sweater, and I focus on the wool instead of my face, neck, and ears, which suddenly feel incredibly warm.

I look away.

I start to walk, and Luke takes his place beside me once again.

Ainsley is now on the playground, going down a slide. We watch as she runs across the drawbridge and stops at the top of the slide. She looks around the park, seemingly for us. When she sees us on the path, she lifts her arm high and waves wildly. Luke and I wave back. Appeased she knows where we are, she slides down and runs around the structure to go up again.

"I'm glad we can talk like this. I didn't know what kind relationship you and I would have," I confess.

"You don't have to do this alone anymore. I know I live far away and can't commit to the kind of time a father should, but I'm here," he says and then adds, "I'd be happy to watch Ainsley. Maybe on those weekends when you're working, I can try to rearrange my shifts."

My feet shuffle as I slow down. "Luke—"

"I love meeting at the park, but I want to visit at your house—or better yet, have her over to my house. She'd love Joe."

"The park is a safe space."

"Exactly." He stops and points around the park, filled with people enjoying a beautiful day. "This is the kind of place men who are court-ordered to have a chaperone for their parental visitations meet with their kids."

"You're a tad dramatic, but I get it. The answer is still no. I'm not ready yet."

"She's my daughter too." His tone rises, and I gasp.

"Please don't take her from me."

My words seem to hit him hard as he jolts back from the power of them. There was something in his delivery that set me off. I hadn't given credence to the fact he could fight me for his rights to Ainsley until now. It was a suppressed thought that bubbled to the surface in a rather forceful and sensational fashion.

"I'd never. I mean it, Jillian. I'd never take Ainsley from you. I wouldn't do that to you or to her. I'm not going to steal her and be on the lam, fleeing to a South American country. France, most likely, because I do speak a lick of it."

I narrow my eyes at him.

"I'm kidding." He places his hands on my arms and gives them a reassuring squeeze. "I know I said and did all the wrong things years ago, but I'm here now. My words mean nothing to you, and I understand that. Let my actions speak volumes. You can trust me."

"Can I?"

His eyes close in defeat.

My gut tells me I need to keep him at arm's length, for fear he'll flake again.

My heart, however, is singing a different tune. It's looking at the pleading in his eyes and hearing the yearning in his voice.

My brain, however, is making a quick appearance and setting things straight.

"Your place is out of the question," I state, and his eyes flicker. "That would require a sleepover, and I'm definitely not ready for that."

"I'll come to your place."

"You live three hours away. That's too late to drive home."

"That's for me to worry about," he says with a reassuring stroke of his hands on my biceps, and I melt into the warmth of his touch but keep my head held high. "Please, Jillian, let me babysit my daughter."

I want to say no. Alone, he has too many chances to say the wrong thing, do the wrong thing. My tongue is on the roof of my mouth, ready to utter the dismissal of permission, and yet he's staring at me with his hopeful, pleading eyes and looking so very desperate.

"You really like saying she's your daughter, don't you?"

"Just as much as I'll eventually love hearing her call me Dad."

I close my eyes from the dagger-like strike those words have on my soul. "Okay. One step at a time. Something easy. I haven't been out to dinner with the girls in a long time, and I owe Tara a thank-you dinner for helping out as much as she has. Maybe you can take Ainsley to a movie? I'll choose a restaurant nearby in case you need me. It would have to be a Thursday because I'm working the next few weekends. And not too late because she has school the next day. If you can rearrange your schedule—"

"I'll be there. Text me the time and place, and I'm there." Luke's devilishly handsome face is smiling like a kid on Christmas morning. "You just made me the happiest man alive."

Just as we're about to step on the grass, a loud roar of a fire engine blazes through the park, causing everyone to look at where the telltale sound is coming from. Over near the street closest to my townhouse is a firetruck, and it's honking loudly even though it's parking at the foot of the park.

I look around for the fire or possible emergency that could have brought a truck to the quiet streets of Greenwood Village.

Ainsley comes barreling through the crowd of kids and over to where Luke and I are standing.

"You brought your firetruck!" she yelps excitedly.

From his wide smile, I know there's no emergency to be had.

"That's not mine, but I made a few calls, and some friends in the neighborhood were able to deliver," he explains, and she squeals with delight. "You asked for a ride on a firetruck, and I always keep my promises."

"When I said the chocolate milk was spoiling her, I had no idea what was in store next," I muse.

Luke lifts Ainsley off the ground. "Come on, Mom. We have a ride to catch. Leave the picnic. I'll get it later."

As Luke starts jogging with her in his arms, I find myself smiling. Smiling can be dangerous.

So can roguish men with firetrucks, chocolate milk, and all the right words to crush a girl's heart.

eleven

"DON'T LOOK, BUT THERE'S a guy at nine o'clock totally checking us out!" Tara waggles her perfectly threaded brows from her seat at Le Amoureux, a French bistro on Main Street.

Her eyes float around the room, mainly to the bar, where many Greenwood Village elite come after a day at the office. It's near the train station and a great place for singles happy hour.

A handsome man near the bar looks our way. With a flirty smile, she brushes her sleek hair over her shoulder. She straightened it tonight, which is common when she is out for fine dining. Tara has different hairstyles for different settings. Tonight, she is dressed in a lace top, skinny jeans, and has the sleekest of hairstyles. It must have taken her forever to straighten the wild mane of curls she usually sports.

I clear my throat and raise my brows to get her attention. "Excuse me, miss, you're here with me tonight. No man-hunting allowed."

"To paraphrase Charlotte from *Sex and the City*, 'I've been dating since I'm seventeen. It's exhausting. Where is he?'" She makes a praying motion and lifts her eyes to the ceiling.

I laugh at her antics. "Okay, fine. But wait until I'm out of here, and then you can go suck face with whoever you want."

"I don't want a hookup. I want to catch that bouquet at Melissa's wedding and then marry the man who puts the garter on my calf."

"Tara, I adore you, but you're a bit too dreamy for me."

She ignores me as she stuffs her face with the truffle fries that came with her steak. "Let's face it. Most of the men who come here are looking for a quick lay or to cheat on their significant other. I know this crowd, and they are not here, looking for a wife."

I take a bite of my tuna tartar. "You definitely don't need a player in your life."

"Cheers to that, sister. I've already been left at the altar by the biggest dick of all. I'm only in for the real deal."

It's easy to forget Tara has a harrowing past. Probably because I didn't know her then. Seven years ago, Tara was dressed in white and having her pictures taken when her groom called and said he wouldn't be at the end of the aisle. Her ex-fiancé had had a change of heart while the guests were arriving for the ceremony. The story goes, she cried for a while, threw a few things, and then pulled up her bridal panties and announced the party must go on.

Yes, Tara was the bride left at the altar who went to her reception anyway.

"I hope it happens for you." My words are honest.

Her cheeks pink with the compliment. "Meeting a man with older kids would be ideal. Hanging out with your and Melissa's kids is fun enough. I like to play with them and then hand them back, all corrupted, like the really cool aunt I am."

"You really have no desire to have children of your own?"

"It's never been the goal. Traveling and enjoying good wine and having laughs with friends—that's my life's mission. Every month, when I get my period, I buy myself an extravagant gift or book myself a unique experience to remind myself what I'd give up if I got pregnant."

I grimace in agreement. "Kids do suck your time and money from you."

"Today, I took a five-hour nap."

"I'm pretty sure that's just called sleeping."

"Exactly." She cheers me, and we drink. "It's exhausting, being me."

"You need to tell me when babysitting is too much. Between your full-time job, your side hustle, and being fabulous, your dance card is quite full."

"I like to keep my dance card jam-packed, thank you very much. Time on my hands is never good. Trust me, I'll let you know when I'm over the babysitting. It's not like you pay me anyway."

"You never accept the money!"

She lifts her fork of escargot. "But I do accept the dinner."

She winks, and I laugh as I bite into my tuna tartar. French food is my favorite, and I don't get to dine at this restaurant too often. Ainsley hasn't developed the palate for this cuisine yet. She's currently into Japanese and Thai.

Tara sips her wine and twirls her glass from the stem. "Because I'm a nosy bitch, I need to know. What's going on with you and the doctor you went out with? Do you ship him?"

"What the heck does that mean?"

"Izzy taught it to me. It comes from the word *relationship*. It means you want to be in a relationship with him."

"No," I state loud and clear.

She takes a bite of steak and then points her fork at me. "You know I Googled him, right? He's like a real-life Ken doll, except he can diagnose diseases and shit."

I take a sip of the crisp Chinon and watch the red tornado in the glass. "He was really nice and—" I stop myself from using the word *lovely*. "He was easy to talk to."

"You make dating sound so dreadful. It's like you've been single so long that you forgot how to find the good in meeting new people."

"Tara," I admonish, tilting back my wineglass and finishing the last drop. "I'm not built like you. I don't have this burning need to be in a relationship. Eric is nice, and he sent a very nice text message, but that's as far as I'm willing to go. My life right now is too complicated for a relationship."

Her mouth opens in a surprised, excited gasp. "Let me see your phone!"

Begrudgingly, I pull my phone out, unlock the screen, and hand it to her.

She reads Eric's text message out loud in a terrible impression of man's voice. "*I'm reaching out to let you know what a wonderful time I had last week at dinner. We said it was a meal between new friends, but I'm thinking about you a week later and I'd be a fool not to try and see if you'd be willing to go out with me again. The odds of you saying no are great. I'm willing to take the chance on having my ego crushed.*"

Tara looks up from the text message with smashed lips and wide eyes, and I can hear her feet tapping on the ground in excitement.

"Jillian, you're an idiot if you don't give this guy a chance. How freaking sweet is this text message?"

"Very sweet," I agree. "What happens when I date him for a while and it fizzles? It'll have been a waste of time."

"Who are you kidding with this drivel? Let me impart some wisdom on you. There's no woman on earth who declares *I don't need a man* unless there's a real-life man who scorned her. Whoever that guy is, fuck him."

"That's your advice," I muse.

"Who are you sticking it to with this *I can do everything on my own* mantra anyway? Not your ex—that's for damn sure. He's probably out living his life and screwing everything that walks. You're only screwing yourself."

The thought of Luke bedding women over the years makes my stomach sour. I haven't given thought to the reality that he's been in relationships since we separated. He could be in one now.

"I'm not like you and Melissa. You rile each other up. I don't need, nor do I want, that for me. Yes, I have issues like everyone else. I choose not to air them. That's not the way I was raised. That's not my style."

"Your biggest issue is, you went too many years without a Tara and Melissa in your life." Her gold bangles jingle as she talks. "You have this amazing, self-empowered aura about you, but that self-reliance can eat you up. Let me explain something to you. When Melissa's ex-husband cheated on her, she gave up on love. Not because she didn't want it, but because she didn't want it to hurt her again. She convinced herself her children's happiness was all that mattered. It wasn't until she met Will that she realized she was still capable of loving despite being hurt."

"Melissa's story is one for the ages. Our stories are different. I wasn't cheated on."

I motion for the waiter to refill my wine glass.

Tara waits for the waiter to finish pouring our wine and then continues, "You're very close to the vest with your past, and I respect that. But I don't understand why you let it alter the rest of your life."

"You're starting to sound like my mother."

"Hell no. Your mother thinks you need a man to conform to societal norms. I'm telling you to stop letting a man dictate how you live. This Eric guy might end up being a dud, but you say you had a nice time, and maybe if you give him a chance, he can turn out to be something more than a good dinner. Don't let being hurt in the past and this drive to be the best mom and an independent woman hold you back from living your fucking life! Don't let some man who made the biggest dick decision in letting you—a gorgeous, successful, talented woman with legs I'd kill for, hair people spend thousands to have, and eyes that are seriously envious—go, impact your life. Fuck him. Seriously, fuck that guy from your past by moving on and living in the goddamn present!"

A woman at a nearby table drops her water glass at Tara's expressive declaration, and I close my eyes in mortification while still getting every word she said.

I take a long sip of my wine and drink in her words.

All these years, I've been closing myself off as a scornful vengeance to Luke. I shouldn't continue to put my life on hold just because he's suddenly made an appearance. If he weren't here and I had that date with Eric, it's possible I would have given Eric a chance for a second date. At least after hearing such a powerful speech from Tara, I'll give it serious consideration.

"I can see why Melissa keeps you around."

She holds her glass in the air and scowls. "There are many reasons, but an elaboration would be nice."

"You know how to strike a match and light a fire under someone's ass."

"So, you're going to go on a second date with the doctor?"

"I'm going to stop letting a jerk from the past decide how I spend my future."

Tar's positively giddy as she takes a drink and lifts my cell phone from the table. My heart races as she looks up from my phone, the light of the screen illuminating her face as she gleams with a devilish grin.

"Sent."

My head rolls back as I close my eyes and hope she didn't just do what I think she did.

My phone pings, and I hear her whistle as her feet keep on dancing.

"You have a date with him next week. Thursdays are best, right?" she says without a care in the world.

I lower my gaze to her and ask, "Did you really just text Eric back and say that I'd go on a date with him?"

She nods with the fierce smirk of a mischievous kid. "Yes! He replied rather quickly, I might add. You're welcome. Don't forget to name your firstborn after me. What's his last name?"

"Hollenford."

"Tara Hollenford," she states dreamily. "It has a nice ring to it."

"You should date him then."

"Nope. He's your future husband. I'm not in the market to take another woman's man. I'm not Maisie," she jokes, referring to the woman who stole Melissa's husband years ago.

"No one wants to be a Maisie," I remark.

"I have an idea. Let's go online and post on Yelp that her salon is doing free haircuts for the next week," she suggests with that devilish look still on her face.

"No, Tara."

Her shoulders fall as her mouth frowns. "Can we at least send a dozen pizzas to the house with crude words written in pepperoni?"

I laugh while trying to keep a straight face. "You're trouble."

She perks up and lifts her glass. "Why, thank you!"

We clink, and then I take my phone, along with hers, away from her.

She grimaces yet declares, "We need more wine. For you. Not me. I'm driving. You are not. So, drink!"

The woman cannot be trusted.

twelve

WHEN DINNER IS OVER, we step out of Le Amoureux and stand on the sidewalk on Main Street. Tara is parked on the street, so I walk her to her sleek sports car. My house is within walking distance, so I'll be going home on foot. Good thing because I had two glasses of wine too many and am a tiny bit tipsy.

As we say our good-byes, something behind me catches Tara's eye. "There's your kid."

I spin around to see Ainsley—wearing the flower dress, pink tights, and denim jacket she picked out for her special date with Luke—strolling down the street. Beside her is the handsome man who picked her up, wearing a black leather jacket and a brooding smile.

Tara grips my arm. "You didn't explain how cute your new babysitter was. Is he single? What's his deal? Would he be a good candidate for me? I usually go for the civil servant types. Cops, teachers, military guys. I like them rough and rugged."

"Luke happens to be a fireman," I state and watch her doe eyes bulge out of their sockets, practically landing on the concrete. "He's not available."

"Taken," she grumbles as she takes out a piece of gum and shoves it into her mouth. "All the good ones are. How do you know him?"

She's putting on her lipstick as I explain with a sigh, "We met five years ago in Aruba and reconnected in Walden."

"And you let him take her out? You had to know me a year before I had the privilege."

"That's because you're trouble. Luke's … a different kind of trouble."

"Interesting." The word is long and drawn out.

Ainsley notices us up the block and waves her hand wildly as she shouts for me. Her other hand is wrapped in Luke's strong one, which she starts to pull in order to run over to us. Luke slows her down.

The amber hues of the gas lamps are showing off the matching highlights in their dark hair. There's a glow about Ainsley as she looks up at Luke and smiles. His eyes, however, are trained on mine as they close the distance. Those golden flecks in his eyes are damn near primal as they lock with mine and send a heated wave of intensity straight to where I'm standing, nearly knocking me over.

And this, ladies and gentlemen, is why I don't over imbibe on wine.

As I mentally right myself, Ainsley and Luke cross the street and walk up to us. Ainsley releases her hand from Luke's to give Tara a huge hug.

"Hey, squirt. Look at you, all dressed up." She ruffles Ainsley's hair, who is looking up at Tara with full cheeks and a bright smile.

"I went on my first date! We went to the movies, and we even ate dinner in our seats. I got a hot dog and popcorn and soda!" Ainsley exclaims to Tara, who places a hand on her hip as she turns to me.

"Why does this guy get to spoil our girl with soda, but I have to keep it under lock and key when I babysit?"

I drop my shoulders and lower my chin at Luke. "Soda?"

He waves me off like I'm overreacting. "I got her the Sprite because it's caffeine-free, and she promised to brush her teeth twice before bed," he explains and then looks at Tara. "If she's mad at that, imagine how pissed she'll be at the R-rated action flick we just saw. Lots of violence and profanity."

"Luke!" I reprimand.

Tara and Luke chuckle like schoolchildren who pulled a prank on the principal.

"Is she always this gullible?" he asks Tara, thumbing toward me.

"Delightfully, yes," she answers and looks at him with her chest raised and hip jutted out. It's her provocative peacock pose and one I've seen her use many times when she's in the presence of a man. "I'm Tara."

"I've heard a lot about you."

"All bad, I hope."

I roll my eyes at the over-the-top way she's flirting with Luke. I've never complained about her flirtatious ways, but this feels out of character for Tara. Like she's trying extra hard on purpose. I give her a questionable stare, and she winks at me.

Ainsley taps Luke on the arm, and he bends down to listen to what she has to say. She whisper-yells into Luke's ear, "This is the one I was telling you about. Mom says she's too boy crazy, but she really wants a boyfriend, and I think you should marry her."

Tara's peacock morphs into a chicken with her head popped forward as she listens to Ainsley's assessment. "Lady, if we are going to be friends, you need to learn to not share the gossip. Besides, Luke already has a girl."

I pull Ainsley by the shoulder and over to me. "Enough matchmaking for you, kiddo. You're only four."

"I'm gonna be five soon."

"Five. Not fifteen," I explain and then kiss the top of her head.

Luke gazes at Tara speculatively. "I don't have a girlfriend. Who told you that?"

"Jillian. She clearly must have gotten her facts confused with another man she lets watch her children." Tara shoots me questioning eyes and then looks back at Luke. Her blue eyes look like pinballs as they shoot from one side to the other. She has a wicked grin on her face as she takes her cell phone out of her bag. "We should exchange numbers. If we're both going to be looking after Ainsley, it would benefit us to be in contact."

"Uh ..." He pauses and looks at me for approval.

I merely shrug my shoulders.

"Sure." Luke slides his hands out of his jacket pockets and takes Tara's phone to input his number.

I assume he's well aware she doesn't just want to talk about Ainsley's child care schedule.

Tara stares at Luke while he puts his information in. Her lashes flutter. "Jillian, you didn't tell me Luke was this handsome."

"You know I can hear you, right?" he asks as he hands her phone back to her.

"Yep." She winks and then puts her phone in her bag. "I'll be in touch."

Ainsley pulls on Tara's dress and points to Luke. "Look, Luke has a butt chin like me."

Tara's eyes squint as she appraises him, bemused. "I told you only good-looking people have chin clefts. Now, do you believe me?"

"Yep!" Ainsley smiles a huge, small-toothed smile. "Luke said his mom had one, and she was the most beautiful woman in the world. Just like me."

"He isn't wrong." Tara squeezes Ainsley's cheek, then looks at Luke. "You're very charming."

"Very," I deadpan, then give them both a closed-mouth smile.

"Jillian doesn't like charming men. She's always warning me that they're dangerous. She even said you were a different kind of trouble."

"Time to call it a night!" I declare with my finger held high and my hand grabbing my daughter's.

Tara grins. "Well, you three have a great evening. I have meetings in the morning. Being an accountant isn't as glamorous as they made it seem in college. Well, actually, they didn't make it seem glamorous at all, but I had higher hopes than six-day workweeks and a never-ending pile of paperwork." She kisses me and Ainsley good-bye and waves to Luke as she gets in her sports car convertible to drive away. "Don't do anything I wouldn't do!"

As she careens down the road with the dual exhaust revving, I turn to Luke and Ainsley.

"I hope I didn't crash your evening. Were you two having a great time?" I ask.

Luke slides his hands back into the pockets of his leather coat. "Yes. We were about to get some ice cream and walk home. Would you like to join us?"

I smash my lips and speak nonchalantly. "If that's okay with you."

He leans down and speaks in that smooth baritone, and his eyes darken with emotion. "I wouldn't have asked if I didn't want your company."

The hairs on my neck rise at the way his voice curls though my veins and settles into every nerve ending in my body.

An unwelcome blush creeps into my cheeks. Wine will do that to a lady. "Ice cream it is."

I take Ainsley's hand and walk down Main Street. She grips Luke's hand in her other one and swings her arms as we walk. Anyone looking at us would think we were the perfect family—mom, dad, and child—walking into the local ice cream shop.

Luke holds the door for us, and when we're inside, he lifts Ainsley, and the two peruse the dairy-free ice cream. It's a limited selection, but it seems to impress Luke.

"Peanut butter and cookie ice cream? I think I've died and gone to ice cream heaven." He licks his lips and places his order, which Ainsley copies because, of course, they have the same favorite flavor of ice cream. "They make soda floats. Vanilla in Coca-Cola sounds like a winner."

I ignore him and order a small raspberry sorbet in a cup.

Luke pays for our treat, and the three of us continue our stroll home. Ainsley skips in front with her cone in hand while Luke and I trail behind her. I run my hand over my arm and fight the evening chill that's crept in. Luke pauses and starts to remove his jacket.

"Here," he offers, to which I hold my hand up and deny. "Jillian, you're freezing."

"I'm fine."

Ignoring my comment, he places the leather over my shoulders. As he does so, I inhale the scent of leather and musk and all things Luke.

"Did you just smell my jacket?"

Trying my best not to drop my cup, I shrug my shoulders inside his too-large jacket and then trip lightly on the curb. He grabs my elbow.

"Think I had too much wine with dinner," I offer in explanation.

"You don't say. You're having a hard time hiding your expressions tonight."

"How so?"

"I think someone is jealous. And by someone, I mean you."

"What in the world would I have to be jealous about?"

"You tell me," he teases and takes a spoonful of his ice cream, lapping the belly of the spoon with his tongue and slowly dragging it out of his mouth.

I take a deep breath and lift my chin. "I knew Tara was going to put the moves on you. I mean, you are very attractive. Could it have killed you to get fat or bald over the years?"

He laughs as he takes a bite, and my eyes linger on that damn plastic spoon as his tongue glides along the bottom of it.

"Although I'm glad you're attractive because …" I point toward Ainsley, who is happily skipping along while humming a tune from *Encanto*—a film that shifts the female paradigm and is on my approved movie list.

"Let's hope good looks are the only thing I passed on to her."

I scrunch my brows. "Why are you always so cryptic? You're like a puzzle I'm constantly trying to figure out."

He points at me with his spoon. "I like tipsy Jilly."

"Don't call me Jilly."

"No problem." He gives me a smile that has my pulse racing. "Jilly."

I growl at him, which only seems to please him as we continue our walk. Ainsley makes the appropriate left at the corner and leads us past the movie theater they just went to.

"This town's cute. Did you go on dates to the movies and ice cream a lot, growing up here?" he asks me.

"George Blinko. Tenth grade. Put the moves on me too hard in the second-to-last row of theater three. I elbowed him in the nose, and that pretty much ruined any chance I had of getting asked to the movies by a boy again."

He laughs. It's deep and boisterous. "Poor George. Did his nose survive?"

"His parents had to bring him to the emergency room. They thought it was broken, but he was just being a baby about it. I think he was more upset that he had been turned down."

"Ainsley's in good hands with you as a role model. You certainly made me try hard for your affection."

"Please note: you are the only man who wooed me as fast as you did. I like to give men more of a challenge."

"I wooed you, did I? I like that I succeeded. Glad I didn't end up with rhinoplasty and a bruised ego."

"I blame the palm trees. They make everything more magical."

He tosses his now-empty cup into a nearby trash can. "If a man were wise enough, he'd plant a thousand palm trees in Connecticut."

"Too bad the weather here would force them all to die."

My comment, although meant to be in jest, causes Luke to furrow his brows as he rubs his chest.

"Yeah. Too bad."

My cup is now empty too.

We stop on the curb outside my house, and Ainsley runs toward the door and waves into the doorbell camera.

"It doesn't work," I remind her as I unlock the door and let her inside. "I have to call an electrician to get it repaired."

"I can take a look," Luke offers.

"That's okay. I can have someone out here this week. I've just been busy ... and distracted."

Lowering his eyes to mine, he grins. "I'll sleep better if I know you two are safe. I have a toolbox in my truck. Let me grab it."

"Of course you carry manly things, like wrenches and screwdrivers, in your truck."

"What's that supposed to mean?" he asks as he opens his back door and takes out a shiny black toolbox from the floorboard.

"You're always ready for anything."

"Trust me, there are some things you need to be prepared for."

I lower my voice. "Like finding out you have a child."

He kneels down and opens the box. "No. That one was easy."

I go inside and turn off the circuit breaker to the front porch. We're now shrouded in darkness, the front porch light off, along with the power to the doorbell. Luke hands me his cell phone and asks that I use the flashlight feature and point it to where he's working. Ainsley is inside, presumably in her playroom. Luke stands and opens the doorbell box and starts adjusting wires.

It's quiet out here.

I lean against the red brick of my home and look up at the stars.

The moon is high and full tonight. It was this big the night we met and danced on the sandy white beach.

"Can I ask you a question?"

"Sure. Just make sure you keep that light pointed at the wires and not the ground."

Realizing I've been distracted by the moon and not doing my job, I roll to the side and point the light at his hands.

"The night after the fire," I start, "you knew how I took my coffee. How did you know that?"

"I remember everything you told me in Aruba," he answers as he works with a screwdriver.

I make a harrumph sound, as if I don't believe him.

He ignores it and casually states, "You hate oranges, but love pineapple. Your middle name is Payne, which was your mother's middle name, and you went to an all-girls private high school and then to the University of Connecticut. You fell in love with wedding planning after watching the aptly named movie *The Wedding Planner* and got an internship with a world-renowned wedding planner while you were still in college. There's a scar in your naval from a belly button ring you got when you were sixteen and was grounded for a summer because of it. Walruses are your favorite animal, and the only thing that scares you are spiders, bathrooms with closed shower curtains, and being seen as a weak female who can't take care of herself."

My jaw is slack from where I froze during his accurate recollection of things I'd once told him.

He lifts his shoulders to his ears. "To name a few. It's weird, I know."

I clear my throat. "It's not weird at all." I lean further into the brick and feel the stone through his leather jacket. "I remember things about you too."

His brows rise in interest.

"You grew up in the country and loved catching frogs, fishing, and riding on a four-wheeler. Broke your arm when you were ten because you accepted a dare from your sister on who could climb a tree higher. You won. Math was your least favorite subject. You were voted homecoming king and were the captain of the soccer team, which was a big deal where you grew up. You have three tattoos—a tribal tattoo you regret, an American flag, and a wolf. You oddly know how to juggle. You can light a match with one hand and solve a Rubik's Cube. And you pretend you know how to speak French, which you do not."

"Glad you paid attention." The smile on his face is so deep that I swear he might have dimples in them.

I never have more than a glass of wine with dinner, yet tonight, I imbibed on three, and now, I'm getting too cozy, too melancholy with Luke.

He closes the top of the doorbell box and screws it back in. When he tests the doorbell, we hear it ring. Ainsley cheers from inside, and we both smile.

"Thank you for that."

"Jillian, I want you to know that you don't have to do this alone anymore. You have me and ... fuck, well"—he runs his hand over the back of his neck and looks back at me—"I'm here."

The way the twinkle of moonlight catches his eye as he glances my way, his gaze smoldering with fire. My flesh is tingling, my belly is swarming, and my heart is swelling.

I wasn't lying when I said he was too attractive for me.

He's too swoony and charming.

He's beyond dangerous.

"You want more time with Ainsley," I surmise.

"That's not all I want."

I run my hand down the zipper teeth of his coat. "I have a date next week."

"You have a date?" His nostrils flare. "New guy?"

"Same. The doctor."

His mouth turns down, and his lip pouts out. "What made you change your mind about the guy?"

"Tara. She had some insightful words to say. I should have asked if she could stay with Ainsley for a few hours."

"If anyone's gonna watch Ainsley, it's gonna be me. I'll move my schedule around."

"What about time with your dad?"

"This is more important."

If I wasn't listening so intently, I would have missed the slight break in his voice.

That's not the reply I thought I'd get. Actually, I didn't know how he'd respond.

I walk inside and turn the breaker on now that he's done with his task, thankful for the reprieve from the way his husky tone made my knees weak. When I come back outside, he's talking to Ainsley on the porch.

"Good night, kiddo," he says.

Her cone is now devoured, and she has peanut butter and cookie ice cream all over her face.

"You're going home?" she asks with scrunched brows.

"I have a cat who needs to be fed."

The sugar rush of ice cream comes out as she exclaims, "You have a cat! Can I meet him?"

"If it's okay, I'd like to bring Joe when I see you next week." Luke looks my way for approval.

I nod because if there's one animal I'll let in my house, it's Joe. I'm actually looking forward to seeing him again.

"I've always wanted a cat. Mom says we can't have one."

He kneels and takes some napkins out of his jeans pocket and wipes the ice cream from her face. "Tell you what. I'll share Joe with you. When you two meet next week, you'll be the best of friends, I promise."

The top and bottom rows of her teeth are bright. "I'm so excited. I'm gonna tell all my friends at school that I have a cat. Wait. What color is he?"

"Orange with white stripes," he says.

"I can't wait to meet him!" She throws her arms around him, and he jolts back, not expecting the affection. "Thank you for taking me on my first date. It was magical."

Luke stiffens for a moment before raising his arms and closing them around Ainsley in a tight embrace. His eyes close, and moisture pools in the pockets. When he opens his eyes, they're glassy and bright.

"Why are you crying, Luke?" she asks him.

"I'm happy," he breathes. "Really happy."

"You don't cry when you're happy. You smile!" She kisses him on the cheek and then skips inside.

With my own raw emotion bubbling under the surface, I let out a few quivering breaths as I go to follow Ainsley inside when Luke calls me back.

"Jillian."

My hand is on the door, and I clench the wooden frame, bracing myself for what he's about say. Because when a man calls your name with the amount of urgency and conviction as Luke just did, you brace yourself to be blown away.

"I lied to you."

Peeking my head in, I tell Ainsley to put her pajamas on and that I'll be up in a moment. As I go back to the curb, Luke is standing in the dark, rubbing his eyes and blinking back his emotions. I steady the quake inside my chest and walk to him with my arms crossed and my chin up, waiting for him to explain exactly what he lied to me about.

"In the car, you asked if I had any regrets—"

"You don't have to explain yourself," I say, trying to stop him. Not because I don't want to hear what he's about to say. It's because

I fear what he says will render me immobile from having him. "What happened between us in the past needs to stay there. All that matters now is Ainsley."

"I understand."

I turn around and walk into my house, leaving part of my heart on the curb and hope he doesn't crush it.

"And ... Jillian?"

I pause, my heart rising to my throat, and I turn around and face him.

"Yes?" I breathe.

"I'll see you next week for your date."

I lift my eyes to the sky as I slide off his jacket and toss it to him ... rather aggressively.

He catches it in the air. As he walks to his car, I'm pretty sure I catch him sniffing it as well.

thirteen

I'M RUMMAGING THROUGH MY closet for a proper dress to wear on a second date.

Appropriate attire for wedding planning is simple and comfortable. That's fine and dandy when you're trying to blend in. Tonight, however, I'd like to not look like I'm about to rob a bank.

The few brightly colored dresses I have are party dresses and a bit too fancy or too sexy for dinner. I enjoyed Eric's company, but I'm not willing to give him the wrong impression with my breasts falling out of my dress or a slit so far up my right thigh that it gives serious Angelina Jolie vibes. I have some pretty camisoles, but I don't want to wear pants either.

My hands stop on a dress on a hanger, still in the dry-cleaning bag and meant to be returned. The long-sleeved brown jersey dress Luke's neighbor Stella lent me is still in my closet. I hold it up and appraise the simple dress. I recall Luke's pupils dilating as they raked over the modest yet revealing neckline.

"At least it's not black," I muse as I pull it on and assess the clingy fabric. It's flattering, and I feel good in it, which is the most important thing.

Deciding this is the best option, I slide on a pair of gold peep-toe heels and matching earrings. I choose to leave my cleavage bare of jewelry, but insert long, dangling earrings that peek through my blown-out hair.

As I do one final look in the mirror, I stare back at the woman I see. Auburn hair, green eyes, and a complexion that is youthful, thanks to my strict sunscreen regimen. I'm not blind. On the outside, I'm an attractive, well-put-together woman. Butterflies swarm through my belly as I wish my insides matched my outsides. Anxiety has always bubbled low under the surface, yet I push it down year after year.

I force the smiles, keep my head down, and do the right thing. If I didn't, my parents would have thought I was crazy when I decided to become a wedding planner after college. They knew I had a vision for my future and the work ethic to balance it. Plus, in their eyes, I was going to marry a physician or a politician and quit my job to rear his babies and be a woman of society.

Clearly, they miscalculated their daughter.

With a nod to myself in the mirror, I walk downstairs and see Luke in the kitchen with Ainsley. They're making chicken cutlets, which Luke has declared his favorite meal in the world.

My nerves sizzle as I watch him teach Ainsley how to roll raw chicken in egg and then in the breadcrumbs. She's giggling at the grossness of the mixture, yet she wants to keep going. While she giggles, Luke looks at her with glistening eyes and a flush to his cheeks despite his smile. He rubs the heel of his palm against his eye and then helps her clean her hands in the sink.

Joe, the cat, who made an appearance at my doorstep tonight with Luke, is on the counter near them, padding his own paw in the flowing faucet.

The three are cleaning up as I make my presence known.

Luke's eyes go from crinkling to completely open as he looks over at me. His chest rises and stays there for a beat longer than a normal breath. His lips are parted as he stares at my dress, starting at my hips and doing a quick yet purposeful appraisal of my attire, stopping briefly at my neck and then landing on my face.

Luke's gaze has me twisting my fingers around each other, and then I wipe my palms down my hips. His eyes roam down and stare at my hands.

"You sure do clean up well," he says, to which Ainsley nods in agreement.

"Like a princess, Mommy."

I give them a wide smile and do a little spin. "I have to return this dress to Stella. It was the only thing that felt right tonight."

"You look good in everything."

Luke's breathy comment, paired with the way he's looking at me with that sinful stare, has me releasing the breath I didn't know I was holding.

"A point to never be forgotten," I joke. "Chicken cutlets?" I ask despite the obvious display on the countertops.

Luke clears his throat. "Yeah. I won't let her use the stove though."

"Mommy! You look so pretty!" Ainsley starts toward me with her wet and half-cleaned hands in the air.

Luke grabs her shoulders and pulls her back to the sink.

"Don't get your mom all messy," he tells her.

Joe hops off the counter and lands at my feet, rubbing his nose against the gold clasp on the front of my shoe. I bend down and pet him.

"Hello, sir," I greet him as he purrs against my palm. "While I'm happy to see you again, I'm surprised to have you on my kitchen counters. That's good for Luke's house. Not mine."

"Joe was helping us make dinner," Ainsley explains.

I rise. "I see. Not exactly sanitary."

"You heard the lady, Joe. No more being on the counters. This is a lady's house, not a bachelor pad," Luke answers easily and then looks down at Joe, who is wrapping his body around my ankles, one at a time. "Joe, stop groping Jillian. She doesn't need your fur all over her before her date."

"You have a boyfriend?" Ainsley asks loudly, and I scold Luke with my eyes.

"No. I am going to dinner with a friend. Just like I do with Tara and Melissa. This friend is named Eric. Boys and girls can be friends, you know. It's not a date," I explain to her sweetly despite the laser beams I'm still shooting at the man behind her. "Just dinner."

"Fuck, sorry," he says and then apologizes again. "I mean, shit— shoot. Dammit, I can't get this right."

I throw my hands up in the air. And start walking around the kitchen island to get my phone from my purse. "This was a bad idea. I'll call and cancel."

Luke quickly dries Ainsley's hands and then brushes past her to cross the kitchen and take the phone out of my hand.

"Don't cancel because of me." His hand is still on mine as he stands close to me. Too close with the way I feel the electricity beating through his body. He keeps his voice deep and low as he looks at me with determined eyes. "I didn't know I couldn't say where you were going. You just have to lay out some ground rules."

"Ground rules," I repeat as I push my hair behind my ear and look over his shoulder at Ainsley, who is playing with Joe on the kitchen floor.

When they went to the movies, I wasn't concerned about all the things he might say to her because they'd be in a quiet theater for two hours. Now, who knows what he could tell her?

"No big announcements. She's not ready."

"Obviously. We agreed to that already."

"You need to know that I don't bring men into my daughter's life, and I have no desire to. For obvious reasons, you're an exception. This isn't a revolving door of strays, which is something you need to keep in mind as well if you're going to be in her life."

"Joe's not a stray cat."

"Stray women," I bite.

Luke's head tilts slightly. "I can't introduce Ainsley to other women?"

"Not unless you plan on marrying them, no."

He mulls this information over. "Will you be introducing her to your date tonight?"

I gnaw at my thumb. "No. Only as a friend. She's never ever seen me go on a date." I rub my hands over my head and down the curls I spent an hour setting. "It's important Ainsley knows that my life is complete with her in it and that I don't need a man to feel validated."

"Validation isn't the same as loved."

"Luke, you're making me nervous. I feel like you're going to say the wrong thing in front of her. Eric might say something insinuating that he and I are more than we are. I don't know why I thought this would work. I shouldn't be going out." My hands rest on my stomach as I curl my brow. "Calling and canceling is definitely the thing to do."

As I'm reaching over to get my phone, his hands rest on my shoulders and gives them a light squeeze. The heat of his hands warms my body instantly, and I stop in my tracks. As his forehead lowers, he penetrates me with his intense gaze, and I find myself being rendered speechless.

My heart, however, is about to barrel out of my chest.

"Breathe, Jillian," he croons, and my lips part, letting out a tight breath.

I feel my chest lifting powerfully high with the deep gasps that follow and settle them into my solar plexus.

Luke's eyes remain on mine.

"It's going to be okay," he says. "Ainsley and I are gonna make dinner, play a few games, and then curl up with Joe and watch a movie on the list of preferred strong-feminist-heroine films you wrote down for me—as well as the number to every doctor in a ten-mile radius, her eating habits even though I have the same allergy, her bedtime routine, quirks and interests, and asterisked points, including no cursing, which I already broke."

My shoulders fall with his words, but I open my mouth to argue, to which he hushes me again.

"You look too pretty tonight to let it go to waste because of a man like me."

"What kind of man are you?"

"The kind that, for a moment, was gonna let you stay home and call off your date because, while I have no right to, I am insanely jealous that a man is going to take you out tonight and it's not me."

"Why are you telling me this?"

"I have no fucking clue."

"Language, Luke."

He glances over his shoulder at the little girl and tomcat, who are too busy rolling around on the floor to notice our conversation.

Luke turns back to me. "The rule is *no cursing in front of Ainsley.* When it comes to you, I want to say all the good words. Including *fuck*. A lot."

My eyes roll to the ceiling as I let out an exasperated sigh. Of all the men to procreate with, it had to be the one who draws me in like no other and makes me want to slap him at the same time. My body ignites when I'm next to him, and it's unfair to my heart. I'd push him away and out of my life forever, but I have to make this work for Ainsley's sake.

The doorbell rings, and I gasp. "I told him to call and I'd come out. He shouldn't be at the door."

Ainsley rushes past me and Luke and barrels tower the door. Joe gallops behind her and hops up onto the banister of the staircase.

"Hey, what did your mother say about opening the door to strangers?" he reprimands, and I stare at him in disbelief. He shrugs. "Told you I read the note."

Shaking my head, I turn to Ainsley and usher her away from the door. "Only adults open the door."

Her tiny lips pucker for a kiss, and then Luke picks her up, taking a step back from the door as I open it.

Eric Hollenford is on the front porch in a dark suit, pin-stripe shirt, no tie, and shiny brown loafers. His short hair is combed back, and he gives that smile I'm sure works on all his patients to put them at ease before a long surgery.

His eyes stay on my face and don't do that long, pausing appraisal of my body the way Luke's did. It sets me at ease.

"You look lovely."

Eric's words are followed by a snicker from behind me. A deep, gruff snicker from a man with a preschooler in his arms. The two look like twins as they giggle. I thought they were disappearing, not staying for an introduction.

I lower my brows at them and then turn back to Eric. "Sorry. Eric, this is Luke and my daughter, Ainsley."

"You're as cute as your mom said you were," Eric says, smiling at Ainsley, to which she smiles back.

Joe hisses from his perch on the banister.

Eric holds his hand out to Luke. "Pleasure to meet you. Are you Jillian's brother?"

"Definitely not her brother," Luke states.

Ainsley beams back at Luke in interest. "Can I call you Uncle Loo?"

"No," he says quickly and shoots me a look.

I explain to Eric, "Luke is watching Ainsley tonight."

"Oh, so you're the manny," Eric states with understanding.

Now, it's my turn to giggle. "Luke isn't the male nanny."

Luke leans forward with a cocky, sarcastic stance. My giggling tops.

"Manny, huh? I could roll with that. I'm a man of manny, manny talents. I tend to all of Jillian's needs." He winks, and I mentally punch him in the face.

"Ignore him," I state, grabbing my purse, and then I point a strong finger at Luke. "Behave. Bedtime is at eight."

"Yes, Mom," Luke and Ainsley reply in unison, causing me to do a double take.

They've only met a few times, and they're already two peas in a pod. Apparently, Incendio genetics run deep with these two.

"Good night. I'll be back as soon as my friend and I are done with dinner." I give Ainsley another kiss, ignoring how close Luke's face is to mine as I say good-bye to my daughter.

I close the door behind me and stop on my doorstep.

"You ready to go?" Eric asks with his hand held out to me.

I stare at it for a beat before taking it. "Lead the way."

As we drive away, I note the sway of the dining room curtain being pushed to the side and the silhouette of a man watching every second of my departure.

fourteen

LOST IN THOUGHT IN the front seat of Eric's Bentley, I look out the window and am surprised when we pull up to the Valor County Helipad on the outskirts of Greenwood Village. There are rows of helicopters lined up in the open lot that is reserved for the town's elite who want a quick commute to Manhattan or Boston. While I've seen the helipad many times, I've never driven past the chain-link fence and onto the tarmac.

"Eric," I say with mild trepidation.

"I know I should have asked you first, but I wanted to surprise you."

"You should know that I am not the biggest fan of surprises."

"Your mother said that. She also said if I suggested this, you'd say no before we got here."

I raise a brow. "Say no to what?"

"Dinner."

I look out the front window. The only building in sight is an office with one rectangular window. "Is there a restaurant here?"

"It's in Manhattan."

"Manhattan is eighty miles away."

"Yet only an hour by helicopter."

"You want to take a helicopter to Manhattan for dinner?" I run the pads of my fingers over my forehead and take in this information. "My mother knows you want to take me on a helicopter to Manhattan for dinner. Sorry, but there are about ten red flags in that comment."

He pulls into a parking spot and puts the car in park. "Flags noted. I happened to tell my mother my plans, and of course, she got yours involved. I just wanted to share with you something that I really enjoy."

"You fly in helicopters regularly," I muse.

"I promise I will have you home at a reasonable hour. I know you worry about your daughter. If we leave now, we'll be at dinner by eight thirty and home by midnight."

"You rented a helicopter to fly to Manhattan for dinner?" I ask, completely dumbfounded.

He grimaces slightly. "I own it. Part of it. It's a helicopter share with some other doctors."

"Oh boy. This is very out of my comfort zone." I hold my palm up to Eric and explain, "It's not that I'm afraid to fly. I'm a single mom, and if I die, Ainsley is left without a parent and ..." My words falter. Actually, if something were to happen to me, Ainsley would have Luke. Not that she knows he's her dad ... yet. I'm still not ready to get into a death trap with the man and risk my life.

Eric nods in understanding. "I understand your concerns. I would like to state that I have a pilot on call with over ten thousand hours of flight time under his belt. I've flown with him countless times, and I promise that nothing will happen to you."

The blades of a nearby copter are spinning with quick, wind-splitting enthusiasm. I look out the window at it and cringe.

"I'm sorry, Eric, but that's a no for me. I'd like to keep my feet on the ground tonight."

He gives a small smile. "That's okay. I have a plan B ready."

"Are you sure? I'd understand if you want to call it a night. You went through all the trouble to hire the pilot. Don't waste your money."

He leans over slightly, and his cologne wafts off the jacket of his suit as he looks at me with his gentle eyes. "I took a chance on this without your permission. It was a poor attempt to impress you. I was going to show you the sunset like you wouldn't believe. You have boundaries, and I respect them. I'd rather take you out to dinner at a fast-food chain in town than bring you home. I like you, Jillian. I just want to show you a good time."

My cheeks heat with his words. They're sweet and something I'm not used to hearing, yet I'm surprised that I like hearing them from Eric. Even if he tried way too hard to show me a fancy night on the town. I can't fault him for that.

"Fast food is definitely out of the question," I say and watch his face morph from hopeful to downtrodden. "However, if we start driving now, I know a great spot where we can see the sunset."

Eric glances up, a wonderful smile crossing his face. He nods as he puts his car in reverse, lays an arm across the back of my seat, and declares, "Show me the way."

I smile, and we set out onto the highway toward the town of Newbury. It's forty minutes away from Greenwood Village, and I'm well aware we'd be almost in Manhattan by the time we pull up to the Mountain View Bistro, a beautiful venue at the top of a hill at the edge of Valor County. I exit the car and walk with Eric up the gently lit path, as the sun has already begun to set.

For a Thursday night, the restaurant is full. I assume Eric slipped the maître d' a tip with how fast we are seated at a table near the window. We each take a seat facing the view, which also means we're seated beside each other at the square table as opposed to across from one another, like we were last time.

We stare at the sky, a canvas of reds, pinks, and oranges as the sun descends below the treetops. The evening sun casts long shadows as setting rays give a warm orange tint to the changing leaves below. There's a glare that pops through the windows, but we ignore it as we take in the view.

"This is no helicopter sunset, but I admit, it is beautiful up here," he says.

"I'm glad you approve."

"Better than what I planned."

"Where were we supposed to eat?"

"I was going to order sandwiches for us to eat on a bench on the High Line. It's a park created on an old New York City railroad line, elevated along the west side of Manhattan."

I lean back in surprise. "I've heard of the High Line. I'm a little curious about the sandwiches on a park bench."

"I figured the helicopter thing was a bit pompous, and I wanted to balance it out by showing you how I could also be down-to-earth."

"That is by far the craziest thing I've ever heard." I laugh loudly and rest my chin in my hand as I look over at Eric —a handsome, kind doctor with gentle eyes and an adorable sense of self. "It's also incredibly sweet. You put a lot of thought into that."

He leans forward with his elbow on the table and closes in a touch. "I'd like you to know, that was the first time I thought of that date. I date a lot, so I don't want you to think I'm recycling date ideas."

"I hadn't thought of that, but thank you for clarifying. What is a typical date for you?"

"Dinner."

"Sorry. I took a very unique evening and made it passé."

"Turns out, dinner is an optimal dating plan because everyone needs to eat. I've never been here before, so that's a huge bonus. This place is stunning."

"Food is amazing too. I mean, it's not sandwiches, but they have an awesome seafood menu. I've been here for brunch a time or two, but hardly for dinner."

"You picked the perfect venue," Eric says.

I sit back in my chair and cross my legs, feeling right about my date with Eric, when my phone buzzes with a text. Seeing it's from Luke, I open it to make sure everything is okay with Ainsley.

On the screen is a photo of Luke, Ainsley, and Joe, all wearing tiaras and holding teacups up to the camera. Well, Joe isn't holding a cup, but he has one in front of him and looks none too pleased with the pink plastic crown on his small dome.

I bark out a laugh at the sight and look down at the comment.

> *Checking in to let you know the house isn't on fire and only mild profanity has been used. By Joe. He's a bastard of a cat.*

I hit reply.

> *Please let Joe know he's in charge.*

> *I trust him far more than I do his owner.*

> *Make sure he stays out of my bed.*

> *By "he," do you mean me or Joe?*

We need clarification as to who is allowed.

Neither of you.

Well ... Joe is a cute snuggler.

So's his owner.

Now, go back to your date.

I'm sure it's riveting since you're texting with me and not talking with him.

Beyond riveting.

He booked a helicopter to fly us to Manhattan.

Seriously?

Currently enjoying a bird's-eye view of the sunset.

Fuck.

Language, Luke.

Fuck me.

"Everything okay?" Eric asks, drawing my attention back to him and away from my phone.

I place my phone back in my purse. "Good. Just an update on Ainsley. I'm all yours now."

He grins. "I like the sound of that."

Three hours later, Eric pulls the car up to my house. I spent the past forty minutes wondering about the inevitable after-date question: *Will I let Eric kiss me?*

It seems like an odd question to ask oneself, but if I'm reading the evening correctly, Eric will most definitely try to kiss me before I exit this car and the question is, *Will I allow it?*

Just as we had the first time we went out, we shared easy conversation, a wonderful meal, and agreed to go out again. I like Eric. He's the finest man I've met in years. He's emotionally available and physically easy on the eyes. I'm attracted to him. In fact, I could imagine going to bed with this man. Not tonight or on the next date, but eventually. The fact that I'm even thinking about this is bewildering to me.

So, why don't I just kiss him first?

"Thank you for a fantastic evening," he says as he places his car in park. "It didn't go as planned, but it was better." His voice is husky as his eyes lower to my mouth.

I let out a shaky breath. He must sense my trepidation.

"I want to kiss you, Jillian. I don't want it to be in my car, but I know you value privacy with your daughter, so I won't kiss you by your doorstep, nor do I expect an invitation inside. But I do want to kiss you."

I swallow hard and lick my lips despite my parched mouth.

"May I kiss you, Jillian?"

I nod because I don't have the words to answer otherwise.

Eric leans forward and presses his lips to mine. They're cool and soft. When I part my lips for him, he takes my mouth in further. Sweetly, gentlemanly.

He pulls back, and I'm grateful he kept the kiss short.

I like Eric Hollenford. He's not only gentle with his physical mannerisms; he's gentle with my heart. I need someone like him in my life. Slow. Steady. Reliant.

I grimace, which has Eric looking at me in confusion. I tell him, "Now, I have to tell my mother she chose a good man for me to go on a date with."

Eric laughs in relief. "Oh, man. I'd hate to have to share the same with mine. They'll be sending out wedding invitations behind our backs before we get to a third date."

The idea scares me because I could see my mother being party to that. I also don't like the relaxed tone in his voice at the thought of it.

"You're right. We should keep this under wraps."

"At least until I propose," he says, and my stomach drops. He must see the shock on my face because he adds, "I'm kidding. I do want to see you again though. Next week?"

"I'll let you know." I open the door and step out of the car. "Good night."

Eric waits for me to get to my door before he drives away. I quietly open the door to my house, hoping Ainsley is asleep.

There's light coming from the living room and the faint sound of a children's cartoon featuring a child doctor who uses her toys as her patients. I march down the hallway, ready to scold Luke for keeping Ainsley up well past her bedtime, but when I get to the room, I'm startled by the sight before me.

Luke is lying on the couch with his feet up on the ottoman and a princess tiara half-hanging off his head of dark hair. A sleeping Ainsley is sprawled across his chest with a blanket over the two of them. Joe is curled up by Luke's feet.

Ainsley's mouth is open, and she's drooling on Luke's shirt.

Standing in the center of my living room, I continue to stare at the way Luke's arm is draped over Ainsley's back. He has a small smile on his face, even in his sleep. A content man.

On the coffee table is a stack of construction paper and markers. The two drew pictures. Luke's is a boat in the sea. A catamaran sailing among the palm trees with a man and a red-haired woman on the bow. It's a poor drawing, but its message is clear.

Next to it is Ainsley's photo. I know her drawings well. In hers is a young girl and a man, holding hands. *Ainsley and Luke* is written at the top. It's the first time she's drawn a picture of herself with someone other than me.

The third picture is a cat's paw print. Apparently, Joe made a picture too.

I walk over to Ainsley and gently lift her off Luke's chest. My action startles him awake because he reaches up to grab her, as if she were falling off.

"Shh. I'm just bringing her upstairs," I assure him.

His eyes are hooded as he sits up. "No. I'll do it." Luke rises from the couch and holds out his hands. "Give me. I'll carry her up."

He practically takes her out of my hands and walks her upstairs. Joe lets out a long stretch and then curls up on the couch again, seemingly not wishing to be bothered. I follow Luke upstairs and peek into Ainsley's room just as he pulls the blanket up to her chest.

"I love you," he whispers to Ainsley as he bows down and gives her sleeping head a kiss on the forehead. "Good night, sweet girl."

I fight the quivering feeling in my chest.

Luke might be a stranger to us in many ways, but he is Ainsley's dad. I'm soon going to have to make the decision on when to tell her. So far, he's been doing and saying all the right things, each visit making it harder for me to deny that he might be true to his word.

I hope it lasts.

As he walks out of her room, I start down the stairs and over to the couch, folding the blanket. Luke stands by the kitchen island and slides his wallet and phone into his pocket.

"We had fun tonight. She was asleep by eight, I promise. I just didn't have the heart to bring her up. She's cozier than a blanket." His voice is groggy, his hair is wildly disheveled, and he has a faint drool stain on his shirt from Ainsley.

"You want a coffee?" I offer. "You have a long drive back to Walden."

He shakes his head and grabs the cat carrier that he arrived with tonight. "Joe and I have a room in a hotel in town."

"You didn't have to do that."

He raises a brow. "Were you planning on me sleeping here?"

"No," I answer quickly. "I know we were joking about you sleeping in my bed, but the thought of you staying here is out of the question."

"I know, Jillian. Relax. That's why I got a room in town—so I could be close. They don't allow pets, so I'm gonna have to sneak this guy in somehow. Come on, Joe."

Joe reluctantly pads over to Luke who places him in the carrier.

As Luke and Joe walk out the front door, I cross my arms and follow them to Luke's truck. It dawns on me that this isn't how I envisioned the end of the night to go. I would have bet money I'd be given the third-degree on every detail about my date. I let out a harrumph sound at how very wrong I was.

"What's that for?" Luke asks as he places Joe's carrier on the front seat.

"Nothing," I say, to which he gives me a look of intrigue. He stands there, staring at me, so I explain, "I'm surprised you didn't ask about my night."

With a furrow of his brows, he stares at the ground for a beat, then looks at me. "That's because I don't want to know."

I purse my lips. "Oh."

"The guy took you on a helicopter to Manhattan. I can't compete with that."

"It's not a competition."

His back straightens, bringing him to his full height, and he looks down at me.

"You sure about that?"

His eyes darken as the weight of his body leans in. I stand tall, not fighting his intrusion, as the man who was asleep not too long ago is now awaken with primal vigor.

"Luke," I breathe out his name as I look up into his face. His eyes yearn and his pleads.

"You want me to ask, which makes me think he tried to kiss you, which can't compare to the way I can."

My heart races in my chest, and a surge of adrenaline pumps through my veins. I press my body against his. My mouth is dry as I breathe heavily.

"I barely remember what that was like."

"Liar."

He leans in and kisses me.

With his hand on my neck, he pulls me in for a kiss that has me sighing into his mouth and relishing in the thickness of his tongue, his hot breath, and his powerful fist on my hip.

I grip his shirt and dip my tongue into his mouth further. My fist pulls his weight into me until I'm slammed into the rear car door. My hand travels down his chest yet goes no further as he grips it and holds it against the cool metal of his truck, holding me in place. His groin presses into mine, and the heavy erection his pants can't contain causes me to whimper as it rubs dangerously close to my core.

Passion exudes from his body, more potent and powerful than those Aruban nights that were the most romantic of my life. I lied when I said I didn't remember his kiss. A woman could never forget the way she felt when an explosion was set off inside of her.

"Fuck," Luke groans as his lips pull away from mine lightning quick.

The warm lips that were on my mouth a second ago are now pressed on my forehead. My own lips rest on his neck, the stubble coarse against my lips as I breathe in his manly scent.

"I'm sorry." He speaks into my skin. "I shouldn't have done that. I blurred the lines."

I close my eyes and nod. My heart is pounding against his which is racing like wildfire. "You're right. That was wrong."

His hands lower from my body, and I release him as well. He pushes himself off me forcefully, running a hand through his hair and clenching his jaw. He doesn't just look like he regrets kissing me. He appears disgusted with himself.

"I'll never do that again."

I cross my arms in front of my chest to protect my erratic and discarded heart. "You'd better not."

I swallow as I watch him run his fingers down the front of his face. The look of anguish is not what a woman wants from a man she just kissed. A woman whose lips are still vibrating with the masculine hum of the man who devoured them.

"I can't be with you. It's wrong on so many levels. I'm also a selfish fuck, and I don't want him to be with you either."

"You have no right—"

"You deserve to be happy," he says with conviction. "I know I have no right to tell you who to date and when, as long as they're good to you and Ainsley. That said, I agree with what you said earlier. Ainsley shouldn't be introduced to any third party in our lives."

"I agree. You don't have the right to say anything about my dating life."

"Jillian, I'm already making mistakes when it comes to you. I'm just learning how to reconnect with you, and it's difficult. I can't make mistakes when it comes to my daughter. I don't want to compete with another man for her attention. Hell, she doesn't even know I'm her dad yet. That's a lot of change for all of us. I think it's best that you keep Eric as just a friend as far as Ainsley's concerned."

I bite down on my lip. Luke's right. He's been a father for a short time, and already, he has his priorities in check. I wish he did when it came to me too.

"You're right."

"You mean that?" His eyes blink up at me.

"I do. This is a big transition for all of us."

"Does that mean we can tell Ainsley I'm her dad?"

"We need a little bit more time."

His posture falls with defeat. "What are you so afraid of?"

I brush my fingers against my lips. "That you'll break her heart."

"I have the same fear," he states, leaning forward and giving me a gentle kiss on my jaw, just beneath my ear. "Good night, Jillian."

"Bye, Luke."

Joe lets out a mewl, so I add, "Good night, Joe."

He purrs in response just before Luke closes the front door and walks to his side of the truck. I watch the man and cat, who are now permanent fixtures in my life, drive away.

Now if only there were a way to forget about that kiss.

fifteen

"COME ON, GIRLS. I want to see you kick the shit out of those bags!"

I do as Tara said and pummel the punching bag with the mighty force of Wonder Woman. That's who I picture I am when I'm at kickboxing class. It helps to imagine I'm the immortal Amazon warrior demigoddess when trying to keep up with the multistep kick-punch combination that Tara came up with.

As our instructor, Tara has whipped Melissa and me into shape, along with the ten or so other girls who frequent this class. We only come twice a week to the only two classes she teaches, but it's enough to keep my waist trim, ass tight, and head from exploding.

"Left foot jab, jab. Straight right hand. Right hook kick!" Tara shouts to the room over the loudspeaker blasting pop music.

I nod and get to work on my sequence.

"What the heck did she say? Left foot jab and then right hand?" Melissa asks from the bag next to me, wiping the sweat off her forehead.

I physically show her the sequence, ending with a roundhouse kick. She nods, and we continue on the bags in synchronized movements.

While Tara is an accountant by day, she started moonlighting as a kickboxing instructor around the time Melissa and I opened our company. I reluctantly came to class because Ainsley was little, but Tara told me to bring a stroller and set her up in the corner. I did, and Ainsley got a kick out of watching everyone work out. Nowadays, she is in school while I work out. It cuts into my productivity, but it's been a godsend for my mental fitness.

"Okay, girls. Water break. Only take a sip! I don't need you barfing on my mat because what I have planned next is gonna really get those abs tightening up!"

At Tara's command, we rise from the floor and walk to the wall, where our water bottles are kept, and drink while we catch our breath.

Melissa looks over at me. "Damn, girl, you're really going hard today. You only pummel that bag like that when your mother is giving you grief."

While my mother is usually the reason I need to let off some steam, my true complication is Luke. If I had known all along he'd be such a sweet dad to Ainsley, I would have forced him to be part of her birth. When he kicked me out of his life—literally blocking me—I knew he wanted nothing to do with her. He told me he didn't want the baby. Now, he's acting like Father of the Year.

Probably because he missed the hard parts. The sleepless nights, the scheduling conflicts, the tantrums, the stress over vaccinations, the sicknesses, the lack of a social life, and everything else that comes with being a parent of a newborn.

Of course, he's happy with Ainsley now. She's a healthy, smart, funny kid. He gets to reap the rewards of hard parenting with some visits to the park and a tea party. He wants to be her dad, but what about when he has to step up and be a father? I have this horrible feeling that she'll disappoint him. He lives three hours away. A once-a-week visit won't be enough for her. When he meets a woman and starts a family with her, will he want Ainsley to be a part of his new life?

There are so many what-ifs that I've been driving myself crazy. Hence why I need to beat the bag the way I have been today.

I'm not imagining the bag is Luke.

I'm imagining it's me.

Because no matter how hard I try to keep Luke at arm's length, he's all I think about.

My sofa still smells of his cologne.

We ate his leftovers in my fridge from when he cooked with Ainsley, and he's a great cook.

Joe left a ball of catnip in the living room.

My freezer is home to a bag of leftover Oreos.

There's a drawing of us on a catamaran stuck to my refrigerator because Ainsley refuses to remove it.

My lips still taste the sweetness of his tongue.

Every reminder makes it harder to ignore that Luke is in our lives. Once we tell Ainsley that Luke is her dad, it's permanent.

It's not just Ainsley's heart I'm trying to protect. It's mine.

Yeah, that's a cluster that messes with my head.

"Earth to Jillian." Melissa's voice knocks me out of my mental fog. "You totally zoned out there."

"Sorry. A lot on my mind."

"I can imagine. With Luke back in the picture, I'm sure you're going through a wave of emotions." She's hit the nail on the head.

Tara gets the class on their backs and says to start with standard crunches. While Melissa and I are lifting our spines off the floor, Tara kneels between us.

"Okay, I need to hear how the date with Eric went. You're welcome, by the way." Tara pats her shoulder for a job well done.

Melissa shakes her head with a laugh. "Will there be a third date?"

"Maybe. We planned on it, but his schedule is pretty tight, and I work on weekends."

"You're not working the weekend of Melissa and Will's engagement party. Bring him as your guest," Tara suggests and then tells the class to start on a different move.

I lift my legs and get to work. "That's too serious of an event to bring a guy to. Plus, Ainsley will be there. It could send the wrong message." Not to mention, I told Luke I'd keep Eric away from her.

"Did you kiss him?" Melissa asks.

"Yes."

Melissa's mouth is agape.

Tara claps her hands in excitement. "Was it a good kiss?"

"Sure," I state as I drop my legs, as per Tara's instructions to the class.

Eric's kiss was fine until Luke dropped that passionate one on me after, and now, Eric's lips are like a wet fish while Luke is a stallion.

"I'm not getting a vibe that it was a good kiss. And if you say, *It was lovely*, I'm going to punch you in the face. Kisses aren't lovely," Melissa says.

I roll my eyes at her. "Not everyone has smoldering William Bronson to kiss on the daily. When Eric kissed me, it was a first kiss. A good kiss. Sweet. Gentlemanly. A promise for better kisses in the future."

Tara twists her mouth. "Even Kent—the guy I dated last year, who refused to go to bed with me—kissed with more passion than that. It's why I kept dating him."

"Did you ever find out why he refused to sleep with you?" Melissa asks as she breathes out the pain from the leg lifts.

"Word on the street is, erectile dysfunction," she replies.

"Who told you that?" I ask.

"This girl who knows a guy, who knows a girl, who used to date him. It's a crazy game of telephone."

I raise my brows and drop my leg to the mat. "That's a shame. He was a nice guy."

Tara places a hand on her heart and the other on her forehead. "A man who Jillian approves of? I am speechless." She pats my thigh. "No quitting. Get those legs up."

"I don't hate all men," I muse, to which the two look at me like I have seventeen heads. I brush them off. "I just … wow, my abs burn … I don't think they're worth imploding your whole world over." I drop my leg again, proud that I was able to muster through another set. I'm huffing as I further explain, "There's nothing we can't do without them."

Tara gives me a high five for my comment and then adds, "True beans. But they are super fun to have around. I was hoping to meet someone at the engagement party, but no-fun Jones over here just informed me it's family only."

Melissa groans. "Family only. Just stay away from his older brother, Rob. He is recently divorced but absolutely angered by all women. He puts Jillian to shame."

"A man who doesn't believe in love anymore? That sounds right up Jillian's alley," Tara jokes and then moves the class to the fourth and final position.

We all groan as we get into plank position, and she starts to count.

My friends might be similar in personality, but they view love in a unique light. Melissa is more practical—like me—while Tara has stars in her eyes. I wish I were more like Tara. The kind that can just throw her heart into the mix and see where the relationship goes, and when it falls apart, she picks herself up by the bootstraps and keeps on going. She's like an evergreen, always changing. Makes me realize I'm not much of one myself, like I thought.

I could tell Melissa and Tara I kissed Luke, but nothing would come of it. They'd have a front row seat to my life's drama, and with the knowledge of your problems comes an invitation for opinions. I don't need their input since Luke made it clear—him kissing me was a mistake that won't happen again.

I push through my crunches and think of the two reasons that hold me back. It's been the same reasons for the past five years.

One of them is a four-year-old miracle.

The other is a thirty-two-year-old grenade.

Class is over, and I walk to the far wall to get my water and then my bag. I'm looking through my bag for my phone, yet I can't find it. "Where the heck did I put my phone?"

"Here you go." Tara hands it over to me with a mischievous, shit-eating grin on her face.

"What did you do?" My tone is one I use when Ainsley is caught doing something wrong.

"Something you're too chickenshit to do yourself. I asked Eric to go to Melissa and Will's engagement party with you. You're welcome."

"Tara!" I reprimand.

Even Melissa's jaw is practically on the floor with Tara's horrible invasion of my privacy.

"You can't just break into her phone and set up dates for her," Melissa yells at her like a parent scolding a child.

"You're acting like that's the worst thing I've ever done. Last week, I pranked Tyler by sending a guitar-playing cowboy, who only wears a thong and a Stetson, to sing 'Happy Birthday' to him at his office because he refused to let you have the kids the weekend of Will's mom's birthday party. I recall you snickering pretty loudly about that one."

"That was mildly funny." Melissa places a hand on her hip and tries to fight her smile, then morphs into her stone-cold mom demeanor. "This is different. Jillian is far more private than I am."

My phone pings the text message alert sound. I look down with bated breath and cringe when I see Eric's name. I open the message.

I'd love to attend. Looking forward to meeting your friends.

My shoulders fall half in relief and a little bit of dread.

"Looks like I have a date to the engagement party." I show the girls the message, and their smiles are huge.

"That's awesome. And he wants to meet us so that's bonus points." Melissa beams.

"I have to cancel. Ainsley will be there."

"So will eighty other people. What's the big deal? It's not like you're going to hump the guy on the dance floor. He's just coming to be adult conversation. Let loose, Jillian. It's great!" Tara says way too enthusiastically. "Just keep your promise and be sure to name your firstborn child together after me," Tara kids, and we both hit her playfully in the arms.

I grab my gym bag and bid the girls good-bye as I head to my car. Today, I'm working from the office while Melissa heads to a new venue to take some pictures as she begins the design process.

At my desk, I open my laptop and start working on an itinerary for a wedding in a few months. I'm deep in the throes of reviewing invoices and contracts when the phone rings on the line to the front door buzzer.

"Lavish Events."

"It's Mother, dear. Let me up."

I cringe slightly as I buzz her up because I'm not in my usual uniform of business attire. Workout clothes and still smelling like a gym rat do not bode well in my mother's presence.

I smooth out my ponytail and look for a cardigan, but to no avail. When my mother appears at the door, she looks like the pristine picture of a high-society member of Greenwood Village—perfectly blown-out hair, navy pants, white silk blouse, silver-and-navy blazer, and Tory Burch flats. Around her neck is her signature Van Cleef diamond clover, and she has three bracelets on, including two Cartier cuffs.

"Heard good news from Jenny Hollenford!" she states like she's about to break out the champagne. "She said you and her son, Eric, have been cozying up quite nicely."

"Hi, Mom. How are you?" I kiss her sweetly and take a step back. "What brings you here?"

Instead of answering my question, she looks down at my outfit with a twist of her face. At least the parts of it that still twist. Her Botox isn't as subtle as it should be.

"You don't dress for the office anymore? Where are your clothes?"

"I came from the gym. I take morning classes twice a week. I don't get a chance to shower unless I have an appointment."

"Smart casual is the only attire acceptable for this office."

"Lululemon leggings don't count as smart?" I joke as I take a seat at the conference table in the main room. "Maybe I should throw on a tie."

She waves a hand in the air at me to ignore my comment. "Smart casual allows you to get funky with your business attire, but this is beyond unacceptable. Next time, change at the gym or run home first. You live close enough."

I take a deep breath and speak through my smile. "It's so great to have you drop by."

She takes a seat in the teal velvet chair. "What kind of host are you to not have offered me a refreshment?"

I stand up. "What can I get you? We have water, sparkling and still, wine, champagne—"

"I'm good, dear. I was just at a breakfast meeting."

I take a seat again.

She sifts through her purse. "You should hear the whispers. It's quite exciting. I knew Eric was going to be a perfect match for you. I just hate that I have to hear the gossip from Jenny. I had to pretend I was already in the know."

As she takes out a box of Altoids, I place my palm out. Rule of etiquette is, never refuse a breath mint. It means someone is trying to politely tell you something.

"I don't want you getting your hopes up, although I'm pretty sure you have the calligrapher on speed dial."

"Why would I need that when my own daughter is a wedding planner? I was just going to use whoever you use."

"That would be Melissa. She does all our calligraphy."

"Good to know. Tell her to keep the spring open. If you play your cards right, you could be Mrs. Eric Hollenford in May."

"Eric was right. Our moms are crazy," I say sarcastically with my hand on my forehead.

"Your attitude is unbearable. To meet a handsome doctor who doesn't have children already and yet is comfortable with your situation is a godsend. You should be grateful."

"Grateful that Eric likes my kid? I'm more hoping that Ainsley likes him."

"I thought Ainsley had met him already. I heard from a woman in my Pilates class that she saw you and Ainsley on a picnic with a man last week."

While Greenwood Village has been a wonderful bubble of a community to raise my daughter in, it is also just that —a bubble. A small town in many ways, where everyone seems to know everyone and word travels fast.

"That wasn't Eric."

Her eyes widen with a mixture of intrigue and skepticism. "There's another man? Who is he? What does he do?"

"There's no other man. It was just a friend who spent the day with us."

"Jillian, I really don't understand why you speak in code."

I laugh to myself since that is what I've been mentally accusing Luke of. I suppose I have always lived in riddles, keeping a greater piece of myself close to the vest, as Tara would say. It's not like I chose to be this way. I just am. *Say please and thank you. Always look someone in the eyes when speaking. Show empathy when taking responsibility for your actions. Never speak about events that happen in the household outside of the house. Smile, even when you're dismayed.*

As a Hathaway, I was bred to exude confidence when I had none. To feign delight when I was distraught. And no matter what anyone asked, everything was always *good.*

My family didn't plan to be fake. They just firmly believed that our business was of no business to anyone else.

The lessons are good, and yet they can make one forget the difference between fantasy and reality.

Tell a lie through a smile enough times, and you start to believe it's true.

I strum my fingers along the top of the table and watch my nails hit the glass one at a time.

"I don't speak in code. I merely tell you what you want to hear."

"That makes me wonder what you don't tell me. You should never keep secrets from your mother."

"The truth often makes you jump to conclusions."

She adjusts her silk collar. "I am very levelheaded. When have I ever overreacted to the truth?"

"How about when I told you I was pregnant?"

Her hands pause as her head swivels toward me. "That was years ago. Why are you bringing that up now?"

"You bring it up every chance you get. You just referred to Ainsley as my *situation*. Do you even hear yourself talk?"

"A twenty-six-year-old woman who goes to a sperm bank to have a child on her own is unconventional."

My fingers stop strumming.

"How would you have reacted if I'd told you I was knocked up by a guy while away in Aruba, who left me the next morning, who I then had to track down like the CIA, only to have him tell me to get rid of the baby because he didn't want it?"

Her shoulders are pressed back as her palms run down the front of her blazer. She purses her mouth as she looks at me with a fraught expression.

"Jillian, you are giving me great cause for concern. If that ..." She swallows as she tries to find her words. "Is that what happened?"

"Just be happy with the sperm bank story."

She takes her purse and stands up, seemingly confused on if she should stay or go.

"Don't tell that to Eric. It's tragic and absolutely horrible. Please tell me that's just a story because I can't fathom you being so reckless as to have been with such a man and then be used in that way. You're a Hathaway, not trash."

I agree. That's why I did to Luke exactly what he had done to me. I blocked him from my life. I had the baby he hadn't wanted on my own. She was never going to live in a world with a father who resented her existence. I moved from my apartment, changed my number, and set up new roots for myself. I let a lie live not just to appease my mother—although that never worked—but because it was easier on my heart.

"Don't call me again, Jillian." His words were pained, but not as much as my heart.

"That's it? You're not going to be there with me when I go to the clinic? You're not going to hold my hand or tell me it's going to be okay?"

"No."

I swallowed my tears and let quivering breaths escape my mouth and responded to him the only way I could.

"I hate you, Luke. I'll hate you forever."

"Don't worry, Mom. It's just a story."

She swallows and rights her posture again, adjusting her strap on her shoulder. "Good. Now, let's try to make sure Eric isn't put off by your callous attitude and ill-fated humor."

"Yes. Let's hope," I say for no reason whatsoever.

My mother leaves, and my stomach gnaws.

Why do I feel like I had it all wrong? And by all, I mean life.

My life just went from complicated to messy.

sixteen

"JILLIAN, CAN YOU GRAB me the tulle in the bin by the grand staircase?" Melissa asks from atop her ladder.

An assistant is standing below it with her hands holding an almost-done roll of tulle and several clips.

I grab the bin they need and walk it into the atrium that's being decorated for a wedding ceremony. Flower vases line the aisle adorned with a white runner, etched with an elegant gold monogram on the end. When Melissa is done adding tulle, she'll incorporate a flower arch to tie it all together.

Once Melissa is set, I head into the ballroom and grab my iPad that I left on one of the tables. I look at the itemized list of things that need to be done. All deliveries are accounted for, the vendors are here, and the event is running on schedule. I just checked in with the bridal party, who are all sipping champagne and getting their hair done. The groom is at a nearby hotel. The photographer is in the lobby, waiting to be welcomed upstairs.

I look at the time and wonder what is taking Luke so long. I panic-called him over an hour ago that we forgot to pack the donation cards we had printed to let the guests know a donation has been made in their name to a blood cancer charity near and dear to the couple's heart. They were ordered to match the menus and were absentmindedly left on Melissa's desk. I blame myself. Checklists are my thing, and I had it marked as being in the bin.

"Ainsley to the rescue!" a tiny voice bellows from the entrance to the ballroom.

I look up to see my daughter wearing a superhero cape, running into the room straight toward me. I catch her with the iPad in hand and lift her in the air.

"We saved the day. Luke has the cards," she explains.

By the entrance is Luke, wearing his jeans and a button-down with leather shoes. I love that he dresses up to spend his days with Ainsley. He hasn't worn a T-shirt once to see her, and it's quite charming.

He's looking around the room, taking in the tall flower arrangements, uplighting on the walls, and the intensive setup of the twelve-piece band. He stands tall, breathtaking in stature.

His hair is wild, different from the combed-back look he had when he arrived at my house this morning. He must have been playing outside with Ainsley because it's finger-combed and ruffled. Magnetic navy eyes lock with mine, and I smile. With his long gait, he walks toward me, and I take a quick inhale.

Yes, of all the men I could have procreated with, I chose a beautiful one.

"Thank you for rushing those over." I motion toward the cards in his hands.

"You caught us at a good time. We were on the carousel, and after five times, I was getting a little motion sick."

"You could have told her."

"Have you met me?" he asks sarcastically, to which I nod and laugh.

"I thought I heard my favorite assistant!" Melissa calls from the room's entrance. Ainsley rushes over to her and Melissa notes me standing here with Luke. She kneels down to Ainsley. "Do you want to see how pretty the altar looks?"

"Yes!" Ainsley says as she grabs Melissa's hand. The two leave with Melissa casting a sly blue eye my way.

Luke takes a step closer to me. "Guess it's just the two of us now. Put me to work."

I show him where on each place setting the cards belong, and we walk around the room together to get them placed quickly. He makes it a game to get each card on the plate before the beat from the music the band is practicing hits the next tempo. He's even dancing as he walks around, and I follow suit.

"Weddings are fun. Do you get to party at all?" he asks.

"No. Starting in about thirty minutes, I'll be on call for the next five hours and loving every minute."

"All work and no play makes Jillian a dull girl."

"I know how to party."

"Three glasses of wine at dinner sounds like a rager."

I twist my lips and think about the last time I let my hair down. "I got drunk at a promotion party last year. It was at Lone Tavern, and I had a few too many tequila cocktails. Melissa's dad had to drive me and Ainsley home."

"Did you ride the mechanical bull?"

I grimace as we move to tables twelve and thirteen. "Actually, no. Although I did get a QVC delivery a week later. Apparently, tequila makes me think ordering three blow-dryers, a year's supply of steaks, and a shake weight was a good idea."

He whistles through his teeth. "That is definitely a wild night."

"I should also add that I got a full set of Baby Shark costumes— for adults and children. They're still in a box under my bed because I have no idea what to do with them."

"Note: keep Jillian away from tequila. I get it. I've made some bad decisions while drinking. Tequila once had me running from the cops in New Orleans. Not my doing. It was all my buddy, who had run his mouth at the wrong time."

We keep our pace and move to the next group of tables on the other side of the room.

"You ever been handcuffed?" I ask, adjusting a napkin that was slightly crooked.

"Sexually or by law enforcement?" he asks easily, which makes me stop what I'm doing. When he looks up from his task, he must see my brows are up with piqued interest, which makes him laugh. "I'm kidding. Not really. I knew you meant arrested. Surprised you haven't vetted me yet."

The idea intrigues me. "I could ask Will to run a background check. He's a cop."

"I'll save you the trouble. I have never been arrested."

"So, metal has never touched your skin," I pry, now slightly more intrigued.

"I plead the Fifth. Like you said, a lot happened before we met at twenty-six."

My lips want to ask more. Like what happened in the years since we've seen one another. Asking questions can be dangerous. The answers might not be what you want to hear.

Still, when it comes to this man, I'm invested. Emotionally. Pragmatically.

Perhaps I don't mind a little bit of danger.

"And after twenty-six?"

The sides of his mouth quirk up, but his eyes don't. "Dating is like real estate. The longer you're on the market, the more people think there's something wrong with you. When it comes to me, they're right."

"You have your flaws," I say, to which he feigns insult, and I laugh. "I'm sure some woman has stolen your heart at some point."

His eyes flicker up, and I feel the acute sense of loss. I take a quick intake of breath.

As casually as I can manage, I ask, "Why haven't you met a good woman and had kids?"

"Because I can't," he answers matter-of-factly.

I tilt my head. "Can't or won't?"

He stands up straight. "Both."

My eyes narrow at him as I try to decode what he's not telling me. With Luke, I often feel like I'm getting half the story.

The words out of his mouth appear to be true. Luke doesn't coat things to make it easy on people. He says what he's feeling without hesitation. He spits out the truth and calls it as it is.

It's the words he doesn't say that you have to be wary of. That's why when he pours his heart out to me in the form of honest words, I don't just listen to what he's saying. I wonder what he's not saying.

Like now.

He looks around the room that's dressed for a spectacular affair. His hands are on his hips, and he looks absolutely amazed.

"I'm proud of you, Jillian. You don't need my accolades, but I remember a girl who said she had a dream of opening her own company, and here you are."

I flush at his words. "I couldn't have done it without my grandmother." With a sigh, I think of the woman who would sit and talk with me for hours on the veranda of her waterfront estate. While everyone else was decked out in designers, she wore jogging suits and red sneakers. "She was a hell-raiser, didn't care about societal norms, and gave it to you straight. She was the backbone of my grandfather's real estate firm, yet never received credit until he died and she took the company over. Her advice was always stern yet understandable. She's the first person I told I was pregnant. She gave me my home. It was an investment property she and my grandfather had, and she signed it over to me free and clear. Told me not to tell anyone because it wasn't their business. Of course, they all found out when she passed last year. It's been an awkward year, to say the least. My family couldn't comprehend why she'd singled me out with the property. They didn't understand we'd had a bond. I was closer to her than my own mother."

He smiles lightly, yet his eyes seem sad.

"She steered you in the right direction. You're a successful single mother."

"It wasn't easy. I used the money I was spending on rent to provide care for Ainsley when I needed it. Worked long hours, took Ainsley with me when I had no one to turn to. Being on someone else's schedule and working on their dime wasn't working for me. I took a small business loan to open my own company. It was risky, but my grandmother had pushed me to be a success. Melissa and I opened Lavish Events together. She's a genius at design and social media."

"It sounds like you're cutting yourself short."

"Where Melissa's great with the creative side, I'm the spreadsheets girl. Finances, bookkeeping, inventory, booking, ordering, planning, and logistics are all me. If I left that up to her, we'd be in a world of trouble. The two of us together make an excellent team."

"Sounds like she balances you well."

"I'm incredibly lucky."

I smile at the thought of how fortunate I am to have Melissa in my life. Some would have said I was crazy to ask a woman going through a divorce to open a company with me, but there was something about her that I knew was exceptional. I'm glad I went with my gut.

"Done," he declares with fanfare as he places the last bit of card stock on the table. "What's next?"

"That's it." I run my hands down my palazzo pants. "I have a small window until I have to go upstairs for the pictures."

"Good. Then, we can dance." He walks around the table in my direction.

I ease my hands over my ribs and belly and the smooth cotton of my bodysuit. "Not on the job."

"You never get to enjoy all the hard work you put in. You should reap a few of the benefits. Besides, we need to make sure the musicians' speakers work properly." He calls to one of the singers who is adjusting her microphone, "Mademoiselle, can you play us a little something?"

Awkwardly, I clear my throat. "Luke, they are professionals and setting up. They don't have time to indulge your whims."

"Any requests?" the singer asks, to which Luke's smile broadens.

"Surprise us," he says as he takes my hand and pulls me toward the dance floor, but not before I place my iPad on the table.

"I don't have time for this."

"Everyone has time to dance."

"Seriously, Luke, if the bride walks in and sees me dancing, it will look utterly—"

"Beautiful," he says as a slow melody plays.

I stand on the dance floor with my hand in Luke's and roll my head to the side. Embarrassment colors my cheeks as the band plays a ballad. It feels odd to be in this room, in the center of the dance floor, dancing alone with this man on display.

"Why do I have the hardest time saying no to you?" I ask, aggravated.

"Because I'm charming." He pulls me closer, sliding his hand along my side and lacing his fingers with mine. "Close your eyes and pretend we're the only ones here."

As the woman begins to sing in a sultry yet silky voice, I fall into Luke's chest. "Something" by The Beatles falls from her lips, and I sway my hips with Luke's to the music.

This is not the first time we've danced together, and yet it feels far more intimate than in the past. Probably because there is a past between us, and there's something potent in this encounter.

"I'm sorry about the kiss the other night," he says.

"You were right. It shouldn't have happened. I think we both had this pent-up desire to see if what we'd had back then still existed."

He hums, "That's probably true."

"The first night we danced in Aruba, you held me just like this, and I remember thinking, *This guy is going to ruin me. No one this handsome with this much charisma, who dances the way he does, can be any good for my heart.* I had no idea what you were thinking."

"I can tell you exactly what I was thinking. I thought to myself, *If I play my cards right, this woman might just be crazy enough to marry me.*"

I swallow hard, lift my chin, and boldly meet his gaze. "That was lust talking."

"There was a whole lot of lust."

"Too often, people mistake lust for love."

"Sometimes, lust leads to love."

My breath hitches, and I lift my chest with the inhale. His body stiffens, and I can feel his heart racing, drumming against my own.

I hate my heart right now.

His expression is one of desire and trepidation. I can't stare at him, for fear I'll fall into the abyss of his heated gaze.

I move my head to his shoulder.

His mouth lowers.

"Do you think about me the way I think about you? Late at night, when the world is asleep and you're alone with your thoughts, do you dream of me? Because I dream about you."

His words tickle my ear and set the hairs of my neck on edge. A tingle radiates down my spine.

"You can't say that to me, Luke."

"I know I shouldn't. I've wanted to say this. For five years, I've thought about your smile, your laugh. I always knew I'd fucked up, and I vowed to stay away, yet there you were one night, wearing that robe and holding that ridiculous ice bucket. I thought I was hallucinating. You were like a damn siren. I let you walk away that night, but I went back because I had to make sure you were safe. I let you walk away the next night because I knew you were better off without me. I know I should stay away now, and yet I can't."

"The only reason you're here now is because of Ainsley."

"She's not the only reason." His words cause me to turn my face to the side in despair. He places a knuckle under my chin and forces me to look up at him again. "I'm grateful not only for her existence, but also because she gives me an excuse to be in your life. I was getting so tired of staying away."

I sigh at his words. My chin rises, and his lowers, drinking in my breath, and I fall hopelessly into his hands that are wrapped around me.

Luke Incendio is fire in the flesh, and if I'm not careful, I'll burn badly. If I fall into his arms—really fall into them—and do something foolish, like kiss him, and if he pushes me away again, it will be my undoing.

"I have to tell you something." I put distance between us. "I asked Eric to attend Melissa and Will's engagement party with me. I know Ainsley will be there, but I'll just tell her I'm bringing him as a friend. Not a date."

"You asked Eric?"

"Technically, Tara did. She has a way of speaking for me when it comes to him. I wasn't going to ask. She ambushed the situation."

"Did you tell him you changed your mind?"

"No."

He repeats my words in silence, slowly letting it in. "You said you'd keep him away from Ainsley."

"He will be one of many people at the event. You act like I'm going to be fawning all over the man and kissing him on the dance floor. What kind of woman do you think I am? I raised Ainsley on my own for nearly five years. I haven't dated a man since before she was born. I'm a successful thirty-two-year-old career woman and a mother. I know how to handle my business."

"Except when it comes to me," he declares.

I hold his steely gaze. "Especially when it comes to you."

"If it wasn't for Ainsley, would you have ever let me back into your life?"

I place a hand over my forever-shattered heart and answer honestly, "No."

His brows draw together in an agonized expression. I counter it with one of defiance. I might fall putty to Luke at a whim, but my head is stronger than my heart.

"Dancing!" Ainsley comes running back into the ballroom and jumps into Luke's arms.

He lifts her and sways her comically from side to side. From the looks of the two, you wouldn't imagine things between him and me were tense a moment ago.

Luke laughs as Ainsley throws her hands up. He spins her around, and her giggle is wild.

"I have to get upstairs," I say to the two of them.

Luke stops spinning and looks back at me with harsh breaths. "We should go."

"Hey, Ainsley. Guess what," I say to my girl.

"We love you, Mommy!" Ainsley declares. "Don't we, Luke?"

He leans forward and lets Ainsley give me a kiss. When he straightens, he looks at me reluctantly and then adds, "Yeah. We do."

A piece of my chipped heart falls to the ground because in another time, I would have believed that.

seventeen

IT IS NO SURPRISE one of Connecticut's most-in-demand wedding designers would have an engagement party so stylish and dreamy that it should be featured in a magazine. Melissa's intentions to keep the event simple are met with sophisticated flair. Her backyard, which is coincidentally Melissa's childhood home in the woods of Newbury, has been completely transformed.

Ainsley and I have been by every day this week to help Melissa and Will decorate the yard, stringing lights around the perimeter of the backyard and setting up a dance floor with heat lamps scattered about to keep guests warm in the evening chill. We have a tent as a backup should it rain.

"Okay, wedding planner, what am I missing?" Melissa asks with a slightly frazzled look about her. "I have propane in all the heat lamps, the DJ is set up in the corner, the dance floor is on the ground. The bar is fully stocked. I'm regretting only hiring one bartender. Should I have gotten another? There's nothing worse than standing in a long line for a cocktail when you really want to dance. Drink and food are huge deal-breakers for guests. Will's mom wanted to do a clambake, but he's a steak-and-potatoes kinda guy and—oh, the bourbon and whiskey. I think there's another crate in the basement. Let me tell the—"

"Melissa"—I place my hand on her arm and smile at her—"everything is absolutely perfect. There's no need to worry."

She lets out a long, shaky breath. "Do I need more heat lamps? I didn't want the tent because the lights look so pretty in the trees, but what if people freeze? It's only fifty-five degrees tonight."

"You have so many heat lamps; it's practically a sauna out here."

"I hate being the center of attention. It makes me nervous."

"You don't say," I tease, grabbing her by the shoulders and spinning her around. "Go. Have a glass of champagne. Only one. It'll help dissipate the nerves, yet it won't be enough to make you do something embarrassing at your party."

"Is that your official advice as the wedding planner?"

"It's my advice as your friend. I'll make sure the final details are in check."

Melissa gives me a hug and then walks over to her daughter, Isabella, who is standing by the favors table, lining it with the small bottles of Whispering Angel Rosé they're giving out tonight as a parting gift.

I check on Ainsley, who is pretend fighting with Hunter. They have foam swords and knight helmets on.

"Hey, you. Don't get that dress dirty," I command as I walk by.

Knowing these two, they'll be filthy before dinner is served.

My expectations of Ainsley when it comes to her manners are the same as how I grew up. Where I've chosen to lighten up are the moments where, sometimes, a kid just wants to be a kid. Tonight, I'm sure her dress will be wrinkled from dancing, and she'll get icing from the cake on her dress.

I kiss her head and walk into the house. Guests have started to arrive and are walking into the foyer. It's a small party of immediate friends and family of the happy couple. Because Will's family is so big, there will easily be sixty people here. Melissa tried to make her wedding this small, but her future mother-in-law isn't having it.

"I don't understand why they wouldn't let me invite the Lalaynes. They're practically family," I hear Will's mother bellow to one of her sons as I pass by.

"Probably because Will broke up with their daughter after he met Melissa in a jail cell and decided to marry her instead," the son explains.

I hide my chortle as I move toward the basement door. I'm almost there when I'm tapped on the back of the shoulder. I turn around and see Eric.

"You're here," I state the obvious. "Did you text? My phone is in my bag."

"I did, but only because I was a little nervous about walking in alone. Wanted to make sure I wasn't overdressed. Plus, I brought a gift."

He's wearing a black suit and a black-and-white tie, paired with Ferragamo shoes with a sliver of argyle socks peeking from the hem of his pants. He looks as handsome and put together as he did for our two dates. The model gentleman that would pass my mother's Emily Post–style rules of etiquette.

"That was very sweet of you."

He takes an envelope from his breast pocket and holds it up. "It's a certificate for dinner. Figured you can't go wrong with gifting a couple a night out." Eric exudes poise as he slides the envelope back into his pocket. "Were you on your way somewhere?"

I motion toward the basement door. "Going to check on a crate of liquor. You can take the walk with me if you'd like."

"Lead the way."

We head downstairs into the unfinished basement of the house. There are boxes stacked along one wall, mostly some of Melissa's father's things he has yet to move into his new home. On the far side of the room are bicycles, old lamps, and a pool table that's covered with a tarp. I look around the floor for where Melissa could have left the box of bourbon and whiskey.

"This house is well lived in," Eric comments. "Reminds me of my parents' house."

"Your parents kept your classwork and all the paintings you did when you were a kid, like Melissa's?"

Eric laughs. "My mother keeps those in a box in the attic, along with bins of my old clothes. She has most of my childhood trinkets. My room still looks as it did when I moved out after college."

I smile at the notion that his mother kept his memories.

"My parents' home is like a museum. Every item is accounted for, polished and on display. If they can't show it off, it's barred from the home. My room is now a guest suite. My mother packed my old mementos up and sent them to my house when she redid the room. She said to keep what I wanted and throw out the rest. She's not a very sentimental woman." I locate the box and raise my hands up in the air. "Found it!"

Bracing myself, I put my hands on the box to lift it.

"Here." Eric places a hand on my back and gently moves me to the side. "I'll carry that for you. Lead the way."

Eric and I walk up the stairs and through the house, which is now filled with party guests. The back door leads to an outdoor firepit, where we run into Tara … and Luke.

Tara looks fantastic in her silver cocktail dress, but it's nothing compared to the sight of Luke.

Navy suit that matches his eyes.

No tie and an open button to show off a sliver of his smooth, muscular chest.

A jawline that's like granite as he glares at Eric.

"Jillian, I love that dress!" Tara motions toward the one-shouldered lavender silk dress I have on.

I look down at it and away from Luke. His arched brows were practically blade-like with the severe way he was staring at the way the silk hugs my curves.

"Thank you." I accept her compliment with a tight smile. "Tara, this is Eric Hollenford. Eric, these are my friends."

I do my job of introducing everyone while my heart is like a train bounding down the tracks. Last I heard, Luke denied Tara's invite to the party, so his presence tonight is throwing me off-kilter.

Eric gives Luke a nod of recognition. "I remember you. The manny."

"Manny?" Tara places a finger to her cheek. "Like a male nanny. That's cute."

Luke's stiff posture shows he doesn't agree.

"I'm not the manny," Luke bites out through his teeth.

Eric clears his throat and gives a forced smile. "If you'll excuse me, this box is quite heavy."

"You need a hand with that?" Luke asks and doesn't wait for the reply. He takes the box from Eric's hands like it's the lightest thing in the world and looks to me. "Where is this going?"

"Right this way. I'll be right back," I say to Eric and leave him with Tara.

Luke and I head toward the bar, and he places it on the ground. I open it and start unloading the bottles for the bartender to stock behind the bar.

"I'm surprised to see you tonight," I state to Luke as I place a bottle of Woodford Reserve in the bartender's hand.

Luke unloads the next two bottles. "Tara asked, so I thought I'd take her up on the offer."

"She's going to get the impression you want to date her now."

"I don't want to date her." He tosses the now-empty box behind the bar.

"Then, why are you here?"

"Why is Eric?" He places his hands on his hips, and a wrinkle cuts across his forehead.

I don't have an answer for him. *Well, I do.*

"I like Eric. He's a nice man and good company. If you hadn't made a reappearance in my life, I might have given him a real shot, not the half-assed one I've been devoting."

"Maybe you should ask why my presence is affecting your love life so much."

My hands ball into fists as I let out an unladylike growl. Luke, however, merely smirks and walks away. I take a deep inhale, pinching the air and bringing it down. Looks like I'm going to have to find my own Zen tonight because Luke is in one heck of a mood.

We walk back to Tara and Eric, who are making small talk.

At our arrival, Eric extends a hand to Luke. "Thank you for taking that box. I could have managed."

"Didn't want you to mess up your pretty little hands. Heard they're important. Geriatrics, correct?"

"Genetics."

Luke's hand grips Eric, and by the surprised, albeit challenging look, on Eric's face, I'd say Luke's handshake is a touch too firm for a greeting.

"Can I get anyone a drink?" I ask the three of them.

Tara lifts her wineglass to say she's good. Luke shakes his head while Eric places a hand on the small of my back.

"Let's go see what they have at the bar," Eric says.

I take the advice I gave Melissa and order myself a glass of champagne. Just one. I don't need to get sloshed at my friend's engagement party.

The layout for tonight's affair is elegant yet informal. There are passed hors d'oeuvres and three dinner stations placed strategically around the yard. It's meant to have friends and family of the couple mingle as they walk about. Eric and I stop at the stations and get food. We sit and talk to some friends of Melissa's. I watch in interest as Tara talks to Kent, a sergeant she dated last year.

I leave Eric to make Ainsley a plate and make sure she stops long enough to eat, and then I have a dance on the dance floor with my friends because that's what one does when you're at a party.

I'm enjoying a second glass of champagne midway through the night when I see Luke and Ainsley take to the dance floor. Her toes are on his shoes, except when she steps down for him to turn her in a series of twirls. Her dress spins out, and her smile widens with each turn she does.

Ainsley looks at Luke like he's her hero. She's always taken easily to adults, but there's something about her bond with him that's kismet and on another level. Her tiny soul knows he belongs to her.

"The manny really has a way with your daughter," Eric says as he approaches my table.

I lift myself out of my chair. "Please stop calling him that."

"I'm kidding. It's a cute nickname." Eric's tongue pokes the inside of his cheek. "They're very close."

"They have a deep bond, yes," I agree.

Tara appears a moment later with what might be her fifth drink of the evening.

"Will's single brother isn't here. I was really hoping to meet him tonight. I tried to talk to his divorced bro, Rob, but Melissa's right. That dude is mean. He practically grunts at you in response."

"Just enjoy the party. You don't need to meet someone," I reply.

"Easy for you to say. You're here with Eric."

"Didn't you come here with Luke?" Eric asks her.

"Yeah, but he's not a date. He's just company. Besides, he's either been staring at Jillian all night or hanging out with Ainsley. Not exactly the kind of man this girl wants to take home at the end of the night."

Eric looks at me over the edge of his glass with a deep scowl written across his face. "Deep bond, you say?"

I give a closed-mouth smile and turn away, not appreciating the way he's assuming things. The music changes to a faster one, and many people take to the floor.

Luke gives Ainsley a kiss on the cheek, and she runs off to find Hunter. Luke's smile is proud, affectionately so, as he watches her run off. When he sees Tara, Eric, and me staring at him, he straightens his stance. His brow quirks, and his smile falls.

With long, sturdy struts, Luke strides over to where we're standing by the table.

"Meeting of the minds, I see," he croons, as if assessing the situation.

"Just watching you have a dance with Jillian's daughter," Eric states.

Tara giggles into her hand. "This is angsty. Someone—and by someone, I mean the hot doc—is way too jealous over there."

I give Tara a deadpan expression despite her accurate statement. Eric is acting a bit bullish, but nothing that bears being called out over.

"I swear, these shoes are going to be the death of me," Melissa yelps as she ambles over to our group, hobbling as she slides her heels off one at a time. "I don't know what I'm wearing to my wedding, but it is definitely not these!"

As she looks at Eric and Luke with their matching stances of aggression, she holds up a finger. "I fear there's something happening here," she states.

Tara leans into her childhood best friend. "There's some weird pissing match over Jillian happening right now, which is a little confusing because Eric and Jillian are dating and she and Luke are not."

"Eric and I are not dating," I answer quickly. Too quickly by the way Eric swivels his body to me, glaring in insult.

"We're not?" he asks, exasperated.

"I mean, we've gone on two dates, but we're not *dating*."

"Do you kiss all the men you're not dating?"

Luke's eyes bulge at Eric's comment. "You kissed this guy?"

"Oh snap, this is getting good." Tara's glass is nearly empty as she takes another sip, downing the rest.

I step toward Luke and speak low yet forcefully. "This is none of your business."

"Kind of is," he retorts with a clenched jaw.

"Wait. Are you two together?" Eric asks.

"No," Luke and I answer at the same time.

Tara giggles. "Girl, I don't know why you went to a sperm bank to have a baby because you have plenty of testosterone in your life to choose from."

Tara's words have Luke's brows furrowing as he turns to her.

"What did you say?"

"Testosterone?" she repeats.

Luke's eyes are hardened as he looks at me again. This time, those piercing eyes are shooting lasers of hurt, disappointment, and pure anger at me. "Did you tell everyone you conceived from a sperm bank?"

The six interested eyes of our audience are staring at me in keen interest, waiting for me to answer him. I swallow as I crane my neck up and stare Luke straight in the eyes.

"I said I had a sperm donor, yes. The rest was up to interpretation."

"This is not a conversation to be had in public. It's no one's business but Jillian's," Melissa states, her tone as sharp as someone trying to be the adult in the conversation.

Tara hits Melissa in the shoulder. "You knew Jillian didn't conceive through medical advancement?"

"I only found out recently," Melissa explains.

"Then, who's the father?" Tara asks.

"Me." Luke's tone is fierce.

Tara steps back to make room for her jaw, which is wide open and falling onto the ground as she points at Luke. "Holy shit! You're Bobo the Sperm Guy?"

I place my fingers on the bridge of my nose and squeeze.

"You call me Bobo the Sperm Guy?"

I'm glad my eyes are closed so I don't have to see the look Luke's giving me.

"Well, this is so not how I expected the night to go," Eric says as he looks at the amber liquid in his glass and takes a drink.

"Please be quiet. Ainsley doesn't know," I plead to my friends. I'm mortified, more so for the folderol this situation is causing. I place my hands on Melissa's forearms and apologize. "This is a nightmare. I'm so sorry this is happening right now on your big evening."

"I'm good. Most people are dancing and have no idea what's happening right now. Besides, I hate being the center of attention. Believe it or not, this is helping. *Me.* Helping me. Not you. Your night is kinda fucked right now. Luke just left. I think you might want to chase after him."

"And say what?" I ask.

"Don't ask me. I'm the worst at this."

I let Eric know I'll be right back and then make my way through the house to find Luke. He's not in the living room, kitchen, or dining room, so I head out the front door and onto the porch. I see him jogging down the final steps to the sidewalk and take off after him. When I get to the sidewalk, I walk as fast as I can to keep up with his long, hurried strides.

"You can't possibly be mad," I say when he is in earshot.

He speaks over his shoulder. "Fuck being mad. I'm furious. Bad enough that I'm the man who didn't know he had a kid, but you told everyone I was some anonymous sperm donor?"

I stop walking. My insides race as anger pierces my gut. My fists are balls at my sides, and the blood that is simmering through my veins feels like it's rushing straight to my head. This is not the time or the place, but the emotions in me are far too powerful, far too hurt, to hold in.

"Fuck you, Luke!"

My words halt his steps. He turns around, his brow raised and his face twisted.

Not caring that I'm on a suburban street in a sleepy neighborhood, I yell at him, "You want me to curse? Well, here it is. Fuck. You! You told me to get rid of the baby. You didn't want her, and I did."

He takes an accusatory step forward, burning eyes directed toward me. "You don't know shit. You won't let me prove anything to you. How many times do I have to meet my own daughter before you'll declare it's a healthy time for her to know? You're trying to keep me at arm's length. From Ainsley. From you. That's why you keep pushing this Eric guy in my face. You brought him here because you needed a buffer. You can't stand what is building between us. You're never going to trust me with my own child because I was an asshole one night after too much booze."

"Whiskey isn't an excuse."

"You don't know what was happening back then."

I throw my hands up and plead for an explanation. "Then, tell me, Luke. What was so monumental, so life-altering that you can't just come out and say it? Tell me what fucking happened!"

Something happened.

Happened to us.

Happened to him.

Happened to our past and future.

He places his hands on his head and turns around. His face is lifted toward the sky as he curses under his breath. As his hands rise, he yells loudly, a feral growl of rage. The sinewy muscles are taut and rigid as he laments the world. His chest heaves with the adrenaline pulsing through his body, and then his shoulders fall, and he rubs his chest.

"She was dying," he says into the sky.

Luke turns around and looks at me. His eyes are glassy, glazed, red-rimmed, the likes of which I've never seen.

"We thought she was sick, but it was pure hell, and it's going to happen to all of us."

"We're all going to die, Luke. You're being dramatic, and frankly, you're scaring me a little."

"I just—" He stops himself from speaking and takes a step forward, his hands out, as if he's trying to explain. His hands rise to his head. His jaw is clenched, and that fierce look in his eye is severe. "I need you to come with me."

"Where?"

"New York. To my father's house."

I take a step back.

"Just tell me now," I demand.

He takes my hand.

"Words never matter with you, Jillian. It's actions. I need you to see what our future might hold."

eighteen

Last night was rough.

Luke left, and I stayed at Melissa's engagement party, doing what I do best—pretending everything's okay. Eric left soon after my and Luke's argument, and I bid him farewell, feeling terrible that he'd left the way he did.

His parting words were, "You told me you didn't have time for a relationship. I didn't listen."

I should have felt worse about his departure, but this hovering news about what disease Luke's family could have had me going down the rabbit hole of WebMD's most horrific diseases.

The unknown had me tossing and turning all night.

Luke meets me at Melissa's to drive the three and a half hours to his father's home. He is bright and cheerful and takes some time to say hello to Ainsley, ending with a hug that is far longer than his previous ones.

Once we get in the car, his smile morphs to a pensive expression as he keeps his eyes on the road and plays upbeat country music.

We haven't said much.

My mind has been running rampant the entire drive, wondering what it is he needs to show me and can't just say. My hands have clenched and unclenched more times than I can count. The roller coaster of emotions has gone through me. Anger, sadness, confusion

… more anger. I've stopped myself at least five times from yelling at him for being so secretive. Not because I'm annoyed. I am beyond peeved he'd keep information about himself that could affect my daughter. I'm enraged.

And yet I'm terrified.

Ignorance is bliss, and once he says whatever it is he's bringing me here to tell me—nay, *show me*—I know there won't be any turning back.

So, I've been sitting quietly for way too long.

Now, we're near his father's home in the country. My heart is racing, my palms are clammy, and I'm pretty sure my stomach is about to expel its contents.

On the eastern edge of the Hudson Valley is a country town, hidden in the thick of ever-changing pines beside lush maples and oaks turning over their leaves at varying rates. Luke's pickup truck bobs on the gravel road. I listen to the small stones kicking up from the ground onto the side of the doors. The pings stop when we hit a dirt road that leads down a long driveway to a home on the hill.

A modern farmhouse with white siding and green shutters sits at the top of a clearing with a long farmer's porch and a detached two-car garage.

Luke parks the truck and exits first. Walking around to my side of the car, he opens the door. He lowers his sunglasses to the tip of his nose, revealing eyes that are serious. "You coming in?"

I take a long breath and get out of the car. My feet are stuck to the ground as I look at the home and the stunning view of the valley below. New England's best autumn foliage is on display with its gorgeous variations of yellows, oranges, and reds. The sun shines bright, shimmering off the treetops and down the valleys and gorges below.

My nerves start to settle.

It's too beautiful of a place for anything bad to happen here.

The front door opens, and a man comes out in his jeans, a button-down flannel, and boots. I recognize Luke's dad from the photo in Luke's house, except he has gray hair now and his belly is a little rounder.

His smile exudes liveliness as he looks at Luke and barrels down the stairs to give his son a hug. I stand idle as the two men embrace as if they haven't seen one another in years when, according to Luke, he visits often. Well, not as often as in the past, I suppose. Ainsley has been his sole focus these days.

His father kisses his cheek and pats his face, appraising Luke from head to toe. "You look good. Drive okay?"

"Yeah, Dad. It was easy. No traffic."

"Excellent." His father releases him with an outstretched arm to me. "Jillian." His greeting is of a proud man who is pleased to see me, as is the twinkle in his eye. "I've heard a lot about you."

I take his hand for a shake and gasp when he yanks me in for a hug. I stagger at the gesture and stand frozen as he puts his burly arms around me and gives me a squeeze.

With brows that twitch toward one another, I look to Luke, who just shrugs. Apparently, his father is an affectionate man.

As a woman who isn't hugged by her own father, I'm taken aback by the gesture. I raise my arms to rest my hands on his back to return the greeting and give an awkward pat, like I'm burping a baby.

"Thank you for having me, Mr. Incendio," I say, clearing my throat.

"Call me Mitch." He releases me yet keeps his hands on my arms, the same way he did with Luke. A glint touches his eyes, sweet and full of admiration with a twinge of moisture around the circumference.

"Thank you for bringing my granddaughter into the world."

His comment sends warmth through my chest. "Ainsley is lucky to have a man who is so excited by her existence."

"Family is everything." Mitch squeezes my arms, and I see the tear fall down his cheek. "When you're ready, I'll be more than happy to play the role of proud grandpa. It's been a dream of mine."

I release a shaky breath at the whoosh of emotion his words bear.

Luke places a hand on his dad's shoulder. "Give the woman some breathing room. She's had a long car ride, and she has a lot to learn today."

Mitch looks at Luke with a distressed expression. "You still haven't told her?"

Luke shakes his head slowly.

The air dissipates from Mitch's chest as he turns back to me, gives my arms one more reassuring hold, and grimaces lightly. "All right, Jillian. Why don't you come inside, and I'll make a pot of tea?

Luke didn't bring you here to meet me. Although I will say, I am quite the good time. Just wait until you hear me play the banjo. I know how to throw it down."

"In the house, old man. No need to have her running down the mountain yet. Grab the box from the backseat. I brought the goods," Luke says and then turns to me as his father walks to the backseat of the truck. He motions toward his dad. "Ignore him. He tries to use his humor to lighten the mood."

"Family trait," I muse.

"Sadly, one of many."

My smile falls as I follow Mitch into the house as he carries the box. Luke places a protective hand on the small of my back. I don't necessarily want it there, yet the heat of his palm feels right.

I want him close.

I want him to turn me around and take me back to Greenwood Village and play tea party with Ainsley and take too many spins on the carousel.

I want him to make this knot in my stomach go away.

Inside the house is bright with sunlight pouring through the back windows. The kitchen is open and airy, overlooking a living room with couches facing the mountain view. Like Luke's home, this one is filled with pictures on the walls and frames on table surfaces. Memories of a family are scattered throughout, beautifully displayed. Luke's parents have wonderful taste, as everything is coordinated in happy hues of yellows, peaches, and navy.

At the far wall, lining the living room, is a floor-to-ceiling glass window and sliding door. The view in the front of the home is nothing compared to back here. It's like the earth has opened up, and I can see the heavens, where the rays of the sun meet the treetops. The sky is a glorious blue, and even the clouds have stayed away just so this scene can exist.

I'm staring at the stunning panorama when Luke takes my hand. I flinch at the touch and then let him grip my hand tight as he nudges his head and guides me through the house toward a bedroom next to the living room. Mitch stays in the kitchen and fills the kettle with water. I stare at Luke's broad shoulders as he leads me through the doorway.

Luke walks in first, relaxing my hand. I stay at the doorway. A hospital bed faces a window with the same view as the living room. On the side wall is a small dresser with a television, which is currently playing a rerun of *Impractical Jokers*. It's a small room with no closet or bathroom, perhaps not initially meant to be a bedroom.

A woman is sitting on a recliner, laughing and swaying. Her torso rocks as her arms move in the air in graceful yet uncontrolled movements. Her hands are curled in a claw shape, and her jaw is in an unnatural open position, fallen, as if she can't keep it closed.

As we walk in, she doesn't seem to notice our entrance.

"Hi, Peyton," Luke speaks softly to the woman as he approaches.

With light-brown hair, blue eyes, and a chin dimple, she resembles Luke despite being very thin and sallow. She looks older than him, yet from the state of her frizzy yet pulled-back hair and clothes that are more for comfort than style, I can't tell by how much.

"Loo," she says with a smile on her face when she looks at him, registering his presence in the room. Her words come out slightly childlike as she moves her body in circular motions.

The two embrace, and he kisses her warmly on the cheek.

"Where you been?"

"I had some things to take care of. Why? You miss me?"

"Yeah. You bring the good food?"

Luke laughs, and she settles into the warmth of it.

I do too.

"Whatcha watching?" he asks as he kneels beside her.

She stares at him for a long beat and then over to the window. Her fingers are making circles in the air as she becomes mesmerized by something outside.

"Peyton," Luke calls to her gently.

She looks at him with a scowl. Instead of love, she's looking at him, confused.

"Do you know what you're watching?" he clarifies his question for her.

She struggles to get her words out. "Why are you here? I don't want you here." The tone of her voice is suddenly deeply angered.

He's unaffected by her change in demeanor. "I came to introduce you to my friend."

Peyton looks over Luke's shoulder, and her eyes bead at me. "I don't want anyone. Go away!" Her irritation is evident not only from her tone, but also from the motions her body makes, even more spastic and uncontrolled as before. There's a determination in her brow though, as if she's trying with all her might to control it. "Go away!"

I press my back against the door frame. Her sudden outburst, paired with the disdain in her voice, makes me want to rush out of the room.

Luke doesn't flinch at her words.

"It's okay, P. You can be mad if you want." He rubs her back and places his head against her shoulder in an attempt to calm her down. "Are you ready to go to the kitchen to eat?" He pulls a walker over to her. "You can get there yourself, or do you want your chair?"

She doesn't answer him for a while. The comedians on TV laugh in the background while we wait in silence for Peyton to make a choice. Eventually, she motions toward the walker.

Luke assists Peyton to a standing position. Her back is hunched as she grips the walker lightly with one hand and struggles to keep upright. Luke places her other hand on the walker and helps her get a grip while holding her hips to get her balanced. Slowly, the two walk through the room, the tennis balls on the ends of the walker gliding softly on the hardwood.

I step back to let them out of the bedroom and follow them into the kitchen. It takes Peyton a long time to walk. Her body sways, yet she maintains a determined gait to make it into the kitchen. I wonder if she'll use a wheelchair to get back because the activity seems to take a toll on her—the journey of thirty feet like running a marathon.

She sits at the table, and Mitch is at her side.

"I have split pea soup for lunch today. Your brother brought it for you from the restaurant you like in Walden."

Peyton doesn't reply to her father, yet she motions for Luke to take a seat. While Mitch warms up the soup, Luke sits down at the table and gives Peyton his attention.

"You good?" she asks him, her body moving less than it was in the bedroom.

"I am." He smiles at the calm tone in her voice.

I wonder if, with Peyton, you never know which version of her you'll get—the sweet child or the angry adult. Growing up with her must have been difficult, and it must have also required a tremendous amount of patience.

Luke leans back in his chair, seeming more comfortable. "There was a house fire last week in my town. I had to rescue two dogs from an upstairs bedroom. You would have loved them. Golden retrievers. Absolute beauties."

Her face lights up. "I love golden retrievers," she says.

Mitch shouts from the kitchen, as if excited she remembered, "Yes, you do!"

The microwave beeps, and Mitch opens the door and takes the soup out of the appliance and then pours it from the glass dish he warmed it in into a rubber bowl. He walks the soup and spoon into the kitchen and sets it down in front of Peyton.

"She loves dogs," Mitch explains to me. "We had one when the kids were growing up. Lady. She was a good girl."

"I miss that dog," Luke muses.

"Surprised you have a cat then," I say.

"A dog is too much maintenance," Luke replies. "Cats can live independently."

Peyton appears to have remembered that I'm here, standing beside the table and watching the family interact. Her head tilts to the side at the sight of me. She looks to Luke, who is scooping the thick soup onto a spoon.

"Who is that?" she asks.

"This is my friend Jillian. I wanted her to meet you."

"To ..." Peyton stammers, her jaw trembling as she begins to rock again. "To show her the freak show?"

"Peyton!" Mitch reprimands her just as the teakettle goes off, whistling as loud as can be.

Luke tries to feed Peyton, lifting a spoon to her mouth. She clamps down her jaw and turns away.

"You have to eat your lunch," Luke says.

Her eyes lock with mine. Her mouth is clenched firmly. She is doubling down on her efforts to be defiant.

Luke's firm with his order. "Peyton, open your mouth."

She turns her chin to the side.

"Peyton, the doctor said you've lost too much weight. You need to eat."

Her eyes narrow.

"Peyton!" he says more forcefully.

"No!" she cries out, her body jerking in a wild motion that sends the bowl of green soup flying across the room and hitting the back of the kitchen island.

"Damn it. That was uncalled for." Mitch is stern with his daughter as he grabs a kitchen towel from the drawer.

"It was my fault," Luke states as he gets up and grabs a roll of paper towels.

Mitch kneels down and starts picking up the bowl and cleaning the mess around it while Luke wipes up the splatters on the table and the nearby wall.

I rush into the kitchen to grab a sponge and wet it. If this incident was anyone's fault, it was mine. Peyton might have trouble controlling herself, but she adamantly did not want to be fed in front of me. I walk to where Luke is cleaning the wall and start to wipe it down.

"No need. We got this," Luke says reassuringly.

Peyton is jerking about in wild movements. Luke gets up from the floor and grips her shoulders, steadying her.

I finish cleaning the wall and help Mitch with the floor. Once it's all cleaned, I get up and make my way out of the kitchen and toward the front door.

Outside, the sun is still shining, and the air is quiet. I take a seat on a sofa at the end of the porch and look out at the valley, wondering if Peyton's condition is what Luke wanted me to see, if meeting her was even the objective. Did she suffer an injury at birth or possibly developed Parkinson's? I can understand how her condition would worry a man with a child. Parkinson's runs in families, but it's not a given for it to be inherited.

My mind is reeling. If Peyton isn't why I'm here, then I am confused as to why I am. I run my hands through my hair and stand and pace the porch, breathing in deeply and calming my frightened heart. I don't know what to do, so I decide to take a seat again and wait.

Twenty minutes or so pass when the front door opens, and Mitch walks out. He has a thick photo album in his hands, the kind that is open, even when it's closed because the pages are so full. He strolls toward me and groans as he takes a seat on the couch, then smiles.

"Sorry about that in there," he says.

"I shouldn't have been staring at her."

"Peyton is like that with or without company. Not usually when Luke's here though. He puts her at ease. He warmed her more soup and is still feeding her now, so we'll give them some privacy for a little bit. He'll bathe her after. She only allows certain people to assist her with that. Luke is one of them."

I swallow and twist my fingers in my lap. "You're an amazing father. Are you her full-time caregiver? I know my parents would have placed me in a nursing home or hired full-time help, not that it's a viable option for everyone. They'd figure out a way—I'm sure of it. They don't have your patience."

"It's ... difficult." He takes a handkerchief out of his pocket and wipes his dewy brow. "As a caregiver, I have it easier than others. I have help. Luke is here on his days off, and the community has pitched in. Peyton has health insurance from her job. She was a schoolteacher, so the benefits help with medications and a nurse that comes by a few times a week. It's daunting for all of us, but no more than it is for her."

I nod lightly and scrunch my brows. "Was she in an accident?"

"No. She's the product of love."

Mitch opens the thick photo album toward the center and shows me a picture of who I can clearly tell is Peyton. Instead of being frail and hunched over, she's standing tall, vibrant ... beautiful. It's her college graduation photo, followed by a series of pictures of the family at her ceremony. I recognize the family of five from the picture in Luke's house. This one is older than the other, yet they look equally as happy.

My finger runs over the photo as I admire Peyton. Her golden skin, her shining smile.

"She was so beautiful," I say and then clear my throat. "Is. She is still very beautiful."

"It's okay. We all see the changes in her. Happened quite suddenly. It's called Huntington's disease. It's the equivalent of having ALS, Parkinson's, and Alzheimer's, all at once. It affects people in different ways, as it's a disease of the body and the mind. For Peyton, the onset of symptoms is occurring rapidly."

"How long has she had it?"

"She was born with it, but was diagnosed five years ago, the same time as her mother."

Mitch flips the pages of the photo album to the front, toward earlier photos. Luke's mom with her three young children fill the pages. He stops at a portrait of Luke's mom with Peyton seated beside her and two babies on her lap. One is clearly a little Luke, a carbon copy of Ainsley at that age. He hands the album to me.

"Annie always wanted to be a mom. On our first date, she said, 'I don't care if we get married. I just want kids.' I told her I'd give her all the babies she wanted, so long as she married me first. We were a little crazy back then. Traveled a lot and partied. We had a good time. We didn't start having our kids until we were close to thirty. Peyton came first, and then it took a few years before Luke and Lauren were born. Once those rascals were here, I knew why God had made us wait so long. Double trouble those two were. We needed the three of us to handle them. Peyton was ten when they were born, and it was all hands-on deck. She didn't mind. Luke was her baby."

I flip the pages of the book. Mitch and Annie raised their children in a home full of laughter. Luke told me stories of his days growing up in the country, but seeing the pictures brings them all to life. Him climbing trees, on four-wheelers, fishing, and frog hunting. He was a cute kid and, not surprising, a very handsome young man. An athlete by the amount of pages that show his athleticism. He and Lauren were the soccer players. Peyton played softball.

The photos are aplenty until around college age. Then, it's sporadic photos from a birthday celebration or holiday. Over the years, there's a change in Annie's appearance. A similar disposition to Peyton's, yet not as severe until I see a photo of her in a wheelchair with Luke and Peyton around her with halfhearted smiles despite her looking toward the floor.

"When Annie started to show signs of anxiety and depression, we didn't think anything of it. In fact, she thought it was because she was going through menopause. The kids were all out of the house by then, so they didn't see her personality alter. I was here, and I didn't realize it in those first few years. She started getting aggressive and angry—kicked me out of the house more than once. I couldn't wait for menopause to be over. It lasted forever. Not consistent, but never-ending, and it got worse."

He flips to a page of her in a hospital bed with Luke's hand in hers and his head on the bed, as if praying.

"Eventually, Annie's speech started to wane. She was forgetful. It wasn't until I got a call that she had fallen at the grocery store and was taken to the hospital did we begin to realize there was something bigger going on."

He takes a breath and continues. "First, we thought it was Alzheimer's because of the forgetfulness. Then, a new doctor diagnosed her with Parkinson's. Peyton came home one day and suggested Annie get tested for Huntington's disease. She had been doing research and learned about it. We had never heard of it before. Peyton was so smart. She saw it before any of us did. She said we should rule it out, so we went to a geneticist. A few weeks later, Annie was a confirmed carrier of the gene."

"A gene?"

"It's a genetic disorder that carries a fifty percent chance of inheriting."

I look down at the harrowing photo and shake my head. "How did she not know? Surely, someone in the family would've had it."

"Annie was adopted. Her parents were amazing people, but they had no records of her birth family. There was no way to have known. Had she known, it would have killed her. Annie wanted to be a mother desperately."

"So, her kids ..." My words falter, as I can't truly get them out.

"All at risk of being carriers. Peyton wanted to know right away. She was diagnosed soon after Annie. Luke and Lauren chose not to find out."

"How could they not want to know?"

Mitch rests his hands on his thighs and looks down at the deck, then up at me. "It's an evil disease, Jillian. Like a snowflake, no one person has the same symptoms, but it eats at you from the inside out. Walking, eating, drinking, swallowing can become impossible. Mental health takes a toll. Anxiety, depression, and OCD are heightened with Huntington's. Peyton's physical symptoms set in earlier than her mother's. The mental deterioration affected Annie faster than it did Peyton. No matter what, it ends in a catastrophic death. Knowing your demise is a terrible way to live."

"Ainsley," I gasp, my hand flying to my mouth as I absorb the information.

"You can't think the worst."

"How could I not? I have a little girl whose life this could alter. I mean, Peyton is only forty-three years old, and her quality of life is already cut short. How early could this start?"

"There is juvenile Huntington's. I beg you not to Google it, or you'll drive yourself mad. Annie was in her late fifties when the symptoms started. Seventy when she passed. Peyton was forty. Sadly, I don't think she'll last as long as her mother."

"Too young. That's too young and too horrible of a demise." I place the album on the couch and push myself up onto unsteady feet, bracing myself on the railing. "Why didn't Luke tell me?"

"Luke …" Mitch sighs. "He went through a hard time, processing it all. He knew his mom was sick, and like all of us, he accepted the Parkinson's diagnosis. When we learned about this, researched it, watched the videos, we all fell apart. He wanted to find out, but Lauren begged him not to. She said nothing good could come from knowing. I agreed. I asked him to wait until he started showing symptoms to get tested. When Peyton found out, it was ugly. She stopped living and started waiting. Waiting for the forgetfulness. Waiting for the tremors. I couldn't stand that for the other two. Luke had dreams, and with that kind of diagnosis, if he were positive, many things in his life would be off the table. Being a fireman, opening up his own restaurant, like he always planned—heck, getting life insurance. Still, he went into a depression for a while. I would have thought it was a symptom showing, except I know my son. He's strong, but he's sensitive. My boy wears his emotions."

"Finding out you could die young would do that to anyone."

"It also had a lot to do with you. He told me he met a girl in Aruba who he thought was *the one*. Told me the same night he found out about Annie's diagnosis and what that meant for the family. Knew he could suffer the same fate."

I look at him. "You knew about me."

"It isn't often a man meets a woman who knocks him off his feet. Trust me, my son always had a girl on his arm, but he never spoke about one like he did about you."

"How's that?"

"Like the idea of not trying for a future with you was worse than the possible hell of a future he had."

I shake my head, liking the words he's saying and hating them at the same time, not understanding them. "Why didn't he just get tested? If he's negative, so much between us could have been different. His future with Ainsley—"

"And if he were positive, well … I'll let him share that side of him. After all, it's his to tell. As you can see, Luke isn't the best with all of this."

"He's always hiding something."

"He's afraid of the truth."

I bow my head. "Where's Lauren?"

"She's in a rehab up near Rochester. When she and Luke decided not to find out, she decided she was going to live her life to the fullest. Started taking risks. The bungee jumping and skydiving I understood. The partying I did not. Got herself hooked on some ugly stuff that almost killed her more than once. She came home for her mother's funeral, but she hasn't been home since." He gestures toward the house. "All of this is a trigger for her. She can't see Peyton, not in this state. It'll set her off. Once Peyton passes, I'll probably sell the house and move closer to her, so long as I know Luke is okay. Find something on one floor in case they get sick too. Hopefully, I'm healthy enough to take care of them."

I take a few steps to the couch and sit myself beside him. This time, it's me who takes his hand.

"Mitch, I know we just met and my words don't mean much, but you are an extraordinary man. You took care of your wife and now your daughter and are planning on spending your last days caring for anyone who might need it."

He pats my hand. "Family is everything."

Luke uttered those words to me when he learned of Ainsley. His desire to be in her life makes sense. He doesn't just want to be with her today. He wants to care for her as his father has for his daughter. Except, if Ainsley has Huntington's, so does Luke, and that would mean he'd need to be cared for. I could do it. I would do anything for Ainsley, and for her, I would care for Luke. I'd move mountains for my daughter.

Mitch looks toward the front door. He smiles. "I might seem like the hero in this situation, but I wouldn't be as strong if it wasn't for Luke. He's my rock, but he doesn't think I see just how soft he is on the inside. We went from a robust, crazy family to one that fell apart in a short time because of an awful disease. I don't know. Maybe it'd be better if he found out. Stop wasting his life away on this horrible disease. He gave up on the dream of having a family a long time ago. Peyton never had children, and Lauren is too frail to. That's why Ainsley is a blessing for us all. I pray with all my soul that she's saved from this. I believe she is. After all, she's our miracle."

My breath is shaky as I agree with him. "She is."

"So are you, Jillian. You just might be the one who saves this family."

I look away and to the door, wondering what Luke and Peyton are doing now. Wondering if the evils of this disease end with Peyton, and possibly Luke and Lauren, or if they live on with my daughter.

nineteen

"YOU WERE TOLD NOT to Google," Luke says as he exits his bedroom.

We spent the day with Mitch. While Luke tended to Peyton's needs, I listened to Mitch's stories of Luke growing up and tried some of his homemade wine. It was bitter, yet I drank my glass so as not to offend the man. When he offered more, I politely declined.

When Peyton wasn't sleeping or in the bed, watching television, she was with us in her wheelchair. It was hard not to look her way, as her constant movements and grunts got my attention. She didn't have any more fits, but twice, she forgot who I was and drifted off during conversations, as if she couldn't remember what she was going to say. As Mitch told stories that involved Peyton, she looked at him like she had no idea what he was talking about.

The mood lightened a lot when Mitch broke out his banjo. I'd thought he was joking, but the man does like to play on his porch and sings rather huskily. It reminded me of Luke serenading me on that catamaran years ago. The Incendio men know how to make a woman feel at ease.

I hadn't planned on spending the entire day, but the hours passed easily. When I called to check in on Ainsley, Melissa said to let Ainsley sleep over since we wouldn't get back to Newbury until after eleven. She's even taking care of getting Ainsley to school in the morning—albeit a little late, I'm sure.

Once Mitch learned there wasn't a rush to get back home, he demanded I learn how to make magic bars—a family recipe that was Luke's favorite, growing up. When they were cooled, he packed a Tupperware for me and asked I have Ainsley try them, assuring me they were dairy-free.

Of course, I couldn't get in the car without him thanking me for coming. This time, when he hugged me, I settled into the embrace rather than stiffening from it.

I like Mitch Incendio.

Ainsley is going to love her grandpa.

The ride back to Luke's house wasn't long, and despite the lovely visit, my head is still reeling. That's why I'm sitting at Luke's kitchen table, researching, just as Mitch advised me not to.

Huntington's disease is a rare, inherited disorder that causes nerve cells in parts of the brain to gradually break down and die. The disease attacks areas of the brain that help to control voluntary movement as well as thinking and psychiatric disorders.

Symptoms can develop at any time, but often first appear when people are in their thirties and forties. When symptoms develop early, the disease might progress faster.

There's no cure, and medication can only help manage symptoms, but can't prevent the physical, mental, and behavioral decline. The cost for care is staggering, and I now understand how fortunate Mitch said it was that Peyton had good insurance. It makes sense why Luke said he needed his.

The more videos I watch of families and patients telling their stories, the more I'm going to be sick. These wonderful, kind, beautiful families are all devastated by disease ripping through their families. Even the ones who get a negative diagnosis are riddled with survivor's guilt.

I pray Ainsley's biggest worry is the guilt. To imagine my girl with her sassy flair for life being trapped in her own body, unable to swallow or even think …

I look up at Luke. He's freshly showered since he smelled of pea soup and antiseptic. His thick hair is slightly curled from being wet, and his skin is dewy. He must have dressed quickly because the long-sleeved shirt he's wearing is clinging to his chest, molding the contours of his body.

He's looking at me with a quirked brow and motioning toward the laptop. "Close the laptop. Nothing good will come of it," he says.

"How can I not look this up? It's my daughter's potential future. I have to get her tested."

"You can't. She needs to be at least eighteen unless she shows signs."

"That's insane."

"I know. All of this is a cruel, insane burden. I'm sorry that of all the men to have a kid with, it was me."

"That's a loaded statement. If I'd never met you, I wouldn't have Ainsley. She's who I was meant to have, and no matter what, I'll do anything for her."

"So will I."

"Then, get tested."

"Except that." Luke's eyes are intensely serious. "That kind of information can have terrible consequences."

"Same can be said for Lauren. She didn't find out, and it ate at her."

With his eyes clenched, he nods in agreement. "I know. Lauren's tailspin came with Peyton's diagnosis. It wasn't just Mom's. It was knowing that one of us had it. She decided to live her life as if she had the gene. Imagine how much worse it could have been had she tested positive. I'm convinced she would have overdosed on purpose a long time ago."

"Luke." It's all I can say. There isn't more to add because from what I did see on the internet, suicide is common among the carriers. The thought of the pain and agony they would face with the worst disease known to man or the realization of what they'd put their families through, is enough for some to end their own lives. That must be why it's called the Devil's Disease.

I hug Joe and wish for yesterday.

Heck, I wish for the car ride when I didn't know any of this.

Turns out, ignorance *is* bliss.

Reality is misery.

"You don't want her changing her dreams because she thinks she'll die young. Ainsley is going to live a good life."

"You sound awfully optimistic. You sound like your dad."

"Maybe finding out I'm a father changed my perspective." Luke pushes the computer over. Joe jumps onto the table and finds Luke's hand and seeks his affection. Luke picks him up and cradles him in his arms. "Plus, this guy helps relax me."

"I see how he's a good emotional support animal." I say, eliciting a growl from Joe. "Excuse me. An emotional support man. You are not an animal."

Appeased, Joe leaps from Luke's arms and lifts his chin to me for a nose kiss.

Luke moves his shoulder in a joking motion, circling it back. The tic catches my attention, and I'm quick on my feet.

"Your shoulder just flinched," I say quickly.

"Yeah. My back hurts. Slept like shit last night."

"Oh." I assess his body movements. "You sure?"

"Jillian, I swear, if you start analyzing my every move, you're going to drive me crazy."

My eyes widen. "That could be a mood swing."

"Jillian," he says deeply and in warning.

I hold my hands up, then run them through my hair. I start to move about the table. "I don't know how I'll ever be able to do this. If I'm like this with you, I'll forever be on Ainsley, always wondering and watching and—"

"You know what you need?" Luke places his hands on my shoulders, stopping me from my march around the table.

I lift a brow and hope he has something profound to say. Something to take away this crippling anxiety I feel building deep in my gut and bubbling to the surface.

"You need to go dancing."

There's a fluttering of my lashes as I look at him, stunned and confused. "That sounds like a horrible idea."

"It probably is." He grins, grabbing his keys off the table and shoving them into his pocket. "Let's go."

"Wait." My attempt to halt him fails as he keeps walking toward the front door. "Your dad said you had a hard time with the diagnosis. You got drunk a lot. You ... went off the rails a bit. If we go dancing, you'll want to drink and ..." *I could lose you again.* "You might not stop."

This time, he turns on his heel. Those steely eyes stare at me blankly as his chest rises with a quick intake of air.

"I'm not an alcoholic. I don't have a problem with liquor. I had a life problem."

He takes three steps forward, closing the space between us. The musk of his freshly put-on cologne lingers in the air between us. I try desperately to resist looking at the captivating hold of his stare, deep, apologetic, penetrating.

"I had a *you* problem. Now, you're here, and there're no more secrets. So, we can stay here and think about dying, or we can go out and start living."

From the moment I met this man, he has been incorrigible. It's emotional whiplash at its finest, and yet he has a way of making me do what he says. I know spending more time with him—*alone time* with him—will be my undoing. It's dangerous, as are all things when it comes to him. Turns out, after a day like today, I'm more of a rebel than I thought.

As Luke turns and walks to the front door and opens it, I grab my purse, walk out, and decide, even if just for the night, to focus on living.

twenty

NOT FAR FROM THE hotel that caught on fire a month ago is a bar with an industrial ceiling, red brick walls, neon signs, and a live band in the back. A black board in the front shows the lineup for the night. The band playing right now is branded as a pop cover band.

The only free table is a high-top along a side wall with a clear view of the stage, yet it's far from the bar. The waitresses look busy, so Luke asks me for my order and goes to the bar while I wait at the table. I wore jeans and a V-neck chiffon blouse to Mitch's house, paired with flats. As I look around the room at the patrons who are easily a decade younger than me, I wish I'd worn something a little different. Perhaps a silk camisole and heels.

There's a mirror on the wall beside me. I take a look at my hair pulled up in a bun. It looks pretty, and I'm impressed it stayed so well all day. However, I feel a tinge stuffy. Pulling the bobby pins and elastic from my hair, I let it spill down my shoulders. There's a slight dent in my hair from being held up, so I fluff it out.

"Gussying yourself up for me?" Luke remarks as he returns with our drinks. An old-fashioned for me and an India pale ale beer for him.

I scrunch my nose at him. "I was getting a headache from my hair being up."

"You look beautiful both ways, but I've always been a sucker for your hair down."

As I take the drink, I fight the urge to look in the mirror and make sure my hair looks good. Screw it. Who cares? I'm messing with my hair when Luke stretches his arm across the table.

"Come here." He places a finger by my cheek and brushes the hair behind my ear, weaving his hand through the bottom to curl it at the neck. Seemingly impressed with himself, he leans back in his chair, lifts his beer, and grins. "Perfect."

I release the breath I didn't realize I had been holding and roll my eyes. "Do you moonlight as a hairdresser now?"

"Only for you." He winks.

Taking a sip, I assess him over the brim of the lowball glass. My nerves aren't entirely settled, as my leg is vibrating, and there's a constant dread creeping itself in the front of my forehead. I rub it lightly.

"You need a distraction."

"I thought coming here was the distraction," I surmise.

"We could play a drinking game."

"I don't think getting wasted is a good look for me right now." With a glance at my glass and the way my fingers are spinning it nonstop, I wonder if conversation wouldn't hurt to lighten my mood. "Okay, Mr. Full Of Surprises And There Are No More Secrets Between Us, I want to know all the things. What is something I would never guess about you?"

His eyes stay steady on mine. I watch as his pupils dilate, and his brows lift the slightest touch. He lets out a breath and then shakes his head as he looks down at the table and raises his shoulder. "Probably that I am a plethora of useless information."

I grin at that comment. "Not what I was going for, but I'll bite. Care to share any of this useless information?"

"Hot water will turn into ice faster than cold water."

"That actually sounds pretty useful."

"Okay." He rubs the square of his jaw and ponders for a moment. "The *Mona Lisa* has no eyebrows."

"Everyone knows that," I deadpan.

"No, they don't. Only nerds and idiots like me care about that kind of shit."

"Well, I guess I'm a nerd then. A well-traveled nerd, who's been to Paris four times. My parents love Europe at Christmastime."

He places his elbows on the table and leans in, his beer in his hand. "Well, if you're such a smarty-pants, why don't you hit me with something astounding?"

I accept his challenge. "The human tongue is the strongest muscle in the human body."

He smirks. "That sounds like incredibly important information. And so very accurate."

My eyes close as I reprimand myself for the warmth that travels through my body and down to my core. The problem with his comment is, he's looking at me with the eyes of a man who remembers having me spread-eagle on a bed with the windows open, the curtains blowing in the breeze, and that very skilled, very strong tongue stroking me from the inside out until I was gyrating off the bed.

I clear my throat and regain my composure, taking a sip and then pushing my shoulders back to resume the conversation. "*I am* is the shortest complete sentence in the English language."

He lifts his beer to his lips and takes a sip. "Interesting. Here's one you might like. Did you know Coca-Cola was the first product featured on a magazine cover?"

"Thought you were gonna say it once contained cocaine."

"It still contains a non-narcotic extract from the coco plant. Maybe there's still a trace, and that's why you can't kick the habit."

"Fine. So, I like to imbibe on a soda every once in a while. It's my guilty pleasure."

The side of his mouth tips up into a devilish grin. "What other guilty pleasures do you have?"

"None of your business."

"I already know you love *Bridgerton*. Any other sexy streaming?"

"Again, none of your business."

"True, but if I'm correct, you have a pin password on your Netflix account so Ainsley can't see what you watch."

I tilt my head at him. "You only know that because you looked on my account when you watched TV."

He takes a long gulp, his throat bobbing with each sip, widening his neck and accentuating his jaw. Those eyes remain on me, and I start to question exactly what else he might have snooped through in my home when he was with Ainsley.

My eyes bulge out of my head as I lean into him and reprimand, "Luke Incendio, don't you dare tell me you went through my bedroom when you were at my house."

He coughs with a swallow and nearly spits his beer. I have to lean back and cover my chest as I look back at him, grinning like a fool and laughing.

"I did not go through your room, but now, I can only assume you have a treasure trove of kink in there."

I cross my arms in defense. "Do not."

"It's okay. You're a single woman who admitted she doesn't sleep around. How else are you supposed to get yourself off?"

"None of your business." I finish my drink.

His eyes sparkle as he watches me in my discomfort. He leans forward again, this time with a more sincere yet amused grin.

"It's natural to seek pleasure," he says.

"Not everyone sleeps around to get their rocks off."

The amusement dissipates from his face as he lifts his finger and curls it in my direction. With defiance, I meet him halfway across the table. With our faces much closer, he stares at me with molten sexuality and a deep brooding. My lips pout as I look at that intense glare.

"Make no mistake," he says, his tone commanding, "I do not, have not, and will not sleep around."

My brows curve as I look down at the table and assess his words. When I look up, it's with a slight tilt of my head and narrowed eyes.

"When's the last time you were with a woman, Luke?"

"Now, who's asking things that are none of their business?" he teases lightly.

"Respond to the question."

His face straightens. "You already know the answer."

The club is loud with speakers blaring, patrons chatting, glasses clanging, and feet stomping. The volume is amplified, yet not as deafening as the intense silence of our stares. Luke and I locked on to one another and asking all the questions we're too afraid of asking and knowing all the answers neither of us is brave enough to accept.

He breaks the silence. "I think it's time we have that dance."

"I'm not wearing the right shoes."

"Then, take them off."

He gets up and takes my hand, slipping me off my stool, and guides me to the center of the dance floor. People are around us, dancing to a Taylor Swift cover.

We move to the music, our feet in sync as the beat shakes the floor and vibrates through my feet. My shoes slide to the side and back in a typical mom dance as I snap my fingers. It feels silly, dancing as we are. I fight eye contact, catching quick glimpses as I move my head from side to side, taking in the room, the people around us, and even the wax on the floor.

We circle each other. I make the mistake of holding his gaze a touch too long, and our eyes lock. As the song progresses, he lifts his arms and dances carefree, like he does this often. Luke is a good dancer, strong hips circling, biceps curling as he makes a fist and moves his feet to the tempo. His smile is addictive, as are his sparkling eyes, shining as he realizes I'm far more timid of a dancer than he is. I recognize that look of mischief and take a step back.

Luke places his hand on an imaginary handlebar and starts moving forward, and with his other hand, he imaginarily picks cans off a shelf. I widen my eyes and look around, hoping no one else is watching him do the shopping cart dance. A few people laugh, give the thumbs-up, and mimic him with their own version.

He looks at me and waves me closer.

I wave my hands, as if to say, *Absolutely not.*

With a laugh, he goes back to regular dancing. Just as I'm getting more comfortable dancing with him again, he stops, drops to the ground, and does the worm. Yes, the larger-than-life man drops to the floor and does push-ups into a squirmy backward motion through the crowd that parts like the Red Sea for him.

As everyone has now moved, a dance circle of sorts has appeared. Luke hops up, and a girl moves into the circle, doing a sexy little dance with him. He takes her hand, gives her a quick twirl, and then moves himself out of the circle to stand next to me. He hip-checks me, and I laugh despite myself.

The lawn mower, then the sprinkler, and lots of twerking have passed before a guy comes over to me and pulls me into the middle of the dance floor. I turn to Luke for help, but he just laughs and shakes his head, feeding me to the fiery pits of hell that is a dance floor circle.

Despite my protests, I'm out here in my ballet flats and staring at the crowd, who is cheering me on. My cheeks redden with embarrassment as I panic, not knowing what to do. I shimmy my shoulders and then do a walk in a circle with my hands over my head because that seems like the thing to do. No one seems to be impressed by my move, so I walk back to my spot, but the crowd pushes me back, clearly wanting something more.

I place my hand on my forehead and look at Luke. He's smiling and nudging me on with his eyes to try again.

With a huge, puffed-out breath, my right foot up on my toes and my left leg flat, I push off the floor. My shoes glide across the dance floor as I moonwalk around the circle. The crowd cheers, and I even find myself laughing in response, dancing and gliding, dipping my head forward and holding an imaginary hat in a Michael Jackson pose. Then, I do a fast spin that has everyone cheering in response.

My face is flushed, and my cheeks hurt from smiling. When Luke grips my shoulders and pulls me into him, I feel lighter than air.

The song ends, and the music changes to a slower tune. Most people leave the floor, as do I, until I'm pulled back with the warm, callous hand of a man I long for and fear intimately dancing with.

He doesn't give me a chance to dispute him as he pulls me into his chest, placing a hand on my back and closing the distance between us. My hand melts into his as I settle my other one on the space between his heart and shoulder. Together, we dance to the music, our feet in perfect sync to the beating of my heart. He turns elegantly, his body in tune with the slow music. Yet there's a sort of harshness to him, like he wants me closer, tighter … forever.

I allow him to move my body anywhere he pleases. After all, tonight, we're supposed to be living.

He leans his head toward my neck, his breath tickling my ear. "Who knew you knew how to moonwalk? Any other surprises?"

"It's my only move. I went to a slumber party in grade school, and my friend was desperate to teach me."

"So, that's what you girls do at slumber parties. Here I was, thinking it was about pillow fights and braiding hair."

I giggle. "There's a little of that too. Mostly, we talked about boys."

"Oh, yeah? What kind of guy did a young Jillian like?"

There's a pause as I groan a little. My mouth skims his collarbone. My lack of heels puts me at a height disadvantage, and yet it's a blessing, as I don't have to look at him when I sigh into his chest.

"Brown hair, blue yes. Likes to dance. Charming."

His mouth moves to my cheek, and I feel his smile graze my skin. "I always liked blondes."

My heart falls to my stomach, and I feel my body give way to his words.

The vibration of his chest dances against mine. "Until I met a fiery redhead with piercing green eyes and the most gorgeous smile I've ever seen. Even since then, I've only had eyes for red."

My eyes lift to his.

This is where I stop breathing. Stop living and give my soul back to Luke.

I don't want him to have it, but damn if this man doesn't know how to steal it.

With the smolder of his stare.

With the lick of his lips.

With the twist of his hips and tightening of his arms that pulls my body closer to his.

To his body.

To his heart.

To his every panting breath.

Nothing seems to matter as I follow him around the dance floor. His heart is racing in his chest, and I feel the power of it charging toward my palm, into my veins, and into every vessel of my pulsating body.

I move with him. He dips left. I fall into him.

We become one with the song. One with each other, basking in the heat of our flesh, igniting in a fiery storm, billowing heavier than the flames the moment we reconnected. My arms glide up to his neck, and I weave my hand in the curls of his hair. His hands move to my hips and dig into my jeans, gripping me with a fierce desire.

I lift my chin. He dips his.

Our mouths are closer as I drink in his breath and look into his eyes. Those soul-searing navy eyes that look as intense as the intimacy of a kiss.

Except we're not kissing.

We're dancing.

And when the song ends, the spell breaks. Luke blinks at me and slowly moves away, taking five steps back, furthering the distance from me.

"I'm sorry," he broods.

His hands are in his hair, and he's looking at me like a man who crossed the line.

I'm looking at him like a woman who is done with men who pull me too close and push me away without an explanation. I've had enough.

"Not again," I declare.

Now, it's my turn to walk away.

twenty-one

I STORM OUT OF the bar and onto the main street of Walden. My chest is heaving, and my pulse is racing.

I can't blame the alcohol because I only had one drink. No, this fury swimming in my veins is the cause of my intoxication of Luke.

My hands fly over to the door handle of his truck as I try to get inside, where I hid my purse under the passenger seat. The door is locked, so I slide my phone out of my back pocket and pull up the Uber app. There are cars in the area, but no one accepts my request to drive to Greenwood Village. I refresh my request and get a ping.

Thank goodness.

The car is ten minutes away.

The steel doors of the bar bang open, and Luke steps out. His footsteps heavy, he walks toward me and hits the unlock button on the car. I open the door, take my bag out, and then slam the door.

"Get in the car."

I turn to him with a fierce defiance. "There is no way I'm going home with you. I've found my own way home."

"You're taking an Uber? Absolutely not." He runs his hands over the back of his neck. "You're coming back with me. It's late."

"You don't have the right to tell me what to do. You never did, and you never will."

Pacing toward the sidewalk, I stand on the corner and watch as the Uber driver draws closer to my destination. He's still eight minutes away.

"Jillian, please, if I gave you the wrong impression back there, I'm sorry."

His words have me spinning on my heel and gunning at him with an evil glare.

"Wrong impression? Since the day we reconnected, you've taken every chance to drop these emotional bombs on me. You say the weekend you met me was the best three days of your life, you drank because you had a *me* problem, and you haven't been able to stop seeing red since the moment we met. Hell, Luke, you haven't been with another woman in five years!"

I run my hand through my hair and pull at the ends. Passersby stop and stare at me like I'm crazy, but I wave them off. This makes two nights I've been unhinged, and the need to maintain decorum dissipates with every second that passes.

"I'm not the kind of woman who becomes unraveled. I'm pristine, poised, and the epitome of etiquette. Except when it comes to you. You have me in knots. So many knots. I didn't grow up in a picture-perfect country life like you did. I had a family who held me ten feet away at all times and saw me more as a product than their child. My success is theirs. My choices are theirs. Who I love is their choice. I decided a long time ago that I was my own master until, one day, I met this man at a bar, and he swept me off my feet. Literally. You think you had to work to get me on that catamaran. I was putty in your hands from the moment you looked at me, Luke. Because when you look at me, it's like I'm the only woman in the room. You did it to me then, and you just did it to me now, on the dance floor in a stupid kind of bar that I don't even like."

I look at my phone. The Uber is still five minutes away. I turn away from Luke and will him to say something. *Anything.*

Another minute passes, and there isn't a word from him. His silence is crashing waves to my ego, and I feel the moisture of tears threatening to fall from my face. I breathe in sharply through my nose and will myself not to cry.

Instead, I turn around, and with my fiercest expression, I say, "How could two people who had an intense connection over a three-day weekend, who were so enraptured by one another and destroyed at the same time, both have given up on intimacy for over five years?

All these years, I assumed you were sleeping around, and yet you were just waiting. For what? I have no idea because you only give me what you want me to hear. It's what I don't hear that frightens me."

"Jillian, if you wanted me to kiss you back there, I would have. If you want me to kiss you now, I will." He lifts his hand in the air and punches the air. "Fuck, I've been dying to kiss you again since I saw you outside in that robe, holding that damn ice bucket. I'd take you in my arms and kiss you right now, but we both know that would be a disaster."

"I don't want you to kiss me! I want you to stop pushing me away. When I woke up in that hotel room to a text message that you had to leave the island for a family emergency, I still held hope. The entire day, I had hope that you and I had something special. You pushed me away. Time and time again, you push, and I can't take it anymore. And then you say you'll do me the favor of kissing me. Well, I won't let you close enough to kiss me."

I swallow and squish my brows together as I bring my fist to my mouth. Two minutes to go.

"You're Ainsley's father, and I can't change that. You have the key to her future, yet you won't get tested. You're selfish, Luke Incendio. You're a selfish coward of a man, and I'm embarrassed to have ever thought I could fall in love with you. Every step of the way, you've only thought of yourself. What you want. What your feelings are. You never think about us."

"Jillian—"

"Stop." I hold a hand up and halt him from approaching. "I don't want to hear your words because while I know what you say is the truth, it's the words you don't say that I want to hear. Like, why I had to learn that my daughter might have a deadly genetic disease from your father? Why did I have to meet your sister to understand? Why won't you ever tell me why you pushed me away before you even knew about the pregnancy? And why the hell did you tell me to get rid of the baby, and now, you are playing Father of the fucking Year?"

His mouth parts, and his eyes glisten with dampened emotion. There's an arch to his stance, as if I hit him in the gut. He lays a hand on his chest and rubs it in circles.

Tears spill down my cheeks. I curse their presence, and yet I can't stop them.

Today has been too much. Too many revelations, more questions, and a heart that's currently shattering on the street because Luke is still standing there, staring—pensive and passionate with a frown of remorse. His mouth though says nothing.

After all that, still, he gives *nothing.*

The Uber pulls up to the curb, and I stare at him another moment, giving him one more chance to, please, tell me why he continues to push me away, just like everyone else in my life has.

Just as I've been trained to do to others.

It's a vicious cycle, and there's no ending it.

I do my best to pick up my own pieces and carry them with me as I step back toward the curb.

Luke finally takes a step forward, his hand outstretched. "Please, don't get in. I'll drive you back. It's safer."

I shake my head. "I have to get home to my daughter. Good night, Luke."

As I slide into the car, I push the tears back into my heart. I've only cried four times in the last decade. Sadly, I dare to look out the back window and see him still on the curb, his fists tight and his head down. I doubt these are the final tears I'll ever cry for Luke.

twenty-two

"YOU SHOULD CUT HIS balls off," Tara demands from her place around the firepit in Melissa's backyard.

"You should drink more wine." Melissa holds the bottle up and refills my glass.

It's been a fun day since I left Luke on the curb and drove away from him. I slept in way too late this morning, buried myself in work, and then played with Ainsley in the park. I needed some girl time, and my beautiful daughter and I went on a scavenger hunt. She even put on a show for me, belting out her favorite songs from *Moana*.

My head has been a mess, so I asked the girls for a get-together. Melissa and Tara were quick to respond with a place and time—Melissa's house, seven p.m.

I stare at Ainsley through the window. She's watching a movie with Hunter and eating popcorn on the couch in the living room while I'm outside in an oversize sweater and an undersized attitude.

"She has no idea her entire life could be plagued." I hug my sweater as I curl my feet under me. "You wouldn't believe what this disease does to people, and the thought of her losing her mind and control of her body to this *thing* is frightening."

"Is there a cure?" Melissa asks with her most worried mama-bear expression on her face.

I know she's thinking of her own children and how she'd react if this were a possible reality for them.

I shake my head and sigh. "Not even close. But there is research in gene therapy, stem cell therapy, deep brain stimulation, medications, supplements … organizations raising awareness and fundraising for a cure. Maybe by the time she shows signs, there will be one."

Melissa places a hand on my thigh and gives it a squeeze. "There will be a cure. You have to believe that. Until then, you can't get ahead of yourself. Right now, you don't even know if Luke has it, and if he does, Ainsley still has a fifty percent chance of evading it."

"She has the same chance of getting it as she does evading it." I droop down with the thought. "You're right though. I have to just focus on the moment. I can't mourn what's not even happening. Still, the anxiety of the unknown is overwhelming."

Melissa places a hand on my back and rubs deep circles. "Luke needs to get tested."

"I know."

"Hell no," Tara states from her seat. "That kind of information could mess with your head more than wondering. At least not knowing, you have hope."

"Ninety percent of people with a parent with Huntington's disease don't get tested for that reason. I keep thinking, if they did and tested positive, they'd be able to be part of research and clinical trials. Instead of thinking about dying, you could help find a way to live."

Tara twists her mouth. "You can't undo that knowledge. If there's no effective cure, why riddle yourself with that? I couldn't do it."

"Yeah, I don't think I could either," Melissa admits.

I nod. "I would. Knowledge is power. I want to know everything I can." With my head in my hand, I feel the tension build at my neck. "If I never ran into Luke that night of the fire, I'd never have known. Ainsley would have gone her whole life with zero knowledge of this disease."

"You'd be more carefree," Tara suggests.

"Ainsley could have had a family and started a life, only to be completely unprepared. Just like Luke's mother. None of them were prepared," I say.

Melissa sits back in her chair and warms her hands in the fire. "You know, it really is amazing how you two ran into each other that night of the hotel fire. It was kismet. You being outside and desperate. Him being on duty. If one thing had gone differently that day, you never would have run into him. Life is amazing that way. We don't realize the small choices we make every day impact the big things that transpire in our lives."

"I suppose I could say the same thing about the weekend I met him. If I hadn't been in that restaurant, needing an old-fashioned, then I wouldn't have met him."

"How did you end up in his bed that night in Aruba?" Tara asks with unbridled interest.

My teeth skim my bottom lip. I haven't spoken out loud about Luke, and now, it's all I want to do. "It was impossible not to. The night after he took me on the catamaran ride, he crashed the wedding I was working. Dressed in linen pants and a peach button-down, he was all suntanned golden, and those eyes of his sparkled. He was so beautiful, but it was his charm. I'd never met anyone like him. He kept his distance, staying by the bar area. Every once in a while, he'd pull me to the side, and he'd kiss my neck." I touch the soft spot of skin just below my ear. "The shivers he sent with that simple touch were nothing compared to the way his smile made me feel. Special. Gorgeous. Empowered. When the cake was served and the night was winding down, he took me outside to the veranda of the restaurant. We danced in the dark, under the palm trees and the brightly lit moon. We kissed and laughed and sang. When he walked me back to my room that night, I asked him to stay. It was the first time I had ever been so brazen with a man. But Luke, he was ... mine. I wanted him. I needed him. Not just for the night. I wanted to keep him. I didn't know how, but if there was a way, I was willing to try."

"And he left the next morning," Melissa finishes the story.

I rest my ear on my shoulder and place my wineglass on the table. I don't need wine to make my heart feel better.

"It was all so confusing. When I woke up, he wasn't there. I had a text message from him, saying that he had to catch an emergency flight home. He left a voicemail too. In that moment, I believed there was a future for us. Later that night, he didn't answer my calls, nor did he on the third day. On the fourth, he blocked me."

"This is some heavy stuff, Jillian. Melissa and I have been bitching about our lives since we met you, and here you've been, carrying this crazy story. Why haven't you told us?" Tara asks.

Melissa agrees, "We're here for you. I don't know if you've ever had anyone in your corner before, but we're here for you."

Tara brushes her curls from her face. "I'm sorry for the trouble I caused, inviting Eric to the engagement party for you and bringing Luke. I had a feeling something might be going on with Luke with the way he looked at you that night on Main Street. I can be a bit of a shit stirrer, but I mean well. I didn't know it would cause such a problem."

I laugh lightly at her description of herself. "Tara, you might not mean to cause problems, but sometimes, those problems lead to greater solutions. Don't change, okay? And you guys … you're absolutely correct. I've never had anyone in my life I felt close enough to share my thoughts with. I've had friends but always traveled this road where my personal life is my own. At least, that's what my mother always said. 'Don't air your dirty laundry where you don't want it seen and be careful who you confide in today because, tomorrow, they could be the one you need to complain about.' I've always wanted that though. A friend who I could tell my deepest, darkest, most wicked thoughts to and not be judged."

Melissa takes my hand and then Tara's. "Well, it's a good thing you have two then. From now on, all the evil, horrible thoughts can be said around this fire."

Tara uncrosses her legs and takes my hand. "You know I'm in. No judgments."

I grin. "Well, I might judge at little, but I won't stop loving you both, no matter what is said."

We all laugh and squeeze one another's hands in solidarity.

"Can we drop hands now though?" I suggest. "This is starting to feel like some weird *séance, witchcraft voodoo* thing."

Melissa gives Tara the side-eye. "Perhaps we shouldn't tell Jillian about the voodoo doll we made of Maisie last year and set on fire."

My eyes widen in horror. There's a short silence, and then we all burst into a fit of laughter.

Yes, this is what I needed.

Friends.

They weren't in my life when I had Ainsley, but came just at the right time. Perhaps if I had confided in them long ago, I wouldn't have felt so alone. Being alone can be unhealthy for a girl like me. You can convince yourself you need it in order to survive. Turns out, I don't quite like being a pillar of a woman. I enjoy having a friend to push me up when I fall down.

As I rub my eyes with the happy, laughter-induced moisture that is around my eyes, I look into the living room window at Hunter and Ainsley passed out on the couch, popcorn kernels on their bellies.

"They look so cute, sleeping with their heads together like that," Melissa coos.

"Hopefully, she doesn't wake up on the car ride home," I hope.

"Leave her here. I'll put her on the trundle in Hunter's room."

"You had her last night. I can't leave her again."

"And you had a terrible night's sleep on my couch. Go home, recharge, and I'll get her to school in the morning on my way to work. Whatever she doesn't have here I can get from your house. I have a spare key."

"That's too much," I state.

"Jillian, it's fine. That's what friends are for."

With my hand on her shoulder, I give her a hug. "Thanks, but I want to bring my girl home. I need her tonight."

I carry Ainsley to the car and buckle her into her booster seat. Melissa gave me a pillow for her head.

It's a decent drive back to Greenwood Village. A good thirty minutes at this time of night. I listen to Niall Horan. His grainy tenor soothes me. As he sings, I become melancholy when I think about life, love, the stars, falling in love, magic, and electricity.

"Do you believe in love at first sight?" Luke asked as we held each other under the moonlight.

"Not at all," I sighed as his finger stroked my arm sensuously.

"Me neither." His grin and the way his eyes crinkled gave me a flicker of electricity that shot up my spine. "Until I met you."

"When are you going to learn that your corny lines have little effect on me?"

His lips rested on mine. "When they stop making you smile."

He kissed me.

His lips were warm and soft as they parted, and my tongue slipped inside.

"I'm crazy about you," he whispered before his tongue dipped into my mouth.

I gripped the fabric of his shirt in an attempt to steady myself. He was a great kisser. The kind that had me standing on my toes, not just to meet his height, but because I felt like I was flying.

A groan escaped his mouth as he gripped me with his hands, one firmly on my back and the other on the side of my face, bringing me into him as he savored every caress of our lips and flick of our tongues. The sensations traveled straight down to my core. I gripped the side of his neck and felt the throbbing of his heart under my thumb, and the need in his groin pressed against my belly.

This wasn't just a kiss.

It was a promise.

I wanted to keep the promise.

Forever.

My memories are of perfect moments when I was blissfully happy.

And as I pull up to my house, I'm surprised by the sight of the man who elicits these beautiful memories.

Seated on the stoop. Head in his hands. Looking distraught and devastated.

Luke is here.

twenty-three

As MY CAR PULLS into the driveway, Luke looks up. The headlights catch his glassy eyes. He's wearing the same clothes he had on yesterday, and his face is worn.

Luke stands up, brushing the gravel off his pant legs.

I stop in my place as I close my car door and approach him tentatively. "What are you doing here?"

Luke's eyes are sullen and heavy with emotion. He takes a deep breath, and when he lets it out, I start to hold my own. His hands splay out wide in the air, as if offering himself. He takes a beat to start, as if the weight of his words is hard to lift off his tongue. His red-rimmed eyes look deep into mine, and I know what he is about to say is going to be potent with meaning.

"I'm scared."

I let out the breath and sink into his words.

He shakes his head and closes his eyes for a beat before opening them and looking at me. "I'm not scared of Huntington's anymore. I watched my mother battle it and my sister fight it. If that's the disease meant for me, I can take it."

I hug my sweater to me, protecting myself from the evening chill.

With a tentative step forward, he continues, "When I woke up with you in Aruba, it was before the sun rose. I just stared at you for an hour, gazing at your soft, porcelain skin and the red hair on the pillow. God, you're so beautiful, smart, funny. You weren't just a perfect ten. You're a one in a million. I would have been an asshole to not realize how lucky of a bastard I was to have made love to you the previous night. I made a vow that morning that I was going to figure out any way to make you mine. It sounded crazy, but after three days, I felt something. Some spark. Hell, I knew I was falling in love with you."

I gasp at his admission. My hand rises to my mouth, yet I don't say a word.

I let him speak.

"I went back to my room to change my clothes and charge my phone. I was going to bring you breakfast in bed. Coffee with French vanilla creamer and a croissant. When I got out of the shower, I had these text messages on my phone from Peyton. I called back, and she was frantic. I mean, *screaming through the phone* frantic. My mother was in the hospital. She had taken a fall at home and hit her head. It wasn't the first time, but it was the worst. She was in intensive care; the doctors didn't think she was gonna make it. I've told you how I feel about my mother, and I mean it. She was my whole world. Her health was declining, but this was the first time I thought I would lose her. I threw my things in a bag, hailed a cab, and I ran to my mother."

Family is everything, I recall the Incendio mantra.

He runs his hand over the back of his neck and then down to his chest, clutching his shirt, as if his heart is about to beat out of his chest.

"There were two flights leaving that morning, and I got a seat on one. I left so damn fast. I texted you on the way to the airport because I didn't want to wake you. I stared at my phone all morning, and when I landed, I saw you had called, but you didn't pick up when I called back, so I left you a message. I needed you to know what you meant to me, but I didn't want to say too much. I was scared as shit for my mom, and yet I wanted to hear your voice. That sweet, sultry voice that makes my whole damn chest vibrate.

"When I arrived at the hospital, we spent hours worrying about my mom, and when she came to, we were all saddled with an even greater pain. The results from the Huntington's test came in. I didn't even know she had taken it. I didn't know what it was. When I found out, I felt like the ground had been swept out beneath me. It didn't just sound like one disease; it was a million terrible ways to die at once. The Devil's Disease.

"My plans to be with you vanished when the doctor said the odds of each of us inheriting the gene were great. Peyton wanted to find out, but Lauren begged me not to. I wanted to, but I was too damn scared. Scared of what my mother's future would look like, of losing her, of possibly having the same disease.

"You called. Jillian, I saw your calls, and I couldn't pick up. I didn't want to fall in love with you and then have to give you up. I hated my family. I hated myself. I was too much of a goddamn chickenshit to take the damn test. I went into a downward spiral. I drank so much. Not because I didn't want you. I didn't believe I deserved you. I couldn't risk you telling me you'd be there for me, no matter what, because I would have been too weak and let you, possibly ruining your entire life.

"When you called to tell me you were pregnant ... fuck. The horrible words I said to you on the phone, the guilt that I told you to get rid of the baby over the goddamn phone, it kills me. There was no time for me to take a test because time was running out for *you*. My mind was a mess; my body was a fucking earthquake. I was convinced I had the disease. Drove myself mad with every second that passed. I was convinced our baby had the gene too. I didn't want the baby, and in that moment, I meant it.

"No amount of whiskey can be blamed for the reaction I had. I woke up the next morning with a clear head, realizing what an idiot I had been, and I ran to you. You said you were going to a clinic, so I looked up every one near Greenwood Village. I took a chance on where you'd be. Three fucking hours, I sped to you. I tried to call, but I shouldn't have been surprised that you'd blocked me back. That's what I get for being a fucking idiot.

"I didn't want you to do it. I was going to ask you to wait. To let me take the test before you decided. I was going to fall to my knees and beg for forgiveness. Beg you to keep the baby, no matter what. When I got there, the receptionist said you'd already left. You took a cab home. I thought ... I fucking thought you had gone through with it."

The breaths in my chest are erratic as I feel his story in my bones. He was cruel, and he was mean. He was also scared.

"I couldn't do it," I say. "I sat in that back room and saw the equipment and the posters and the sterilization, and I couldn't do it."

"I thought you had," he cries.

"You should have told me, Luke. I should've been able to make an informed decision."

"You should have. If you had called at any other moment and I wasn't half a bottle deep in Jack Daniel's and deep in woe, I would have told you."

"I wish you had," I say.

"When I left the clinic, I looked up your address. An apartment building in Greenwood Village. When I got there, I saw you on the fire escape. Your head was in your hands, and you were sobbing into your palms. I thought that meant you had let the baby go. Let me go. My beautiful, full-of-magic girl, who I was falling in love with, was destroyed because of me. I had done that to you. I'd made you destroy the life we'd made together.

"I made a second vow in that moment. I'd stay away from you forever. I thanked God you hated social media because I tried to find you over the years, and it would have killed me to see you with another man. Kissing another man. Having his babies. I couldn't bear to see you in the life that I'd imagined us having just two weeks before.

"It's why I came here that night all those weeks ago, after the fire. The night I met Ainsley, I came here to tell you the truth and never did because I was so thrown off by her existence. I came here because you had asked a question and I'd lied to you. You asked if I had any regrets. The answer was always yes. There is no excuse for what I did. I just ..." He hesitates and swallows hard.

Luke closes the distance some more. "I'm not just scared. I'm fucking frightened because I made so many horrible choices in a short time frame, all because I was half a man who couldn't do the right thing. I ruined your life. I ruined Ainsley's."

He falls to his knees.

On the pavement before me, Luke Incendio collapses to the ground and looks up at me with eyes so remorseful and pleading that I feel like I'm the altar on which he prays as a man of immense sin. His hands rise to his lips as his eyes water with conviction.

"I love that little girl so much, and if I take that test and I'm positive, I'm petrified that she'll be at risk of having it. If I do, I don't want her giving up her life to take care of me. I'll kill myself before I lade her with that burden."

"Luke—"

"I love her, Jillian."

I drop to my knees, the skin of my knees scratching against the hard concrete, and yet it's nothing compared to the pain my soul feels at the break in this beautiful man's soul. I place my hand on his face as he looks down in defeat.

"What if you're negative? You're *both* negative?"

His lashes glisten as he looks up at me, his eyes hooded and defeated.

"Then, I almost killed my daughter because I was too much of a goddamn pussy to take a test. I gave up being there when she was born, the first time she crawled and walked. Birthdays and holding her close to me and telling her *I love you* over and over—because I do. I do."

He breaks down in tears, and I lean forward to hold him. Luke buries his head into my neck and grips my clothes, sobbing into me. All the questions I have are answered in the form of love.

"People born with passion react in the moment. You are a passionate man, Luke. You made mistakes, but no one knows what it's like to experience your pain."

"You can't make excuses for me."

"If it wasn't for you, Ainsley wouldn't be here."

"I'm going to get tested."

He looks up at me, and I swallow down the shock that I, too, might cry in this moment. He places a hand on the side of my face. His thumb grazes my cheek, running small circles over my skin, as he stares into my eyes.

"I will do it for Ainsley. I will for you. We need to know what her future holds. If I'm positive, we'll let her decide when she's grown if she wants to find out."

I stare down at this man, his navy eyes that burn deep into my soul. He's beaten and broken, and yet my heart is practically aching for him. As he looks at me with a yearning ache in his pout and the vulnerability seeping from his skin, I fall for him.

Yes, there was always something about his light and charm that swooped me in, but there's more about him in this moment. This raw, passionate man that has me willing to give him my whole world.

"Are you sure?"

He leans his forehead against mine. "You're my family. I'd do anything for you."

I close my eyes and let the rush of relief fall from my chest. "You're a good father, Luke." He blinks up at my words, and I grip his neck as I declare, "It's time we tell Ainsley that too."

"You mean it?"

I smile through almost-fallen tears. "I do."

His grin is luminous as he brushes a tear from his own cheek and then kisses my forehead. "Where is she?"

"In the car. She's a heavy sleeper. You want to carry her in?"

"More than anything."

He wipes his eyes with the backs of his hands, and he stands. He helps me up and then walks to the car and opens the back door. Ainsley is still curled against the pillow, heavily sleeping in her seat. While I open the front door, he scoops her up and cradles her in his arms as she lays her head against his chest.

I hold the door open for them, and he walks her up the stairs to her room.

Together, we undress her from her play clothes and change her into her pajamas. When she's all settled, Luke kneels at her bed and rubs her head.

I move to the doorway and rest against the doorjamb.

The moon is shining through the bedroom window as he bends his head down into his hands—a father praying for his daughter, asking for forgiveness for his sins and pleading for a bright future.

When he looks up, those desperate eyes seek mine for more than forgiveness.

They're asking for everything.

twenty-four

WHEN I TOLD LUKE I had a doctor in mind to do his testing, he immediately grunted at me.

"Do you know any geneticists in the state of Connecticut who take your insurance and will squeeze you in as a favor?" I smirk at him.

"Takes my insurance, *plus* a twenty-five-hundred-dollar fee." Luke glares up from his seat in the office and the wall of degrees and plaques. "He could calm it down with the showy display of accolades. I mean, how many times does *US News & World Report* need to list him as a top doctor? Is there a shortage of doctors so others can't win or something?"

I snicker as I admire the wall.

With a fellowship and residency at Duke University, followed by a master's from the University of Massachusetts, Eric Hollenford is a clinical geneticist who specializes in treating people with rare, inherited genetic disorders. He's even received honors from the American Society of Human Genetics and Yale University.

"You're nervous," I state.

"I am, but that doesn't mean I can't be annoyed that this was where you brought me."

I place my palm on his hand that is drumming manically on the handle of his chair. I'd be concerned it were a symptom, a tic of sorts, but Luke has every right to be anxious in this moment. Calling to attention his tapping or that he can't sit still wouldn't make matters any better.

With a gentle squeeze of his hand, I lean into him. "It's gonna be okay."

He turns to me and sighs, rubbing his finger over my hand and lifting it to his mouth for a kiss.

The door to the office opens, and Eric walks in. He notices my fingers wrapped around Luke's. I don't let go.

Eric extends a hand to Luke, who keeps mine in his left while accepting Eric's greeting.

"I'm sorry to hear about your mother and sister," Eric states with empathy.

"Jillian said you made a miracle happen by seeing me so soon. I can see you're a big shot in the world of genetics."

"I'm also a teacher at the university, so my office hours are limited, and I tend to book months in advance. When Jillian called with your story, I promised I'd help in any way I could."

Eric walks around the desk and takes a seat, resting his folded hands on the desk. He explains, "A test of this caliber isn't taken lightly. First, you'll undergo genetic counseling. Once all the benefits and risks have been explained and you're ready, we'll conduct a physical. We'll examine your thinking, balance, and walking ability. Sometimes, we do a brain scan, but I don't think that's necessary at this time. Then, we'll test a sample of your blood for the genetic mutation that causes the condition. It can take a few weeks to get the result."

Luke looks down at his jeans and beats his thumb along the seam. "If it's positive?"

"You're getting ahead of yourself there. One step at a time."

"If it's positive?" he asks again more sternly.

I rub my thumb along Luke's while looking at Eric. "He's worried about Ainsley."

"I understand." Eric nods. "Well, when she's of age—and only if *you're* positive—we can explore those routes. Look, Jillian, Luke, I know your concerns. This disease is like a freight train with no brakes. There are medications that help relieve symptoms, and we've found that many people who test positive spend their healthy years getting in peak physical and mental shape in hopes of slowing down the decline. Many people are worried about having children." Eric lowers his brows. "Luke, have you considered having more children?"

He clears his throat and sits up straight. "No, and I haven't given it a chance to be possible."

Eric nods, not finding the comment odd in any way. "There are medical advancements in that field. Donor eggs, sperm donation, and even in vitro fertilization to pretest the DNA of each embryo is a reality. It comes with a cost, but should you test positive, you can have more children guaranteed to not have Huntington's."

I smile in relief. If they're making breakthroughs of that caliber, then maybe they will explore the DNA and find a cure.

Luke doesn't seem as optimistic. "Right now, my only focus is on Ainsley."

"I understand," Eric says and clears his throat. "Well, let's get started. I'll be right back."

As Eric rises and walks out of the room, I twist in my chair and appraise Luke. "How are you feeling?"

"I guess pretty good since I'm more focused on the fact that Eric isn't a total asshat, like I hoped he'd be."

"What you said back there, about children not being an option. Are you really celibate? Haven't you ever thought that you might be negative and could live a healthy life with a family?"

He takes our joined fists and lifts them to his lips, holding them there. "After making you give up our child, I never thought I had the right to ask a woman to make that choice again. Besides, no woman has ever measured up. There's no comparison. Not even close."

I don't have time to ask more because Eric returns with a woman in a red blazer. She introduces herself to Luke as a counselor who will be working with him.

"Wish me luck," Luke croons as he walks out of the room.

I grab my purse and coat and start to leave Eric's office to wait for Luke in the lobby when I turn around.

"Eric," I say, only to find he's already standing in front of his desk and looking at me as if he, too, wanted to say something.

I speak first. "About how things ended at the engagement party, I apologize. My life is messy, and it's in no way conducive to a relationship. I led you on at a time when I'm not ready. Not for a proposal or a one-night stand—or as it turns out, for a romance of any kind. My friends thought I was, and my mother prays I am, but

I'm just not there. I haven't been for a really long time. You deserve to meet someone wonderful. I hope you find her."

"You were always honest with where you stood. I pushed a bit."

"Maybe in another time, I would have given myself more freely, but the truth is, I've been tied up for a long time."

"I can see that." He moves closer as he slides a hand inside his suit pants. "Jillian, I do want you to be aware of what a diagnosis like this could mean. Caring for someone with Huntington's can destroy even the best of hearts."

"Ainsley's my daughter. I wouldn't blink at tending to her."

"I'm not talking about Ainsley."

I understand what he's referring to. "As you said, Eric, one step at a time."

He grimaces in understanding. "I wish you the best. The next time I see Luke will probably be for his blood draw, so long as he passes our examination. I don't give these tests lightly. If he's positive and already made such rash judgments in the past, be careful of what he could do if the worst turns out to be true."

His warning is felt through my soul, like a vise is gripping it tightly. "I know."

I head down to the lobby to get a bottle of water.

As expected, the appointment is long, and Luke texts that he'll meet me when he's done.

I take a seat at a table near the hospital's café near the main entrance.

I'm sipping my latte and scrolling through a website discussing the use of in vitro fertilization to eradicate genetic disorders when the nearby elevator chimes. It's sounded quite a few times since I've been in here, but the clanking of heels, paired with the intense smell of Baccarat permeating the air, I look up with a snap to see my mother approaching me.

She slides her sunglasses off her face and looks down at me with disdain. "What are you doing here?"

My phone falls off my leg and onto the floor. I retrieve it and place it in my bag. "How did you know I was here?"

"I didn't. Are you here to see Eric?"

"I just saw him."

She folds one arm and gestures with the other with the flick of her wrist. "That's wonderful. I'm glad to see you're getting further acquainted."

I sit back and cross my legs. "Actually, we won't be seeing each other anymore. I'm here with a friend who has an appointment with him."

"With a geneticist? What kind of friend?"

I lift my chin and declare, "Ainsley's father."

Her perfectly squared, chiffon-covered shoulders drop. "Ainsley's father. Please. I've had enough of the theatrics from you, Jillian. You ..."

She blinks excessively while fiddling with her sunglasses. Her shoulders curl in as she opens her hands and waits for me to tell her I'm joking. Her eyes dart around the room and then back to me as she squeamishly lowers her head, angling it out and waiting for me to continue.

I don't.

She takes the seat beside me and leans in real close. "That ridiculous story you told me the other day. That ..." Her brows lower as she tilts her head and keeps her voice even lower. "That story wasn't true, was it?"

"It was," I say with a deep exhale.

Her sunglasses fall to the table as her hands splay out while she processes this information. The cringe of disgust in her face is evident.

"What kind of man would abandon a woman like that?"

"It's a long story, but Luke is in the picture now. You're going to have to deal with it."

"Are you here, getting a paternity test?"

"We're here to ensure that everything with Ainsley is in tip-top shape."

I'm selective with the information I provide her. Kathleen Hathaway can be dramatic. She'll either fall to the floor in a fit of dramatic tears or start planning a multimillion-dollar charity event for Huntington's research. I'll be happy to let her plan that in the future, but first, I need to process all of this myself.

I look down at her black leather loafers. "The better question is, where are you going in Gucci?"

She lifts her chin. "I have a lunch with Frank Hollenford, Eric's father."

"Do you always dine with your friends' husbands?"

"You make it sound tawdry. We're just having a casual lunch. You mind your manners. *See not, say not.* Gossip is beneath you."

I uncross my legs and place my hands between my knees. "What's the big deal if people know you went to lunch with a friend?"

"Perhaps I don't want anyone to know. Maybe we're throwing Jenny a surprise party, and this is our big meeting," she says, flabbergasted.

"When's Jenny's birthday?"

"When did you become an interrogator for the FBI?"

"*Wow*. And I wonder where my issues came from. Everything you and Dad do is so hush-hush. For all I know, you could be having an affair with Dr. Hollenford."

"Jillian Payne!"

"People are flawed, Mom. It's okay if everything isn't perfect. You know, I was so afraid to tell you about Luke that I lied about myself for so long. There is no shame in getting pregnant and that it didn't work out with the dad. It never bothered me. It hurt me that you couldn't accept it."

"Darling, I accept Ainsley. I love my granddaughter. We are private people because the folks in this town are judgmental."

"Private doesn't mean shamed." I rise from my seat, taking my latte and my purse. "I'm done with lies. I'm a thirty-two-year-old mother, I own one of the most successful wedding and design companies in the county, and I have an absolutely amazing daughter and group of friends. And for anyone who asks, Ainsley's father is Luke Incendio, and he's in the picture."

I start to walk away when she shoots up from her seat and grabs my hand.

"Wait."

Her word has me pausing. My mother never shows eagerness.

"I worry about you," she says. "How do you know he won't abandon you again?"

"I don't," I answer honestly. "But I'm tired of pretending my life is perfect. It's messy, and it's mine."

twenty-five

"I'M READY!" AINSLEY CHEERS as she charges into my room, wearing her sparkliest unicorn dress with a blue tutu bottom and a coordinating headband.

"You look beautiful, my baby."

Twirling in her dress, she raises her arms and does a ballerina pose. Her Chiclet teeth are all on display as she smiles.

"Come here, sweet girl."

I take her hand and walk her to the bed so the two of us can take a seat. She saddles up so close that she might as well be on my lap.

"Ainsley, are you happy?"

"Yep!" she declares easily as she plays with her headband to make sure it's straight.

"I have always loved having you all to myself. For a long time, it's been just us," I say, and she looks up at me with big doe eyes. "Luke is going to be spending a lot more time with you."

She holds her hands up and claps them together. "Can he live here?"

"No," I say rather adamantly. "You might be spending some time at his house now and again. How do you feel about that?"

"Can I play with Joe?"

I laugh that her main concern is not about being apart from her mother. It's whether or not she can play with a kitty. Four-year-olds are amazing.

"Yes," I say. "Joe will be there." Resting my hand on her back, I rub it up and down. "Why do you like Luke so much? You've met lots of adults, and yet you gravitate toward him."

"What does grave-tate mean?"

"It means you are drawn to him. Pulled to him. You like being with him. *Want* to be with him."

She nods her head dramatically. "I like Luke."

"Why?" I ask curiously.

She lifts her shoulders. "I don't know." The question seems to intrigue her because she places a finger to her lips and thinks about it. "Maybe it's because we have matching butt chins. It's a special club."

Pulling her tight, I kiss the top of her head, careful not to mess up her headband. "I love you so much."

She jumps off the bed and scurries out of the room.

I finish getting ready myself in a new dress I purchased this afternoon for our special dinner—a strapless, plum-colored dress that hits just above the knee. I had my hair blown out and am wearing my best jewelry—my tennis bracelet, a diamond pendant, and matching earrings. All gifts I received from my parents and grandparents throughout the years.

I slide into my heels and head downstairs to the kitchen. When the bell rings, I allow Ainsley to answer it because I know it's Luke.

I hear them barreling down the front foyer as I'm putting my things in my purse. Luke has Ainsley in his arms, and they're laughing as he bobs her up and down like she's a unicorn on the run.

When they get into the kitchen, Luke sees me and stops.

The smile on his face morphs into an irresistibly devastating grin. His eyes smolder with fire as he takes in my appearance—the exposed calf, the fabric of my dress that hugs my curves and clings to my breasts, and the bare shoulders that give way to my neck, which he appraises. When his eyes land on my face, it's with a dreamy gaze that's sweet and sexy.

"You're beautiful." His voice is deep.

Warmth creeps up my cheeks. "Thank you."

He places Ainsley on the floor and adjusts his suit. Black satin lapels line the suit jacket, which is cut to precision to accentuate his broad shoulders and the gentle lines of his waist. His callous hands look smooth as they peek out the French cuffs of the shirt he's currently adjusting. His tie is slim and narrow yet slightly crooked.

I close the distance between us.

"Here," I offer, taking the tie in my hands and straightening it for him.

Luke raises his chin, yet his eyes remain trained on mine. He smells divine, like musk and man. I trail my hands down his tie and feel his chest rise with a deep inhale.

I leave my hand there a beat too long.

"A tuxedo?" I lift a brow. "Where exactly are you taking us tonight?"

"A special evening for my girls."

Every time he says things like that, my heart turns over in response.

I spin around and grab my purse, then walk with Ainsley to the coat closet. She puts her furry pink dress jacket on, and I slide on my wool overcoat but leave it open.

We drive in Luke's truck with Ainsley in the booster seat he purchased for her. We don't travel far, and I'm stunned when he parks the car near the entrance of Greenwood Village Park. The vast space that is usually crowded is empty and dark. I can hardly see a thing, except for the town carousel that is uncharacteristically lit up and glowing.

Luke gets out and then walks around my side to open my door. He takes my hand and escorts me outside, then gets Ainsley from the backset.

He takes her hand and guides us toward the carousel.

"Is that for us?" Ainsley asks, pointing wildly at the amusement ride that is playing traditional merry-go-round music.

"I rented it just for us."

She starts jumping up and down, and her excitement reflects onto Luke's face.

The carousel operator greets us through the gate. To the left of the ride, under the building structure the carousel resides in, I see a table set up for dinner for three. I turn to Luke with my mouth parted.

He smiles. "A slight upgrade from our picnics."

The three of us board the carousel. Ainsley selects a brown horse with flowers along its mane. I take the one beside her—a gray pony with blue feathers in a cap. Luke is on the other side of Ainsley on a black stallion.

The ride starts, and we take a go around, the three of us laughing and talking. The music is joyous, as is the beam on Ainsley's face. When the ride ends, she scurries to another horse and settles on that one. Luke and I follow suit and take other horses as well.

For the third ride, Luke asks if we can take a seat on the ornate bench on the ride. It's long enough to seat five people, but only Ainsley and I take a seat. Luke opts to stand.

When the ride starts, this time at a slower speed than before, he takes a knee in front of Ainsley. The horses move in an almost-still pace, and the music is a softer tune yet still magical.

"Do you know why your mom and I asked you to get dressed up extra special tonight?" he asks Ainsley, who shakes her head. "Because tonight is extra special."

He looks to me, seeking permission, and I nod slightly, taking a long, shaky breath.

The confidence of Luke falls a little as he swallows hard and looks at Ainsley like a man about to promise marriage to a woman— nervous as hell.

"Ainsley, have you ever wondered about having a dad?" he starts.

She nods. "Mommy said I don't need one, and that's okay because all families are different. I have Mommy and Grandma and Grandpa."

"You have a daddy, Ainsley," I explain gently.

She looks from me to Luke with a confused squish to her face. "Are *you* my daddy?"

"Yes." His lips puff out, and his brows form a deep V. "I'm so sorry I haven't been there for you. That's why I wanted to make tonight so special. I plan to make up for all the time we've lost because you are the most special girl in the world, Ainsley. If it's okay, I want to be the best dad in the universe for you."

Her wide eyes continue to stare at him with a blank expression.

"You're my daddy," she states.

"I am your dad," he confirms cautiously, tears building on the inside of his eyes.

Four-year-old eyes look at him from one eye to the next. She's appraising him from deep in her soul in a way I didn't know a child could. As she stares, Luke waits, and his face flushes.

Ainsley's shoulders fall. His do too. The moment is fraught with tension as they look at each other—his face sad and hers confused.

Then, she lifts her arms up in the air and brings them down in a fierce fist pump as she declares loudly, "Yes!"

Luke sits back on his heels and looks at her with trepidation. "Yes is good?"

"Yes is so good!" She jumps up and throws her arms around his neck and gives him a hug bigger, tighter, and full of more affection than I've ever seen her give.

Those tears that pooled in his eyes are now spilling down his cheeks as he wraps his hands around her and pulls her in tightly.

My own view of the father and daughter is clouded in tears as I see the union of the souls that were meant be together. Even before they knew they belonged to one another, they fit.

Ainsley kisses Luke's cheek.

"Guess what," she says to him.

"What?"

"I love you, daddy."

"Fuck me," he declares, and before I can yell at him for profanity in front of our daughter, he lifts her up and spins her around on the carousel, causing her to squeal with laughter. "I love you too, kid."

I sit back on the ride, rubbing my hand over my mouth as I try to catch my breath. The sight of Ainsley as happy as can be makes my heart soar.

The carousel ride ends, and Luke motions for the conductor to let it go one more time.

"You really like this ride," I tease.

He sets Ainsley beside me and then takes a knee again. "One more thing. I had this all planned out in my head, and I just need to get one more thing done. Man, this is nerve-racking."

Luke takes a deep breath. From inside his breast pocket, he takes out a square black velvet box. Opening it, he shows Ainsley the contents—a small, heart-shaped gold locket, etched with a piece of glass in the front.

He takes the locket out of the box and holds it in his palm as he shows her the inside. A photo of Luke is on the left, and one of me is on the right.

"In this locket are the two people who love you most in this world. No matter what happens, you should always remember that you were created with love. That love will make you stronger than anything."

He closes the locket, and she places a finger on the front design. It's a glass heart with what looks like white grains inside.

"What's that?" she asks him.

"Sand. From a place called Palm Beach in Aruba. Someday, when you're much older, Mom will tell you all about it. Maybe she'll even take you there."

"Will you be there?" she asks.

"Maybe," he states gently. "Until then, you can have this."

He places the necklace around her neck, and she looks at it with a smile.

"It's so pretty. I want to wear it every day."

"I hope you do." He grins and accepts another hug, kissing her cheek and soaking in her love. He rises to let the conductor know we're ready to get off. "Now, I have a special meal planned for my girls. If you're lucky, there might be some peanut butter and cookie ice cream."

"This is the best day ever!"

Ainsley runs off toward the dining table, leaving me and Luke under the lights of the glowing carousel.

"You did good, Luke Incendio."

"About that," he starts and croons, "Ainsley Incendio has a great ring to it."

I place a hand on his chest. "Okay, caveman. What happened to saying you weren't going to brand her like cattle?"

"Turns out, I've been wanting to brand a lot of things lately." He winks.

twenty-six

I PUT AINSLEY TO sleep with her locket hanging from an old jewelry holder of mine that's sitting on her end table. She wanted someplace special to lay her necklace at night because it is her most favorite thing in the world.

As I lie in her bed a few extra minutes, as I do every night to make sure she's sound asleep, I look over at the locket. When I showered at Luke's house weeks ago, I saw a bottle of what looked like white sand in the cabinet under the sink. I was curious about what it could be, and now, I wonder.

I wonder how long he's had it there.

I wonder if he gathered it after our feet touched the sand.

I wonder if he did it for me.

I close my eyes and shake my head. There is no way he kept a memory of me after the way we parted. Sometimes, I wonder if I've been watching too many romance stories on Netflix. For a woman who has stated time and time again that she doesn't need love—and I know without a doubt that I certainly do not *need* it—I often wonder if I'm fooling myself because, like most people … *I want it.*

If I didn't want love, I wouldn't have given myself so freely to a man the way I did with Luke. I wouldn't slowly be welcoming him back into my heart despite how I vowed never to think about him again.

Oh, how I fooled myself. Luke's all I've ever thought about. Especially in moments when I'm curled up with our daughter, listening to her deep, slow breaths as she falls into slumber, smelling the sweetness of her skin, watching the fluttering of her lashes, and staring in awe at the beautiful miracle that she is, I think about him.

I think about Luke when I'm working a wedding and how he showed up that night in Aruba, all clad in linen and his shirt unbuttoned just a touch, revealing that smooth chest, and showcased his award-winning grin. He had his eyes on me all night. While I pride myself on professionalism, I'll never deny that I kept looking his way too.

I think of him when I'm by myself. In the car. In the shower. The bed. Hell, he's even on my mind when I'm eating a bowl of cereal.

Perhaps that's what love is. Echoing the spark that once was in order to keep that inner flame burning.

After I told Luke I was pregnant, I went to my grandmother for guidance.

Her words were simple.

"You don't need a man to accomplish anything in this world. If he doesn't want you and he doesn't want that baby, he doesn't deserve either of you. He gave up his right the moment he told you to abort. You want that baby, then you keep it and keep it on your terms. You accept full responsibility, and you can because I'm going to give you the means to make sure you don't ever have to crawl to a man again."

I was never concerned about being able to provide for my child. Yes, finding care for Ainsley while fulfilling my career desires was a worry, but it wasn't what I immediately thought of. She convinced me that was my only concern. I never went back to bang down Luke's door because I believed this was *my* choice. Something *I* wanted alone.

I never wanted to be alone.

I never wanted to do *this* alone.

I never wanted to give Ainsley half a household. If I had known all these years that Luke was going to love her the way he does, I would've barged down his door tenfold.

I was so scared he wouldn't want her. Devastated he didn't want me. Even after he knew we were both here and so very willing, he turned us aside, and my heart couldn't take it.

Now, I have regret.

The Luke I thought he was and the man he is now are the same, and I'm understanding the many facets of his soul. He's complex—a charismatic and charming man, who is burdened with a truth that frightens him.

He reacts on impulse, driven by emotion. If you look closely, you'll see those emotions written on his sleeve, so very available for you to read if you only take a glance.

I have always been the opposite. I hold my emotions back and only give a fraction of myself to others because I believed no one cared to be bothered. Because my business was no one else's, I needn't rely on anyone.

The truth is, I do need people.

I need friendship.

I need family.

I need love.

I slide out of the bed and head down the stairs in my bare feet. My plum-colored dress drags on the floor as I walk into the kitchen. Luke is leaning on the island, looking through his phone. He's still in his tux, except his jacket is slung over one of the stools. His tie is loosened, hanging idly from his neck, with the top two buttons of his shirt undone. Silver cuff links are on the countertop as his sleeves are rolled up, three-quarters length on each side, revealing golden biceps.

His thick, styled brown hair is windswept from several spins around the carousel. That masculine jaw, roguish cleft chin, and that twinkle ... *damn*, did the golden flecks of his eyes twinkle under the carousel lights this evening. He was so carefree and disarming that I felt all the butterflies in my stomach, as I had the night we met.

The difference is that smile, charm, and charisma are all meant for our daughter. They aren't for me. I have to remember that. While I have him here in the present, the moments that we shared in the past are merely left to memories I carry with me.

"Your daughter was exhausted. She fell asleep quickly."

He looks up from his phone. The sharp line of his jaw softens as he smiles at the sight of me. His eyes, however, don't seem so carefree with the way they drink me in. I swear, the man has a way of making me quiver with a simple look, whether he intends to or not.

"*My daughter.* I loved saying it before, but now that it's all happening out in the open and she knows ..." He places a hand on his chest. "Did you hear her call me Daddy? That was single-handedly the greatest moment of my entire life. I mean it, I could drop dead right now. That is the most fantastic feeling in the world. I wish I had been here for all the firsts."

"You're here now."

I stand next to him at the island and place a hand on the counter.

"I am," he murmurs. "So are you."

I clench the cold granite countertop in order to cool the way his baritone heats my skin.

He must feel something, too, because he pulls in a sharp, short breath. He moves his body closer to mine.

"I've been so enamored by my child's existence that it's overshadowed why I came here in the first place. Weeks ago, when I showed up on your doorstep, it wasn't with the knowledge I have today. I came here, scared and with my tail between my legs, because I had to see you again."

"I know. You came to apologize."

"I came to see you again," he repeats.

His body grows ever closer, and I suck in a breath. The stone against my palm does nothing to cool the ever-flowing blood from boiling over in desire …

For his words.

For him.

"Jillian," he breathes. "I was enraptured by you the first moment I saw you. Your fierce personality. Your self-assuredness. You think I've aged well? You're the most stunning, captivating woman I've ever met."

As if traveling on its own, my fingers rise and touch his jaw. I lay my hand on his face and he falls into it. A deep, ragged breath expels from his mouth as he does so, looking back at me with hungry eyes.

"You can't say words like that to me unless you mean them," I plead.

"I've meant every word I've ever said, except one. The answer was never no." His fist grips the fabric of my dress at my hip and pulls me in. "I should have said yes."

I tremble as the coarse fingers of his other hand travel slowly up my arm.

"Yes, to being with you."

His palm glides up to my bicep, leaving trickles of shivers on my skin.

"Yes, to having a life with you."

I whimper as he caresses my bare shoulder and skims the skin of my neck.

He tips my chin and forces me to look into his eyes.

"Yes, to being the man of your goddamn dreams because you sure as hell are the woman of mine."

He grips my face and brings my mouth up to his. We're breaths apart, and I drink in his scent, his air, his desire.

I might question his need for me, but in this moment, there is no sense of wonder left. Especially when his body edges close to mine and I can physically feel the desire in his bones.

Wanton in Luke's arms, I melt into him, gripping him firmly by the back of his head and bringing his mouth to mine. A guttural moan sounds from deep in his throat as his lips part, and his tongue invades my mouth, penetrating and lavishing me in the sexiest kiss of my life.

My hooded eyes flicker up to see him. His eyes are closed, yet desire is written all over his face. I close my eyes again and get lost in the heat of his kiss.

I slip my tongue inside and out. His lips are soft and full, and he meets every wet, hot glide of my tongue with a more demanding one of his own. Our lips weave as we lap and suck. He tastes divine, and I savor every flick of his tongue.

His mouth moves to my neck, and he devours my flesh, taking wide-mouthed kisses up and down the artery. As his teeth skim my ear, I pull him close and feel the bulge of his arousal against my belly, my hips seeking the steel. I love that he's aroused from our connection.

Desire pools at my core, and I inhale a shaky breath as it sends shivers up my body and out in a quivering gasp.

Luke pushes me against the counter and uses the leverage to smash his body to mine. My hands roam his hardened chest. I undo more buttons so I can slide my palms against it, breaking our kiss long enough to admire his beautiful skin and the husky muscles he's acquired even more of since I last touched him.

"You're gorgeous," I say and look up to his eyes that are glazed over in lust.

He places his hands on my hips and hoists me onto the counter. My legs are spread so he can find a place between my thighs. My counters are extra high, so I cry at the loss of the feel of his erection. His mouth is on my shoulder, licking along my clavicle, as he slowly unzips the back of my dress until the strapless top falls and my dress pools at my rib cage, exposing my bare breasts.

"Luckiest man alive," he says as he licks at my nipples, sucking and lavishing at the buds one at a time, paying homage to the other with deft fingers.

A desperate whimper escapes my throat. Desperation drips down to my core. I grip his head and hold him in place, begging him to bite and suck and have his wicked way with me. I grind against him, seeking friction to my ever-aching clit. I grip his hair and pull his head back for a soul-shattering kiss.

"I need you, Luke."

"You have me," he declares. His hands rise to the sides of my head, and he kisses me with strong strokes and sultry swipes.

"We can't stay here," I say. "Ainsley will wake up."

"Do you want me to leave?" His question is asked as he moves his mouth back to my neck and caresses my breast with his hand.

"Upstairs. Bedroom."

He lifts his head. "Are you sure it's okay with her home? Maybe we should wait. Fuck, I really don't want to stop, but I will."

My chest is heaving, and my core is throbbing as I slip my arms around his neck. "Parents have sex all the time with their kids home."

"Thank God for door locks." His full lips swiftly turn into a smirk.

In one fell swoop, Luke places a hand under my knees and another on my back and lifts me off the counter. I hold the top of my dress to my chest as he carries me up the stairs. His sense of urgency makes me laugh.

"Be quiet, or you'll wake our daughter," he says as he walks past Ainsley's room and then stops at the bathroom, only to realize it's the wrong room. Then, he toes open my bedroom door. "Jackpot."

I'm placed on the bed, and then he walks over to the door, double-checking it's locked.

I sit up on my elbows, my dress falling down in front, and admire the sight before me.

Luke Incendio.

The man who wooed me in Aruba, rescued my heart in Walden, and claimed it on a carousel hours ago is standing before me, strong and sexy. His shirt is almost entirely unbuttoned. There's an obvious form of arousal in his pants. As his teeth skim his lower lip, there's no missing the awe in his eyes as he looks at me lying on the bed.

He slowly steps toward me, his shirt falling open, allowing his ridges of muscles to come into view. I want to feel that skin against mine.

"Are you just going to stand there all night?"

He blinks a few times. "I'm just waiting to wake up."

I tilt my head. "You dreaming?"

"If I am, I don't ever want to wake up. You. On the bed. Like this?" He bites his fist. His eyes close as he tries to compose himself. They open, and it's with moist lips and a primal yearning. "Best fantasy of my life."

"You always were one for cheesy lines."

"That's not a line, baby." He takes five long strides toward the bed. His feet stop just before me as he looks down.

"What is it then?" I rise to my knees and meet him at the edge of the bed.

"It's just me. I've wanted this so fucking bad. I still can't believe you're here. Even after all these years, all that's happened, you're—"

His words are silenced by my finger on his lips.

"No more words."

I move my hand to the back zipper of my dress and lower it to the end, just above my ass. My dress falls to the duvet, and I shimmy out until I'm left in nothing but a thong. My hair cascades over my shoulders. My full breasts are exposed and puckering in the cool breeze despite the intense heat pouring from his stare.

"Actions, Luke," I whisper. "Show me."

His chest rises and falls with wild breaths as his nostrils flare and pupils dilate.

"Show me what you do to me in your dreams," I demand.

I've had this man before. It was intense and earth-quaking, yet nothing compares to the reconnection. Two people—shattered by the past and coming together in the present with apologies, forgiveness, pain, and desire—as our chests collide. His mouth is back on mine, and his fingers bite into my skin. My hands work to remove his jacket and tie, tossing them over his shoulder, while he makes quick work to rid his torso of his shirt.

Skin to skin, we rub against one another. Fingers explore, and mouths cherish. His callous fingers dig into my waist. The dominant hold he has on me shoots through every nerve in my body. His fiery mouth works perfectly against mine before finding its way to my ear, my throat, my breasts, nipping and soothing.

Luke lowers me to the bed, and I shimmy up toward the headboard as he crawls over my body. He's still in his dress pants, and I want them off yet am silenced as his hands take mine. He pins me to the bed. The weight of his body is possessive as he controls me with the force of his groin grinding against my panties. I open my legs wide, lifting my hips into him, letting him know exactly what I want.

Possessive hands glide down my arms as he drags himself south. He teases a finger along the lace, skimming the edge of my core. My back arches, and I spread even further, quivering in need. Gentle bites along my flesh through the fabric have me crying out and lifting my knees to straddle his head.

Luke's laughter is felt against my thighs. "I miss the way you fuck my face with your pussy. Suffocate me with your orgasm."

I blush at the notion.

"I'll kill any man who touches this. It's mine." His growl radiates as he sucks on me through the lace.

"There's no other man, Luke. No one could ever do to me what you could."

"What have you been doing all these years without me?" He lifts a brow with a devilish grin on his face. He moves toward the side of the bed, stretching an arm toward my nightstand and opening the drawer. "Bingo," he declares as he removes my vibrator—a purple personal massager.

I cover my face with my hand as he lifts it up in the air.

"Single woman, you've used this for pleasure for far too long," he drawls.

I think he's going to toss it onto the floor like garbage. Instead, he turns it on.

"What are you going to do?"

"Make sure that when you use this when I'm not here, you remember how good it can *really* feel."

He lowers the vibrator to my clit and presses down. I see stars and the gorgeous smile of the man moving the pleasure tool in long, slow circles.

His mouth moves to my breast, and he sucks hard, far more vicious than I would think I could handle, but with the intense pulsing of the vibrator on full blast, his sucks and bites are potent. His free hand moves to my underwear, shifting the fabric and inserting a finger inside my core.

I whimper in pleasure. My head falls back. My hips rise. There's a bead of sweat dripping down my spine as my body is heated, blood circulating through my body like a current greater than the ocean as it rolls in, the tide building. The sensation of his hand, paired with his mouth and the vibrations, is too much. The curling and pressing rhythm of his fingers, now two of them gingerly caressing me from the inside out, are more than I can stand.

Toes curling.

Legs shaking.

The arches of my feet cramp.

The waves building inside me crash in an erotic explosion as my orgasm gives way, rushing through me as my core clenches around his fingers. I writhe on the bed.

His fingers are dewy with moisture when he removes them and lifts them to his lips, sucking every drop of my arousal from his flesh.

"So fucking good."

His hair is falling down his forehead as he looks at me, dreamily handsome and the epitome of a Herculean male.

I might have just had an orgasm, but I'm still thirsty for more. I throw my arms around him and kiss him senseless, tasting the arousal of my pussy on his tongue. His arms wrap around me. We move until we're on our knees, clawing at one another.

I undo his belt buckle and push his pants down. Luke helps me remove his pants and boxer briefs. Now, completely naked, I stare at his large, swollen cock. It's impressive in length and, from what I remember, impressive in action. I remove my lace panties and throw them on the bed.

We stare at one another, naked and straddling the bed.

My hand reaches out, and I touch the top of his thick cock, rubbing my thumb along the head, and then massage his shaft, stroking his length. His head leans back as he groans in pleasure.

I kiss his chest and the space above his heart. I kiss his ribs and then down to the sinewy muscle of his abs. He clenches his body with each featherlight kiss, pushing the hardened muscle against my soft lips.

I get lost in the trail that leads down to the massive erection bobbing against my chest with each pump of my hand.

I wet my lips and take his cock in my mouth. Breathy moans escape him. Sliding my tongue down the veiny shaft, I widen my mouth to accommodate the girth, opening my throat to take him in.

"Baby," he drawls, "you're amazing."

Long strides of my tongue elicit sweet curses to the heavens as he calls out my name, caressing my head and rubbing circles along my cheeks.

My tongue circles the tip of his cock before running up and down the pleasure vein and dipping back into a rhythmic pace up and down. I reach out and cup his balls, caressing the thin skin. He leans forward at the touch, so I replace my hand with my mouth, gently sucking them one at a time and then going back to his shaft for a long, hard inhale of his dick.

"I'm not going to last long." His breathing is heavy.

I want his pleasure for myself. It might be selfish, but I want him inside me, all heated, hardened energy buried deep within me.

Leaning back, I look up at him. He wipes the bead of moisture from my mouth. I suck on his thumb.

"Sweetest fucking mouth." He shivers as he speaks, and I reward his reaction with one more run of my tongue over the pleasure vein.

When I see his eyes are closed, I grin at the way I'm able to make him feel. *Alive.*

I fall to the bed, spread my legs, and hold out my hand to him. He takes it and kisses the inside of my palm.

"We need a condom," he says. "I don't have one on me. I haven't done this in years. I didn't expect this to happen. I hoped someday, but not tonight."

"I'm on the pill," I state, my pulse racing. "I have been since I gave birth to Ainsley."

"I can't."

I pull gently on his hand, forcing his weight to fall on me.

"There's nothing to be afraid of. Live, Luke. You said we should live, so do what it is you want to do the most."

"Do what I want to do the most, huh?" He smiles as he brushes my hair from my forehead. "How did you know what I want to do the most in this life is make love to you?"

I bite my lip and stare up at the man who holds my heart.

"Because it's exactly the same for me."

His mouth sensually comes down to mine. I shift my hips and lean up into him. His chest comes flush with my bare breasts. His hand runs the length of my rib cage before digging his fingers into my lower back. He lines himself up with my core, thrusting his cock against me.

We hold each other's gaze as he enters me and sigh at the same time. My eyes hood over as he repeats his movements. I lift my clit toward him for friction as he rolls his hips in a surreal, shiver-inducing motion. The sensation of our union is so powerful; it's like an electric current has bolted between us and shocks through our bodies.

"I missed you," he whispers in the dark.

"I need you."

"I'm here."

His hips move, more frequent in rhythm. Our silent sighs became panting breaths. I grip the headboard, knuckles white. His hand on my back digs deeper. Intense gasps of pleasure echo in the room and radiate through our bodies. Over and over, he fills me. He holds my hand again above my head, and the other grips my hip. As he moves in and out, I follow his lead, meeting him thrust for thrust.

From the bottom of my toes to the tips of my fingers, I release myself to him.

I feel him giving his heart up the very same.

Our hearts let go of the tension.

Our bodies give way to ecstasy.

Our souls unite, like a fire ignited in a haze of attraction, ready to combust in an outpouring of desire. Yearning, wanting, needing, throbbing. We speak to each other through caresses.

With every thrust, he rubs against my clit.

With each pull, he takes the air from my chest at the loss of him and replaces it with a new thrust deep into my heart.

He speeds up, and I meet him. My palm grips his neck, and I feel his pulse throbbing against my thumb.

Pressing my mouth to his, I cry against his mouth as the firestorm inside my soul burns. He swallows my cries with a kiss until we can't breathe. Our mouths move and gasp together as we ride out our highs.

I feel the heat of fire growing inside of me. He leaves me, and every time he enters again, it's like a match lighting the flame once more. It's an explosion of my heart and my body. When my orgasm rips through me, it's like a volcano erupting. My body shakes. My fingers grip his shoulders and dig hard into his skin.

Luke is unrelenting, a madman chasing his own orgasm, running into the fire with me, ready to get burned.

As he spills his release deep inside me, I come with a curse, a prayer, and thanks to heaven and hell and anything that made this moment real.

Because this time, neither of us is dreaming.

twenty-seven

"Morning, Mommy."

Ainsley's sweet voice ushers me out of my slumber as I roll over and hug my pillow.

"Hello, my baby," I say sleepily. I'm still too tired to get up.

"I see your boobies!"

My eyes bolt open as I pull up the duvet and cover my naked body. I shoot upward on the bed, looking to the place beside mine. There's a large divot in the bed where a man slept. A gorgeous, tall man, who, if my daughter were to see him right now, could be in for a very life-altering surprise.

I look around the room for signs of Luke.

We made love two more times last night—with me on top and another with him taking me from behind in the shower. I hadn't made love to a man in years, and here I was, having the most intoxicating sex of my life. To say I was starving for the man would be an understatement. I craved him something desperate. I got my fill tenfold, and if I'm honest, I hope there's more of what we did last night planned for the future.

When I last looked at the clock, it was two o'clock in the morning. Luke was still here, neither of speaking on what the morning would bring us. We were too lost in the sensual shadows to burst *that* bubble.

While I'd like to sit here and reminisce about the most intense sexual encounter of my life, I'm having quite the out-of-body experience as I sit in my bed, naked, with my four-year-old staring at me with doe eyes, mussed-up bed hair, and a crooked smile.

"Your hair looks funny," she says.

I run a hand through my damp hair that must have started to dry in my sleep.

"I took a shower before bed last night," I explain to her.

She lifts her shoulder. "You forgot to put on your pajamas, silly. Can I have cereal for breakfast?"

With a yawn, I nod. "Yes. Just give me a minute to get dressed."

Ainsley runs out of my room, and I walk over to my dresser to take out panties, a bra, and a jogging suit. In the bathroom, I brush my teeth and look at my reflection. While my hair is all matted and sticking up from falling asleep with it the way I did, my skin is glowing. I suppose good sex will do that to a woman.

I don't remember falling asleep. It was foolish of me to have done so with Ainsley in the house. Her waking up to him in my bed would have confused her. Luke must've been wiser and gone down to the couch.

As the thought arises, I wonder why I don't hear Ainsley talking to him. I put my hair up in a bun and then walk downstairs. Ainsley is in her playroom, talking to her stuffed animals. I look in the living room and in the bathroom, then glance outside to see Luke's truck isn't there.

I didn't expect Luke to stay in my bed, but the fact that he left the house completely sets an unnerving feeling in my belly. My phone shows zero messages, and there's an odd sense of déjà vu in the air.

Luke left.

That's okay. He's a grown man, and he can do as he pleases. I gnaw at my thumbnail and wonder if I had greater expectations at what this morning would be about. Truth is, I wanted Luke to be here. The idea of waking up to him in my home and having breakfast with our daughter is something I secretly craved.

I hate myself for having that expectation.

Sex doesn't equal love.

I'm getting a bowl from the cupboard to pour Ainsley a bowl of cereal when the doorbell rings. I advise my daughter to keep playing while I look to see who it is.

As I open the door, my heart skips in a way that makes me roll my own eyes.

"Morning," Luke says, standing in my doorway in fresh clothes and holding a brown bag in his arms. "Thought my girls might want bagels this morning."

"You changed," I state, taking in his jeans, long-sleeved shirt, and freshly shaved face.

"I had a hotel room and figured it was better to go there last night."

"That was smart. She woke me up and commented on my lack of sleep attire."

His laugh is light. "Good thing we didn't damage her with the sight of me in my birthday suit as well." There's a shift in his stance as he stands there, looking down at me with an arched brow. "Can I come in?"

I blink and then hold the door open, nodding as I welcome him in. "She'll be excited to see you."

"Only her?" His lips smash together as his hands fiddle with the bag.

"Well, I might have hoped you'd be here this morning. It was smart you left. We don't want Ainsley to get the wrong impression."

He swallows. "Agreed. We shouldn't give her false hope. But I wasn't asking about her. I was asking about you."

I smile and then take a deep breath. "I don't bullshit with men. If I don't want them around, I tell them. I just don't have a lot of experience with men I *do* want around. It makes me feel vulnerable. Correction: *you* make me feel vulnerable."

"No bullshit, huh? I like that." He walks in the door and waits in the foyer while I close it.

"Do you have any admissions for me?"

"I didn't realize I had to explain myself. I'm scared of you, so knowing that I make you feel vulnerable is a relief."

"Why would I scare you?" I ask, dumbfounded.

He takes a step closer, his mouth inches from mine. That uncertain stance he had in the doorway is now replaced with the strong stature of the confidant man he is. "You're the only girl I've ever woken up, thinking about, and fallen asleep, dreaming of."

"That makes you scared of me?"

"Fucking frightened."

He leans in and gives me a chaste kiss on the mouth and then holds up his bag. "Bagels for three?"

I trace my lips with my fingers and watch him walk down the hall, stopping at the playroom. Our daughter rushes into his arms.

As they select their bagels and spread vegan cream cheese on them, I lean against the doorframe and sigh.

Maybe things will be okay.

"Thank you so much for making this the best day of our lives!" my client gushes as we wrap up her elegant afternoon wedding.

This was a unique affair, slightly different than what I'd been planning the last few years. The couple wanted a simple yet exquisite afternoon affair at a vineyard in Wallingford. They didn't need Melissa's designs, yet booked me to coordinate the vendors and logistics for their affair that required everything to be brought in, even the catering.

"It was an honor to work with you. I wish you the very best. I'll be in touch with the photographer so you have samples to choose from when you arrive home from your honeymoon. I know you want those thank-you cards in the mail soon," I say.

"You've made this process seamless!" The bride smiles as her new husband shakes my hand and thanks me profusely.

Planning weddings is a rewarding career. Even on my bleakest days as a single mom, I always enjoy the radiant glow of a bride. Heck, I even find the tantrums amusing. As a young girl, I loved weddings, picturing myself as a future Jennifer Lopez, falling for a Matthew McConaughey. After enrolling in college and choosing hospitality management and communications as my major, I thought I'd find a niche in hotel management or museum gala planning. That was more in line with my parents' objectives of having a daughter with a footprint in Greenwood Village society. There are many elbows to rub in those positions. Then, I got an internship for a celebrity wedding designer, and I was hooked. I never thought I'd be thirty-two years old and having the career I do.

Being fulfilled.

Being so happy.

Yes, I have an extra click to my heels today as I leave the wedding and slide into my car. The sun has just set, yet it's still early. I enjoy the dusk over the hilltops on the drive to Walden. I listen to the radio and think about how different I feel today compared to yesterday. To last week. To last month. To last year.

I'm surprised I'm not currently agonizing over Luke's test results. I am not this optimistic. In fact, many would say I'm a scowling realist. If I think of the test for too long, I might start to get that jittery feeling in my legs, paired with the sweaty palms that come with worry.

Those anxious thoughts aren't with me right now. For the first time in years, life feels like it's going to be okay. Ainsley is happy with a father who loves her beyond measure. Luke and I have shouted our secrets out in the open. We've rekindled.

It's been a few days since our carousel ride and subsequent bagel breakfast. Luke offered to keep Ainsley this weekend while I worked. He has a rotating schedule and has demanded that he have Ainsley on the weekends when I'm working and he's not. When I agreed she stay at his home, he was elated, showing up at my house yesterday to pick her up for their first sleepover. Since he drove to pick her up, it's only right I do the return trip.

Luke texted throughout the day. His father went to Walden to meet Ainsley. He sent a video of Mitch as he streamed tears of joy down his cheeks at the sight of his first grandbaby. The man fell to his knees and hugged our little girl, who seemed a bit confused by the reaction. Ainsley, like her mom, isn't used to the overly affectionate Incendio clan.

Before the visit was over, Ainsley was playing catch with her grandfather while wearing her Rockford Peaches costume—from a movie Luke had her watch last night in preparation for the costume. Mitch stayed for lunch but couldn't stay longer, as he had to get home to tend to Peyton. Before he left, Luke sent me a selfie photo of the three of them—three generations of mischievous smiles.

When I show up at Luke's house, I stop on the pavement and breathe in the evening cold. Last two times I was here, we were not on the best terms. The first time, I had so much animosity toward him. The next, I was distraught by the secrets he held. Now, I'm walking up the path to Luke's home with a smile on my face.

Country music is playing on the radio, loud enough that no one notices me walk in, except Joe, who is at my ankles and serenading me with a deep purr as he nuzzles my legs. I place my bags on the floor by the door and scoop up Joe, walking into the room of two unhappy faces at a table.

Luke and Ainsley are playing a board game in the dining room. She has a scowl on her face, deep with dark eyebrows, just like her father.

"You look like you're having a blast," I comment.

"I want to have babies, but I skip over them every time." Ainsley pouts from her chair in the corner.

Luke throws his arms up. "I tried to let her win, but it's the spin of a dial. The number is the number. Now, she's refusing to finish the game."

I put Joe down and stand next to Ainsley with my hand on my hip and my chin lowered. "Ainsley Lisette, you cannot throw a tantrum when you don't win. No one's going to want to play games with you if this is how you behave."

She folds her arms and pushes her chin into her chest.

I look at Luke. "Told you parenting isn't as fun when she's losing at games."

"Trust me, I'd let her cheat if it were possible."

I laugh at the seriousness of his expression. "Don't give in to her. She's being bratty."

He stands up and explains, "I'm not upset because she's having a fit. I'm upset about *why* she's having a fit."

I look at Ainsley and her sour expression. "She's mad because she wants to fill her car up with kids. That's what everyone wants to do in this game. She's had this fit before, and I never let her off the hook. She has to finish."

I lift a finger and am about to scold my child when it dawns on me what Luke just said. He's not upset because Ainsley's upset that she can't fill her car with pink and blue pegs. She's upset because … *she can't fill her car up with pink and blue pegs.*

My heart drops at his forlorn gaze. Looking back at Luke, I tilt my head.

With a soft voice and in wording Ainsley wouldn't understand, I say, "It's just a game. Not real life. You heard what Eric said. There're options for that. She won't have to give up anything."

His chest collapses at my words, and I see the relief slowly crawl over his expression. "You're right."

The next week is going to be long and difficult. I try to maintain the positive focus I had on the drive here. I can only control the things I have control of. In this moment, it's these two and their painstaking personalities.

"As for you, young lady, it's just a game, and you have no right to sulk. Besides, you know I hate this game. It sets up unreal expectations. You shouldn't even have to stop at the Stop sign to mandatorily get married before making babies. And, yes, some people have babies, and some don't. That's just life. As the game says. Now, get up, give your father a hug, and apologize for ruining his evening."

With the speed of a sloth, she slips off her chair and then pads over to Luke with her mouth in a steadfast frown and her eyes looking up through her lashes.

"Sorry, Daddy."

Luke, true to form, lifts her into his arms and hugs her. "It's okay, kiddo. You didn't ruin my evening at all. I'm sorry your mom yelled at you like that. I'd never."

My mouth falls at his words, and I watch as they both look at me like I'm the big bad wolf. My hands fly to my hips again, and I give them a mean mom stare.

"You're scary when you go all hard mom on her." He smiles at me. He puts Ainsley on the floor and then pats her toward the bathroom. "Get ready for bed. I'll tuck you into bed in a few."

Ainsley looks up at him with a grin, clearly no longer upset about the game. "Can you read me my *Molly, by Golly* book? I want to hear about the first female fire girl."

He laughs and kisses her head. "Absolutely. Go wash up, and I'll be right there."

She scurries down the hall, and I watch as Luke cleans up the board game by himself.

He grins. "Let me guess. You make her clean up her games after playing."

"Especially after having a fit the way she did, yes."

He leaves the pieces scattered on the table, takes me by the waist, and kisses me deeply. His mouth has me melting into his tongue, lips, reveling in his hands, and forgetting where I am.

"Man, you're hot when you're mean."

Snapping out of my little haze, I reprimand him, "I'm not mean. I'm a mom. And what about not doing anything with Ainsley around?"

He groans. "This is gonna be difficult." He places the board game pieces in the box. "I set the two of you up in my bedroom. I'll sleep on the couch. You're welcome to visit me in the middle of the night."

He winks, and I walk to my overnight bag by the door.

He's still talking as I bring my bag into the dining room. "I have to find a place to put my treadmill if I'm gonna make the guest room a proper room for her."

I unzip my bag and unfold the dry-cleaning bag with a garment inside that I gently laid on top of my things.

"Are you getting dressed up tonight? I wasn't planning on going out."

"This is Stella's dress I borrowed months ago. I think it's time I return it." I take a gift bag I brought in with me and hold it up.

"Do you have to? I love that dress on you."

I smile. "I can't very well keep something that belongs to another woman. I'll be right back."

Leaving Luke to finish cleaning up, I head across the street to knock on Stella's door. I can hear the ruckus of her children inside and her asking them to stop wrestling. She opens the door, and her expression shows she's quite surprised to see me.

"I came to return these." I hand her a bag with the shoes and the hanger with the plastic still on it and her freshly laundered dress inside.

"Jillian, it's wonderful to see you. Would you like to come inside?" She thumbs toward the inside of her house.

I can hear her sons laughing as they topple to the ground.

"Just dropping by to say thank you for helping me when I was in distress."

She lifts the shoe bag, clearly feeling the weight of it is far heavier than a pair of size-nine shoes.

"There's a bottle of wine and a box of Amy Morgana Chocolatier truffles inside," I explain.

"That's too much for a used dress."

"Don't forget about the trip to the drugstore. The makeup and underwear—"

"That wasn't me. Luke went to the store. He told me to say that was all from me. Thought you might find it odd. I know I did. Not because he was a man who was running to a store at six o'clock in the morning to get you mascara. You see, I've lived on this block for four years. Not once in that time has he brought a woman home, spoken about one even. Suddenly, you show up, and he's had a smile on his face for months now. Luke always smiled, but these smiles are different. Most smiles we give are to make other people feel at ease. These smiles were his. Genuine grins of a man who was happy to be alive. It's been nice to see."

"I'm glad you've seen a change in him." I smash my lips and take a step back.

Her mouth purses as she twists the hanger in her hand. "I hope I didn't overstep or make you uncomfortable."

"The opposite actually. He's lucky to have you looking after him."

"He's lucky to have you. I hope to see a lot more of you."

"I do too," I answer honestly.

As I turn on my heel and head back to Luke's house, I'm surprised it's so quiet inside. He's straightened up the dining table. Everything in the home is set as it was the first night I came here—clean and barren. I hear the faint noise of him in the bedroom with Ainsley. I peek in the half-open door at Luke in the bed, Ainsley curled up into his arm. The lamp's light casts them in a golden glow as he lies above the blankets while she's underneath them.

They're a sweet sight. He's reading a story to her, and she's looking at the pages with half-closed eyes.

I want to kiss her good night, yet I don't want to disturb their moment. I've had Ainsley all to myself for too long. Learning to share her will be difficult, but I'll make do. She's half his after all.

I take a shower and change in the bathroom, happy to get comfortable after a long day on my feet. This time, instead of just Old Spice, I find feminine shampoo and body wash and a kid-friendly three-in-one bottle with a picture of SpongeBob on it. I make a smiley face on the mirror and get ready for bed.

When I exit, Luke is on the sofa, his feet propped up on the coffee table, and he's watching television.

I walk farther into the room to inspect what he has on television. "*Bridgerton?*" I ask, intrigued.

"Started watching it a few weeks ago. Some old ladies in the park got me hooked. There's some intense sex in this show."

"Not what you thought, huh?"

"So much better."

He pats the spot on the couch beside him, and I bite my lip in trepidation.

"I don't know if that's a good idea. Ainsley could wake up and come out here and—"

"See us watching TV together? I'll change the channel if that's what you're worried about."

"This isn't one of those Netflix-and-chill moments, is it?"

He twists his face, as if the expression is foreign to him.

"It's when you pretend to watch TV, but you're really fooling around on the couch," I explain.

"Oh. I've heard of it. We can mess around if you want, but I was just thinking we could spend the night cuddled in each other's arms."

"I thought Joe was the affectionate bastard in the house?" I balk.

"He learned it from his father. Now, come snuggle with me."

I fall to the sofa and take a spot in Luke's nook, the same spot our daughter was in a short time before. Luke takes the afghan off the top of the sofa and lays it over us. Once we're settled, Joe leaps over and curls his body into my hip.

My hand lies over the wool of the blanket. "I like this. Handmade?"

He gives a soft smile. "My mom made it when she was expecting me. We each have one. Peyton's is pink, and Lauren's is peach."

"Tell me about your mom. She sounds very loving."

"Annie Incendio was the greatest mom in the world. My sisters said I was a mama's boy. They were correct. I might have been a mischievous little boy and a hellcat of a teen, but I would drop anything when my mother called."

He pulls me in closer and plays with a loose tendril of my hair. "You would have loved her. When I was a kid, she'd take us out on adventures. She'd fill the car with gas and drive as far in any one direction, wondering what town we'd come across. She was a country girl, but she loved the city. We'd go to Manhattan, Philadelphia, Boston, and Rochester, to name a few. From trying the different foods to visiting the zoos or museums, she wanted us to get out and experience the world even if it was only for a day."

"I love that idea."

"She had a love of learning, always wanting to visit the historical sites. I didn't need to open a book to learn about Niagara Falls. We drove there on my day off from school. When I had a research paper to do on Ulysses S. Grant, she took me to Grant's tomb. Lauren did hers on the Statue of Liberty. The family went together to learn as much as we could."

"Makes sense why you're a country boy who loves big cities and travel."

"It was all my mother's doing. She also loved to dance and insisted we each learn how. Friday nights in the winter were reserved for dance parties in the living room. She had this incredible smile that lit up the room—always when she was looking for me, Peyton, and Lauren. We knew she loved us because she told us every chance she had. I have dozens of cards, all with long write-ups of how proud she was to have me as a son. How much she loved me. Those cards stopped a few years before she passed—when her hands started to cramp and her mind began to wander." He sighs, deep and heavy.

I look up at him and watch his eyes close with a loose tear falling down the side.

"How someone with so much joy in her smile, who moved with grace, and had a voracious passion to learn could turn to jelly before our eyes is something I will never understand. The fact that I was too preoccupied with myself to not care as much as I should have, until it was too late, will live with me forever. I was too young and dumb to understand."

I lean up and wipe the tear from his face.

He looks down at me with a sad yet loving crinkle to his eye. "I'm going to give this blanket to Ainsley. I think my mom would have loved that."

I kiss him on the cheek. "She'd have loved everything about it. Ainsley will too."

With a shimmy into Luke, I sigh as I watch a tale of unrequited love, a man traumatized by his fate of having children, and a woman desperate to keep him forever.

I know how you feel, girl. I know how you feel.

twenty-eight

"CHEERS TO ADULTS' NIGHT!" Melissa hollers as she holds up her glass close to her chest. On her count, we all move our bottles and glasses toward the center as we cheers for her Boomerang video. "Wait! Don't go anywhere." She looks at the video and then declares, "I cut out Tara's glass. We have to do it again."

We all groan at having to retake the video yet laugh because, aside from Luke, we're used to Melissa's antics. She takes her social media accounts very seriously, whereas I absolutely despise it.

"My arm's longer." Will grabs the phone from her hand and holds it up high. "Let's try this again."

We do the cheers push-in-and-pull-out motion again and wait until Melissa shouts, "This is a good one! I'll tag you guys."

Luke and I flop down in our seats at Lone Tavern, a country bar in the nearby town of Castleton, and drink from our respective glasses—a wine for me and a beer for him.

"Is she always like this?" Luke asks, motioning toward Melissa, who's thumbing away at her phone, posting her video onto her stories.

"Delightfully so. She's a genius at wedding design and manages our social media."

"Good thing since you don't have it. Or has that changed? I tried to find you over the years. See how you're doing. I couldn't find you."

"My parents forbade it when it first came out, and after seeing how it's ruined people's lives, I've stayed away. I don't even like to get in shots on the company page. Thank God for Melissa. She loves to get on camera, and her social media magic is what put us on the map."

I smile at the thought of how fortunate I am to have Melissa in my life. As I watch Will slide an arm across her chest and pull her in for a backward hug, I beam at how happy I am that she's found her happiness.

Luke glides his arm across the back of the booth. I settle into his side as he pulls my chin toward him and kisses me on the lips. "I'm glad you went with your gut on a lot of things."

"Look at you two, all cute and kissy!" Tara gushes, about three drinks deep. "So glad we didn't have to chop your balls off."

Luke lifts a brow, and I rub his thigh as I explain, "It's her favorite appendage to verbally attack when she's upset with men."

"I get that. Just keep her away from my appendage." He takes a draw of his beer.

"Don't worry, man. Tara's threatened to cut mine off more times than I can count," Will says.

"That's because you have been a shit more times than *I* can count," she counters.

"And she's an accountant, so she knows her numbers," Melissa jokes, to which Will playfully squeezes his bicep along her chest in response.

We're out tonight for the first time in a while, as Melissa and I hardly get a Saturday night off. Lone Tavern is a raucous bar with a band playing music at the far end of the room, which is blaring through the bar. We're lucky we secured a booth because the place is jam-packed with young locals, all decked out in their hippest attire. If it were up to me, we'd be at a wine bar or someplace a touch more refined. Still, the fact that everyone is out tonight and having fun makes this the perfect choice.

"Luke, do we know if you're gonna die from some crazy, horrible disease yet?" Tara asks, to which Luke nearly spits out his drink.

"Tara!" Melissa gasps.

She shrugs. "It's a legit question."

Luke swallows. "Not for another week."

"Decorum, please," I ask her, but Luke kisses my head to let me know it's okay.

"No more talk about blood tests, or balls being chopped off, or anything negative. Tonight, we are out to celebrate." Melissa is rather cheeky tonight.

"How did you guys get away anyway? Tara's here, so who has Ainsley? New babysitter?" Will asks.

"My parents," I say.

"Oh, man. Poor Ainsley. She's probably going to be balancing a book on her head as she gets ready for her future cotillion," Tara says.

I laugh. "My mother is big on etiquette, but she never made me do that," I state and then sway my head. "Well, once. Before my sweet sixteen. Yeah, Ainsley is most definitely walking back and forth with *Moby Dick* on her head."

I look at the glass in Melissa's hand, a highball with a clear liquid and a lime wedge.

"What are you drinking?" I ask her, knowing she's usually a white-wine gal.

"This?" She lifts her glass and takes a sip from the black straw. "Just some seltzer with a lime."

I narrow my eyes as I tilt my head at her. "Are you the designated driver?"

"Yep," she answers, yet there's something mischievous about her grin.

It's as if she's keeping a secret that she really wants to let us in on. When I look to the side and see Tara is giving me an equally curious side-eye, our jaws drop with the revelation as we turn back to Melissa in unison.

"No way!" Tara shouts.

"Are you?" I ask, sitting up and forcing Luke's hand to fall from my shoulder.

Melissa nods her head rather forcefully and starts to smile and cry as she confirms, "I'm pregnant!"

Tara is at her side lightning quick. It takes me a second to get out of the booth and over to my friend, who is carrying life inside her. I throw my arms around her, and the three of us hug, blissfully happy for this news. Luke gets up and shakes Will's hand in congratulations. Will's smile is bigger than beaming as he talks to Luke, who seems genuinely happy for Will and Melissa.

It's too early to know what the future holds for me and Luke as a couple, but soon, we'll know what it holds for his health. If the result is negative, then he doesn't carry the gene for Huntington's disease, and if this thing between us blossoms, I'd love to give him another child. I'd love for him to experience it all—the announcement and the hugs, the growing belly, the birth and all the firsts that come with a baby's first years of life.

I never thought I'd have more than one child, but for Luke, I would.

My insides flop with the romantic notions in my head.

What has gotten into me?

Luke Incendio.

That's what.

As Melissa gushes about her news to me and Tara, the guys talk. Soon, Will whisks Melissa onto the dance floor, and Tara finds herself a handsome man at the bar.

Luke and I slide back into the booth, side by side. He rests his head against the leather and turns to me. "Do you want to dance?"

I shake my head. "Not really."

"Good," he croons. "I just wanted to sit with you in the quiet."

I laugh and look around the room. Young coeds are screaming over the music as they share conversation and shots and dance to the band. *Quiet* is the antonym.

I angle my legs so they're facing Luke, crossing them in his direction.

"It's not very quiet in here."

He rubs the tender spot beneath my ear and holds me there. "When you're in the room, your voice is the only one I hear."

I roll my eyes at his cheese.

His eyes capture mine. "I never told you this, but the first night we met, I looked over and saw this gorgeous redhead. Then, I saw you," he jokes, and I slap him in his chest. "I'm kidding. I'm trying to keep your ego from getting too big. You know you're beautiful, so I don't have to prop you up with compliments. Good-looking girls are a dime a dozen. But when I saw you, I damn near fell to the ground. It wasn't just your hair, the piercing green eyes … it was this mouth." He runs his thumb over my bottom lip. "When you spoke and this sexy, sultry voice came out, I was entranced. And your words ... fuck me. You were witty and confident, and when you laughed, I swear it was the only sound I ever wanted to hear. It's *still* the only sound I ever want to hear."

My chest quivers with his words, paired with the way he has a hold on my neck, powerful, like he owns me. It's potent energy that shivers down to my core.

"You always have the right words."

"I'm lucky that way, I guess." His hand lowers to mine. He takes it and rests his palm against mine. Our fingers weave in and out of each other's, teasing with the slip of the finger across the other. "So very lucky."

He leans in and kisses me.

I whimper in response as he dusts his lips across mine. He pulls me tight against him, gripping my hand in his. A current of electricity swims through me, sparking every sensual nerve ending and singeing me down to the very core.

When Luke kisses me, I not only get caught in the lustful haze, but I also fall deeper under his spell, the kind that makes me forget where I am and why I ever gave up on the idea of love. I know I should tread lightly with this man. The future is uncertain, and yet in many ways, we are destined to be together. As I push my tongue into his mouth, I feel how very well we belong together, right down to my toes.

"I love your mouth," Luke growls as his mouth moves to my neck. He sucks along my pulse line before kissing his way back to my lips. "Do you hate that I'm devouring you in the booth in a very public place?"

"Yes," I gasp as he grips my hair and pulls back, giving him a better angle to suck along my collarbone.

I release my hand from his, lowering it to his thigh, and rub the severe bulge in his jeans. His throbbing erection pulsates as I rub it up and down.

"Jillian, what are you doing?"

"Behaving like the kind of woman I despise."

"What kind of woman is that?"

"One who craves a man desperately."

His pulse quickens. A primal need hisses through his teeth. He takes my mouth again, our kiss frantic. My nipples harden as I brush up against his chest, desperate for the connection, yet I'm confined by the angle of the booth and the table that's too darn close.

Luke must feel the same way. He breaks our kiss and takes my hand, leading me off the leather and out of the confines of the booth.

He leads me past the dance floor, a mechanical bull with a line wrapped around it, out down a corridor toward the exit, and out into the parking lot. His truck is in the corner of the lot, one of the farthest spots, as the lot was full when we arrived. As we approach, he hits the unlock button, then opens the back door, and practically lifts me inside.

The car smells like pine, musk, and, when Luke enters, feral man. It's a heady combination. He closes the door and sits on the bench seat.

"Your house is way too far away, and I can't wait that long to touch you," he groans.

"Then, get your hands on me now."

That's all he needs. His hands are in the tendrils of my hair. His mouth is on my neck. I lift my blouse and toss it into the front seat, giving him free rein to lower those lips. My bra is pushed down, springing my breasts free. My nipples pucker at the cool air around us. I cry out when he sucks on the bud.

Luke's mouth is on mine again, and we make out in the backseat of his truck like teenagers—me topless and him wearing way too many clothes. I grip the cotton of his shirt and motion for it to rise. Sensing my urge, he moves his hands behind his head and removes his shirt. Inch by glorious inch, I get to see his rippled torso and chiseled chest as he removes his shirt, joining it with mine.

I love Luke's body. I bless the gods of the fire department for making him the stealth Adonis he is. Beautiful, smooth tan skin, carved pecs, and a six-pack, smattered with a thin line of hair that leads from his belly button to down into his boxers and jeans. I want inside those clothes. So much so that my hands work quickly to undo his buckle and unbutton his pants.

As I'm lowering the zipper of his crotch, Luke takes my head in his hands, cradling my skull and kisses me gently. The passion in his mouth is no match for the fury of my fingertips as they seek his hardened cock and free it.

I break our kiss. And look down. The sight of his erection makes me salivate. My hand runs up and down the length, feeling it engorge with every stroke, growing and pulsating against my skin as I wrap my fingers tightly around it. I give a firm squeeze and lick my lips.

My breathing is erratic, but nothing compared to Luke's. His cheeks are flush, his lips parted, and the steely gaze in his eyes says he loves the way I'm making him feel.

I love that I can make him feel this way.

I bend down at the waist and slide my tongue across the crown of his cock. He groans as he slides his fingers in my hair. With my jaw lowered, I take him into my mouth in one smooth motion.

My eyes are open. I want to see it all. See the base of his member as I glide up and down. The swollen top as I slide up and run my tongue down the underside. Look up and watch his eyes as they glaze over, sexy and hooded.

I lap at his length, sucking and moaning and loving the feel of steel in my mouth. His nails scratch my scalp, and his thrusts become powerful.

My back aches, as the position is an unnatural one. I lean back for comfort, whimpering at the loss of my full mouth but I don't get to pout long. Luke directs my head back up to him and kisses me with more passion and vigor than before.

We make quick work of removing our pants fully. The glass is fogged, providing protection from outside eyes. I'm not worried though. The dark and out-of-sight parking spot affords us privacy as we sit here, naked—him on his knees and me now on my rear.

His head hits the roof as he leans toward me. His hand is outstretched, rubbing his deft fingers over my folds.

"Ahh," I gasp when he circles the sensitive bud. Shivers course up my body.

A devilish grin crosses his face as he lowers his body to the floorboard. He moves my right thigh to the side and settles his face in between my thighs. The backseat isn't large, and yet the two of us make it work. He nudges my legs wider and tosses my foot over his shoulder.

I'm sitting here, bare to him as he stares at my pussy like a man salivating for a meal. Flattening his tongue, he dives in with long strokes, licking from one end to the other.

"Luke." My voice is husky as I clutch the back of his neck and pull him closer. "Don't stop."

There is nothing slow or teasing as he buries his face between my legs. He is rough and desperate, sucking my clit and pushing his tongue inside of me. My head falls back, and I begin to tremble.

Luke was always a fire, burning hot and singeing down to the embers. Spark after spark, he reignites this passion in me that's more dangerous than before. I feel that heat build within me. My ears are hot, my back sweats, and when he gives one last hard suck, I come undone.

Wave after wave of pleasure overwhelms me, overtakes me, until I'm quaking with it, shaking and sobbing into the silence of the dark night.

He doesn't relent. Luke laps at my core, drinking in every bit of desire I give him. My body is limp yet invigorated. No sooner does he sit on the bench seat than I am on top of him, straddling my thighs over his hips and kissing him.

I kiss him with fervor.

I kiss him with excitement.

And as I lower my hips and take him in, I kiss him with devotion.

"Jillian," he breathes against my lips.

A hoarse moan escapes his mouth as my hips roll up and down his length. He feels so good inside me. I lower myself again and push down, reveling in the intoxicating shivers he sends through me.

"I don't ever want to lose you." His words are deep. He grips my hips.

I take his mouth in mine again and speak against his swollen lips. "Don't let me go," I breathe.

He looks up at me, vulnerable and panting.

"You look so free right now. You don't have to hide anymore. Not with me. That show you put on for everyone, where you pretend everything's perfect, ends now. Let go, Jillian. Let it all go with me."

His kiss is hot as we join again, not letting go this time.

With our bodies, we make love in the dark.

With our souls, we give ourselves fully to one another.

Our breaths are one when we gasp.

Our heartbeats are in sync as we fall.

Fall into lust.

Fall into passion.

Fall into love.

When we come, it's together.

I sigh. I'm happy. Too happy for my liking. I can't help it. His mouth kisses my décolletage as we catch our breaths, glowing and sated, holding on to one another in our postcoital bliss.

"What are you smiling for?" he asks, rubbing my hair off my forehead.

"Can't a girl smile after good sex?"

He kisses my nose and traces the bow of my mouth with his fingers. "Absolutely. I love your smile."

Love. The word sends a quiver through my heart.

I rub my teeth over my lip. "I love your smile too." The sound of my own voice, all mushy and sweet, has me rolling my own eyes. Still, I don't let it up. "You're gorgeous—you know that?"

"I believe that's something I'm supposed to say to you," he says.

"Then, say it."

He rubs my cheek and looks up into my eyes. His navy eyes are darkened in the shadows, yet I see that sparkle, the twinkle of gold that radiates through his soul.

His lips part, and he's about to speak when a cell phone rings. It's mine, as I know the ringer I use.

We grin in unison as our foreheads fall to each other's.

I fish my phone out of my purse and look at the phone. I answer because it's my mother.

"Hello?" I answer.

"Jillian. Jillian? It's me. There's something wrong with Ainsley!"

twenty-nine

"AINSLEY!" I BARGE INTO my parents' home and rush through the marble foyer, calling out her name.

Luke is behind me, nearly barreling into my back in his urgency to get inside.

"Jillian," my mother says as she sashays down the staircase. "I'm so glad you're here. She's been sick to her stomach something awful for the last hour."

I meet her at the center of the staircase. "Where is she?"

"Upstairs. She hasn't stopped. It's a mess upstairs, and I have no help to clean it up."

I ignore my mother's care about the mess that is my daughter's violent illness. I'm more concerned that she's forty pounds and she has been vomiting nonstop for the last hour.

When I get to the bathroom that's connected to one of the guest rooms, I see my small daughter lying flat on the bathroom floor, limp and lethargic. Luke lifts Ainsley into his arms and cradles her. My mother stops in the doorway.

"Jillian, I didn't know you were on a date. You're a handsome man. Where are you from?" she asks.

Luke ignores her question. "She's pale."

"We should take her to the hospital."

He checks her airway and heartbeat. "She's okay. I think she's dehydrated." He looks to my mother. "I need ice chips and something for her to drink. Flat soda, apple juice, even a Popsicle."

Mother places a hand on her chest and looks at us like she has no idea what kind of drinks she has in her refrigerator or how to move in order to obtain them.

"Charles." She eventually calls my father's name. "Get drinks."

Her order down the stairs is said like she's ordering a scotch instead of getting hydration for her severely ill granddaughter, who isn't even talking right now. Her lack of urgency is disheartening. I get up and run downstairs myself, fetching a bottle of water and a gourmet ice pop from the freezer.

When I get upstairs, Luke is in the bathroom by himself, and my mother has disappeared. I hand him the supplies. He lifts Ainsley upright. She groans, upset to be woken up from her sick-induced sleep.

"Kiddo, you have to sit up and have some of this ice pop." He watches me open the ice pop haphazardly. He smells it and asks, "Lychee?"

I shrug. "Lychee, coconut, and lime. There were no kid-friendly flavors there."

Knowing this is the best option, he prods Ainsley to open her mouth. He wets her mouth with the cold sugar. She seems to like the sweetness and sucks on the pop some more before falling to his arms and curling up again.

My mother reappears with a towel and a plastic spray bottle. "Jillian, clean up the bedroom, will you? I can't stand the smell. I'm gonna gag."

I drop the towel and bottle on the floor and look back to Luke. "See if she'll drink water."

He gets her to take a sip and shakes his head in disappointment. "What did she eat tonight?"

"I already told you on the phone, she had nothing out of sorts." Mother's hands are held up in explanation as she looks down at Luke. "You look very familiar."

"I'm Luke. Ainsley's father."

"Daddy, I want to go home," she sobs as she takes another sip of water.

"This is the man who left you?" Mother gasps, and Ainsley looks up at Luke with urgency in her voice.

"You're leaving? Can I come with you? I want to leave." She pouts quietly.

"I know, kiddo. We'll get you home as soon as you have something to drink. You threw up a lot."

The water in her stomach must trigger something because she grips her stomach, rolls over in Luke's arms, and vomits into the toilet.

"What did she eat tonight?" I ask incredulously.

"A lemon ice sorbet. That's all."

"There had to have been something else," Luke bites out as he holds Ainsley's hair back.

My mother seems exasperated at the inquisition. She tosses her hands up and looks at the ceiling with annoyance. "Fine. I had her try Nutella."

"You know she can't eat that." My disgust radiates through my body. Ainsley's intolerance to it is something we've discussed many times before.

Her hand rests on her hip. "Jillian, this dairy thing is very inconvenient, and frankly, it's quite disruptive. She can't grow up without eating dairy. That kind of dietary restriction is the kind of thing that burdens those around you. Frank Hollenford was telling me how some people can build a tolerance toward their food allergies by being exposed to them a little at a time. Tonight didn't go as planned, but getting her to try some dairy is good for her."

Steam, metaphorically, pours from my ears. "You can't play God like that!"

"She's lactose intolerant, not anaphylactic." Her tone drops. "You're very dramatic. It's just vomit, which will pass."

"You could have killed her," Luke chimes in as he holds a wet cloth to Ainsley's mouth.

"Says the man who wanted her dead to begin with."

"Mother!" I'm beyond shocked and outraged by her lewd comment.

My blood runs cold, yet as revolted as I am by her comment, she looks at me with an air about her, as if my disdain is bothersome.

"Please, don't act all self-righteous, Jillian. It's unbecoming," she says, and then she turns to Luke, who is on his knees with Ainsley. She looks down at him like he's a wasp she's ready to step on. "As for you, I heard the sordid details of your past. What kind of man abandons a woman who is having his child? And what kind of disease do you have that my daughter had to accompany you to Valor County Hospital?"

I take her by the elbow and escort her into the bedroom. "This is not for Ainsley to hear."

"Why not? It's the truth. He's a deadbeat who didn't want to care for his child. I know you were at the hospital to see Eric. What kind of genetic condition is he carrying?"

"A horrible one if you must know. Huntington's disease."

Her face morphs to absolute horror, causing lines to form on her face that even her Botox can't numb. "Jillian, that's … that's a …"

"You've heard of it?"

"By the time you get to be my age, you've heard of it all. I saw it on *60 Minutes* once. It's the absolute worst genetic disease someone can get. When will the results be in?"

"Soon."

She paces her bedroom and looks at the plush carpet as if it has the answers. "You knew about this when you slept with him? Have you known all these years?"

"I just found out."

Her pacing stops. There's a sinister straightening to her back as she looks at me with a stern expression. "How convenient."

Now, it's my turn to place a hand on my hip. "What's that supposed to mean?"

"He all of a sudden reappears in your life. Comes back to make *my* daughter, the one with a successful business and property, the one who has the means, take care of him."

My jaw drops at her insinuation. "Those are cruel accusations, even for you."

"He went out and had his fun. Now, he needs to make sure he doesn't die alone in some state-run nursing home. He knows you have money. It's written all over you."

"This is deplorable." My raised voice is shaky.

"That disease can last a decade. Is that what you want for yourself? For your daughter? To play nurse to an invalid for years?"

"I can't hear any more."

"It's honesty, Jillian. You give me grief for wanting you to meet someone and settle down. I choose good men for you. Successful men. Not ones who turn their backs when you're desperate and alone. Not ones who rebuke their fatherly duties. Even if he doesn't have this gene—and let's hope he doesn't because that could mean your daughter is cursed—what kind of man are you teaching your daughter to admire? Not him. Not a lowlife."

If I thought my mother had an actual caring bone in her body, I'd be open to her concerns. If she showed more depth of feeling for the situation and what it could mean for Ainsley's well-being, I'd understand. She doesn't care about my and Luke's story. Yes, it's fraught with misery and untold truths, but it's our story. It's Ainsley's story. I'll be damned if she destroys my daughter's view on this world with her own sinister one.

I turn my back to her and open the bathroom door. Luke is standing with Ainsley in his arms. She's finished the ice pop, and her coloring looks a touch better.

"We're leaving."

I usher them out of the bathroom and into the hallway.

My mother is fast behind us on the stairs. "Where are you going?"

"Taking my family home," I answer her. "Since Dad is so concerned about us, please let him know Ainsley is fine and we left."

"What am I supposed to do about the bedsheets?"

I stop on the landing and turn to her as she lays a hand on her necklace. "Clean them yourself."

"You are just rotten. I should tell your father about this attitude. Just like your grandmother. You think the rules don't apply to you."

"Grandma might have been hard, but she didn't take shit from anyone, and neither do I."

Luke, Ainsley, and I walk down the front steps. He lays Ainsley in the backseat, but leaves the door open, then walks to the front seat.

"She gave you a false sense of self."

"She helped me when no one else would. I had to lie to you and Dad in hopes that you'd accept my mistake, and you still shunned me all those years." I'm fired up as I take a step toward her and look her dead in the eye. "You care more about optics than reality. I'd rather be a poor wedding planner who lives in a shack with a man who is about to die a horrible death that will waste away my own days than play Stepford wife to one of your doctors. I'm done trying to be this perfect picture for you to showcase to others when you don't even care enough about what's right here in the flesh. Hell, Dad wasn't even up there while his granddaughter was practically passed out on the bathroom floor or even down here since I've been shouting at you in the foyer. He's probably on the back veranda, having a cigar, ignoring the fuss. No wonder you're having secret lunches with married doctors."

"Jillian Hathaway, rumors are beneath you."

"I don't know what to believe, Mother. Everything is shrouded in secrecy. I'm done being that secret. I'm proud of my life. I'm proud of my choices. I'm proud of my family. No more secrets. Ever again."

"Would you prefer our secrets be aired out like dirty laundry on the clothing wire?"

"Yes," I state easily, catching my breath and calming myself. I get into the backseat of the truck and lay Ainsley's head on my lap. "Good-bye."

I close the door and nod to Luke that I'm okay and he can start driving. My parents' home is lit up with bright lights in the entryway, and I see my mother staring at our car as we drive away.

I never fight with my mother. All these years, I've done as she said, believing she had the best intentions for me. I still believe that, I suppose. I might hate my mother, yet I love her. In her own weird way, she looks out for me. The fact that I disagree with everything she says is a problem.

The drive back to my townhouse is short, as we live a few miles away, toward the heart of Greenwood Village. Ainsley is asleep when we get back. I carry her to her bedroom and lay her on her side. I place a bowl on the floor near her bed in case she gets sick again. A glass of black soda from my secret stash is on her nightstand. Hopefully, it will be flat by the time she needs to drink it.

I leave her door open and walk downstairs.

Luke isn't in the kitchen or living room. I look up in my bedroom, and he's not there either. I find him outside, leaning against his truck. His hands are in his pockets as he looks down at the pavement.

"She's in bed. I'm gonna sleep in her room tonight in case she gets sick again," I state, rubbing my arms against the evening chill.

Luke nods yet keeps his eyes trained on the ground. "Does she do this often?"

"Not since she was diagnosed as an infant." I take a step forward. "I think she's okay. She just needs to rest and get some food and drinks in her. Her coloring looked good when I just laid her down. Come inside. It's cold out here."

He shakes his head. "I'm leaving."

"Why are you leaving?"

"I don't think I should stay tonight." His voice is calm. There's a sadness to Luke's tone, similar to the night he showed up on this very doorstep, groveling. This rugged man, who can be so strong and commanding, has a vulnerable side that radiates through his pores. "She was right, Jillian. I'm a lowlife."

"Not this again." I fall back on my heels and rub my palms together. "The past is the past. Unless what she's saying is right and you did seek me out because you know you're dying and want someone to care for you—"

"No. Never. I'd rather kill myself than have you waste a day looking out for me."

My stomach drops with his words. "Luke," I breathe.

"I messed up in a way a man should never. If someone did to Ainsley what I did to you, I'd kill them." He rubs his hand against his chest and looks at me. Those golden flecks are hidden by the darkness in his gaze. "I'm Ainsley's father, and that will never change. But my life with you ... you see a future with us. I see it in your eyes. I did a disservice by letting this thing between us grow before we know what the future holds. I was selfish. I should have stayed away from you."

"You didn't, and here we are. We can't go backwards."

"We can't move forward. A lot of where we stand depends on the test results."

"You're the one who didn't even want to take the test, and now, you're throwing it in my face?"

"The stakes are even higher now. This thing brewing between us ... I was a fool, living in this bubble, thinking that none of it mattered. For years, I lived my life as if I had the gene and vowed to never let it taint anyone else. I broke my own vow. I spent the last week thinking I could love you the way a man should without the knowledge of the future mattering. It does. It's *all* that matters. I love you, Jillian. So fucking much that it hurts." He grips his chest with a firm grasp. "Right here. Every time I look at you. When I hear your voice. When you laugh. When I think about you. It hurts right here because I know there're so many reasons I don't deserve you."

"If you believe for a second you get to choose who and why we love one another, you're crazy."

"Nor can I choose when. But I can control how I love."

"Love is what keeps people together."

He pauses, hesitating. "Perhaps my love is great enough that I know how to keep away."

Love. I've equated the word with Luke for years, using it in all of its powerful forms when I think of him—good and bad. Yet here he is, throwing it in my face once again, blaming it for his bad choices.

A long silence lingers between us.

His throat contracts as he frowns and speaks. "If I have the gene, there is no us."

I run my hand over my head and close my eyes. When I open them, I'm damned to feel tears falling onto my face. Hate that he makes me cry. I hate that I feel so much emotion when it comes to Luke.

This time, instead of holding my tears back, I let them fall and use them as my power.

I back away from him. The words I want to say on the tip of my tongue, and yet I can't say any more. Words mean nothing. It's only actions. For me, the action is to go inside my house, slam the door, and lock it.

If only he wasn't the one holding the key.

thirty

LUKE

"HI. IT'S ME, LUKE. I'm sorry I had to run out on you this morning. I hope you got my message. My mom is in the hospital and I'm on the first flight back to New York. I know you probably think I'm some guy who got you into bed and then took off, but this is all real. I'm sorry I wasn't there when you woke up, but I hope to be next time. I'd really like to see you again. Boston and Greenwood Village aren't that far. At least for me, it isn't. If you're willing to take the drive, so am I."

Those were the words I spoke on a voice mail five years ago to the woman I fell in love with over three days in Aruba. I was panic-stricken and sick with worry about my mother, and yet I still wanted to hear the voice of the girl who I vowed to make my own.

Life didn't work out the way I'd planned. In fact, it all turned to shit pretty quickly.

In movies, men are always the heroes.

The army grunt who carries seven of his fellow men out of a burning, ravaged city.

The officer who dismantles a terrorist operation to save an arena threatened by a nuclear weapon.

The man who jumps through hoops to make the ransom payment to save his daughter.

The homeless guy who works three jobs to get his son out of poverty and provide him with the world.

When I was a kid, I knew I wanted to be that man. The one who would drop anything to save others. I never cared for the accolades. The total badassery of being sweaty, covered in soot, and shouting shit like, "*Yippee-ki-yay, motherfucker*," was all I needed. Actually, I'm kidding with that. Maybe I never knew exactly what kind of man I would be, but I knew I was going to be one of the good ones.

Life in the country afforded me a bit of that opportunity. I learned from a young age to have unlimited freedom yet be responsible to do the right thing. I can hunt, fish, and build. I'll take your dare and give you the God's honest truth, and I'm not afraid to take a risk. And I was always down for a party.

While many men in my community took to farming and livestock, working at the gas company and becoming law enforcement, I worked at the local pub. I dreamed of someday owning my own bar and restaurant, where the locals could come and put their feet up after a long day—that was my kind of living. To fulfill that hero thirst in me, I figured I could become a volunteer firefighter, like most men in my town, including my own father.

I hadn't thought about college until my older sister, Peyton, decided to become a teacher. I hated school. Playing soccer and hanging out with my friends were the only bonuses. The thought of going longer than I had to sounded like the worst kind of living one could do. Still, I enrolled because that was what my mother wanted me to do.

"Just do two years, and then you can go off and do whatever you'd like," she said.

"What's the point? I want to own my own bar someday."

"Accounting and entrepreneurial courses would do you good."

"What do you know?"

"Everything, Luke. I'm your mother."

After getting my associate's degree, I moved to Boston with my friends. My twenties were fun, to say the least. The drinks flowed, the jokes roared, and the women were easy. I was a line cook during the day and a bartender at night. My buddies and I joined the Boston volunteer fire department because we were tough enough, smart enough ... and loved the excitement of running to the rescue. Like I said, *yippee-ki-yay*.

I dated a lot in those days. I had a few relationships, but nothing that went past a few months. After twenty-five, women started to hear wedding bells when you took them to bed. I learned to be up front with anyone I dated. Life was good, and I was in no rush to settle down. None of the guys were—until that one summer. I went to my first bachelor party, and my life changed forever.

A three-night bachelor party in Aruba. The first night, I was excited to party. The second night, I was in good spirits. The third night, I was over the need to see another pair of naked tits. The guys went out to a strip club, but I decided to hang back. It's not that I don't enjoy a good show, but after three nights of debauchery, I was ready to just have a drink at the bar before my flight the next day.

When I headed down to the lobby, I was followed by the groom's brother and brother-in-law, who were also eager for a low-key drink. We were at a bar in the hotel restaurant, talking about the Red Sox, when there was a flash of red that caught my attention.

Porcelain skin, an oval-shaped face, the perkiest of noses, and a mouth so full that women would pay money to have lips like hers. I was lost in the sea of her emerald-green eyes and her auburn hair that I wanted to run my hand through. As if her face wasn't stunning enough, she had this body that was a man's wet dream. A curvy ass, full breasts, and a narrow waist you could grab on to.

I made her laugh that night, and I swear I felt that laugh vibrate in my chest. I had to rub the space above my heart because every time she laughed or sighed or giggled, I felt it right down deep in there. I thought it was indigestion or perhaps too much booze over three days in Aruba. Whatever it was, I couldn't ignore it. I put on the charm. All the lines and bravado I had was laid out for this girl.

By the night's end, I had her on the beach. I had no clue what the fuck I was doing, but she seemed like she needed to have a good time. When I walked her to her room, leaving her to have a good night, I pulled out my phone and changed my flight home. I couldn't leave the next day, not without knowing more about Jillian, the beautiful woman I had only known an hour.

I knew there was something more.

I felt it.

My friends thought I was crazy. It cost me a grand to get a room for one more night because the hotel was full and they only had suites available. I put it on my card without a second guess.

The next day, I booked a boat and prayed she'd take me up on my offer. She did, and that was when I knew I had one chance to see if this girl was real. Didn't help I'd never sailed before. I'd figure it out.

The sun beat down on our skin, hot and inviting against the constant breeze of the Caribbean island. She stunned me by wearing a black bikini that I could see through the thin fabric of her cover-up. Catamarans aren't that big, so I was pleased she had to sit close to me. The constant erection I was trying to hide wasn't pleased, but I made do with some serious shifting.

We talked about simple things. I wanted to know why she had become a wedding planner. She asked me my favorite hobby as a child. Our conversation was easy. It flowed.

I started to sing. Tim McGraw's "Live Like You Were Dying" is what came out, and I just let it all belt out as I navigated us around the island. I had no idea where I was going so when the wind started to pull us toward an inlet, I let it, for fear of her noticing what an idiot I was.

There was a cliff with people jumping off. I thanked the gods of sun and wind for dragging us in that direction. When we got close, I dropped the small anchor that came with the boat.

"Lunch?" I asked as I opened a cooler of sandwiches and fresh fruit.

"A meal and a show, huh?" she teased as she took the sandwich, I'd made her. "You're a good singer, Luke. Between your voice and the wind in my hair, it felt like I was on a real vacation for a minute."

I took a seat beside her with a tangerine. "You mean to tell me you didn't book an extra day onto this trip for pleasure?"

"Who has the luxury to take time off like that?"

I laughed, knowing my own secret. "Someone who takes chances."

"These are my years to work hard and prove myself. I'll party when I'm settled in my career."

"Not a risk-taker, I see." I punctured the skin of the fruit with my thumb.

She balked as she looked at the water and the people floating at the foot of the cliff. "The way I grew up, you weren't to make a splash, for it might disturb the swimmers around you."

"I was raised to cannonball through life."

That comment made her laugh. "You're funny. Cheesy and charming."

"Not the two adjectives a man aims for, but I'll take it." I popped a piece of tangerine into my mouth and grinned.

The Cupid's bow of her mouth pursed as she raised her brows. "What adjectives would you use to describe yourself?"

"Gallant. Alluring. Prepossessing," I say and then explain, "It means highly attractive. My sister is obsessed with words. What else? Captivating—"

"Vexing," she adds.

"Tenacious. I think that's the right word."

Her eyes rolled. "Untiring."

"I could definitely tire you out." I winked as I popped in another piece of fruit. That comment had her lifting her chin and narrowing her eyes.

"I'm not into playboys."

"What are you into?"

She bit her lip and curled her knees to her side. "Sensitive men who aren't afraid to show a woman his feelings."

"Women always say that, but they go for the alpha asshole. Just like men think they want a complacent woman so they can domineer when what we're really looking for is someone to help us through life because we're fucking clueless."

She giggled, deep and throaty. Damn, the sound of that voice and the way she radiated with that smile that reached her eyes ... it had me rubbing my heart again.

"I can't tell if you're full of shit or the only man who says exactly what's on his mind."

"I can promise you one thing—the words out of my mouth will never be a lie. Now, skirting around the truth, that I can do. I have a way with words."

"All right. Use your words. Tell me what you want from me. You said you don't lie. Be honest."

Fuck me. I was being called out on my own admission.

I placed the now-empty peel into the cooler and leaned forward. I didn't want to scare her away, and yet she'd asked for the truth. If she couldn't handle it, then I'd bring the boat back to shore and catch the next plane home.

"When I saw you last night, I thought you were the sexiest woman I'd ever laid eyes on. I wanted nothing more than to talk to you because you were attractive. Then, I got to know you a little, and I found myself smiling when I walked back to my room last night. I was daydreaming about you, fantasizing about getting to know you better—intimately even."

Her eyes widened at my admission, but I kept going.

"Just as much as I find you attractive, I enjoy talking to you. You show confidence on the outside, yet I can see that uncertainty in your eyes. Last night, it was about work. Today, it's about me. The thing that strikes me is that in either situation, you haven't backed down. You never let people know how unguarded you are on the inside because you wear your brave face on the outside."

A light breeze came through the air, pushing her hair off her shoulder. Her mouth was parted as she stared at me with cautious eyes. She didn't say anything. I wasn't sure she knew what to say. I stood up and offered her my hand.

"Let's go."

Her soft, small hand slid into mine. "Where?"

"We're gonna jump."

She looked up at the cliff. "I don't jump."

"With me, you do."

I didn't know if it was my admission to her on the boat or the way she'd felt when I practically threw her off that cliff, but something had sparked in Jillian. She kissed me. Yes, she kissed me first. It was the greatest kiss of my goddamn life because it wasn't just with her mouth. It was like her entire body was telling me she wanted me. Like she was giving me every ounce of that unguarded wall she kept erected and letting me tear it down brick by brick.

We made it back to the boat and kissed some more, talked some more, and on the way back to shore, I sang some more.

At the hotel, I canceled my flight and extended my room for one more day. When she left the rehearsal dinner she'd worked that night, I was waiting for her with a bottle of gin and chocolate cake. We drank and ate by the pool, sharing stories, laughing, sneaking kisses and cheap feels. I was falling hard for her.

I left her doorway a chaste man that night with a wide grin, whistling as I walked to the beach and filled that empty gin bottle with sand and headed back to my room.

I couldn't wait to see her, but she was working a wedding, and I had to give her space.

Halfway through the reception, I slid into the room and kept my place by the bar. As she worked, I observed her from afar. A woman or two came up to me at the bar and introduced themselves. I wasn't interested. I only had eyes for Jillian.

She was amazing. Organized, kind, and stern when need be. Her smile radiated when she spoke, and she managed to make a beachside wedding look like it was out of a movie.

When she passed, I touched her. When she looked, I grinned. And when she finally had a chance to step away, I danced with her. Under the stars, in the moonlight, I held on to the girl of my dreams.

When she asked me back to her room, I made love to her like a man who had finally found his way home. It was a cool night, so we opened the windows and let the breeze come in. We started with a kiss, and soon, our clothes were in a pool on the floor, and I had my thumbs kneading her perfect breasts and my fingers skimming against her clit, circling, as I placed featherlight kisses along her skin.

Her hands on me explored.

My mouth on hers savored.

I slid into her, and she whimpered. Our chests rose and fell in sync as our hips rolled with one another. Her breathing became my own, and I'd never felt more connected to someone in my entire life.

That was the past.

Now, I'm saddled with waiting for the results that can decide my future with the woman I love. Of all the places I could go to think, I chose my father's front porch.

Today is one of my three weekdays off, and Jillian is back in Greenwood Village working. I asked to have Ainsley for the day, promising my father he'd get some one-on-one time with her. Peyton is inside with a home health aide, which means my dad can relax and enjoy his granddaughter.

"Pop!" Ainsley calls for him from the grassy area where she's playing with a turtle he found for her in a nearby lake.

I'm glad my dad chose Pop as his name. It was what I called my grandfather, who was a great man.

"Can I keep him?"

My dad looks over the railing at her holding the turtle by his shell. "No. He belongs in the lake with his family. You can visit him whenever you'd like."

She sticks her bottom lip out and looks at him with her muddy face. "I'm gonna name him Hunty after my friend Hunter. Hunty the turtle!"

Dad laughs as he looks at her with softened eyes. Ainsley puts Hunty back in the bucket Dad brought out and grabs her bubble wand, making bubbles for her new reptilian friend.

"She's beautiful, son. Enjoy every minute with her."

"That's the plan. I can't believe I missed so much of her life already. These days of waiting are killing me. Jillian is barely talking to me. It's for the better. I want her to keep her space."

"Son, you have done many things in your life I'm proud of, and this is not one of them," my father says as I sit on a rocking chair on his porch.

"Tell me how you really feel."

He sits beside me. His bones creak as he does so, age catching up with him in a way I don't think he prepared for. "Now, I can't ever imagine what your life is like. I've never had to endure the kind of pain your mother and sister have. I won't imagine to know how I'd behave in your shoes."

"That's right," I say to him. "You have no idea what this feels like. I know your feelings about Jillian, but I can't pull her further into this. It's bad enough that Ainsley is. Her genealogy is something I have no control over. We'll help her as best we can. But Jillian? That I have control over."

"Can you?" he challenges with a laugh. "Boy, you're a good son, but a stupid man. I don't know what it's like to be you, but I know what it's like to be me. I had a great wife. A top-notch, *broke the mold when she was made* kinda wife. We didn't know all this was going to plague us, but I'll tell you what. I'd have loved her to the end, no matter what."

"You're one of a kind."

"Would you be there for Jillian if she had this disease?"

"I'd be there to the bitter end."

He gives a harrumph. "Maybe you're not as stupid as I thought."

"Okay, you'd love Mom to the end, no matter what, but would you have had children with her? Knowing what you know now, would you still have had Peyton, knowing the life she lives?"

"Probably not. But I have no regrets. Peyton had a beautiful life before this. I wouldn't have given up her healthy years and knowing her, being her father, for anything. I wouldn't have given up the chance of having Lauren as my wild-child daughter. Most importantly, I'd never trade a day of having you as my son, Luke. Of all things this crazy life has brought us, having you by my side has been an absolute honor. I love you. No matter what happens, no matter what you need from me, I'll take my last breath, being by your side, because that's love."

He pats my back, and I shake with emotion. I wipe my eyes with my pointer finger and thumb.

"Damn you, old man. You like to make me cry, don't you?"

He pats me again and laughs. "You were always a big softie. Just like to pretend you're all hard sometimes."

"I always thought I was like Mom. Free-spirited and always wanting to see the world. I guess I'm like you too."

"How so?" He raises a bushy brow.

"Now that I know Ainsley, I can't imagine life without her. No matter what happens, I'm happy she's here."

"Me too, Luke. She's a miracle." He sighs as we watch Ainsley running in the grass, chasing bubbles. Her brown hair dances in the autumn wind. "Do you want to be with Jillian?"

"More than anything." My words don't take more than a second to say.

"What would you have done if you'd never run into her that night of the fire?"

I sigh as my daughter looks over at me with a huge smile. "I'd never have known Ainsley existed. I'd never have known this life with Jillian existed."

"You'd still be wandering around, waiting to die. Like a phoenix rising from the ashes of a flame, you came back. Looks like those two taught you how to live again."

"You believe in fate, old man?"

"Hell yeah, I do. I'm a romantic, you know." He winks, and I roll my eyes. He settles into his seat and sighs. The weight of the last decade has taken its toll on him. "I'd like to see you settle down. Be in love. It's a good thing, you know. Not worth running from."

"I know love. This is how I show it. If I'm positive, I can't be with Jillian. She's the mother of my child but it ends there. She deserves a good man who will take care of her. Love her for eternity.

She deserves someone to be with her when she's old and gray. I don't want her wasting her good years taking care of me. And I couldn't stomach having her devote her world to me and I choose to end it early. Leaving her like that would destroy her."

"Leaving her now isn't?"

"She has years to move on. Some lucky bastard will sweep her off her feet. I'll hate it, but on my dying day, I will know that those three days in Aruba and these last few weeks being with her have been the happiest of my life. I'll be assured she's in good hands and living her fullest life."

"Now, who's the romantic?"

"She made that possible."

"A good woman will do that to a man."

Now, it's my turn to sigh. "For me, it's always been her."

I lean back in my rocker, and the two of us, side by side, rock in our chairs and yearn for love and life just as we always wished it could be.

We enjoy the rest of the day with my dad. He takes Ainsley for a ride in his pickup truck while I stay with Peyton once the aide leaves. There's no manual for this situation. No course in school or college lecture. Our youth is spent planning for the future which is wild because no one knows what the future holds. Somedays I long to be the ignorant boy who only cared about soccer and girls. To be the man in the backseat of his mother's car with the window open and driving to our next adventure.

The days of being a boy are long gone. Men are the heroes. We act it in different ways. For me, it's doing what I see best for the woman I love. It's being present for my father and sisters. It's putting out fires. It's keeping my head down and living in the present.

When it's time to leave, Ainsley and I head into my truck and drive back to Greenwood Village. She watches a movie on her iPad for most of the drive and falls asleep during the last hour.

When I reach Jillian's house, I see her car is in the driveway. I park on the curb and lift my daughter from the cab. Jillian opens the front door, already in her pajamas. I walk Ainsley up to her bed. Jillian takes Ainsley's locket off and hangs it on a jewelry holder by the side of the bed. As she dresses our girl in her pajamas, I watch from the doorway.

Jillian looks beautiful tonight. Makeup-free and wearing green polka-dot pajamas. The moonlight casting in through the window makes her glow as she kisses Ainsley on the cheek and pulls the covers up to her chin.

As she steps out of the room, I move closer to the doorframe to make room. She brushes past me without a glance. I inhale the faint scent of her vanilla lotion as I follow her down the stairs and to the front door.

I'm not wanted. I understand that. I asked for that. And yet I'm devastated by it.

We stop at the front stoop. Her eyes are looking down. Placing my knuckle under her chin, I turn her face up to me. She flutters her lashes up as I rub her chin with my thumb.

"I love you," I tell her.

She falls into me. Her hands wrap around my back, and I pull her in tight, resting my hand on her waist and in her hair, kissing the top her head and lavishing my love onto her.

"I love you so much, Jillian."

"I love you too," she says against my chest.

We stand here, under the moon and the stars, gripping each other for dear life. When she tilts her head, her lips are close to mine. Lifting up onto her toes, she kisses me. When her sweet mouth presses against mine, I part my lips and kiss her back. Her lips are soft, almost silken and pillowy against my own. Warmth fills my body as I groan when her honey-like tongue glides into my mouth, and I savor every bit of love, passion, and dedication she's giving me. I could die kissing this woman. I'd be happy to.

"Do you want to come inside?" she asks.

"You know I can't stay," I say and watch as her chest shivers with a deep exhale.

I hate this wall I've put up between us. I hate that I'm forcing her to be vulnerable in a way she's not comfortable with. Still, I love her more than I hate any of those things.

"If it's okay with you, I'd like to hold you. Until you fall asleep."

She shakes her head as she takes a step back. "I don't want you to do what you don't want—"

"Jillian"—I take her hand and pull her against me, walking us into her house—"there is nothing I'd rather do than hold you right now."

A small smile of relief appears on her face.

I guide her into the living room and take a seat on the couch. She curls up on my side. There's a white faux fur blanket beside me.

I place it over her and watch as she snuggles into my side, warm and bone-tired.

"Go to sleep, baby."

Her body relaxes with the weight of a long day on her feet.

She mumbles against my chest, "I wish we could have this forever."

I kiss her head and keep my head against hers. "Me too."

thirty-one

IT'S RESULT DAY.

The lobby to Valor County Hospital is crowded today as I make it to my appointment to see Eric Hollenford. I can't stand that guy. He's okay as far as doctors go, but it bothers me he kissed Jillian and she actually liked him. He's the kind of man she should be with if the results are positive and that pisses me off even more.

I'm a selfish bastard, I know.

So much counts on today. Ainsley's health. My future with Jillian. I understand why Eric put me through a psychological examination before getting tested. This news could kill a man—literally and figuratively.

There's a trash receptacle nearby, and I resist the urge to lean over and vomit my guts up. I run my hands through my hair and head toward the elevator.

That's when I hear my name.

"Luke."

It's said by a woman. Sultry, raspy … Jillian.

I turn around and am surprised to see her here. Her hair is in a bun, and she's wearing a jogging suit, the kind she hates to leave the house in. Her skin is splotchy, and those gorgeous green eyes are bloodshot.

My girl's been crying.

I want to walk up to her, hold her, kiss her soft lips, and ask her what's wrong. But I know the answer. What's wrong is me. Until I get upstairs and learn the truth, I can't be with her. Sill, I'm relieved as fuck that she's here. I need her like a dying man in the desert needs water. I can't take a damn drink though. Still, I told her not to come today.

"Jillian, you can't come upstairs with me. The results could be horrible, and I don't know if I'll be able to look at you and brace for what they have to say at the same time."

"I'm not going upstairs," she says sternly.

I nod. Understanding. I don't want her upstairs, and she's honoring my request.

"Neither are you," she adds.

I'm confused by her statement, and I'm pretty sure the expression on my face says just that.

She shifts on her feet, then takes a step closer, closing the distance between us. "I told you that knowledge is power, and I was right. The knowledge of this disease has the power to heal and the power to destroy. If you find out you're positive, you'll never love Ainsley as freely as you should. You'll keep her at arm's length, waiting for your first symptoms to start, panic that she has it too, and never forgive yourself for potentially giving her the gene as well. You'll run away before she has a chance to know you—to truly love you not only as her father, but also as a man. I won't let you do that to her."

I rub my hand along the back of my neck. This wasn't the plan. I was supposed to go upstairs and find out the results. She's not supposed to be here, messing with my head even more.

"What about her future? Ainsley needs to know."

"If you show signs, we'll get you tested. When she's eighteen, she can make the choice herself to get tested."

I swallow down the emptiness and regret. "No. We chose this for a reason. I'm doing this for you."

"I was wrong to convince you that this was the only solution. Luke, you've given up so much, stayed away from us for so long. Even if those results come back negative, you'll never stop blaming yourself for the past. You'll be even angrier at yourself for wasting time on a disease you never had. Positive or negative, whatever's on that paper will only destroy you."

She's right. No matter what the results are, I'm damned either way. There's no changing that because it's the way I'm built as a man.

She takes a step forward. Her small hands fiddle with one another. "If you do have the gene, why waste the next ten, twenty, thirty years on something that will destroy you whether you want it to or not? Live in the moment. Love in the moment. Love Ainsley." She swallows down the shakiness in her throat. "Love me."

"I do love you, Jillian. That's why I'm doing this. I love Ainsley beyond measure because I'm her father, but you … I choose you. You're the only woman who will ever be right for me. The only woman I love enough to walk away."

"I don't want a conditional love. Even if you're negative, you'll love me like it's an apology to a wrong. One you'll never forgive yourself for. I want us to love one another fiercely, whether it's for one good day and a million bad ones."

"You don't know what you're signing up for."

"I know what I'd be losing if I let you walk upstairs. Positive or negative, it doesn't matter. It's never mattered. All that matters is us."

I told myself I'd stay away from this woman until I knew my fate, but she makes it fucking impossible. I never knew I could love someone so much that I'd risk staying away from them in order to make them happy. What I didn't realize was that she loves me just enough to keep me just as I am.

My beautiful, sweet Jillian Hathaway.

I let go of her hands and stare at her and her wide, determined eyes and lips pleading to be loved. Forever. Unconditionally.

"Jillian. Luke." Eric Hollenford is standing in the lobby with his suit jacket on and a coffee in his hand. "I was just on my way back upstairs. We have your results in. Are you ready to come up?"

I look at Jillian, who is running her hands on her jogging suit.

"Just tell me now, Doc. I can't handle the wait," I say to Eric with my eyes glued on hers.

"I can't. You have to be upstairs. There's a protocol."

Jillian's eyes are pleading with me. Her frown prominent as she begs me to stay with her. She reaches out for my hand and squeezes it. That little squeeze sends a bolt of electricity up my arm and straight for my heart.

I let out a heavy breath.

"I've changed my mind. I'm not going to find out," I say to Eric.

Jillian's head jumps up as she looks at me in elated shock.

"Really?" Jillian asks.

"Really."

She lays a hand on my chest, pulling on my shirt. "Are you sure?"

Am I sure? No. I'm not sure about anything except the fact that I love this woman. This wild madwoman who has me thinking in circles when I'm around her. She's right; if I find out, I'll never be the same. We'll never be the same. Maybe just living is what's best for us … for our family.

"Yes, I'm sure."

"What about Ainsley?" she counters, making sure I'm positive in my decision.

"Like you said, we'll let her decide when the time comes."

She lifts up onto her toes, throws her arms around my neck, and kisses me. I take her by the waist and kiss her back for what is the first of many kisses for the rest of our lives, no matter how long or short that might be.

A clearing of Eric's throat has me letting my girl go yet taking her hand.

"Sorry about that. Must be awkward with you liking my girl and all," I say.

Jillian elbows me in the gut.

Eric nods with an awkward yet matter-of-fact expression. "A little, but it's cool. I just want to say …" He pauses with a smile. It's big and reassuring. "You two enjoy a very long life together." He winks and walks away.

Jillian lifts a finger and points toward Eric. "Did he just wink?"

"He did."

"Was that a good wink, like *enjoy your long life together because I know you're negative?*"

"It could have been a *ha-ha, sucker, you're gonna die early* wink."

"I don't think it was," she says.

"Fuck. I don't think it was either. We should ask him."

I start to walk away, but she pulls me back.

"Oh no, you don't, Luke. He winked. I'm good with a wink."

I blow out a huge breath and run my hand through my hair. "I think I'm good with it too."

She runs a soothing hand over my bicep as she stretches onto her tiptoes and begs me for a kiss. "Now, take me home and start enjoying that long life with me, please."

"Yes, ma'am." I cup the back of her head, holding her to me, and kiss this beautiful woman in a crowded lobby without a care in the world.

"Yes, ma'am." I cup the back of her head, holding her to me, and kiss this beautiful woman in a crowded lobby without a care in the world.

epilogue

"HAS ANYONE SEEN MY black shawl?" I ask as I exit my bathroom.

Joe purrs from his place on my bed, smart enough to keep his distance, as I'm in my dress, ready to head to Melissa's wedding.

I was at the barn earlier today to set up but came home for a shower and to do my hair and slide on my dress. We have to be back there within the hour because my pregnant business partner shouldn't have to work her own wedding, no matter how good she is at her job.

I text the assistants we recently hired as full-time employees and make sure they have everything under control. They respond that they are ahead of schedule. I breathe in relief and look up at Joe.

"Where are they?" I ask him, referring to Ainsley and Luke.

In the months since Luke and I have been together, many changes have been made. He still works as a fireman, but was able to be transferred to a firehouse in the town of Castleton. Will was able to use his connections to get Luke a transfer. It's a long commute but much closer than Walden. Now that Luke is working in the area, he's moved into my townhouse, along with Joe who has made himself quite at home. It's nice having Luke here. Not only do I get to spend my nights with the man I love, but Ainsley has a household with her father and mother who idolize her. Luke could work on being the disciplinarian though. It's a good cop bad cop scenario that leaves me as the bad one. I don't mind. He's still making up for lost time with her.

Each day that passes, father and daughter grow closer. He takes her on a date once a month, and me once a week. We've even embarked on some family road trips like the kind his mother took him on when he was younger. We visit Mitch often, and have even made slight amends with my mother having spent Christmas Eve with her and my father.

My heart beats happier, and life moves at it should.

I find my shawl on the floor of my closet. It must have fallen off the hanger when I got dressed. I call out for my family once again. They couldn't have gone far, seeing as they should be dressed in wedding attire and ready to go.

Joe leaps off the bed and onto my nightstand, where a red can of Coca-Cola is sitting. I look at it curiously, as I never have soda in the house. At least, not anywhere Ainsley can find it. There's a Post-it note attached to the can.

> *Once, there was a girl who craved a Coke and found herself in nothing but a robe, rescued by a devastatingly handsome fireman. If you love me more than you love this can of soda, open the door.*

Joe leaps off the bed and onto the floor, padding at the door for me to open it. I open the bedroom door and look down the hallway to see the gold ice bucket from the Walden Hotel on the floor with a Post-it note attached.

> *Confession time. I know you didn't actually need this ice bucket. When a man wants to see a woman again, he'll use any excuse to do so. I'm glad you left it in my truck. I'd have looked like an idiot if I showed up here that day just to tell you I missed you. If you missed me too, come into the kitchen.*

I pad down the stairs and into the kitchen and find a box on the counter. I place the bucket and soda on the island and stare at the bottle of white sand with another Post-it note on it. It's the same bottle I saw under the bathroom sink the first night at Luke's house. The sand inside matches the sand on the outside of Ainsley's locket.

I've kept this sand all these years because I never wanted to forget falling in love with you in Aruba. Now, I get to fall in love with you every day if you'll just come find me.

Joe is standing by the French doors in the living room that lead to our small courtyard-style backyard. I open it and gasp at the sight before me. The yard is decorated with Christmas lights, and vases of ranunculus flowers in various shades of lavender and purple cover the space.

Luke is in his tuxedo, strong and handsome, combed-back hair and a devilish grin. It's chilly out here, but the heat from the smoldering gaze of the man with navy eyes that breathe fire, setting everything they look at to dust, warms me in more ways than one.

Ainsley is by his side, wearing her party dress and looking like an angel with her hair brushed and decorated in a floral headband.

Luke smiles from the far end of the courtyard. "You got my notes."

I smile. "They were clever."

Ainsley takes my hand and moves me toward the center of the pavers. She's smiling from ear to ear. "Mommy, Daddy has something very special to ask you."

The butterflies in my stomach rumble as I place my hand there to calm my nerves. Luke looks the pillar of confidence as he swaggers my way, one step at a time.

Luke looks good tonight. Too good in his tux, pristine and polished. He looks like a gentleman instead of the roguish charmer he is. My charmer. I love charming. In the time since he's been back in my life, there hasn't been a day where he doesn't make my pulse race, head spin, and body radiate with the heat of his gaze.

"Jillian," he croons as he closes the distance between us.

I raise a brow and look up at him. "Yes, Luke?"

"I thought I loved you in Aruba. I thought I loved you when I saw you on the main street of Walden in that ridiculous robe. I thought I loved you when I found out you had given me the most beautiful daughter in the world."

Ainsley giggles by my side. I smile at her and then turn back to Luke.

"The truth is"—he takes my hand in his—"I couldn't have loved you then, not nearly as much as I do today. Tomorrow, I will love you even more. An unwise man once said, love is knowing when to walk away. A wiser woman taught me that true love means staying, even when it's the hardest thing to do. I'll stay by your side through the thick and thin, the easy and the hard. I'll be yours, Jillian, if you'll have me, for the rest of your life and beyond because I couldn't fathom loving anyone ever again as much as I do you."

Luke falls to his knee, and I gasp despite the fact that I felt this was a proposal the moment I stepped foot in the backyard.

"Jillian Payne Hathaway, will you do me the honor of being my wife?"

He holds a hand out to Ainsley, who places a diamond ring there. He slides it onto my left finger. It's a simple, elegant round-cut stone on a rose-gold band. It's perfect and stunning. Everything I could have ever wanted.

"Yes," I cry out as he stands, and I throw my arms around him, wrapping him in my body. With my lips on his and my hands in his hair, I kiss him endlessly.

We take a breath, and his forehead rests on mine. "Yes?"

"The answer has always been yes." I grin and kiss him again.

Ainsley sandwiches herself between her mom and dad.

"We can be a family!" she squeals.

Luke lifts her and holds her with one arm while sliding his other arm around me. "That leaves one more thing up for asking," he says to our daughter. "How do you feel about being Ainsley Lisette Hathaway-Incendio?"

I shake my head. "No way."

Luke's elated features fall. "Why not?"

With a shrug, I state, "Ainsley Lisette Incendio sounds better."

He smiles bigly and kisses me on the mouth, and then he gives his daughter a kiss on the cheek. "What do you say, kiddo? Wanna be an Incendio?"

She places a finger on her cheek and looks up to the sky, as if she's thinking really hard. When she's done, she lifts her chin and then drops it dramatically as her arms shoot up with a, "Yes!"

Luke laughs. "You like to keep me on my toes, kid."

"Are you happy, Daddy?" she asks, pulling his head to smoosh it with her face.

"I am. You know why?" he asks, and she lets go of his face. He looks down at me and grins. "Family is everything."

I sigh into his arms and place his hand on my belly, the one that now holds more than nervous butterflies. It holds new life. New life he hasn't heard about until now. "Family is everything."

Luke's brows shoot up and his jaw drops. "Really?" He looks down at my stomach and then to my face that is now simmering with tears. I just finished my makeup and wasn't planning on ruining it before seeing Melissa take her vows.

"Really," I state with a nod and a smile. "Are you ready to do it all from the beginning?"

Luke places Ainsley on the floor and then takes me in his arms, placing a hand on my stomach and another on my back. He kisses me long and hard, and I melt into him as I have time and time again. I'm swept up in his kiss and the outpouring of love he has for me, Ainsley, and our growing family.

"I'm ready for it all, Jillian. I love you so much. Thank you, Jillian, for giving me my family."

Luke and Jillian's story isn't done!

Read the extended bonus epilogue at www.jeanninecolette.com

Tara and Rob's romance is available for preorder.

Love ... It's Wild

Melissa and Will's story is available now.

Love ... It's Complicated

ALSO BY JEANNINE COLETTE

THE ABANDON COLLECTION

Pure Abandon
Reckless Abandon
Wild Abandon
True Abandon
Sinful Abandon

STAND-ALONES

A Really Bad Idea
Just Ten Seconds
Wrecked
Body of Trust

SEXTON BROTHERS

Austin
Bryce
Tanner
Layover Lover (Spin-Off)

FALLING FOR THE STARS

Naughty Neighbor
Charming Co-Worker
Rebel Roommate
Arrogant Officer
Bastard Bartender
Loyal Lawyer
Heartbroken Hero

WWW.JEANNINECOLETTE.COM

acknowledgements

It's hard to write a novel and have it live up to the expectations of those deemed *the greatest book you've ever written!* and be better than *yeah, that wasn't your best work.* Love ... *It's Messy* was a story I knew would be difficult to tell yet was the only one that dared to be written.

After writing *Love ... It's Complicated*, I knew I had to tell Jillian's story. I immediately started to ponder: *Who is she? Why is she still single? Who is the man who ruined her? What made a twenty-six-year-old woman have a baby on her own?* The answers to the questions answered themselves. I paused my attempt to write due to nerves about what readers would think of the storyline. These characters are flawed, and the simple question of *why didn't they just tell each other their feelings* is a common concern in romance. It's cliché, I know.

While being an adult and speaking your feelings is the obvious choice in situations, we tend to hold in our true selves due to pride or to protect our feelings. Jillian and Luke aren't perfect and the path to their happily ever after is rife with complications. They might be adults, but like many of us, they are still teenagers at heart, trying to find their way in the world. I hope you enjoyed their journey.

Whether you loved this book or not, I'm honored you read to the end and even made it through these acknowledgments. **Thank you from the bottom of my heart for reading my words and for your ever-growing faith in these stories. You, the reader, are amazing!**

To Autumn Sexton of Wordsmith Publicity, the woman who told me to write the book as I saw it, no matter what doubts I had. You are why I continue to tell the stories in my head even if they don't always fit into the current reading trends.

To Wilmari Delgado, my alpha forever. Your dedication to the storylines and finding the missing link is crucial. The book community is blessed to have you as their own. I'm blessed to call you my friend. To my beta readers, Maria Black, Carey Sullivan, Erika Van Eck, Nadine Killian, Paramita Patra, and Nicole Westmoreland. Your insight and wisdom into character development is what made this book work!

To Lauren Runow. Your invaluable conversations and analysis of the characters I write is something I will cherish forever. To Stefanie Rose, for every being the one I look forward to connecting with and chatting story plots, life, and books. Thank you for always checking in. To Melanie Moreland, Jane Anthony, A.L. Jackson, K.K. Allen, Ginger Scott, and Dylan Allen, for being class acts.

To Janine Infant Bosco. My writing partner who grew a forest with me as we kept each other focused. Thank you for your ever interest in Jillian and Luke's story. And for the love of artichokes. Did you finish your book yet???

To Jessica Botero, because I forgot her in the last book's acknowledgments and no one loves the word *glistening* as much as she does.

To the Bookstagram community, Goodreads community, and the members of Jeannine Colette's Army of Roses on Facebook—You are the reason these books are being read. Thank you for every share, like, and love!

Thank you to the dream team!!! Sarah Hansen of Okay Creations, for yet another spot-on outstanding cover. Jovana Shirley of Unforeseen Editing, for making me look like a well-polished author. Twenty-one books later, and I still make the same mistakes. Courtney DeLollis, for finessing this book down to the last letter with your stellar proofreading.

My husband, Bryan. My forever hero and the one everyone asks if he's the inspiration to my books. The answer is always ... yes.

My kids, Jake, Everly, and Aliette. My biggest supporters, who have grown to the age where they're excited to tell people their mom's an author. I love you more than all the words in my stories.

To Joey Stanton, who has given more passion to moving my books off the pages and (hopefully!) onto the big screen someday.

To my family, because I always believe they are worth mentioning, including Marilyn Thompson, Stephen Thompson, Kathy Curro Thompson, Lynn Distefano, Jim Distefano, Michelle Worden, Nicole Lancellotti, Tara McCormick, Nicole Parsons.

Finally, to Jill Meister, for lighting the fire under me last year because she believed I was special enough to do it. She was my coworker, my production tutor, and now my forever friend. And to Nanci Weaver, who had the office I ran to when I needed a place to hide and is now the other end of the line when I need an ear. You two are my constants. The family I choose. I love you both so much.